DIRTY LITTLE SAINT

M VIOLET

A NOTE FROM THE AUTHOR

Dirty Little Saint is book two in the Devils of Raven's Gate Duet. It picks up right where book one ends. So, if you haven't read *Pretty Little Psycho*, I highly suggest you do so before continuing on. The ravens will thank you.

Dirty Little Saint is darker, grittier, and unapologetically filthy. This is a pitch black romance. The MCs are not redeemable. If you have any triggers, please read all the CWs below before diving in. There is graphic SA (not from the MCs) that happens within the first few chapters.

CWs

Graphic sex
Sex rituals
Graphic language
Graphic violence
Physical assault
Sexual assault
Extreme Bullying
Public humiliation
Somophilia
Gaslighting
Kidnapping
Captivity
Murder
Blood rituals
Cult practices
Forced bathing
Forced orgasm
Grooming
Menstrual sex
Fisting
DVP
DP

Forced masturbation
Sacrilege
Dubious consent
Non consent
Group sex
Sword crossing
Coercion
Manipulation
Bondage
Sadism
Masochism
Submission
Domination
Stalking
Torture
Mutilation
Sex while getting mutilated
Trauma
Abuse by a parent
MFMMM
MFMM
MM
MFM
Choking
Spanking
Restraints
Sensory deprivation
Poison play
Knife play
Blood play
Praise
Degradation
Breath play
Gagging
Spitting
Anal sex
Object play
Voyeurism

PLAYLIST

Psychotic—SkyDxddy

Lavenders—Rivals

MASOCHIST—Ellise

Psycho Crazy—Halestorm

Grim Reaper—bludnymph

Cowardly Lion—Grace Blue

NO HANDS (SIDE A)—UPSAHL

Self Destruction Mode—The Chainsmokers & bludnymph

Bad 4 Me—DeathbyRomy

Chemical X (feat. TIMMS)—UNDREAM

Red Flag—Cloudy June

Hellhound (feat. Jazmin Bean)—DeathbyRomy

Ruthless—Bookish Songs Collective, Kendra Dantes & Nino Tosco

MOURNING—Ellise

Lunatic—Elly Eira

Buried (feat. Katie Herzig)—UNSECRET

Knives—Neoni & Savage Ga$p

Monster—Chandler Leighton

Lights Out—bludnymph

Body Bag—Neoni

Bad Girl—AVIVA

Devil Is A Woman—Cloudy June

V.A.N—Bad Omens and Poppy

Bullet with Butterfly Wings—Violet Orlandi

he loves me, he loves me not—Jessica Baio

Horns—Bryce Fox

Cold Blooded—Chris Grey

Nightshade—The Lumineers

Sinner—Diamond Eyes

For everyone who gets up every day and keeps going,
even when the going doesn't always want to get got.
I believe in you.
I believe you.

But the Raven, sitting lonely on the placid bust, spoke only
That one word, as if his soul in that one word he did outpour.
Nothing farther then he uttered—not a feather then he fluttered—
Till I scarcely more than muttered "Other friends have flown before—
On the morrow *he* will leave me, as my Hopes have flown before."
Then the bird said "Nevermore."—The Raven, Edgar Allan Poe

DIRTY LITTLE SAINT

PROLOGUE

Maureen

SOME BELIEVE THAT RAVENS ARE THE HARBINGERS OF DEATH. THAT they're damned souls. Others believe they can summon the ghosts of murdered wolves. I'm not sure what to believe anymore. But when a raven dies, their coven mourns them by mimicking their cries. Tonight, I can hear those cries in the distance. It's like nails on a chalkboard.

Up at Valentin's cabin, we are far from Tenebrose, yet still tethered to it. An unkindness of ravens forms a wall in the front yard. They weep for their fallen. They mourn the shifting of the bond. Three weeks ago, we were at their mercy. Slaves to their every whim. But all that changed when I took the mark and pledged my oath to Nocturnus.

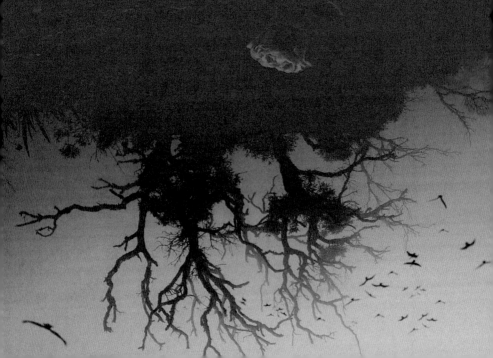

"Come away from the window, Maur." Valentin snakes an arm around my waist, and I almost cum from his body heat.

I lean my head back against his chest and close my eyes. "The ravens... they're still out there."

He dips his fingers inside the waistband of my jeans. "They envy us. You should be more concerned about what I'm going to do to *you* right now."

I let out a soft moan and arch back. He pushes two fingers inside my slick pussy, and I can barely breathe. His scent invades my senses. I want to taste him. To bottle up his essence and drink it while he fucks me.

"It's time for your next sacrament, Firecracker." He presses his thumb against my throbbing clit and drags me backward.

My heart races. It's been weeks since I pledged my oath to them. When I sprawled out on Riot's bed and let the three of them mark and defile me. We've been nesting here at Valentin's cabin while the three of them have taken sick pleasure from edging me ever since. *I want to explode.*

Another moan erupts from my throat as he pulls me down the stairs. The darkness begins to cover us, and I start to panic. But he knows the way to the crypt beneath this house better than anyone. He can navigate it with his eyes closed. So I let him guide me down with his fingers still working their magic inside my pussy.

"Do you want me to fuck you?" he growls in my ear.

"Yes," I plead.

He gives my clit a hard pinch. "Such a needy fucking slut."

As soon as we get to the bottom of the stairs, the sound of a match against stone breaks the silence followed by the stench of sulfur, and the whole room lights up.

My ache for them festers as I come face-to-face with Riot and Atlas. All I can see is their eyes behind their bronzed masks. They stare back at me with a crazed hunger, a reminder of who they are deep down.

Fucking psychos.

Dressed in all black, they pull up their hoods before giving me their backs. They move like predators as they stalk down the tunnel.

Valentin pushes me forward as we follow them.

"Please, Val. . . I *need* to cum." His fingers are torturous, teasing my flesh with the promise of release but never allowing me to reach it. I don't even care where they're taking me. Or what they plan to do to me. The pain is always worth the pleasure.

As he withdraws his hand, I shriek in protest. He grabs the back of my head and yanks on my hair. "You're not in control tonight, love. So shut the fuck up and *stop begging.*"

The tunnel dead-ends in a small cavern. Its stone walls are lined with sconces and stained with blood. The cold draft that seeps between the cracks sends shivers down my spine.

A large stone altar sits in the middle of the room, similar to the one back at Nocturnus, except this time, there are no initiates watching. No one's eyes on me but theirs—my three devils of Raven's Gate.

Atlas's pet snake, Zeus, slithers around his shoulders, its body hanging five feet to the ground. I shiver as the memory of the reptile sinking its fangs into my thigh rushes forward. The pain had been excruciating, the paralysis that followed terrifying, but the sweet ecstasy that enveloped me after Atlas sucked the poison out was a pleasure that I struggle to find words to describe. It was ex-quisite torture.

Riot stalks behind me, his fingers dancing across my shoulders before dragging my top down to my waist. He presses a cold blade against my belly. "Before this year is up, every inch of your skin will bear our marks."

My nipples swell as he drags the tip of the blade in circles around them. It takes my breath away. "I'm ready," I murmur.

He steps back. "Take off your clothes and get on the altar."

My teeth chatter from the cool, damp air but also from

anticipation. I slowly finish removing my top, then my pants and shoes. The cement floor is like ice against the soles of my bare feet. A spasm flickers in my core as I slide my panties down and off.

They watch me with a feral hunger as I climb the steps of the altar, their need growing like a raging fire. I gasp as the freezing stone meets my flesh when I lie down across it.

But I know I won't be cold for long.

Their silence sends a flutter of nerves to the pit of my belly. I don't know what will happen next. I never do with them.

"Spread your legs, open up for us," Riot orders. His voice is hoarse and gravelly at the sight of my soaking wet pussy.

Valentín and Atlas move in closer, flanking me on either side.

I'm about to be devoured.

The snake hisses and lunges toward me as if he remembers how I taste and craves another bite.

"Don't make any sudden moves, love." Atlas towers over me, his blue-green eyes glowing like fairy lights.

Fuck.

I tense, every muscle in my body going rigid. With Zeus firmly in his grasp, he brings him closer.

Valentín clasps my head in his hands. He leans over, kissing my cheek as he whispers, "Mor tua, vita mea." *Your death, my life.*

I whimper and brace myself for the bite.

Riot caresses my thighs. "Don't fight it, Firecracker."

Zeus slithers up my leg, returning to the spot he's tasted before. The sigil on my neck burns as if it were freshly carved. A bolt of electricity shoots through my veins like a power growing inside me.

I close my eyes to escape the madness that threatens to consume me, but all I see are angry ravens. "F-fuck," I stammer. Panic rises in my chest.

"Shhh," Valentín coos. He softly rubs my nipples between his fingers. "Stop trying to be in control. Let it happen."

I open my lids and lock eyes with Atlas again. Satisfied that

DIRTY LITTLE SAINT

I'm not going to freak out, he loosens his grip on Zeus. The impatient reptile darts forward and doesn't stop until its fangs are sinking into my thigh.

I gasp and arch my back. "Oh, no," I cry out. "It burns."

An eruption of moans echoes in my ears as they watch. My vision starts to blur, and it feels like an eternity before Atlas pries Zeus off me. I feel the poison barreling through my veins like a freight train.

It moves fast, making its way to my heart. True fear consumes me, and I start to doubt whether he'll be able to suck the toxin out in time.

I try to scream, but my tongue feels like a bowling ball in my mouth.

The wound on my thigh grows hotter. Through my haze, I can see Atlas's head between my legs.

I blink a few times, and it becomes clearer. A light swirls around us. An energy that crackles in between each limb.

I swallow hard as every nerve in my body prickles. I feel every-thing, but I can't force any part of my body to move. *I'm not in control.*

Atlas licks his lips. "Thatta girl. You did so good."

Riot traces my open wound with his thumb. "This is where it should go."

Valentin nods in agreement. He kisses my cheek again. "*The power of Serpentis.*"

Oh, fuck. He's going to carve the sigil on top of the snake bite. No. I try to sit up, but my body feels like dead weight. "Wait," I whisper.

Riot drags a finger down the center of my pussy. "Relax. It will only hurt a little. Let me show you how pleasure eases the pain."

I let out a moan as he rubs my clit in circles while plunging his

5

other finger deep inside me. He pumps in and out slowly. Every flick is heightened under the paralysis.

"Mmm, yeah. That's it. You look so fucking hot with my fingers inside you."

Valentin takes over as Riot goes for his knife. "Keep fucking her just like that."

I want to roll my hips and spread my legs wider. "More," I whine.

Atlas joins him as they take turns sliding their long smooth fingers in and out of my throbbing pussy.

I'm consumed. Wild with lust and need.

So much so that I don't initially feel the sting of the blade ripping into my flesh.

But when I do, it's fucking horrific.

I gurgle out a scream as he digs into my skin, carving me up like an animal headed for the slaughter.

Val and Atlas thrust harder, sending spasms to my core. I'm being pulled in two different directions—on the edge of coming and dying at the same time.

"Almost done, Firecracker." Riot works the knife like an artist painting a masterpiece.

I want to jerk my hips, and this time, my body actually obeys me. The toxin must be wearing off.

The pain and pleasure intensify tenfold.

"It's done," he growls. "Open her up for me."

Atlas and Valentin pull my pussy lips back. Riot licks his lips and eyes me like prey. "In absentia lucis, tenebrae vincunt." *In the absence of light, darkness prevails.*

I flinch as he wraps his lips around my clit and sucks. A burst of adrenaline and spasms rush through my core like an explosion, as if I'm erupting from the inside out. I cry out as the orgasm I've been craving finally unleashes.

I don't care about the pain anymore. I grab the back of his head

and grind against his face. He chuckles, taunting me even more. Knowing they've been denying me for this very moment.

Atlas squeezes my nipples hard. "Say it, Firecracker."

Riot scrapes his teeth against my swollen nub as he sucks, humming and moaning. I clench, then release, chasing the high as far as it will take me. "Mors vincit omnia," I murmur. *Death always wins.*

They are devils. They are death itself. And they always get their way. They always win.

Another moan erupts from my chest, and I cum all over his lips.

CHAPTER ONE

Maureen

T HE GRAVES ESTATE MAKES NOCTURNUS LOOK TINY IN COMPARISON. I can smell the hemlock even before we approach the thick iron gates. The fumes stick to my throat like sludge, burning my nostrils and making my head pound.

The tension builds between us the closer we get to the main house. I peer out the window, straining my eyes to see what lies beyond the darkness, searching for any flicker of light or life. A deep sense of dread settles into my bones. There is something not right about this place. *And I thought Tenebrose gave me the creeps.*

Atlas squeezes my shoulder. "Don't be afraid, love."

"Understatement of the year," Valentin mutters from behind the wheel.

A chill snakes up my back. If fear were a living, breathing entity, then this is where it lives. "How angry is he?" I murmur.

"I don't remember a time when my father wasn't angry," Riot hisses. "We killed Zeke. Bastard or not, he was still his son. There will be consequences."

Fuck. "I killed his son . . . I'll accept the punishment."

The three of them collectively tense. Valentin jerks his head, finally looking at me for the first time since we embarked on this journey. "If Holden Graves touches a fucking hair on your head—"

"He won't," Riot snaps. "I promise you . . . he won't."

Atlas rubs both my shoulders as if he could miraculously massage the anxiety right out of me. "We stand together. Zeke tried to take our coven and our girl. According to the Nocturnus bi-laws, we did nothing wrong."

I clasp my neck as my freshly carved sigil starts to burn. The stench of hemlock thickens, and I can barely breathe. "*Fuck.*"

"You'll get used to it," Valentin quips.

His body is rigid, his tone icy. If I didn't already know him, I'd be downright terrified. "Get used to parts of my flesh randomly catching on fire? No, I don't think so."

Atlas kneads his fingers deeper into my muscles. "Pain reminds us we're alive, Maur. It connects us. Here, dab this on your neck and thigh."

I take the vial of poison from him and nearly pass out from the scent. "What the fuck is this?"

"Nightshade. It will temporarily deaden the nerves around your sigils." Even Atlas's tone is darker than usual. He's usually the most cheerful of the three. I guess no one is safe from the ominous vibes of Riot's family home. *I can't believe anyone grew up here.* But it's starting to make more sense as to why he is the way he is. I imagine the hell would feel more welcoming than this place.

The ravens squawk alongside the car, bound to us by an unseen cord. Their power over us has weakened, but it still hangs by a

VIOLET

delicate thread. Valentin says that once I get more sigils, we'll be able to overtake them completely. But the curse my family has placed on Nocturnus still clings to our souls like a whisper.

It's the middle of the day, but the darkness hanging over this property threatens to engulf us. Through the beam of the headlights, particles of dirt and dust swirl in the wind. Dead leaves rustle and crunch under the tires as we race toward the house. I'm on edge as we finally cross the long stretch and pull into the front drive, not knowing what we're about to face.

Two gargoyles perch atop the large stone fountain in the center. I shiver under their glare. "Well, that's not creepy at all," I snicker. Riot sighs before sliding out from the back seat. He stalks around the car to open my door for me, offering me his hand. "My father has a tendency for drama. But it's not all smoke and mirrors. Don't ever let your guard down here."

I swallow hard, nodding as I slip my fingers inside his. An instant surge of heat transfers between us. Ever since they marked me, our connection has grown stronger. Every touch drives me wild with lust and ache. But it also pushes me further down into the darkness that surrounds them. It's like having invisible hands around my neck, their grip firm, reminding me they could crush my lungs at any moment. Or send me into the most primal state of pleasure that I've ever felt. It's divine torture. A constant state of pain and ecstasy.

There's an electricity in the air as the four of us approach the monstrous house. Every inch of it is cold, made of stone and iron with barred windows, covered in emerald-green ivy—the only pop of color that I can see. It hugs the walls, plastered to it like it's been there for a thousand years.

I don't let go of Riot's hand when the door swings open. A pale old man in a crisp black suit glares back at us. His eyes harden even more when they land on me.

"Romulus," Riot greets him, his tone devoid of any emotion.

"Mr. Graves," he replies. "You are looking well."

"Call me Riot, old man. Mr. *Graves* is my father."

The tension thickens, and I don't even realize I'm holding my breath until I feel Atlas's hand on my lower back. I exhale and lick my lips, willing moisture back into my mouth. I look past Romulus to see a tiny woman leaning on a cane in the foyer. Her platinum blonde hair is cropped short and styled in finger waves like the flapper girls of the 1920s. She wears a plain black dress and black pumps, elegant but as cold as this house.

Romulus steps aside and motions for us to come in. "Mr. Graves is occupied at the moment. He'll join all of you in the library for cocktails before dinner. Do not be late."

Riot snorts. "Wouldn't dream of it." He pulls me into the foyer, coming face-to-face with the woman. "Mother."

She's a pretty woman with very few wrinkles on her pale face. But it's the absence of joy in her eyes that makes her look aged and hardened. Like someone snuffed the light out of her.

"Welcome home." Her voice matches her blank expression. She turns to the rest of us and forces a tightlipped smile. "Atlas, Valentin. How is Tenebrose treating you?"

Valentin snickers. "I'm sure you—"

"Fine," Atlas cuts him off, giving him a warning look. "Everything is fine at Tenebrose, Mrs. Graves."

Riot's grip on my hand tightens when his mother's gaze locks onto me. "This is Maureen. I expect she will be welcome here."

She sticks her free hand toward me. "Clover Graves. Nice to meet you, Miss Blackwell."

My stomach turns. She cannot mask the disappointment in her voice. "Thank you for having me. You have a lovely home."

Clover Graves smirks at Riot. "Your father wants to speak with you. Alone. He's waiting for you in his office. The rest of you know where your rooms are. Go clean up and meet us in the library in an hour."

Riot clenches his jaw. "Whatever you say, Mother." He lets go

of my hand, and I almost snatch it back. There is nothing tethering me to this house but him.

I start to follow Atlas and Valentin up the stairs when Mrs. Graves sticks her cane out to block my path. "Not you. This is a house of decency. You will not be staying with the boys. I have prepared you your own room."

My stomach sinks even deeper. Fuck. I understand respecting their rules, but I'm not a fucking child. Does she even know I'm with all three of them? She's looking at me like she thinks I'm the biggest joke she's ever laid eyes on.

Valentin steps in front of me. "With all due respect, Mrs. Graves, Maureen should stay with us."

Her eyes narrow, and I swear I hear her hiss under her breath. She raises her hand, and I think she's going to slap him, but instead, she caresses his cheek. "We have rules in this house, Val. Rules you have always obeyed. Don't start breaking them now. I would hate to have to call your father and tell him of your defiance."

Atlas sighs and places a hand on Val's shoulder. "It's all good, Mrs. Graves. It's just been a long drive." He whispers in Val's ear. *"Let it go."*

I kiss them each on the cheek, much to Mrs. Graves's displeasure, and step away from them. "It's fine. I'll see you all in the library later, okay?"

Atlas nods, but he has to physically drag Valentin toward the large marble staircase.

"This way," she quips. I follow her down a long corridor, amazed at how fast she moves with a limp.

I can't believe she used Val's father as a threat. *Their families are fucking crazy.* She doesn't speak to me again until we reach my room. She turns an antique skeleton key into the ivory doorknob before spinning back around. She studies my face for an uncomfortable amount of time.

"You will not behave like a slut in this house, Miss Blackwell. I won't tolerate it. Especially when it comes to *my* son."

My mouth drops open. "You don't even know me. I... . I am not a slut." Every ounce of shame and rage that I've felt since last Halloween comes rushing back.

She chuckles. "Well, you're certainly no saint. I've seen your type before, my dear. You have those boys wrapped around your traitorous finger like a snake in the grass." She slams her cane down hard against the marble floor as she takes another step toward me. "You don't want to know what we do to snakes around here, Miss Blackwell. I urge you to heed my warning... or you'll find out."

I want to cry, but I won't give her the satisfaction. So I bite my tongue and nod. "Yes, Mrs. Graves."

She backs off and motions for me to enter the room. "Romulus will fetch you in an hour for drinks." She starts to leave but pauses at the door. "There are dresses in the closet. *Decent dresses.* Make sure you wear one of them."

She eyes me up and down one last time before leaving, taking stock of my short skirt and crop top. When the door closes behind her, I hear the click of the key slide into place and turn.

My stomach drops as I bolt to the door and turn the knob. I can feel all the blood rushing to my feet. It's fucking locked.

Fuck.

My heart sinks. I knew the Graves were not going to roll out the red carpet for me. Riot's hatred for my family wasn't born out of thin air. His parents probably poisoned him against us from the moment he took his first breath. But locking me in my room like a child... Clover Graves has managed to make my own mother look like a fucking saint.

As I sift through the elegant closet, my mind races. What has Riot told them about me? How did she get that cane? Are they going to murder me in my sleep tonight? Why do they have a closet full of plain as fuck dresses all in my size?

Ugh.

I pick the least revolting one—a black knee-length sweater dress splashed with red roses. I step into a pair of black pumps, also in my size, and smirk as I admire myself in the mirror. She can force me to wear her clothes all night long, but it doesn't change the fact that there's nothing *decent* about me. I'm still *their* little slut.

I was going to be respectful, but suddenly, the thought of the three of them defiling me in his parent's home, in his mother's dress, makes me feel so hot and depraved that I'm tempted to finger myself right now.

I'd love to see the look on her face when she spots cum stains on her *decent dress*.

I take a deep breath as my clit starts to spasm. I wonder if they have cameras in here...

I'm tempted but think better of it. I don't know what their powers are. And until mine are stronger, I need to try to be on my best behavior. I have no idea what the Graves family is capable of.

A knock on the door interrupts my plans of masturbation, further sealing my decision to act like a well-behaved lady.

I take one last look in the mirror, fluffing my waves out around my shoulders, and start for the door.

"I'm ready. You can let me out now," I grumble.

The key creaks as it unlocks the door, and I'm once again face-to-face with the creepy butler. His lips curl up in annoyance. "There are initiates in this house. Ones who may have impure thoughts. The lock is to keep others out for your own safety."

I snicker. "Well, then she should just let me stay with Atlas or Valentin. They can protect me."

Romulus is careful to keep his gaze on my face, but I know he's already stolen glances at my body by the way he sneers. "We have rules about fornication in this house, madam. You will learn them soon enough."

A chill trickles up my spine. His tone isn't threatening, yet it's

still ominous and foreboding, I can't imagine the horrors he's seen, and may have even been a part of, in this house. I'm not naïve to what Nocturnus is. I tried to run from it myself. But my dumb ass had to go and fall for the three of them.

I nod while trying to swallow down my apprehension. "Fair enough."

He locks the door behind us before spinning on his heel.

"Follow me. I'll show you to the library."

The only thing I'm looking forward to now is the many cocktails I'm about to imbibe. Lord knows I'm going to need them to get through this night.

CHAPTER TWO

I FEAR NOTHING. NOT EVEN DEATH. MY FATHER IS SOMEONE I SHOULD fear. Holden Graves is a monster. But I stopped being afraid of him a long time ago.

And he fucking hates me for it.

I pause before entering my father's office, taking one more peaceful breath before the torture begins. But no matter what he does to me, I have to keep the target off Maureen. He can't know what she means to me. Fuck, I'm still figuring that out my-self. All I know is that the thought of him harming her in any way lights the poison in my veins on fire. I'll burn this whole fucking compound down to keep her away from him and his sick games. I'd be lying if I didn't admit that looking at my father is a bit

like peering into a future mirror. I am my father's son in many ways. From our tall, lanky builds to our jet-black hair, although his is now peppered with grey, to our sharp jawlines, angular noses, and bright-blue eyes. But that's where the similarities end.

Holden Graves is a terrible husband and an even worse father. My mother and I have the physical and mental scars to prove it.

I enter without haste, pushing the door open like it owes me money. I can never appear weak in front of him. He'll find some way to make me pay for it. Every step, every breath has to be calcu-lated around him. Everything I do is deliberate and with purpose. Just one wrong move is all it would take for him to gut me open and feed me to the wolves.

I stand rigid in front of his desk, careful not to make eye con-tact until he addresses me.

"At ease, Riot. Sit the fuck down."

I don't relax, but I sit immediately. My shoulders are so tight, my bones feel like they might crack.

We lock eyes, and a shiver passes through my lips, down my spine, and spreads to every inch of my body. This man is murder in the flesh. Pure fucking evil. It's no wonder I have anger issues. The devil's blood runs through my veins.

It makes me fucking sick to my stomach.

"What do you have to say for yourself?" He leans back in his black leather chair casually. But it's an act. The second I let my guard down, the moment I start to think he's being chill is when he'll strike. He lures his prey into a false sense of safety before ripping their throats out with his bare teeth.

I press my shoulders back and stand my ground. I don't have the luxury of being a normal son. "I assume you're referring to your bastard, Zeke. He's dead. I killed him. There's not much else to say."

My father's nostrils flare even as a twinkle of amusement flit-ters in his eyes. But he doesn't break. "You did *not* kill your brother. Your new slut did. And what I'm *referring* to is how in just one

short semester, you've managed to lose complete fucking control of Nocturnus."

My brother: Fucking pathetic. Atlas and Valentin act more like my brothers than Zeke ever did. That bastard snuck into my coven, staged a coup, and went after my woman. But my father wants to blame me? Nah. Fuck this.

"Maybe if you had better control over your dick, we wouldn't be in this predicament," I bite back.

He doesn't even have to move an inch to bring me to my knees. Without making a sound, he attacks.

A blast of heat hits my chest first, then a barrage of needles stab at my throat. He's always careful about not leaving marks. Physical scars can be covered up with tattoos and clothing. No, he goes for where it hurts the most. He hits the innermost parts of you that you can never escape from.

"You were saying?" His eyes turn black as he continues to assault all my nerve endings.

I don't push back. I'd have to lean on my thread to Maureen, and I don't want him tasting that. It's not his to know. So I stifle my own power and take his punishment like a true fucking Graves.

When I was a kid, my mother tried to stop him. She'd get in between us and beg him to show me mercy. It worked a few times. But eventually, he said that she was making me soft. And he was right. If I had been able to defend myself, my mother wouldn't now need the assistance of a cane to walk. She wouldn't have been robbed of every ounce of joy in her life. He beat it out of her the same way he beat it out of me.

I'll be fucking damned to hell if he thinks he's going to do that to Maureen. Not to mention her ever-growing hold over Atlas and Valentin. Holden Graves will have to get through all three of us, and it won't be pretty.

"Your resistance is futile. I will break you open and take what I want," my father growls.

I smile back at him and continue to hold my position.

He releases me with a snarl. "Do not underestimate me, son. That was just a taste of what's to come if you don't get in fucking line." He smooths his scarred hands down the front of his shirt. "How did you lose control of Nocturnus?"

I have to swallow a few times before I can speak without my voice cracking. He did a fucking number on my throat. "I *didn't* lose control. Zeke and the others failed. The ones I didn't kill are rotting in Absentia Asylum."

He sighs. "And the Blackwell girl?"

I hate that he even knows she exists. "She had nothing to do with it. Wrong place, wrong time," I lie.

"Bullshit," he yells and slams his fist down on the desk. "Have I taught you nothing about that wretched family? They are the rea-son we've been cut off from the source of our power. You and your friends wanna play with her cunt? Fine. But bringing her into this house... marking her with our sigils... you have crossed a fucking line."

I feel the poison in my veins surge. "The Blackwells didn't raise her. They kicked her out of Ever Graves just as they did us. Maureen is nothing like them."

Holden snickers. "Or it's a trick. A lie. It seems you're the one who should have better control of his dick. You're letting it make decisions that affect this entire family. This isn't about me father-ing bastard sons. No. You have brought the enemy into our house. There will be consequences, Riot."

Fuck.

Nothing I say is going to convince him. I need to get her the fuck out of here.

I nod. "You're right. I'll take whatever punishment you see fit."

Keep the focus on me, you fucking tyrant.

He smirks. "Oh, it will be more than fit." The chair screeches against the hardwood floor with the force of his pushing back on

M VIOLET

it as he stands up. "We'll discuss this more later. I'm ready to meet this little temptress of yours. Shall we?"

My stomach turns. "Finally. All this talk has made me fucking parched." Never back down. Never show weakness. Never fucking show emotion.

He nods. "Good. Let's have a civil drink together. You're not going to like me very much after tonight."

Was that a fucking threat?

I snicker back at him. "I don't like you very much right now."

It's a game we play. A battle of wills and wit. We've been doing it my whole life. It's like our entire world is one big game of chess, and my father controls the board. He doesn't see me as his opponent but as his pawn. If he's not careful, I'll have to take him out instead.

I'm uneasy until I see her. She sips on an ice-cold martini by the fire, her warm fingers leaving condensation prints on the glass. Valentin and Atlas flank her on either side, dutiful and loyal like guard dogs. Romulus hands me a single malt scotch as I stalk toward my coven. I've been drawn to Maureen since the moment I saw her in Wickford Hollow. But nothing could have prepared me for how I feel now. The sigil on her neck glows in recognition of our bond as soon as I breathe the same air as she does.

"Hello, Firecracker. You look tasty as fuck," I whisper in her ear, which elicits a shudder from her lips.

"I don't think your mother's very happy about that," she teases.

"Did you know that they locked her in her fucking room?" Valentin barks.

They are playing a dangerous game with me. I try not to show a reaction but simply nod. "Typical. My mother still thinks we're teenagers."

Atlas laughs. "Fuck, remember those days? Sneaking out of your fifth-floor window to go party in the woods. We had to make so many fucking bargains with the ravens so they wouldn't rat us out."

Valentin steps in closer, his nostrils flaring. "This isn't a joke. She should be with us in our room. Not locked away like a prisoner."

I smile and swirl my drink. "Keep your voice down, Val."

Maureen squeezes his hand. "Don't worry, I'm fine. Their house, their rules."

Before Val can get another protest in, a cold draft sweeps through the room, and Holden Graves makes his grand entrance.

"Where's your mother?" Maureen whispers.

I tighten my grip on my glass. The absence of Clover Graves could only mean one thing. This cocktail party isn't a party at all. It's business. And Maureen is the whole fucking agenda.

CHAPTER THREE

Maureen

EVERY CELL IN MY BODY WANTS TO GET AWAY FROM HOLDEN GRAVES. On the surface, he looks like an older version of Riot. But his energy is black and toxic. It oozes out like tendrils of smoke, threatening to suffocate us all.

The guys are on edge, wound tight. As if this man could deprive us of oxygen with just a flick of his fingers. There's a pit of dread stewing in my belly that tells me maybe he could. It's already getting harder to breathe from the tension.

Holden Graves narrows his eyes at me, his gaze traveling up and down the length of my body. I fight the urge to hide behind Riot. I'm not a shrinking violet, but this man's energy is dark and

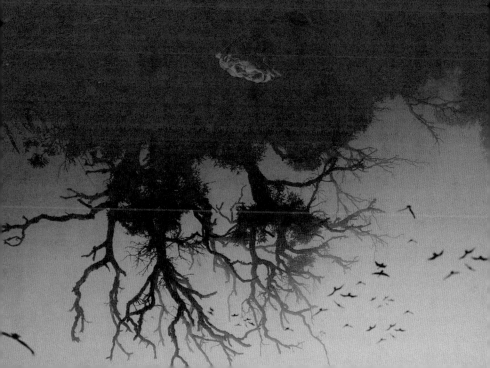

Atlas. How could I say no?"

Holden forces a smile. "No one crafts poison quite like you,

new batches of oleander I'd love to have you try."

tour of your new lab last time you came to Tenebrose. I have some

Atlas smiles and slaps him on the back. "You promised me a

guys are connected to me, and they can feel it too.

up my arm. I hitch my breath, trying not to show a reaction. But the

My heart races as he flexes his power, and a sharp pain travels

of this."

elbow as he notices the sigil on my neck. "And I didn't approve any

"Well, she hasn't earned my respect either." He pinches my

Maureen doesn't deserve your disrespect."

too, incurs the wrath of Holden Graves. "Don't be a dick, Father.

Valentin growls next to me, but Riot cuts him off before he,

never said anything about working for the Blackwells.

I feel my cheeks burn. What is he talking about? My father

your mother couldn't keep her legs closed."

groundskeeper. Such a shame you had to grow up in squalor because

betrayed Val's uncle all those years ago. Getting knocked up by a

arm. "I'm well aware of the scandal your mother caused when she

elbow in his hand, and a slight ping of electricity shoots up my

tice his pupils dilate. "I'm just testing our new friend." He cups my

Holden throws him a dismissive look, but I can't help but no-

Riot hisses. "I already told you she's never been to Ever Graves."

murmur.

and vibes of the *stab you in the back* variety. "I've never met her," I

I don't like the gravel in his voice. It's laced with quiet threats

How is Penelope doing these days?"

copper on fire. That's how she got her nickname, you know? *Penny.*

to us. "You have your grandmother's eyes… like burnt honey or

He strolls over, taking a drink off Romulus's tray on his way

I've been through, there's not much left that scares me. Until now.

sinister. His power looms over us like a black cloud. After everything

Behind that Adonis smile and those sparkling, ocean-colored eyes, Atlas, too, is a predator. A psycho who's not just immune to poison, he drinks it for fun. And right now, with Holden's fingers digging into my arm, I can feel Atlas's crazy going up a few notches in my bones.

When Holden finally lets go, I cradle my arm to my chest. I rub the tender spot he pinched and feel a knot already forming. Fucker. I wonder if he's the reason why his wife walks with a cane.

Riot rests a hand on my lower back in warning. As if my thoughts are too loud.

Atlas reaches into his breast pocket and pulls out a vial. "This one is fucking fire. It will keep your cock hard for hours."

Holden smirks. "I'm sure Maureen appreciates that."

My face flushes again. "Not sure that's any of your business," I snap.

"Oh, you're fiery. Have to be to keep these boys' interest. They get bored rather fast."

"So do I. Kind of like now with this conversation."

Holden steps toward me, and the guys close in around us. "You're right. I'm faking pleasantries when what I really mean to do is get down to business."

"Father," Riot warns. "Leave her out of this."

He shoves a finger in his face while keeping his gaze locked on mine. "Shut your fucking mouth."

Chills race up my back.

"You have pledged yourself to Nocturnus, have you?" Holden asks me.

I nod. "I made an oath to Riot, Val, and Atlas."

He snickers. "They belong to Nocturnus. So now you do as well. As the eldest living Graves heir, I am Nocturnus."

Riot snorts. "Yes, we know, Father. You're the fucking king of the castle."

"What do you want from me?" I whisper. There is no way this man is going to let me walk out of here unscathed.

Holden snaps his fingers and Romulus scurries over like a lap dog. He places a dagger in his hand. The hilt is the same as Riot's.

"A ceremony. It's Nocturnus law for female initiates to submit. In order to be fully accepted into our coven, you will need to take part in this most sacred rite."

"No," Valentin barks. "No fucking way."

Atlas sighs. "We've already done it, Mr. Graves. She's been initiated by us."

Riot stays quiet, but the look in his eyes toward his father is murderous.

"She has not been initiated properly," Holden snaps back. "All your former members are either dead or locked away. It must be done again. I must bear witness. Or I will strip her of her sigils right now."

I clasp my sigil as a warning shot fires up my neck. My skin crackles, and I know that he's holding back. I can feel it. This is just a teaser of what's to come if I don't comply.

"Fine. I'll do it."

"Maui, you have no idea what you're agreeing to." Valentin grabs me and pulls me into his chest.

"I don't think I have much of a choice. Don't forget who I am." I wink at him even though my insides are curdling with fear.

Holden nods. "Good. We'll do it tonight. I don't want you in our house any longer until you've been cleansed. Romulus will get you ready for the ceremony. And your punishment for Zeke will follow after."

Wait. What?

"Punish me," Riot roars. "It's my fault he's dead."

What in the fuck is going on? Punishment? I can't breathe.

Holden grabs Riot by the back of his head and pulls him. "If that's the case, then I'll have to enforce the rule of Hekate."

Riot's face pales. He gathers his composure. "No. That won't be necessary."

"What is the rule of Hekate?" I whisper to Atlas.

"You don't wanna know, Firecracker."

My stomach flips.

He shakes him. "Say it out loud then. I want to hear it from your lips."

Riot's jaw clenches. "She's just a toy for us to play with. I accept whatever punishment you see fit."

I wince. How did he go from begging for my mercy to making me sound like I'm nothing but a whore? He's just lying. But why? What has him so scared that punishing me is the least fucked up thing Holden Graves could do?

Valentin bows his head. "*Bastard*," he curses under his breath. Atlas hands me the vial of poison instead. "You're going to need this."

Holden claps his hands together in delight. "You'll get your toy back soon enough. I'll deliver her to you myself when it's done."

"Wait." My heart hammers. "They're not coming with me?" Having them there was the only way I knew I'd get through this.

"They don't have clearance. This rite of passage is to be witnessed by elder members only." His lips curl up into a smirk.

Fuck. Me.

"Sex is magic. Power. The initiates must bear witness before whatever *this* is can be taken seriously. Those are the rules of old. One of our most sacred rites." Holden Graves hands me a black hooded robe.

I want to be numb. To feel nothing like he does. A part of me wants to run back to Wickford Hollow and hide in Bailey's basement

for the rest of eternity. But I'm in too deep now to turn back. There's too much blood on my hands.

And I can't imagine a life without Riot, Atlas, or Valentin in it. As psychotic as some might think that is, I'll do whatever is asked of me to keep the four of us together.

"You don't have to do this, Maur." Valentin is a towering beacon of rage and sorrow. The darkness takes over his eyes, pitch black and murderous.

Riot stares straight ahead, solemn, refusing to look at me. While Atlas has numbed himself into a stupor, his eyes aglow with poison swirling around his pupils.

I nod. "Yes, I do."

Holden whispers in my ear, *"Your cunt has broken them. Now it's your turn to be humiliated."*

His nostrils flare in my direction when I peel off my dress and panties as I was instructed by Romulus earlier. When I put on the robe and pull up the hood, Holden knows he's won. But he's sadly mistaken if he thinks that he owns me. I'm not doing this for him or his initiates. I'm doing this for us. For my devils.

I follow them down the stairs, leaving my guys behind. I shudder when the heavy metal door closes, cutting me off from them completely. We travel so many levels down I think we might be entering hell itself. The air is thicker the farther we get. The scent of oleander is cloyingly sweet, tickling the hairs on my nose as I try not to inhale too much of it.

My heart beats faster with each step I take, the silence of my sins permeating the spaces between us. Holden leads the way through an intricate maze of tunnels and caverns, a whole other world that exists beneath his estate. Terror begins to creep into my bones as we pass group after group of masked figures.

The initiates at Tenebrose were fledglings. Amateurs. These are not the same. They stand tall and powerful, unafraid. As if they could squash me with just a flick of their fingers. They have all pledged

oaths long ago. And in their callous glares, I detect the disgust for a girl who's broken all their rules. Who took one of their own from them and sent the rest scattering.

We reach another cavern, and my jaw drops open. There must be at least thirty masked initiates standing watch. They hold torches to light the room, casting an eerie glow on their bronzed masks, their eyes demonic.

I shiver and instantly regret agreeing to this. Fuck.

Holden walks around before stopping in front of me. "It's time to learn our true ways now, Miss Blackwell. I'm going to show you how we deal with murderous little whores."

I clench my fists and fight the urge to deck him in the face. He doesn't know shit about me or what the four of us have together. But I bite my tongue. I just want to get this over with.

He snickers, thinking he's won yet again. "As soon as you take off your robe, the ritual will begin. I will give you another sigil. But you will only receive its power when the ceremony is complete in its entirety."

I swallow down the lump in my throat. "What kind of sigil?"

He smirks. "Virility. You like to wield your cunt so badly, I will give you a sigil that lets you do just that, my little temptress."

I have to choke back the bile that's rising in my throat. This man is a fucking monster.

"What do I have to do to complete the ritual?"

His eyes darken. "Sexual surrender is the lifeblood of this ritual. The carnal release of one's essence and nectar is demanded to fulfill the transfer of power. It lives in that fleeting moment of euphoria. That moment of weakness. When you open up your body and soul to receive it."

I look around the room at the initiates. They stand stoically and without expression. This has been done before. That I'm certain of. It's too late to turn back now . . .

"I'm not fucking any of you."

He laughs. "No, you're not. We don't want your filth on us. As I said, when you take off your robe, we will begin." He points to the center altar as an initiate lays a black cloth over it.

With shaky fingers, I untie the robe and let it fall to the ground. I resist the urge to look down. I need to appear strong. He thinks I'm weak, but I'm far from it. So I raise my chin and make eye contact with every single initiate.

Their silence begins to break as they ogle my naked body. They step forward, forming a tighter circle around us. Tiny little breaths escape their tightly controlled lips, floating to me like demonic whispers.

"Lie down on the cloth and spread out. Legs open and hands above your head."

My nerves are shattered, but I lie down and do as he says.

"Very good." With a blade twice the size as Riot's, Holden Graves moves down between my thighs. His eyes narrow when he spots the sigil and snake bite. "Blasphemous," he curses and glares back up at me.

I can't stop shaking now. He looks like he wants to tear me to shreds.

He nods to two initiates. "Hold her down."

One grabs my wrists and pins them while another does the same to my ankles. I take deep breaths and will my heart to slow down so I don't have a fucking heart attack.

"I guess virility will have to go here instead." He grabs a hold of my unmarked thigh and pins it back. He rests one hand against my pussy, shifting his body weight onto it. "For leverage."

My blood is fucking boiling.

Without warning, he digs the knife into my thigh. "You will bleed for me."

I scream as he carves into me with zero care or concern for my flesh. It feels like he's fucking butchering me. This isn't sacred or special like the way it was with my guys.

Saliva drips from his mouth as he swirls the knife around for what seems like an eternity. "Such a beautiful sight, little temptress. Red is a good color on you."

I arch my back as the burn spreads through my belly and then shoots up my spine. This feels different than Riot's marks. There's an underlying current of evil that runs through Holden's blade. It scratches and claws at my bones like a pack of angry wolves. I grunt through it, refusing to let him see me cry.

He steps back and nods to the initiates once more. They release their hold on my wrists and ankles, but I stay still. I don't trust this monster, and I don't want to give him a single reason to torture me some more.

He holds up the knife, showing it off to his initiates. "The gate is open. It's begun."

"What now?" I breathe.

He snarls down at me. "Now, you will bring yourself to release."

My stomach flips. Oh, fuck. No, this can't be happening.

"In . . . in front of all of you?" I knew he was going to mark me, but this level of depravity is on another level.

He smiles when he sees the horror on my face. "Yes. A woman's juices are like sweet nectar from the gods. You will release them in this sacred room." He beckons to his initiates. "Come closer."

They inch in, making room for each other to get a better view.

Fuck.

When I hesitate, he leans down and whispers in my ear, "*Do it, or I'll do it for you.*"

Fuck. Why is this happening?

I gently slide my index finger down the slit of my pussy.

Holden sighs. "Don't be shy now, little temptress." He digs his thumb into my freshly carved sigil, and I scream. "Act like you mean it, or this will burn you from the inside out."

And I believe him.

I pull my pussy lips back, rolling my hips as I stroke myself.

Despite my rage, it sends spasms deep inside me. I can't stop the moan from leaving my lips as I feel the pleasure take hold of me.

"Bear witness to the mark of virility," Holden shouts. Then he leans down and whispers again in my ear. "You need to touch that spot deep inside you, little temptress."

The sound of his voice in my ear makes me want to puke, but the pressure building in my core overpowers it. It's the fucking sigil making me crave release. Fuck.

I try to ignore him and continue to fondle myself. I go back and forth between rubbing my clit and my lips. I hate how fucking wet I am.

Holden grabs a fistful of my hair. "We are entitled to watch you fuck yourself. Now, get those fingers in nice and deep before I flay the skin off your back."

The heat from my thigh surges, and it really does feel like he's lit a match underneath me. I grunt in frustration, not wanting to give him what he wants but knowing that I have to.

I push my finger all the way inside my pussy and let out a deep moan. I arch my back, rolling my hips up as I press against my G-spot. Fuck. It feels so fucking good. I try to pretend they're not there as I add a second finger, flicking wildly against my core.

I pump in and out as the initiates watch me, breathless and silent. It's fucking creepy as hell, but I don't even care anymore. My orgasm is starting to build, and all I want to do is surrender to it.

He laughs in my face. "You're not just *their* little slut anymore, are you? No, you belong to Nocturnus. To all of us. *To me*." He motions to an initiate. "Show her. Mark her with your virility."

My heart races, but I can't stop chasing my high. The initiate pulls his robe open, revealing his hard cock. He doesn't utter a sound as he strokes himself. The vein in his shaft pulses right before a stream of cum bursts out. He shoots it onto my belly.

I scream and try to roll away from it, but Holden pins my shoulders down. "You will take a mark of virility from each one of us. And

if you stop fucking yourself one more time, I will let one of them cum in your fucking mouth."

Fuck. Panic mixed with pleasure sends me into a tailspin. I need to cum and get this over with. I need to show him that the ritual is done.

I work my fingers in and out as my orgasm starts to climb again. I try to ignore the sticky cum on my belly, I try not to touch it too.

"Oh, fuck," I cry out as I clench around my fingers. A deep spasm reverberates through my core, sending tingles to every inch of my body.

"That's it. Surrender. Give your power over to Nocturnus." He sends another initiate up as I ride it out, who does the same as the last. This time I feel the thick cum dripping down my calf.

All I can do is moan as my orgasm climbs into another one. The sigil on my thigh sends what feels like little electric shocks straight to my core. Riot's sigil flares in response and mimics it. I can't stop bucking like a wild animal now as, one by one, all the initiates jerk themselves off on me.

I'm covered in their cum.

A gurgling cry escapes from my throat as I come down from the rush.

Fuck. It's fucking over.

Holden raises his hands above his head. "The first two who step forward will get the honor of bathing our little temptress."

I roll over and try to cover myself with the black altar cloth. "Just let me go back to my room. I can clean myself up."

"You think it's over?" He lets out the wickedest laugh I've ever heard. "We are far from done here, Miss Blackwell. We will get you cleaned up and ready for the next part."

Oh, fuck, no. "What's the next part? How many parts are there?"

"You'll see," Holden sneers right before two initiates step forward and clasp onto my wrists.

There is a bucket full of water at my feet. The two masked initiates take turns dipping their sponges into it. I am beyond fighting now. There's nothing I can do but surrender.

"Cleansing is a powerful part of any ritual. You must wash away your sins and start anew," Holden spews his bullshit like he thinks he's a god.

The sponges are rough and scratchy, but it's better than being covered in initiate cum.

They take turns scrubbing me. I flinch every time one of them rubs their sponge over my breasts or down my ass crack. But I grit my teeth and continue to bear it.

And Holden enjoys every second of my displeasure and humiliation. "Make sure you clean all of that disgusting cum from her pussy," he commands to one of the initiates.

My stomach turns. Fuck. "No."

He arches an eyebrow at me. "How dare you tell me no, temptress. You agreed to this punishment. I know you're a traitor, but are you a liar too?"

My cheeks flame, but I shake my head. "No, I'm not." I let out a deep breath as he nods for them to continue.

One of the initiates separates the folds of my pussy back while the other slowly swirls the sponge inside me, forcefully raking my tender flesh with it in a circular motion. I have to lean back against the other one so I don't lose my footing. I feel his hard cock poke against my ass through his altar robe, and my stomach knots.

Holden laughs. "Yeah, that's it. Clean that filthy cunt."

The one standing behind me lifts my leg, opening me up wider. I hear the other one's breath hitch as he drags the sponge up and down the length of me, his gloved fingers grazing my folds.

Holden shakes his head. "Lie her down."

I have to fight back the bile because fuck knows what he'd do to me if I puked all over them.

They urge me down, and I lie back without protest. The one from behind grabs a sponge and starts on my breasts again, working it in slow circles.

Holden claps in delight. "That's it. Wash away all that filth."

The other one gawks at me through the mask, his eyes glazing with lust and depravity. He's enjoying every minute of my humiliation. All of them are. Especially Holden.

Holden snaps his fingers, and another initiate stalks over. He pushes my thighs apart while the new one pours water from a pitcher down my slit.

Holden snickers. "This is Nocturnus holy water, little temptress. It's going to sanctify that blasphemous cunt of yours."

This is all for Zeke. I get that now. This isn't about recognizing me as a Nocturnus member. No. It's about punishment and revenge. It's about control.

As if he can read my mind, the nightmare begins again.

Holden motions for them to stop wiping me. He paces in circles around me, appearing as if he's deep in thought. "You took something from us, Miss Blackwell. Rather, someone, I should say. If you weren't under Riot's protection, you'd already be dead."

Fuck.

"It was self-defense—"

"Quiet!" Holden slaps me across the face so hard I lose my breath. "I don't want to hear traitorous things about my son. I can't kill you, but I will dole out a punishment."

I fight back the tears, but it's getting harder not to fall apart.

"What are you going to do to me?"

He chuckles. "It's what all of us are going to do to you. For my son, for their fallen brother... One lashing from each of us. They get to choose your ass or your cunt. You think you can handle thirty-five lashings, Miss Blackwell?"

The tears stream down my cheeks. "Please..."

He swipes his thumb across my wet cheek. "The best part is that I get to watch you cum again.

"What? Are you crazy? You think I'm going to get off on this?"

He sucks my tear off his thumb. "Oh, that sigil I gave you will make sure of it. You're going to beg for each and every lashing."

My face burns with humiliation. I want this to be over so fucking bad. But he just keeps making up new rules as we go along. I'm at the mercy of a madman.

"Get on your knees, temptress." As I turn over and shift to my knees, he pushes me down hard. I catch myself with my palms just before my face smashes against the cement.

I'm on all fours, shivering as I wait for whatever happens next.

I cringe as I hear him slide his belt out of his pants. He drags the end of it down the length of my back before letting it rest on my ass.

"Widen your stance." He watches my every move as I spread my legs farther apart. "Yes, like that. Angle your ass up and get down on your forearms. Press your face against the ground."

The cold cement touches my cheek first and then grazes my nipples as I lower myself down to the position he demands of me.

I take deep breaths, readying myself for the world of pain this maniac is about to bestow upon me.

"I will inflict the first lashing and the last. *For my son*," he growls.

And I'm not entirely sure which son he's referring to at this point. For killing Zeke or claiming Riot.

Without warning, I feel the woosh of air before the belt snaps down on my ass.

"Fuck," I cry out. It stings and prickles.

He ignores my cry. "Next."

The first initiate steps out of the circle and stalks toward me.

Holden hands him the belt, and he cracks it down just as hard, wielding it with the same undercurrent of anger. My knees are already starting to throb as I try to hold myself up.

After three more initiates inflict their lashes, I am almost pos-itive that I'm swollen. I'm shaking all over. *Only thirty more to go.*

"I think she could use a few on the other side, don't you think?" It's a rhetorical question posed to a group of psychos who will al-ways agree with him. "Get on your back, temptress."

I whimper in pain as I lie back on the cold ground. While I'm grateful to give my knees a break, it hurts to put weight on my ass.

"Please . . . show mercy."

He snarls down at me. "I'm getting really tired of having to tell you to open your fucking legs."

This man fucking hates me.

I spread my thighs apart as far as they'll go.

He smirks and hands the belt to another initiate. "Now, this is where we'll get to see her unravel."

The initiate towers over me, readying himself. I can almost feel the sick pleasure twisting in his gut. He drags the tip of the belt down my slit. I don't look away.

"That's it. Do it for Zeke," Holden coos.

The initiate grunts right before he jerks his wrist up and smacks my pussy with the end of the belt. I cry out and buck my hips. The sting of the leather sends a spasm to my clit. The fresh sigil on my thigh burns and weeps as if it's thirsty for more.

Fuck.

One by one, they continue. I am rabid, feral, and depraved. With each sting, the tingling in my core builds. I can't stifle the moans. Each break in between edges me closer to release. I hate that I need it.

I'm on my back again as Holden stands over me. "Time flies when you're having fun. I have to say, I'm impressed. Thirty-four lashings and you're still conscious. I'm gonna give you your final one. But I want your cum leaking out when I do."

I want to cum so badly, just not in front of him. But I have no choice.

He nods to two of his initiates, and within seconds, they're attaching cold metal clamps to my nipples. "For the final blow . . . a final mark." They bring him a mortar and pestle. I can smell the cloyingly sweet mixture as he mashes it up.

He kneels over me and begins drawing markings on my flesh with the thick paste. "Nightshade, the crushed bones of a raven, and my precious Zeke's blood."

I jerk my face away as he paints my cheeks. "*No.* I don't want his blood on me!" I scream.

"Hold her down!" One of the initiates who bathed me charges forward and pins my arms above my head. Holden pinches my chin hard and roars back, "His blood *is* already on you! It's all over your traitorous hands."

The tears I've been holding finally spill out. The shame he's marked me with threatens to eat me alive.

Holden laughs as he stands up and readies the belt. He drags it up and down my slit, stimulating all the nerves in my pussy. My clit begins to spasm. "That's it, little temptress. We're almost done. Relax and surrender to the power of Nocturnus."

I blink back more tears, and as I gaze up at him, I swear he has two horns on his head and a raven's beak. Or am I hallucinating from the poison that's seeping into my skin?

I can feel my orgasm building, and it makes me sick. But I can't control it. The sigil sends spasms to my core in waves, faster, harder, over and over until I can barely hold back any longer.

Holden raises the belt. "I spilled your blood. Now, I will spill your nectar." He lashes down, slapping the belt hard against my throbbing pussy. I buck at the contact and gasp as a deep orgasm takes hold. Like a feral animal, I break free from the initiate and snatch the belt away from Holden. I squeeze my thighs around it and feel instant gratification. *I need this release.* I rub the belt back and forth between my folds as I ride out each wave of pleasure.

He steps back and watches, satisfied that he's turned me into

M VIOLET

this crazed wild thing. "Don't ever forget who you belong to, tempt-ress. I can take away your freedom *anytime* I fucking want. No one will stop me. Not Valentin. Not Atlas. And especially not Riot. They bow to me. Now you do too. Welcome to Nocturnus."

The room empties out, and I'm left alone on the cold hard ce-ment. I lie there for what seems like hours, teetering on the edge of consciousness until someone picks me up and carries me out. Before we reach the top of the stairs, I black out.

CHAPTER FOUR

Valentin

I CAN'T HEAR HER SCREAMS, BUT I FEEL THEM. THEY REVERBERATE underneath my skin, seeping into my bones and blood. They're torturing her... *our firecracker.* And I can't do a fucking thing. It's ritual. Tradition. An oath that we all pledged, including her. But someday, when we have more power than Holden Graves, *I will seek* retribution for this night.

Riot is locked away in a cell down below. He went mad after they took her down the stairs. He wanted his father to punish *him,* not Maureen. And so that's exactly what Holden did. There is no pain you can inflict on Riot Graves that will make him break. But hurt his firecracker, and it will send him into the deepest depths of hell and despair.

"We should have fought harder to keep her out of this," I grumble.

Atlas sprawls across the bed next to me. "You heard him. If we pushed, he'd enforce the rule of Hekate. Holden is stronger than us here. With all his initiates around him . . . they would be doing much worse to our girl right now."

What a dumb fucking rule. I want to set this entire house on fire.

The rule of Hekate is as old as Nocturnus itself. A clause put in our bylaws to keep initiates from running off for love. We don't have many women in our order, but this rule exists for the ones who manage to slip through.

Fall in love with a female initiate, and you will be forced to watch every other initiate fuck her. If you have any ounce of decency in your bones, Nocturnus will make sure to flay it out of you. We're taught that love is weakness. Marriage is for duty and carrying on our bloodlines. And female initiates are not fit to be wives.

Only playthings.

So we can't fucking show how much we care about Maureen while we're in this house.

"Your pupils are the size of golf balls, Val. She's going to be fine. You need to relax before you have an aneurysm." Atlas hands me a vial of nightshade. "Drink."

I gulp it down in one sip. I've always hated this house. Even more so than my own. The energy here . . . it pulls at my darkness.

"Why are you so fucking cheery right now?"

Atlas sits up. A blue glow flashes through his eyes, his pupils dilated. His smile fades, a snarl replacing it. "I can feel her pain. Her sadness. But I'm trying not to betray my oath."

I nod. "Why are we letting him do this to her?"

He sighs. "The ravens can't control us anymore, but Holden still has more power than we do. If we try to go up against him now, we'll lose. We need to wait until we're stronger."

He's right, but it still makes me want to stab people. "She's going to need extra care after this. I'm… afraid of what this will do to her."

Atlas swills another vial of poison, taking it back, his gaze hardening on the ceiling as he lies back down. "She'll be fine. It's just an initiation ritual."

The door bursts open just before Riot stalks through. A fire blazes in his eyes. "She's back in her room. Resting."

Atlas and I shuffle off the bed and go to him, each grabbing one of his hands. I feel his anger surge through me. "Have you seen her?"

He shakes his head. "Not yet. I don't want to face her alone."

Atlas grabs the back of his head and pulls him close. "Let's get our girl and get the fuck out of here."

Romulus unlocks Maureen's door for us and for a second I contemplate bashing his head in. But he's not the one keeping her caged like an animal. He's a pawn like the rest of us.

My breath catches in my throat when I see her. She's curled up in the fetal position on the bed, naked. The flesh on her ass is bruised and swollen. A dark energy passes through us collectively. A rage that's about to spill over.

"Ah, look how innocent she looks while she sleeps," Holden snickers from behind us.

The three of us whip around and block her from his view.

Riot clenches his fists. "What the actual fuck did you do to her?"

Holden stalks toward his son, his gaze hardening with each step. "I marked her. Broke her. And then I punished her for her treachery. We all did. You didn't really think I was going to let her get away with murdering Zeke, did you? Bastard or not, he was my flesh and

blood. And he was Nocturnus. Your little temptress is lucky I didn't snap her fucking neck."

"Don't call her that," Atlas growls. I glance over to see him practically foaming at the mouth, the first show of anger he's displayed since we arrived here.

Riot takes another step toward his father. "I will never forget this."

He chuckles. "No, you won't. And neither will she. Every time you lick her cunt, you'll see my sigil on her creamy white thigh."

Bile rises up in my throat. I almost choke on it. There will be a time and a place for us to mend Maureen's scars, but we can't do that here. "So we're square then," I say in the most monotone voice I can muster. "We're free to leave." *I'm not asking.*

He smirks, satisfied that he's fucked us all up for life. "You can go if you like. But don't ever defy me again. If you had killed this slut when I told you to, your brother would still be alive."

What the actual fuck? I look over at Atlas to see he's just as startled as I am. Riot never told us Holden wanted Maureen dead. Fucking hell. It's going to be a long fucking night.

Riot starts forward, and I place my hand on his chest, preventing him from knocking into his father. "That *slut* is with us now. She took your mark and did everything you asked. You will not touch her ever again."

Holden laughs. "Relax, son. I'm not going to take away your toy. I just wanted to play with it for a while."

One more word out of this asshole's mouth, and it will be the end of us. I am shaking so hard that I'm nearing convulsions. "Let's go," I growl.

Without hesitating, Atlas throws a blanket over her and gently scoops her off the bed, cradling her to his muscled chest. She looks like a tiny doll in his big arms.

I grab her bag and nudge Riot toward the door.

As we make it into the foyer, Holden's sick laughter echoes

from behind us. I keep pushing Riot forward. We can't fight his father. Not like this. Not with our strongest link broken and unconscious in Atlas's arms.

And he knows this. He taunts us with it. But what he doesn't know is that there's a deadly storm brewing in each of us. We are all breaking tonight. But when we heal, there will be fucking hell to pay. The second Holden Graves touched our girl; he made the worst mistake of his life.

I swallow back my anger and keep walking toward the front door. Clover Graves waits for us.

"Leaving so soon?" She leans heavier on her cane tonight.

Riot shakes his head and sighs. "I will protect Maureen in all the ways that you couldn't protect me, Mother."

She raises her chin, her eyes cold and glassy. "You were always different, Riot. I'm not sure if that's to your benefit or detriment. I guess we'll see what you're made of sooner or later."

He leans in and lays a soft peck on her cheek right before he snarls in her ear, "*Plan for sooner.*"

CHAPTER FIVE

Alice

"SHE HAS A FEVER," I CRADLE HER HEAD IN MY LAP IN THE BACKSEAT of Val's car.

Riot grunts as he pounds his fist down on the dashboard.

"I swear to the fucking raven I will kill him for this."

"She did this for us," I murmur as I stroke her cheek.

Valentin grips the wheel, taking the turns through the back roads of Raven's Gate like a race car driver. "And we fucking let her. After everything she's already sacrificed for us. Now this? It's unforgivable."

He's partly right, but this is the world we live in. This is what it means to be Nocturnus. "Maureen knew what she was getting into with us."

"Did she though?" Riot roars. "Did she even have a choice?"

She's always been meant for us. There's no escaping that fate.

Maureen knew it the second she saw us. We knew it. Even as much as we all tried to fight it. "No. None of us had a choice. The ravens set this path in motion a long time ago."

"Fuck the ravens," Valentin grumbles.

"I wish I never went to Wickford Hollow that night." Riot glances back. The pain in his eyes is palpable.

"You killed for her that night," I remind him.

He reaches out to touch her, then shrinks back. "And I will again."

We all will.

I didn't grow up with the same violence that Val and Riot did. Their fathers are monsters. Mine was just never around. Even now, I barely speak to him. But you know what they say about idle hands. I got really fucking good at hiding my true nature.

While my father, Pisces Thorn, is a part of Nocturnus, he's always been way too narcissistic to take any of it seriously. He'll show up if Holden demands it, but he's always got one foot out the door. Holden doesn't give a fuck as long as my family keeps supplying him with poison.

The farther away we get from the Graves Estate, the lighter my chest feels. Or maybe it's the copious amounts of nightshade I've been downing. I watch her take shallow breaths while she sleeps, her shoulders twitching under Riot's leather jacket. But she *is* breathing, and that's all that fucking matters. Although, knowing Maureen . . . she's going to be feral as fuck when she wakes up.

Riot shakes his head. "What the fuck have we done?"

"Nothing," I bark. "She paid a price just like we all have. And now it's done. Get a fucking grip, Riot." The poison is almost out of my system, and my patience is wearing thin. This is who we are. Devils. But these two suddenly fucking think they're saints.

Val glares at me in the rearview. "Forgive me for forgetting how unstable you are, Atlas. Thanks for the reminder."

I can't help but chuckle. "You love my chaos. And so does she. What you two don't seem to get is the fact that Holden Graves may have just created the monster we need to defeat him and the Blackwells."

Riot's head jerks back, his eyes glowing bright blue. "So, she's just a pawn to you?"

A wave of giddiness rolls through me. My cock instantly hardens at the idea of what dark and depraved things will come from our little firecracker in the nights to come.

I stroke her cheek, relishing the warmth it brings to my icy fingertips. "She's whatever we want her to be. Don't you see? Everything she does is for us. Every limb in her body aches to please us."

Valentin sighs. "You're an asshole."

"I'm a fucking god. All three of us are. And she's our dirty little saint. How quickly you forget that it was only a few weeks ago when you forced your cock into her mouth. And *you*," I smirk at Riot, "shoved your fingers inside her bloody cunt. You might no longer hate her for being a Blackwell, but she's still our doll to play with."

For fuck's sake, do they think we were going to hold hands and dance around a campfire together? These fucks need to be reminded of who they fucking are.

"I don't give you enough credit, Atlas," Riot mutters. "Your brand of psycho scares even me sometimes."

I laugh as Valentin pulls into the driveway of the cabin. People always think I'm the sweet one. When your eyes sparkle like the ocean, it lures them in, makes them trust you. My level of depravity simmers. It hides behind my charming smile, sculptured cheekbones, and pretty blond hair. And just when you think you're safe, I'll strike. But Maureen isn't some wilting flower. She's strong and beautiful and feisty as fuck.

They'll see."

After tending to Maureen's wounds with various ointments and salves, we dress her in a loose T-shirt and sweatpants. I place her

on the couch, cover her with a blanket, and plant a soft kiss on her cheek before joining the others in the kitchen.

Riot sits on top of the granite counter, taking long pulls from a bottle of bourbon. Even with his dark hair matted and sweaty, his skin sallow from his father's parlor tricks, he's still one of the most striking men I've ever seen. A kind of strange, beautiful that takes your breath away. His cold demeanor only enhances his looks more. My cock begins to swell. It's been way too fucking long since we've made each other cum.

Valentin snickers. "I can see your fucking hard-on from here, Atlas."

"When is he ever *not* hard?" Riot hops off the counter and stalks toward me. He cups my dick through my pants. "We'll play later, okay?"

I nod and take a pull from the bottle. "I'll find other ways to amuse myself until then."

Valentin pats me on the back. "I'm going down to the crypt." Broody fucker. He always did prefer his own company to ours. Maybe a few hours down in the dark with his dead relatives will settle him.

I toss him a vial of wolfsbane. "Don't have too much fun without us."

Riot arches an eyebrow at me. "You're still hard."

"I am." A mischievous grin spreads across my face.

"Fuck," he mutters. "I'm going for a walk. Don't come crying to us when she wakes up and stabs you."

I laugh as I watch him leave through the front door and turn right toward the forest. The ravens squawk at him but he's unfazed. That man's shell is impenetrable.

Now, I'm going to go remind our girl that there's no fucking rest for the wicked.

I pick her up off the couch and carry her upstairs to my room.

She smells like soap and firewood. "Mmm, you're so fucking pretty," I whisper in her ear. She whimpers slightly but stays asleep.

I lie her down on my bed. A rush of adrenaline shoots through my veins. This is devious and twisted and fucking hot. I pull her sweatpants down, taking her panties off along with them.

My breath hitches at the sight of her bare pussy. I want to devour it. "I'm going to get you so wet, love."

I kiss her neck as I carefully pull her arms out of her T-shirt before getting it over her head and off. I toss it to the floor. I watch her for a few minutes, admiring her curves. Her nipples are hard and red, swollen with lust that she's not even aware of yet. It's like her body knows what it wants even when her mind is asleep.

"I'm going to have some fun now." I push her legs apart and kneel in between them. She arches slightly in response. "Thatta girl." I slide my finger up and down her slit. "Oh, fuck you *are* soaked."

Fuck. I hadn't expected her to be that wet so fast.

Her pulse quickens, and she lets out another little whimper just as I slip my finger inside her pussy, inching it all the way in. "Mmm, so warm and slick." I'm on the verge of losing control. I pump my finger in and out, watching how her belly trembles with each thrust. To have this kind of control over her... it makes my cock twitch and ache to be inside her. But I want to play with my doll first.

I pinch one of her nipples, and she bucks. Her eyelids flutter, but she stays asleep. Fucking hell. Her chest flushes pink as I work my finger deeper inside her. I press my thumb against her clit. "Fuck, I love touching you like this. You're doing so good."

Her pulse jumps again when I shove a second finger in. "Mmm, you like that. I know your body better than you know it yourself."

She lets out a moan.

It's taking everything I have not to stick my cock inside her. I push her legs wider apart and peel her pussy lips back so I can get a better visual of my fingers sliding in and out. "I can't wait

DIRTY LITTLE SAINT

to see the look in your eyes when you wake up with cum dripping down your legs."

She rolls her hips up and rides my hand. "Oh, baby... fuck yeah. Just like that."

Her juices begin to trickle out. I lean down and lap them up, licking from taint to nub. "You taste like the sweetest sin."

She moans and tosses her head from side to side. So close. Any moment now, she's going to wake up and see what I'm doing to her. This makes my cock throb in my pants. I pump my fingers faster.

"Atlas..." she murmurs.

I take off my shirt. "Is my pretty little psycho awake?"

Her eyelids flutter again before opening to half-slit. She blinks a couple of times. "What... oh, fuck."

I pinch her nub. "You're so fun to play with."

Her eyes widen. I can almost see her brain catching up with her body. "Where are we?"

I don't stop fucking her with my fingers. "In my room at the cabin."

She bucks again as I hit that sacred spot deep inside her. "What the fuck are you doing?"

"Getting you ready for me to fuck you."

"You couldn't wait until I was awake?"

I take off my pants and kneel in between her legs. "No. Feel free to return the favor to me anytime."

I squeeze her clit, and she loses it. The second her cum squirts out, I thrust my cock inside her, filling her tight little hole to the brim. She screams as she clenches and then stretches around me.

"You're a fucking psycho," she growls as she cums all over my dick. I can't hold back any longer. I wrap my hand around her throat and give her pussy a hard thrust. "And you're my fucking drug," I howl as all the blood rushes to the tip of my cock. A spasm shoots down my shaft right before I explode inside her.

CHAPTER SIX

Maureen

I LOOK UP AT THE FERAL PREDATOR BETWEEN MY LEGS AND WANT TO scream. He's more unhinged than I thought he was. Should I really be surprised? And yet my body is tingling, spasming with pleasure. Every inch of my skin is on fire. His cock twitches against the sides of my pussy, reminding me of the control he has over me.

How I'm a slave to this desire.

Atlas leans over, pressing his chest against mine as he pins my wrists above my head. "I'm going to be greedy now."

He rocks into me slowly, his cock hardening again. And I can't help but rock with him. He feels so fucking good. He moves slower this time, gentler. I can feel the entire shape of him, every ridge and vein, as it throbs inside me.

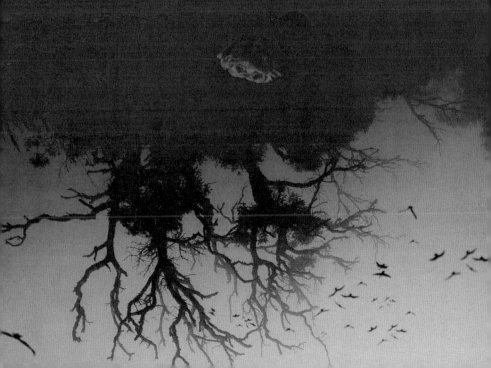

"Fuck," I moan as he burrows in deeper. I can almost feel him in my stomach.

He covers my mouth with his. We both gasp when our tongues touch. He kisses me hard, desperate to swallow me whole.

"I will fuck you like this all night. Deep... and *slow*." He rolls his hips up and down in a tortuous rhythm.

What the fuck is wrong with me? I should be furious with him for touching me while I was asleep. But instead, I'm opening my legs wider and praying he never stops.

I don't even care about my tender flesh and aching muscles. My heart rate jumps as images from last night flash in my mind. I close my eyes and try to block out the lashings. The humiliation of being tortured in a room full of men who were aroused by my suffering.

"*Harder*," I demand.

Atlas slams into me. "That's it, my love. Let me help you forget."

I wrap my legs around his waist and squeeze, desperate to feel every inch of him. I bite down hard on his ear before I whisper, "I hate what the three of you have done to me."

He pulls out and violently thrusts back in. "You fucking love this. *That* is what you hate."

Is he right? Am I ashamed that all this sickness actually turns me on? "I want a drink."

"Right now? While I'm fucking you?" Atlas laughs and reaches for the half-empty bottle of bourbon on the bedside table.

I grab his wrist. "No. I want what *you* drink."

His gaze heats with desire. "That's my girl." He picks up his jeans from the bed and gives them a shake. A vial of poison falls out of the pocket and into his palm.

"Come get it, then." He fists his cock and pours out a few droplets of nightshade onto his shaft.

I lick my lips and get on my knees, panting over his glistening cock. Thirsty for his sweat and poison. I drag my tongue up the

length of him and feel an instant burn. But it numbs the pain every-where else. *It quiets the demons in my head.*

He hums in appreciation when I take all of him into my mouth.

"Oh, shit... Yeah, just like that, baby. Suck me as hard as you fuck-ing want."

I slide my lips up and down while he threads his fingers in my hair. The salt from his skin mixed with the toxin sends my pulse into a frenzy. He grunts and pulls my hair as I scrape my teeth across his shaft.

Without warning, his cum bursts into my mouth, his cock puls-ing against my cheeks as I swallow it down. He grabs the nape of my neck and thrusts all the way to the back of my throat. My eyes water and I have to breathe through my nose as he gags me.

But it feels so fucking good.

He chuckles as he pulls out. "Fuck, that was good."

I lick my swollen lips as I come up for air. "You better sleep with one eye open, Atlas. I will get you back for violating me."

He squeezes my chin and then gives my cheek a playful slap. "I can't wait for your revenge, Maur. I'm sure it's going to be fuck-ing epic."

I roll my eyes and slide off the bed. "Where are the other two psychos?"

He hands me the sweats and T-shirt I'd been wearing before he ripped them off me. "They're around here somewhere. Hey... are you okay?"

I glare at him as I dress. "Okay? You have no idea what they did to me. I thought you'd be more concerned."

He sighs. "I was. But I knew you could handle it. I won't let them hurt you, Maur."

I charge forward and give him a hard shove. "But they did fuck-ing hurt me, Atlas. Didn't you get a good look at the welts on my ass? Or were you too busy staring at my pussy?"

He tries to hug me, but I push him away. "Maur—"

"*Thirty-five lashes.* Front and back. For killing a man in self-defense. A man you all hated and were going to kill anyway. Tell me,
what would Holden Graves have done to *you* if you'd been the one
to shove the knife in Zeke's chest? Hmm? I bet you wouldn't have
had to strip naked and make yourself cum in front of a bunch of
creepy old men."

Atlas's nostrils flare. "They made you do what?"

I snicker. "Oh, you didn't know they were going to do that? You
must have missed the memo. What the fuck else did you think was
going to happen? I'm a woman. I knew what was in store for me the
second I saw the way Holden looked at me."

He's pacing around the room now, sweat beading at his neck.

"Then why the hell did you agree? We would have gotten you out
of there if you asked."

I throw up my hands, frustrated with how simple-minded and
naïve he's acting. "Because he would have punished Riot instead!"
I yell. Tears start pouring down my cheeks before I can stop them.
"I ... didn't want him to get hurt because of me."

I wipe my face with my arm, the rage building again when I
think about Holden's hand on my pussy, the way he cupped it while
he mutilated my thigh. "But the three of you let me go in there alone.
You let it go on for hours. Didn't you think at any point that, hey,
maybe we should go check and make sure she's still alive?"

Atlas's chest heaves, his breathing erratic. "I'm sorry ... we didn't
think. This life is all we know. I forget that you're not used to all this."

I snicker again and head for the bedroom door. "You're right.
How could I forget? The three of you did the same fucking thing to
Libra. And she's your own flesh and blood. I knew there was going
to be some fucked up weird shit that I had to do to be *initiated*, but
that ... what they did to me ... it was a joke to them. A game. They're
probably all laughing about it together right now."

Atlas reaches for me again, but I slide out of his grasp. "Maureen,
I'm sorry. Please. Fuck. I didn't know."

I laugh in his face. "Holden Graves said that I belong to him now. To all of those bastards. He let them jerk off all over me. I was *covered* in their cum. It leaked into every fucking crevice of my body. Deep down, you had to fucking know."

Before he can say another word, I open the door to find Valentin glaring daggers in our direction. He braces himself against the door-frame, his arms shaking. "I'm going to fucking murder all of them."

An ache forms in my chest. Fucking Val... The violence that breeds in his eyes has always been my salvation. He's the only one who said I didn't have to go through with the ritual. That he'd take me away. But the sight of him still makes me angry.

I shove him out of my way. "*You should have come for me*," I snarl.

He nods. "You're right. I failed. Tell me what to do."

My heart breaks for him. I know he will let this guilt destroy him. But I'm too angry to show mercy right now. "You can both go to hell. I'm done."

Atlas's eyes widen. "You aren't leaving, are you?"

"Let her go if she wants. I don't blame her," Val sighs.

I shake my head. "I'm not leaving. I just need some air. And to be alone."

"I'm so sorry, Maur..." Val looks like a wounded puppy. It's al-most endearing until I feel a twinge in my ass cheek. And I remem-ber that I'm not going to be sitting down comfortably for a while. I brush past them both without another word. I need to get the fuck out of this house for a while. Or I might be tempted to burn it down.

I'm still fuming as I stomp through the front yard and head for the forest. My tightly laced boots are the first comforting thing I feel as

they carry me. I'm so angry I don't even flinch when a raven swoops down to squawk at me.

"Fuck you!" I scream and shove my middle finger toward its face. "And fuck you too, Riot. I know you're following me."

He huffs but continues to hang back, preferring to stalk me like a serial killer instead.

Whatever.

The tree line thickens as I move deeper into the forest, darkening my path. But it doesn't deter me. In fact, it spurs me on. I want to be bathed in darkness. It's the only thing that calls to me. The only feeling I want to embrace.

I slow my pace as the branches thicken out of their stumps, tangling and twisting on the ground. I almost trip as I step over them. But I am focused, pissed off, and on a mission to sink as deep into the gloom of this space as I can get.

My sigils flare, singeing my flesh with every step I take. Riot's boots crunch behind me. He's keeping his distance, but it's only a matter of time before he corners me. I look forward to when he does so I can hurl all my anger at his emotionless fucking face.

I come to a clearing where the trees have slightly pulled away, but the sky is still obscured from my view enough to where I can't tell if it's day or night. And I don't care.

My stomach knots as images of last night's ritual replay in my mind. The mix of emotions makes me want to vomit. I wasn't initiated. I was punished, humiliated, and then left in a pool of my own cum and blood. I shiver at the memory of their masked faces, their gloved hands... Shame fills me as I remember being turned on by the sadistic act.

I flinch at the touch of a hand on my back.

"It's just me, Maur," Riot huffs.

I spin around to face him, my mouth full of venom. "Get away from me."

His blue eyes harden. "No."

"How could you let them do that to me?" I hear the ache in my own voice, and it makes me sick.

He closes the gap between us, towering over me. "You don't understand the power my father has."

I fight back tears. There's no way I'm fucking crying in front of him. "You're fucking crazy. All of you. I'm done. Take me back to Raven's Gate."

I'm overwhelmed. Ashamed. *So fucking angry.* "You know what? Fuck that. Take me to Wickford Hollow. I don't want to see another raven ever again."

Riot wraps a hand around my throat, and it feels like salvation even as his arrogance irritates every nerve in my body. "*No.* You're ours. *Mine.* And we will help you get through this. Help you understand. But leaving is not an option."

I hate that I love the way his grip feels around my neck. "Maybe it should be. If we're not together, we can all go back to how we were before. *Safe.*"

He blows out a deep breath as his lips inch closer to mine. I try not to inhale that familiar scent of tobacco and coffee. Try not to swallow every particle of it even as it gives me life.

"There is no *before*, Firecracker. There is only us. And whether you believe it or not, what happened last night will *never* happen again."

Why does my heart believe every fucking word he says? My brain is screaming at me, but my heart, my body, just wants to lean in. Like every fucking word out of his mouth is gospel.

"You're going to have to do better than that if you want me to trust you, Riot."

His grip tightens on my throat. Shivers race down my back from the pulse of his fingertips. He weaves his other hand into my hair and gently tilts my head back. Like my soul wants to fly out and meet his.

"I'll explain everything," he purrs. "But right now, I just want

to give you a new memory to replace the last one that's on repeat in your head."

I swallow hard, my need for him outweighing my temptation to destroy everything, my traitorous heart and body choosing him instead of my own sanity. "You've ruined me. And I hate you for it."

He glides his hand up my neck, leaving tiny sparks in its trail. "The feeling is mutual, Firecracker. It's a *sickness*. But my craving, my obsession, my need for you is stronger."

His heated breath puffs out like smoke in the cold air between us right before his lips graze mine. "Eternity is our curse and our salvation. Over and over again until the ground opens up and swallows us whole, we will ruin each other. Because any other fate would be worse than death. Because no other fate exists."

Fuck.

He's right. I know this in the core of my being.

I clench my fists in frustration and open my mouth to scream, but I'm cut off by his kiss.

We both gasp as we release quivering breaths inside each other's lungs. His tongue dances around mine, sending sparks of electricity over every inch of me. My sigils flare and burn as our ache collides.

He tips my head, arching me back as he probes deeper, kissing me harder, desperately. Violently.

I moan. I cry. I drink his saliva down like holy water.

A gust of wind circles our limbs, and I can hear the ravens cry on the fringes. As the link between us grows, our unforgiving hearts beat faster, sending another crushing blow to the nature we fight against.

Riot pulls back, but only to leave a trail of kisses up my aching jaw. "You're my *violence*," he whispers in my ear. He scrapes his teeth across my lobe, nipping and sucking like a starved animal.

"*Mors tua, vita mea.*"

Your death, my life.

I understand more than ever now.

And I know that another piece of me did die last night. Just as each of his brutal kisses brings another hidden part of me to life.

He slides his hands down to my waist and pulls me hard against him. "Let me worship you here for all of nature to witness."

I let out another whimper, my heart racing. When I meet his gaze, an unspoken question is answered. I can't fight it or deny it any longer. I don't want to escape him.

He swoops me up and lays me on the ground. I gaze up as he takes his shirt off, mesmerized by how his sigils glow like the blue neon in his eyes. The light swirls and pulsates, weaving in and out of his corded muscles. I follow the glowing path of his blood as it pumps ferociously through each vein.

This man is the absolute definition of haunting beauty.

He pauses, and I'm confused for a second. Until I realize what he wants. My consent. For the first time since I ever laid eyes on Riot Graves, he's asking for permission to touch me.

In response, I unbutton my pants and slide them off along with my panties.

His arms tremble as he kneels down between my legs. "You are my goddess. And this is my sacrament."

A tiny shiver snakes across my belly as he circles my clit with his thumb.

"And you're my penance. You've damned my soul, Riot."

He licks his lips. "Shhh, let me feast now."

I arch back, grinding my hips into the ground as he drags the tip of his tongue up my slit. "Oh, *Fuuck*," I whine.

He plants soft kisses on my pussy, his lips hot as he savors me. Every gentle flick of his tongue tickles my core. *Fuck.* The agony sends me to the edge, and I almost cum. No. It's too soon. I want to relish every second. To draw it out. I tangle my fingers in his black strands, take a deep breath, and unclench.

He hums as he pushes his tongue in deeper. I roll my hips and rub my pussy against his face, moaning like a cat in heat.

"Mmm." He digs his fingers into my ass and pulls me tighter to him.

"Riot... fuck. I need... you." I'm coming unhinged; sick and starving for his brutality.

He slides out and runs the length of his tongue up my slit. "I know." He sucks on my nub before nipping it with his sharp teeth. I buck as it sends a spasm straight to my core.

"Oh, no," I cry out—not in protest but in disbelief. This man knows how to push every one of my buttons. He knows what makes me come undone. Every. Single. Time.

I claw at his skull, rabid with lust. Like a fucking masochist.

He grunts and lifts my hips off the ground as he thrusts his tongue back into my greedy pussy. His hands are underneath my ass, my legs around his neck. And it breaks me. A force gathers inside me and unleashes as my essence explodes like a pressure cooker overflowing.

"Riot!" White stars blur my vision the second my juices flood his mouth. He clamps down harder as I cum all over his feral tongue. He drinks from my pussy, sucking and swallowing every drop. And all I can do is writhe and moan as I ride his face.

The sigils on my thighs smolder, sending shivers up and down my body. My pleasure is bittersweet, mixing with rage as memories from last night threaten to surface. I shake my head and pinch my eyes shut.

Riot replaces his tongue with his fingers. "Look at me, Maur." I shake my head as he pumps his fingers, drawing my orgasm out.

"Look at me right fucking now," he demands.

I open my eyes and gaze into his. My breath catches in my throat.

"Good girl. Tell me what I am to you." Another orgasm takes hold of me as his fingers probe deeper, hitting my G-spot. "You... are my penance. My... devil." I can

barely get the words out as he adds a third finger, stretching me wide around him.

"Yes. Right now, *I'm your devil*. No one else. You will only think of me when I'm inside you."

I nod as I drown in his murderous blue eyes and surrender again. I let it all fade away. Nothing else exists but this moment. And like a switch that I now have access to, the sigil that Riot carved into my thigh burns brighter. And the other sigil... goes dark.

Riot nods as if he sees the realization, the relief in my eyes. He stills his hand as I try to catch my breath. "I can do more than just ruin you, Maur. All you have to do is let me."

He's the only one who can. It's always been this way. Since the first night we met, I lurch forward and crawl into his arms. I bury my head in his neck and breathe in his scent as he holds me tighter than anyone ever has. "Can we stay like this forever?" I already know the answer, but I want to pretend for a little longer.

He kisses my cheek. "No. But now you can come here in your head whenever you want."

The ravens shriek through the trees.

"They're getting desperate," I whisper.

"They aren't the only ones, Firecracker. Our enemies gather as we speak." He stands us both up and helps me with my pants.

"Ready to go back?"

Not even close. But I nod. "I guess."

We walk toward the cabin in silence, shrinking back into our own sacred spaces. Those spaces that we use to shield ourselves from being too vulnerable with each other. But after tonight, neither one of us can deny that this thing between us... is something like love.

Valentin is pacing the front porch while Atlas slumps back in a rocking chair. "There the fuck you both are. We're gonna have some unwelcomed guests soon."

The hairs on the back of my neck prickle. "What?" I thought you said we were safe out here."

Riot stiffens like a statue as he grips my hand so tight I'm afraid it might snap in half. "Who?"

Val's eyes darken. "My father. If you think Holden Graves is a monster..."

I shudder.

"Fuck," Riot mutters.

Now I'm the one squeezing his hand for dear life. "What does he want?"

"The same thing they all want," Atlas quips. He won't look at me. "To feast their eyes on the girl who broke the curse."

I swallow hard, my anxiety kicking into high gear. "No, I'm not staying here."

Val stalks toward us. He grabs my other hand. "I'm not leaving you alone this time, Maur. I swear on the fucking corpses of ravens, he will not lay a finger on you."

Riot's rage is palpable, soiling the air around us like a toxin.

"How much time do we have?"

"A few hours or so?" Val shrugs.

Riot nods. "Then we better be quick." He turns to me, his lips still coated in my juices. "You need another sigil."

"It's too soon, Riot. She can't handle it," Atlas pleads, his blue-green eyes bloodshot from what looks like crying.

That's odd. That man usually thinks funerals are funny.

He still won't look at me.

And I can't resist another dig. "You clearly have no idea what I can or cannot handle, Atlas."

He throws his hands up in defeat. "You're right. I'll shut the fuck up now."

Val and Riot exchange an uneasy look.

I lift my chin with confidence. "I don't ever want to feel powerless again. Besides, what's the worst that could happen?"

Atlas groans. "You could die."

I glare at him and hiss.

VIOLET

"I know, I know. You hate my voice right now."

"He's right," Val quips.

Riot lets go of my hand so he can move behind me. He pushes my hair to the side and tilts my head, exposing the first sigil he gave me. "He's also wrong. She's Nocturnus. Our power is also hers."

He turns to face me and gives me the same look he did in the clearing. He's waiting for my consent.

I blow out a deep breath. "You know I'm ready. But I want to hear the truth about what happened last night."

CHAPTER SEVEN

Maureen

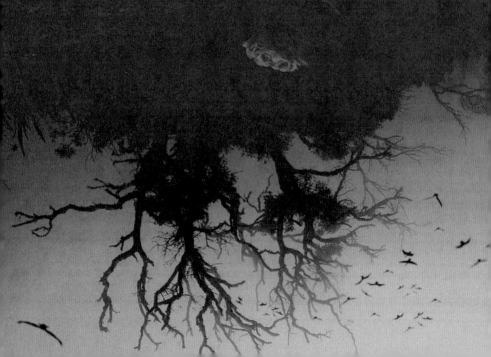

S ITTING IN VALENTIN'S KITCHEN, I'M FLOODED WITH MEMORIES OF that one special night we shared here. Back before I murdered Riot's half-brother. Before all the things that I will never be able to shed, or be free from, happened. That night was the first time I'd seen Val smile. I haven't seen him smile like that since.

As we sit across from each other now, every traumatic emotion he's ever felt sprawls across his face. His father is a true monster, hurting him since the moment he took his first breath. Valentin isn't scared of anything or anyone except Laurent Erebus. And he is currently on his way here.

I'm sandwiched between Riot and Atlas, my nerves shot.

"Did you know they were going to make me touch myself in front of them? That they were going to lash me?"

Val's nostrils flare as he white-knuckles the edge of the break-fast table. "No. That level of depravity shouldn't have been in-flicted on you."

Atlas sighs. "Our rituals are sexual, Maur. I knew you were getting a new sigil and figured he'd parade you around a bit. But Val's right. We wouldn't have let you go down there if we knew how fucked up things would get."

I take a long pull from the whiskey bottle that he passes to me. "I've played all your sick and twisted games, Atlas. But last night was not fucking fun."

Riot fidgets with the bottle before taking a drink, his mind seemingly a million miles away. He sighs in remorse even as his gaze hardens on me, his blue eyes almost black with rage. "I un-derestimated his deviancy. If I pushed too hard, he would have overpowered us all and invoked the rule of Hekate. Which, trust me, would have been much fucking worse."

"You think we have power, Maur?" Atlas interjects. "You have no idea what power is until you experience our fathers. They're Nocturnus elders who have been controlling us our whole lives."

Val snickers. "That needs to end now. They think of you as a pawn, Maur. Women are always pawns in our world. I guess that's why my mom left."

His eyes are sunken, and he looks like he hasn't slept all night. My heart aches for him. It truly does. But they've been keeping too many secrets from me. "What is the rule of Hekate?"

The three of them look at each other like they're collectively about to throw up. This sends a cold burst of dread straight to my belly.

Riot spins the whiskey bottle on the table, rolling it back and forth between his palms. "It's a clause to ensure that the male initi-ates don't get too attached to the female ones."

"He means fall in love," Valentin mutters.

Riot throws him a dirty look before he continues. "They usually have plans for who they want us to marry—women who aren't in the order but come from good breeding. So, if we get distracted by a female initiate, if we start thinking thoughts about choosing her as our mate instead . . . they invoke the rule of Hekate."

He takes another pull of whiskey. Sweat beads on his forehead. "The woman would be forced to fuck every initiate whenever they wanted. Indefinitely."

My stomach knots. I saw how those men looked at me the last night. They would have given anything to do more than what they did. "That's disgusting. How many times has this happened?"

"Never," Valentin shakes his head. "It's never been enforced."

My cheeks flame. "But last night, Holden threatened you with it because of me. He's not going to stop coming after me, is he?"

"No," Riot murmurs. "But he doesn't understand the bond the four of us share. He knows you broke the curse and opened the gates, but he has no idea how powerful you are. We sensed it every time. You unsettled the ravens just by being here."

Atlas pulls out a vial of poison and chugs it back while looking at me, his eyes aflame with the toxin. "As I said, it could have been much worse."

I roll my eyes at him. "Thank you for your commentary, Atlas. Let's switch places next time and see how much worse it is for you."

He chuckles. *This asshole actually chuckles.* "I like that kind of shit, Maur. You forget my nature. Don't get soft on me now."

And here, this whole time, I thought he was the sweet and gentle one. Fuck me. He's more unhinged than Val and Riot put together. And my traitorous pussy spasms at the thought.

Fuck, now all I can think about is his hands on me, making

M VIOLET

me do things my mind doesn't want my body to do. And my body is saying *fuck you, brain, this man's cock is my medicine.*

Atlas smirks as if he can read my mind. We can all sense each other's moods and emotions now that I've received two sigils from them. It's like getting imprints of thoughts and words with-out full sentences. But they're better at it. It frustrates the fuck out of me when I can't read them as well as they can read me.

"I want some of that." I motion to the vial.

He pulls out a fresh one, and I drink it down in one sip. I jerk forward as the poison burns my throat. A metallic taste fills my mouth as if I've swallowed a thousand needles.

I cough and lean over the table, my vision blurring.

"*Whoa. Fuck. Maui,* you're not supposed to drink the whole thing," Atlas rubs my back as I gasp for air.

"I thought you were teaching her moderation," Riot growls.

"She doesn't know what that is," Val adds. He removes a tin box from his jacket and offers me a joint from it. "Have a few puffs. It will take the edge off."

I've never been happier to see weed in my life. Back in the old days, my bestie, Bailey, and I would get so fucking high there wouldn't be a single snack left in the house at the end of the night. I let Val light it for me and relish a deep, long drag, coughing a few more times as my chest expands, and the fragrant smoke fills my lungs. "What did I just drink?"

"Pure uncut nightshade," Atlas announces with pride.

"You're an imbecile," Riot barks at him.

My head is fuzzy, and my limbs feel like dead weight, but I can't stop the lazy smile from stretching across my cheeks. I'm definitely fucking high.

Val glares at me. "I'm going down to the crypts."

"*Again?*" Riot and Atlas bark out at the same time.

He scoffs. "Yup. I need to clear my head before dear old Dad arrives."

"Want some company?" I ask, my words slurring.

He grinds down on his teeth, flexing his jaw. "Maur... I've reached my quota of pleasantries for the day."

My stomach flips. "What the fuck is that supposed to mean?"

Less than an hour ago he expressed remorse for leaving me alone with those bastards. Now, he can't get far enough away from me. I'm starting to get whiplash from his mood swings.

He bolts up out of his chair. "Riot sulks into a bottle of whiskey, you two have your poison, and I enjoy my solitude. Not sure why that's so hard for you to grasp."

I snicker. "Well, you don't have to be a fucking dick about it. A simple no would've been fine."

I lurch back as he rushes forward and grabs the sides of my chair. "Do not think for one second that I am any different than the man you first met. Just because I don't want an entire coven of initiates coming all over you doesn't mean that I'm going to let you determine my existence."

The fucking nerve. My cheeks flame as I glare daggers at him. "Fuck you, Val. Go exist somewhere else then."

His lip curls up into the nastiest snarl as he shoves my chair back, slamming it to the ground with me still in it. My back hits the floor and knocks the wind out of me.

He kneels down to straddle me, wrapping his hands around my neck. "One more word out of your mouth, and I will fuck it so hard, you won't be able to speak ever again."

I bite my tongue, wheezing as air slowly reenters my lungs. *The look in his eyes is vicious.*

"Relax, Val, she's just worried about you," Atlas chirps. He chuckles again as he lips the vial, rolling his tongue around the edges to milk every drop.

Val pinches my chin. "I don't want her worry. I want her to fucking do what I ask."

I swallow hard, my throat still burning from the poison and the weed.

We stare at each other for what seems like an eternity, both fighting the urge to either kiss or kill each other.

Riot and Atlas say nothing. They do nothing. This is just what we are.

Val lets me go with a grunt but doesn't bother to pull me back up. "Let me know when *he arrives*."

I stare at the ceiling as I listen to him stalk off. It takes Riot a few minutes before he offers me a hand up. "He's just angry about his father coming. It's not you."

The fuck? "So now I'm his fucking punching bag?"

Riot shrugs. "You're whatever we want you to be, Maur. And in turn, we are yours to do with whatever the fuck you want."

A fire burns in me. A deep rage mixed with a craving to defy and destroy. "Is that true? Well, I'll see myself down to the crypts then. So I can do whatever I want to him."

Atlas stands up and yawns. "It's your funeral, Maur. I'm going to take a nap."

Riot cups my face in his hands. "After he kicks you out, come join us upstairs."

I have a twisted longing for all of them. It's undeniable. I'm their greedy little slut who can't get enough. But neither can they. They take what they want when they want it.

Well . . . then so will I.

And right now, I want Valentin on his fucking knees.

It's dark and cold as fuck down here. Here I go again, getting my ass in trouble. This addiction to it. *To him.* It's like a gun, and I can't take my finger off the trigger.

I haven't been down here since he locked me in that coffin. Shivers tickle my thighs as I remember the way he controlled the little bullet vibrator he shoved inside me. And when he closed the coffin lid, the rush of adrenaline consumed me. It was terrifying and exhilarating at the same time.

But now my stomach twists with fear and anxiety as I stumble through the dark, wondering what state I'm going to find him in. A sane person would have walked away after getting their chair kicked over. But no, not this bitch. I'm just a glutton for more punishment.

When I get to the bottom of the stairs, the door's ajar. Either he knows I can't resist coming down here to piss him off some more, or he's just that fucking confident that I'll obey him.

Sometimes, I wish I didn't want him so badly. He's more than a walking red flag. He's the ink, the cloth, the whole fucking flagpole.

I tiptoe through the doorway like a timid mouse. Candle-filled sconces line the entire perimeter, shedding some light onto this windowless and otherwise pitch-black crypt. The flames flicker rapidly as my presence shifts the energy in the space.

I drag my fingers across the stone walls as I walk, careful not to take too many deep breaths. Afraid that this crypt will some-how suffocate me.

I didn't give much thought to what he's doing down here. If in fact he's enjoying his solitude. He could be jerking off in a cof-fin or hanging from the ceiling like a bat for all I know. I chuckle to myself as I picture it.

A soft breeze brushes past me, sending my pulse into a frenzy.

Oh, shit.

I try to swallow down my fear, but my throat feels like sand-paper. My heart beats loud and fast in my ears. It's too quiet in this crypt. So quiet that the tiniest pin-prick of a noise rattles me. *Oh, fuck, there could be rodents down here.*

The air thickens as I move toward the center of the crypt. I have to squeeze in between the rows of coffins to get any farther. I look around, trying to guess which coffin he made me cum in. Maybe he's resting in that one. That night was such a blur. We were drunk on wine and lust for each other.

A loud screech makes me jump. Another subtle breeze tickles my skin, sending all the hairs on my neck straight up. Fuck this. I spin around to go back the way I came when I walk into a wall of solid muscle. I gaze up at him, my lip quivering. Fuck. *He's so fucking pissed.*

Val wraps a hand around my throat and backs me up against one of the coffins. "You never fucking do what you're told, do you?"

The corner of the lid presses into my back, sending sharp pains down my spine. "Haven't you learned that by now?" I taunt. A golden light swirls in his dark-brown eyes. He clenches his jaw. "I should bend you over my knee and spank you for being such a fucking brat."

My belly flips as I glare back at him. "Don't tempt me with a good time."

He curls his fingers, applying more pressure to my throat. "You might be in over your head right now, Firecracker. I'm not in the fucking mood for one of your games."

I wrap my hand around his wrist and yank him closer. "My *games?* I came down here so that you didn't have to be alone. Because I know what you're feeling right now. But you lashed out at me instead of the person you really want to. *Your father.*"

He shoves into me, pressing his muscular chest against mine. His eyes blaze with a fury that could make your bones jump out of your skin. "You don't fucking get it. The second he gets here, I cannot look at you. I can't speak to you. *Because he will fucking know.*"

What the actual fuck?

Something shifts in his eyes. Something sad and and lost flickers

behind his long black lashes. I don't even care that he's squeezing all the air out of my lungs.

"He'll know what, Val?" I manage to squeak out, my heart hammering.

He lowers his face, his lips hovering over mine. "That I will want to skin him alive if he tries to pull the same shit with you that Holden did last night. And then he'll laugh in my face because he's stronger than me. It will make him want to hurt you more. I can't let him see."

"Fuck," I breathe as he loosens his grip on my neck. There's no doubt in my mind that Valentin wants me. The chemistry between us is an explosion every time we're near each other. The craving to touch and kiss and fuck consumes us at all times. It creates a palpable tension that we fill with hate and anger so that we don't spontaneously combust every time one of us walks into the room.

I remember the night I stormed into his bedroom after they left me stranded on the side of the road. I stole his car that night. But, to be fair, they tampered with my car first. Val and I went from screaming at each other to fucking each other's brains out all night. There's this obsessive and toxic desire between us.

But the way he's looking at me now... It feels different. He lets me go, and I almost whine from the lack of contact. I reach out and snatch his wrist back and clutch it to my chest. "When you don't look at me, I physically ache... So, look at me now. Give me all of you right now. Before we have to go back up-stairs and pretend we don't care about each other."

He drags the tip of his tongue across his lip. "I really fucking hated you at first. I was worried you were going to ruin what Riot, Valentin, and I had built. And I didn't fucking trust you. You were just an obstacle I had to move in order to get Riot's attention back to Nocturnus."

From the moment I bumped into him on my first day at

Tenebrose, I sensed he hated me. Even when he defiled me in the mud, his lust and anger worked in unison to fulfill and humiliate me at the same time. But this magnet . . . it pulls us in deeper and deeper every time we touch.

"And then you stopped hating me. What changed?"

He takes a step toward me again, this time not backing me into a sharp-edged coffin but embracing me. He snakes an arm around my waist. "The day you were arguing with your mother outside my uncle's classroom. When I saw her hit you . . . I knew. An unexplainable need to protect you came over me. You were broken just like me, sad and lonely and starving for affection. The same way I was. So I decided in that moment that if I was going to ruin you . . . I had to let you ruin me too."

My eyes water. All those warm fuzzy emotions I usually loathe, the ones I push down, are washing over me in waves before I can even brace myself for impact. Knowing that the two of us have been hurt the most by the ones who are supposed to love us is a bond no man, woman, or raven can break.

I plant a soft kiss on his cheek. "You're always safe with me too, Val."

We look at each other. Like, really fucking look at each other. He brushes a strand of hair off my shoulder. "I'm never going to be tender with you, Maur. That's not who I am. The Erebus sickness has nestled in my bones. It's diluted the blood in my veins with a brutality not fit for polite society. I will not apologize for who I am. But I'll never truly hurt you."

I slide my fingers around his throat, loving the way his pulse ticks up at my touch. "And I'm never going to be some docile obedient doll that you can just toss aside whenever your mood shifts. I am yours. *But you're also mine.* And I like the way you ruin me."

He crushes my lips with his own, snarling as he plunges his tongue inside my mouth. We moan in unison, our pulses

quickening. The heat in our bodies rises as we cling to each other like feral wildlings.

I grab at his T-shirt, fisting it in my palms, clawing at it because it's in my way of his skin. I push it up and over his head. I pause for a moment to gaze at his chiseled body, letting myself take in every sigil and scar. He's beautiful. And he's all mine.

But I haven't forgotten the way he pushed me over, making the air whoosh out of my lungs. "Get on your knees, Val," I command.

He arches an eyebrow. "Careful, Maur. I'm on the fucking edge right now."

I peel off my jeans along with my black lace panties. "So am I..."

I slide my hands down my belly and spread my pussy lips open.

His eyes darken. "I won't be gentle."

"I fucking hope not." My juices glide down my thighs as I slowly rub myself. I let out a whimper as he watches.

"You're the only one I'll get down on my knees for, Maur," he growls in my ear, his breath hot and unsteady.

A smirk catches my lips as he lowers himself to the ground. He yanks my right leg up and tosses it over his shoulder, opening me up wider.

A deep moan erupts from my throat as he licks me from taint to clit. I lean back against the coffin and close my eyes. "Val..."

"Mmm." He thrusts his tongue inside my pussy, lapping at my walls like a starved animal. "You taste so fucking good," he rasps after he slides back out. He scrapes his teeth across my swollen clit before taking it in his mouth. A deep spasm spreads through my core as he sucks it.

My fingers tremble as I pull my lips wider apart, desperate for him to fill me again. "Please, Val..."

He lifts my other leg over his shoulder so I'm straddling his

face. The back of the coffin digs into my back again. This time, I don't mind. This time, I barely feel the burn of its edges searing into my spine.

He pushes my hands away from my pussy and plunges his tongue back inside, filling me to the hilt. I throw my head back and scream as another spasm rips through me, sending me over the edge.

I arch back and thrust his face against his face with so much force the coffin creaks and rattles. He holds me up with his arms, pinning me to him as he devours me. I lock my legs around his neck as my juices spill out onto his tongue.

"Val," I whine. "Oh, fuck."

He laps up my cum greedily as he moans. The heat from his breath sends me into a frenzy as another orgasm thunders through me.

"Fuck," I cry out again.

When he comes up for air, he licks the remaining cream from his lips. "I'll get on my knees for you anytime if it means you're going to cum as hard as you just did." He slides out from under my legs and sets me back down carefully. My knees wobble, and I have to lean on him so I don't collapse.

"The way you make me cum . . . it's like a fucking drug. I'll never stop craving it." He uses his shirt to wipe my legs and pussy before I pull my panties and jeans back on.

The more he touches me, the harder I fall. *Fucking phero-mones.* It's everything—his scent, his voice, the way he looks at me . . . It's stronger than a drug. There is no rehab for this addiction. He leans over and kisses me. I moan again as I taste myself on his lips. "I just want to hide down here with you all night. The guys could tell your father we aren't here. That we ran away."

Val sighs. "You know that won't work, Maur. He'll sense you before he's halfway up the driveway."

I shrug and force a smile even as the anxiety builds in my chest. "It was worth a shot."

He runs his thumb across my lips. "Someday soon, there will come a time when he'll want to run from us."

The sigil on my neck pulsates, reminding me of the oath I made to him, Riot and Atlas. It comforts me as much as it terrifies me. We're bound together by blood and ritual now. The sigil that Holden carved into me also awakens but only for a moment. I'm getting better at controlling it instead of the other way around.

"You're right," I murmur. "I can feel a shift in me."

Goosebumps pebble my flesh.

He nods. "Which is why we need to give you another sigil tonight."

More blood and pain. I'm not sure how much more my body can take. But being powerless is not an option for me.

I lace my fingers through his, sending a bolt of electricity through us both. "I'm ready."

CHAPTER EIGHT

Riot

"I'M GOING TO GIVE MAUREEN THE SIGIL OF EREBUS TONIGHT." I THRUST the dagger into the flame, sterilizing it for the ritual.

Atlas hovers by the fireplace, watching me work as he's done a thousand times before. "Val's sigil? That's a fucking dark one."

The Erebus sigil stems from shadows. It can bring nightmares, but it can also help one shift matter and energy to bend to their will. The three of us were marked with it a long time ago.

I lay the dagger on the altar and pull up the hood of my robe. "The longer Maureen is with us, the less light she'll need to see."

Atlas sets out three vials of poison next to my blade. "Where will you mark her?"

I press my fingers against the back of his neck. "Here. Her hair

will hide it from Laurent. And she will have deeper access to its power with it being at the top of her spine."

I place the traditional Nocturnus mask on my face, a symbol of tricks and illusions. The bronze chills my nose and cheeks, reminding me of the ice that runs through my veins. I am not a good man. Never have been. I was raised in my father's likeness. Though I'm nothing like him, there isn't much good in me either.

Maureen is my salvation. But she's also my curse. I succeeded in capturing her, but now I have to make sure she stays. There is no me without her anymore. All my life, I felt that missing piece. My dark queen. The thought of carving another sigil into her flesh, marking her with more of our essence, makes me so fucking hard I can barely walk.

That's what she does to me. To all of us. Her pretty pink nipples and perfect pussy make each of us feral as fuck. And her mouth . . . fucking god, those full lips and sharp tongue wrapped around my cock are better than any poison I've ever tasted.

Atlas nods as if he can hear my thoughts. "Let me get you ready for her."

We lock eyes and the temperature in my body rises like a fucking inferno. I take off my pants and nestle back in an iron chair. Atlas shoots back a vial of poison before stalking over to me. He hands me one too, which I knock back just as quickly. He kneels down between my legs and pushes my robe back, exposing my massive erection. "You're going to cum hard and fast for me so you can last longer with her later."

I let out a moan as he rolls his thumb and index finger around the tip of my cock. "You're so good to me, Atlas."

He chuckles, his blue-green eyes brightening, pupils dilated and pitch black. "Shh, close your eyes and relax."

I do as he says, allowing my body to unclench. I quiver as he takes the entire length of me in his mouth. "Oh, fuck."

He slides his thick lips all the way down to my base, coating

M VIOLET

my shaft with his hot saliva. Spasms tingle throughout every vein as he works his mouth up and down.

I dig my fingers into his scalp, yanking on his icy-blond strands.

"Yeah, just like that."

A smirk pulls at his lips as he continues to choke on me. He moans as my cock twitches in his grasp. I white-knuckle the arms of the chair, panting as I my climax builds. "Atlas... fuck. I'm gonna fucking burst."

He slips a finger in my ass, and I lose it. Stars dot the black behind my closed lids. "Fuck!" I roar.

My cum shoots out like a bullet, invading his mouth and throat. He laughs as I shake and tremble, clenching and unclenching my ass cheeks around his thick finger.

"Mmm," he moans as he drinks every drop of my essence.

The high is unlike any other. The poison mixed with sex in our sacred ritual room... it's not just an orgasm; it's transcendence.

I stroke his face as he licks his lips. "So fucking good."

He beams back at me, basking in my praise. "I can't wait to watch you mark our little firecracker. I want to lick her blood from your blade. It tastes so good."

My legs wobble as I stand up, my adrenaline still racing. "I want to watch you and Val fuck her at the same time."

Atlas arches an eyebrow. "You'll think she'll go for that? She's still pissed at me."

"I won't be asking."

"Asking what?" Maureen calls out. She's holding on to Val, her face flushed. My cock hardens again. I can smell the fresh cum on her thighs from here.

I stalk over to her and wrap my hand around her throat.

"Laurent Erebus will be here soon. It's time, Firecracker."

"Take off your clothes," Val growls in her ear.

I hand her a robe to slip into. And a mask. Her eyes widen.

"For me?"

"You are just as much Nocturnus as the rest of us. The mask is an honor. From now on, you will not enter a ritual without one." She's not the lamb anymore. Her power will eventually surpass ours. But even then, she will always belong to us.

The excitement in her breath is palpable as she wastes no time peeling off her shirt and jeans. She slides her panties down to her ankles, and I almost pin her to the wall and take her right then.

Patience, fucker.

She pauses as if seeing my composure crumble. I nod for her to continue, swallowing hard as every inch of me wants to ride her like a fucking animal.

"Before we begin, you need to make peace with Atlas." Her nostrils flare every time she glances in his direction.

Our fiery woman lets out an exasperated sigh. "We're fine. I'm cool. Let's just move on."

Val shakes his head. "No, you're not fine. You're still pissed."

Atlas winks at her and flashes his million-dollar smile. "What's it gonna take, pretty girl?"

The clash of wills between them is going to be the death of us if they don't rein it in.

Maureen slips on her robe and mask before prancing over to Atlas like a cat about to pounce. Without warning, she rips the buttons off his shirt, splitting the fabric wide open. Atlas looks both impressed and terrified as she drags a pointy pink fingernail down his chiseled chest.

She cocks her head to the side. "I want to give *you* a sigil. Something that makes you unhinged if anyone hurts me."

Atlas blows out a shivering breath, his smirk gone. "Oh, you are batshit crazy, and I'm in here for it." He puffs out his chest. "Riot, give her the blade."

What the fuck?

I shake my head. "Maur, you don't know the first thing about carving sigils."

M VIOLET

"So, teach me right now," she quips. "If you want us to be cool again, he needs to wear *my* mark."

"How is this going to solve anything?" I roar.

Her head jerks in my direction. Behind the mask, her eyes glow for the first time. "Because I want to fucking brand him. Just like your father did to me. That will make me feel better."

Atlas nods and licks his lips, excited. "I'm so fucking down. Riot, the knife. Now."

Val sighs and fetches it for him instead. But he keeps his hand on the hilt as she reaches for it. "This sigil will turn him into an even bigger monster than he already is. You know that, right?"

Maureen touches her mask to Val's cheek as if she's giving him a kiss. "We're all monsters now, Val. But this one needs to remember who feeds him."

Every cell in my body sparks with need for this woman. She's beating us at our own game. Claiming us the way we've claimed her. I would get down on my fucking knees right now and let her carve a thousand sigils into my flesh if she wanted me to. And so I concede to her every chaotic whim.

My sigils flare as I stalk toward the three of them. I wait for Atlas and Val to put on their robes and masks before I gently clasp onto Maureen's wrist. She squeezes the hilt as I guide her hand over to Atlas's heart. His nipple pebbles as the tip of the blade grazes the skin below it.

Val places his hands on Atlas's shoulders, and a surge of adrenaline sparks through us, our eyes aglow. The connection is consuming, and I have to fight to keep my heart steady.

I hold up the palm of my hand, showing her the sigil. It's raised and swollen as it never fully healed. "I got this the night I first saw you in Wickford Hollow. When I got back to Tenebrose. After I murdered the creeps who defiled you. I was drunk off the scent of your wet pussy and their blood that was still on my hands."

She runs her slender fingers over it. It burns under her caress

as if her hand is a torch. "Why did you get it? You didn't even know me then."

I squeeze my hand around hers. "Because I wanted to make sure that no matter who you were or where you went, that I would always kill for you. That I would never let anyone else outside this circle lay a hand on you."

She drops her head, her hand going limp in mine. "But you did... last night, you did nothing to stop them."

Fuck. I wasn't going to tell her. The last thing I want is for her to pity me or think I'm weak.

Atlas tilts her chin toward him. "They locked him up, Maur. Riot went on a psychotic rampage last night, so his father locked him away until they were done with you. I'm the only one who didn't put up a fight. I'm a narcissistic asshole. Now take it all out on me, pretty girl."

A painful sob lodges in my throat. My sigils dig into my flesh, coming alive as the memory of being ripped away from my fire-cracker surfaces again.

"Oh, Riot," she whimpers.

I clear my throat. "This is the mark you will give him. And then next time, he'll be locked up alongside me."

"After tonight, there's not going to be a next time," Val snarls. She sniffles under her mask. I can't tell if she's crying or if it's just an allergic reaction to the thick layer of dust that has settled into every brick and stone. "I... *I don't know if I should do this now*," she whispers.

Atlas grips her masked face. "I'm ready to bleed for you, Maur. Make me your fucking slave."

CHAPTER NINE

Maureen

M Y HAND TREMBLES AROUND THE KNIFE. SUDDENLY, I'M NOT AS brave as I was a few minutes ago. My flight-or-fight response has me wanting to throw up. I still don't understand Atlas's nature, but the idea of carving into his beautiful body sends my pulse racing. There's too much adrenaline coursing through my veins.

Riot steadies his hand over mine, guiding the blade to Atlas's chest. "This is part of who we are. You can do this."

I nod as I lock eyes with Atlas. He still has that shit eating grin on his face. It almost infuriates me but then I remember I'm the one holding the knife. I don't want to hurt him ... completely. Maybe slightly. Fuck. I'm just as fucked up as they are.

I dig the tip of the blade into his chest. He lets out a little whim-per as the first trickle of blood spurts out. I'm not a squeamish per-son. I've killed two people. But those acts were full of rage and chaos. I was in an unhinged state. This is different.

Riot continues to guide my hand as I etch the sigil deep into Atlas's flesh. "Fuck that feels good," he moans.

My breath catches in my throat as a spark of energy shoots up my fingers. It's like a vibration. "Do you feel that tingling?" I ask.

Atlas licks his lips. Desire flickers in his gaze. "Mmm, yes. I feel like I'm about to cum."

Riot steps away as I continue to carve the sigil on my own, my fingers somehow knowing the way without my knowledge. The air is sticky and sweet between us. Without understanding what's hap-pening, I have the strongest urge to make him cum.

As I stare at his mutilated flesh, the vibration in my body height-ens, I glide my hands over his abdomen, smearing his blood in cir-cles around his belly button. He whimpers as I peel his robe back. I slip my hand inside and wrap it around his hard cock.

"Oh, fuck. That's my pretty girl. Taking what belongs to her."

He wraps his hand around my throat. I'll never get enough of this. My control is an illusion, but he lets me have it.

I stroke him up and down with my bloody hands, relishing every ridge on his veiny shaft. It's so smooth and so fucking hard.

I want more.

I push him back, guiding him to where I want him. When the backs of his legs hit the iron chair, I pull his robe completely off.

Riot comes behind me and unties my robe. I shiver as it falls to the floor. Wearing nothing but a mask now, I feel feral and unhinged.

"Come sit on my lap, pretty girl. I know your pussy is aching for my thick cock." Atlas spreads his legs as he leans back in the chair.

Val spins me around so my back is to Atlas. He and Riot hoist me up and then lower me down onto Atlas's cock. I let out a shud-dering moan. "Fuck..."

While Atlas fucks me from behind, Riot spreads my thighs apart and watches him slide in and out. I grind down hard, panting and trembling as Atlas fills me to the brim. "Such a good fucking slut for me. Mmm." He rolls his hips up and down in a rhythm so fucking agonizing I can't contain my cries.

Val kneels down between our legs and plants a trail of kisses up my thigh. He gazes up at me with a look so terrifying it almost makes me cum. "*I want in*," he growls.

Atlas pulls me back and pinches my nipples hard between his fingers. "Yeah, let's see how wide your pussy can stretch for us."

Panic spreads in my chest. I can barely take Atlas. "Wait, no. I'm too tight," I whimper.

Riot fingers my clit. "Shhh... relax and let him in."

Oh, hell no.

I jerk up, but Atlas slams me back down. "*Relax.*"

Val removes his robe before straddling me. He spreads my pussy wide open and inserts his finger next to Atlas's cock. "That's it."

I gasp, shocked that he could get his finger in there. And it feels... fucking incredible. But his entire cock? There's no fucking way.

"This is dirty," I whine.

Val's eyes darken. "Yeah, and you like it fucking dirty." He forces the tip of his cock in next to Atlas. "Mmm, just like the time in the car. You liked sucking my cock while Riot played with your pussy. All that blood."

Atlas lets out a moan as Val's cock rubs against his. "Mmm, I wish you were on your period right now."

Riot holds my shoulders back against Atlas as I squirm. A sharp pain shoots up my core as they stretch me open. "It hurts. I'm too full."

Val pushes in another inch, and it feels like my stomach is going to rip open. "It's going to hurt a little longer, but then... you are going to cum so fucking hard with both of us fucking you."

Atlas licks the side of my neck and up my cheek. "We're going to fill the fuck out of you." He yanks my head back and smothers me with his mouth. Despite the pain, a spasm rocks my core. I buck as I moan into his mouth. His tongue is hot and probing and aggressive. He explores my mouth with a hunger I've not felt from him before. It's not even human.

Riot keeps his finger on my clit, rubbing it in circles as Val thrusts all the way in. A bloodcurdling scream rips from my throat.

"Fucking hell!"

They both slide in and out of me together, and I almost pass out from the pressure. But my juices flood out like a fucking faucet turned on full blast. "Ohhh," I moan. *Fuck.*

Atlas chuckles. "Yeah, that's our pretty little psycho. Letting us split you the fuck open."

"It feels good, doesn't it?" Val glares down at me.

The pain lessens as I find my rhythm. They ride me like a see-saw, slithering in and out, their cocks grinding against one another as they keep stretching my throbbing folds.

My whole body is on fire.

Val digs his fingers into my thighs. "Tell me." *Thrust.* "How good." *Thrust. Thrust.* "This. Fucking. Feels." *Thrust.*

I feel them both in my spine. In my ass. I'm on the verge of losing my mind, and my orgasm is seconds away. "Yes. It feels so fucking good."

Riot pinches my chin between his fingers. "Time for your new sigil, Firecracker."

Fuck. I should have known. They are so fucking depraved. Of course he's going to mutilate my flesh while I have two cocks inside me.

He grabs a fistful of my hair and pulls my head down, exposing the back of my neck. "I'm marking you with the sigil of Erebus because you belong to our darkness. Our depravity. Our sickness."

I cry out as he scrapes the blade across my neck, weaving it in and out as he scars me once again.

Val and Atlas thrust harder as the blood trickles down my neck and back. We are covered in so much of it... like a fucking massacre.

I close my eyes and feel another surge of power enter my veins—something thick and sludge-like. It sends shivers up my spine. I feel cold. Feral. Angry. I open my eyes, and all I can see is them.

A deep spasm rolls through my pussy, and I lose my breath as my orgasm rips into my core. "Fuck!" I yell.

Val and Atlas feel it too. I hear them roaring in my ears even as my soul floats over my body. I am in it but out of it. Feeling every-thing and yet gazing down on myself from above. Watching how their swollen cocks tear into my pussy. Feeling every ridge and vein throbbing against my bruised walls.

Atlas cums first, but Val is mere seconds behind. They rock me between them as their hot, white liquid fills me so full it seeps into my ass crack. It's thick and sticky and allows them to slide even deeper in as they chase their own peaks.

And holy fuck, I can't stop cumming.

Riot pulls my head back up and shoves his tongue in my mouth. He kisses me hard and deep while the other two milk my pussy with their greedy cocks.

"In absentia lucis, tenebrae vincunt," he chants.

In the absence of light, darkness prevails.

Valentín grunts through his clenched teeth, "Mors tua, vita mea."

Your death, my life.

"Mors vincit omnia," Atlas adds as another burst of his cum fills me.

Death always wins.

I clench around them both, shocked that I haven't blacked out

DIRTY LITTLE SAINT

yet. But I've been waiting for this moment. A chance to recite my own vow. My own pledge to them.

"Ruina nostra salus," I moan as another orgasm grips me.

Our ruin is our salvation.

"Yes," Riot coos in my ear. "That's right. We are your ruin as you are ours."

Atlas fingers my new sigil. "You are ours to do whatever we want with, pretty girl. Remember that next time you try to say no to us." Val caresses my cheek. "We always know what's best for you."

I am so irrevocably fucked. Literally and figuratively. They actually own me. There's nothing I can do to release their hold on me. Nowhere I can run to or hide. Our sigils are like tracking beacons, binding us together with invisible cords.

There's no escaping.

And to think that it turns me on. That it excites me . . .

Have I lost my mind?

With my hair down, as Riot instructed, my new sigil pulses on the back of my neck. Although hidden from view, I still wonder if Val's father will be able to sense it. The power is so dark that I feel like there are shadows following me. Then there's the chill I haven't been able to shake. Even after taking a twenty-minute hot shower after the ritual.

The sound of wheels crunching on gravel gets louder as Valentin's father and his entourage make their way up the driveway. Atlas used his power of sight to send a raven down to check earlier. So we know he's only minutes away. The closer Laurent Erebus and his motorcade get to the house, the more I want to run into the forest and hide. If he's anything like Holden Graves, I could be in for another round of humiliation and abuse.

M VIOLET

As the four of us wait on pins and needles in the sitting room, I flinch at the first sounds of car doors opening and slamming. I try not to peer out through the window, foolishly hoping that if I don't look, it's not really happening.

Footsteps click on the pavement, getting closer. My heart is in my throat.

Valentin throws me a look. "Keep quiet until he addresses you."

I nod even though a tiny streak of rebellion surges in me. A temptation to greet this asshole at the door just so I can slam it in his face.

The doorknob twists open, and in he walks with six masked men in tow. Chills cover my body as the cold draft follows him into the room.

Laurent Erebus is darkness.

With black hair and brown eyes, he resembles Valentin, but it's subtle. The man stands taller than my guys. He stands in front of us in a black designer suit. There's a deep scar above his right eyebrow that travels down in a straight line, crossing over his discolored eye. Like a villain straight out of a horror movie, his energy is sinister. His gaze, deadly.

He folds his scarred hands in front of him and glares at his son.

"Such a fucking disappointment."

Val lifts his chin in defiance. "Well, at least I'm consistent."

Riot and Atlas remain quiet. As do I. The exchange between Val and his father is not meant for us.

As Laurent stalks over to the window, his initiates follow him. As if this powerful man needs backup. He peers out between the blinds, his jaw clenched. "Do you know that when a raven dies violently, its soul gets trapped between worlds? It exists in agony, unable to fly up or down."

Val's throat bobs. "What's your point?"

Laurent snaps his head to the side, his lips curling into a snarl. "The ghosts of ravens are everywhere because of what you did."

"With all due respect, Father, we did what was best for Nocturnus. We broke the curse. They can't control us anymore. We can leave Raven's Gate without consequence. I thought that's what you wanted."

He stalks toward his son and grabs the back of his neck. "You didn't consult the elders. You have no idea what you unleashed."

Riot sighs. "Sir, what we—"

"Shut your fucking mouth, Graves," Laurent commands.

I shudder as Riot completely obeys him.

What the fuck?

Val glares back at his father. "We saw an opportunity and took it. The Blackwell heir was in our school. Our territory. Every time we mark her, the ravens' hold on us loosens."

Laurent shakes him by the collar, and my sigils spark with rage. "You got your looks from me but your intelligence from your mother. And she was as dumb as they come."

Val's nostrils flare, but he bites his tongue. I want to run in between them and remove Laurent's grip from his neck. An overwhelming need to protect him consumes me.

"Well, she was smart enough to get the fuck away from you," Val spits.

Laurent squeezes him tighter, his eyes glowing. "Watch your fucking mouth, boy. We had the ravens contained. The second you marked her, pledged yourselves to *her* . . ." He jabs a finger in my direction. "You violated an agreement we had with her family. She is their only female heir, and they believe you've tainted her with Nocturnus blood. Just like Silas did to Jessamine all those years ago. The very reason why the feud started to begin with. You didn't fuck-ing break any curses, you started a fucking war."

Fuck.

Everything's happening so fast; I haven't had time to even pro-cess all the events that have transpired. Jessamine Blackwell—the ghost girl who stalked me all over Tenebrose just so she could hand

deliver me to Riot's brother, Zeke. Tricked and betrayed by my very own ancestor. She believed that if Zeke took over Nocturnus, that if she offered him my blood, she could be free to join her lover, Silas, in the After. But then I ruined her entire plan when I stabbed and killed Zeke.

Val's eyes widen. "So? Let's go to fucking war then. The Blackwells punished the Graves for decades because of an accident. They made the rest of the families choose sides. We chose to side with Riot's family. *We* chose to follow them to Raven's Gate and remain here. Is it so wrong that I would want to help my best friend seek redemption?"

"Accident?" Laurent roars back. "Silas Graves poisoned Jessamine Blackwell. Did he really think it wouldn't kill her?"

"Well, it didn't kill me," I murmur under my breath.

His scowl turns on me. "What did you say?"

Oh, fuck. Apparently, that wasn't as under my breath as I thought. I clear my throat. "The poison. It hasn't killed me."

Laurent glares at Atlas. "You fucking Thorns and your poison. Did you ever stop to think what the Blackwells would do if this one died too?"

Atlas doesn't flinch. He's not afraid of Laurent. I can see it in the murderous look that takes over his pretty ocean-colored eyes. "I know how to administer it properly. Silas didn't. Apparently."

Laurent shakes his head and turns back on his son, whom he's still holding in an iron death grip. "The ravens are dying, the Blackwells are infuriated, and your initiates are either dead or rotting in Absentia Asylum. Give me one good reason not to beat you to a bloody fucking pulp."

His threat sparks my adrenaline. I leap from the couch. "I'll give you two. One, because he's your fucking *son*. And two... because I'll kill you if you hurt him ever again."

"Maur..." Riot warns as he moves to my side. "She's just sleep-deprived," he pleads with Laurent.

Val curses under his breath but doesn't dare look in my direction.

Laurent snickers. "Spoken like a true Blackwell. Congratulations, *son*. You've just made your bed with the devil herself."

"I've been called many things, but devil? That's a new one." Val wrenches away from him, finally finding his strength. "If that's true, then I'm glad she's on *my* side."

Laurent's goons take three steps toward Val, and I lose it. I rush forward, prepared to meet them when Riot and Atlas both jump in front of me. Laurent holds up his hand, stilling them in their place. "Enough. This is a waste of time. You're all too naïve and sex-crazed to understand the severity of your actions. But you will see soon. The mess you've fucking made..."

"We broke the fucking curse," Val growls out.

His father nods. "That you did. The four of you can leave Raven's Gate whenever you want... And now the Blackwells can also come in whenever *they want*."

He snaps his fingers, and his initiates file out. "Some curses punish, and some protect. Remember that when Penny Blackwell comes for you all."

And with that, Laurent and his initiates are gone, leaving us in a state of disarray and self-loathing.

A nagging twinge of dread twists in my gut. A thought that hadn't crossed my mind until now. "What if the curse started long before Silas killed Jessamine?"

Val looks at me for the first time since his father arrived. "What are you talking about, Maur?"

I swallow hard, my mind racing. "There's something your fathers aren't telling us. You think they'd be happy we broke the curse. But they seem terrified."

Riot stalks over to the bar and pours himself a whiskey. "They're just pissed we did it without their permission. They're so greedy, they want their hands in everything."

M VIOLET

I shake my head. He's not getting it. "I think there's more to it. They really don't want us to leave Raven's Gate."

Atlas runs a hand through his blond hair, slicking it back with his sweaty palm. "Maybe they don't want us to go to Ever Graves."

"But why? What don't they want us to find out?" I've been on the precipice of something big. Something important. But I couldn't quite put my finger on it until now.

Riot's face pales. "The curse isn't real."

CHAPTER TEN

Maureen

T HE ONLY THING STRONGER THAN FEAR IS HATE. WHEN YOU LOATHE someone so much, you don't care what they'll do to you as long as you can hurt them first. And if Laurent Erebus hates Val half as much as his son hates him, then it should come as no surprise that he's been lying to us. That they all have.

"You're saying that there was never a curse. Only a lie to keep us from leaving Raven's Gate? That's insane," Val quips.

It sounds even more insane saying it out loud. But it tracks. I twist my hair up into a top-knot and fan the back of my neck. "Is it? My family ran Riot's out of Ever Graves when Silas got Jessamine killed. Except she didn't follow him to the After. They got

separated . . . or she got stuck. Whatever. She was controlling the ravens before I came along. Until I joined Nocturnus."

"Why would our families make up a lie like that? For what purpose?" Atlas leans forward, his interest piqued.

I pace around the room, my pulse racing. "Fear? Greed? Who knows . . . But there must have been something in it for them. Nocturnus didn't exist before the feud. It was born *from* it. Your families worship the ravens and give sacrifices, and in return, they give you power. But where does that power come from?"

Riot places his hands firmly on my shoulders. "Do you hear how ridiculous this all sounds, Maur?"

I shrug him off. "You've never even been to Ever Graves, Riot. None of you have. The three of you were born here in Raven's Gate after the Thorns and Erebuses sided with the Graves. You've said it yourselves. Tenebrose was built on hallowed ground. I think they made a pact, not a curse."

Valentin balls his fists at his sides, the rage building inside him. "So our ancestors discovered a secret, and in order to protect it, they made up a lie to keep any of us from leaving. Is that what you're saying, Maur?"

The new sigil on my neck crackles, stinging the flesh that surrounds it. I pause in my tracks and breathe through it. I'm more confused than ever, but I'm so close to figuring it all out. I can almost taste it. "I think so. I don't know . . ."

Riot flexes his jaw after taking a long sip of whiskey. "They have their secrets. I'm sure of it."

"Maybe they created a fake curse to keep the Blackwells out and *you* in . . . Until I came along and ruined it. And your fathers think *I'm* the fucking devil. I think this has more to do with them not wanting me to control the ravens."

Riot looks down at the floor. "Fucking bastards."

Atlas lines up rows of poison vials on the coffee table. "They're afraid of you, Maur. Afraid you're going to steal it all from them.

That's what last night was really about. The ritual, the punishment for Zeke—it wasn't initiation—it was an effort to make you submissive."

Riot looks up, his eyes glowing. "You're the dark queen on this psychotic chessboard."

"Afraid of *me*? I'm just a hot mess from a small town. The Blackwells might be scary, but I'm nothing like them." I find it hard to believe that little old me could strike fear into the heart of some-one like Holden Graves or Laurent Erebus.

Riot dusts his fingers across the sigil on my neck. "You've killed two men in cold blood, Maur. Maybe you're more of a Blackwell than you thought."

A wave of chills dance on the surface of my skin. I don't want to think about either of those nights. "It was self-defense," I whisper.

"Was it?" Valentin crosses the room and takes my face in his hands. "You and Bailey planned to kill Chad and Billy that night in Wickford Hollow. And Zeke . . . *we were going to do it*, but you flew past us with the knife." He brushes his thumb against my lips. "Don't fight that part of you, Maur. It's one of the things I admire most."

Was he right?

Am I just fooling myself into thinking I was some poor, help-less girl fighting to stay alive? I didn't hesitate either time. A dark rage took over me on both of those nights. A need for revenge and redemption.

I shake my head, my emotions unfurling from the most de-praved parts of me. "I don't know who I am anymore."

Atlas leans back against the couch. He twirls a vial of poison between his fingers. His blue-green eyes sparkle. I could literally drown in the depths of them. I search his gaze for peace, but all I find is a beautiful chaos. It teeters on insanity, pulling me in deeper with every breath. Seducing me every time he flicks his tongue across his perfectly full lips.

He smirks as he catches the way my throat bobs. "We know who you are, Maur. You're our firecracker. Our pretty little psycho. You're

the woman we lay sacrament to and worship. Blood... death... we don't give a fuck about all that. To us, you're just ours."

As fucked up as that sounds, it stirs a little tremor in my belly. A longing in my heart. An ache between my thighs. Fuck, why am I so drawn to their madness?

And at this moment, I realize I'm not angry with Atlas anymore. I don't think I ever was. I just needed to take it out on him. I forgot how hectic loving him can be. He's never shown me to be anything but sadistic. His moods are whimsical, flippant, and unhinged. But he would never intentionally let anyone hurt me. Last night was normal for him. These rituals are all he's ever known. Nocturnus is his life.

I'm the stranger in this world. I'm the one who is getting a crash course in cults and secret societies. Val didn't do anything to stop it either. But he expressed his regrets and sorrow for leaving me alone with Holden.

That's what irks me. Atlas doesn't seem to care. That's what hurts me the most. "I need some air."

I rush out the front door before they can respond. The fog is thick, all the way down to the ground. There's a crisp chill in the air that reminds me of Tenebrose. The way it whips through my hair, biting my flesh. I'm filled with melancholy, a longing to go back. I miss my classes, my friends, and even the unlit paths through the woods. I close my eyes and take a deep breath, sucking down the last traces of winter. When I open my eyes, I gasp and try to remain as calm as possible. Over a dozen ravens perch on the ground, surrounding me. My pulse races.

They don't squawk at me as usual. Instead, they are quiet and still as they gaze back at me. I'm afraid to move. "What in the actual fuck?" I murmur.

"Don't be afraid," Atlas whispers in my ear. I didn't even hear him walk up over the hammering of my heart.

"What do they want from me?" I swallow hard, willing saliva into my mouth.

He brushes his lips across my neck. "The same thing we all want..." He kisses my sigil. "To serve you."

I turn in his arms and have to crane my neck to meet his haunting gaze. "Back at Tenebrose, you told me to come to you after they hurt me. But you never said you'd stop them from doing so."

His eyes light up with approval. He slides his hands around my waist and pulls me to his chest. "Now you're getting it. I will never go against my nature or prevent others from going against theirs. But I can put you back together after they've picked you apart."

I nod. My addiction to all three of them festers like a disease. Our mutual obsession is as twisted as the dead branches beneath my boots, rotting and spoiling anything good left in me. But I don't care. I want them *too* much. This need consumes my every waking thought and impulse.

"Will you ever hurt me, Atlas?" I feel his muscles flex as I run my hands over his chest, wishing I could feel his skin instead of his T-shirt.

"Mmm, only in the best possible way," he purrs. His eyes flash—hungry, feral.

I draw in a deep breath as he crushes his lips to mine. Everything else falls away in his kiss. I forget about the cold, the ravens, and the ritual scars that mar my flesh. He tastes like honey and wine. Like sweet fucking desecration.

I moan into his mouth as I claw at his clothes, desperate to get them off. "Please, Atlas..."

He scrapes his teeth up the length of my jaw until he reaches my earlobe. He takes it between his teeth and nips. I wince as it pinches and stings. He snickers at my discomfort but eases up. I let out a deep breath as his tongue lashes out, the heat from it soothing my tender flesh. He sucks my lobe like he's drinking from a fountain of

eternal youth. Like a fucking vampire drinking blood. It's excruciating and orgasmic. Agonizing yet stimulating.

Pleasure is never without pain. He reminds me of that as he
bites down harder this time. I whimper and dig my fingers into his
arms. "*Get inside me right fucking now.*"

"Not until I've left my teeth marks all over your body." The buttons of my shirt fly off and hit the ground as he rips the fabric open.
With one hand, he unhooks my bra and tosses it.

I shiver and try to cover myself, but he pushes my arms back.
He brushes his palms over my nipples, sending goose pebbles across
my skin. My nipples swell and ache, hardening with each flick of
his hand.

The sound of feathers ruffling reminds me we're not alone.

"They're watching us."

"Let them fucking watch, Maur. Let them see how I destroy
you." He unzips my pants and pushes them down along with my
panties. My pussy spasms as he palms it with his cold hand.

But he doesn't move.

"Atlas," I whine.

He flicks his tongue over my nipple. "I wanna hold my pussy
first." He licks my other nipple, drawing slow circles around it with
the tip of his tongue. "I wanna feel its pulse beating in my hand. The
fucking ache and throb as it begs to be fucked."

Oh fucking hell. I'm going to cum before he even does anything. This man ... fuck. "You're a bastard, Atlas," I breathe.

He laughs, the vibration from his throat sending tremors
through every inch of me. He squeezes my pussy, and I almost black
out from euphoria. "That's my good little pussy. You're fucking hy-
perventilating for my cock, aren't you?" He loosens his grip and begins rubbing his palm back and forth. I shudder as he grazes my
taint. "Or is it my fingers you want?"

I grab his wrist and try to force his hand. "All of the above."

"You're being a bad girl, love." He undoes his belt and slides it out in one swoop. *Why was that so fucking hot?*

He grabs my wrists and fastens them with the belt behind my back. "There. That's better. Now, where were we?"

I almost cry as he slides his palm back over my pussy. My juices leak out and drip down my thighs. I'm fucking rabid for this man right now. "We were at the part where you were going to stop edging me and start fucking me." I jerk my hips forward.

"Don't you dare fucking grind against my hand until I give you permission." He slaps my pussy. "Now beg for release, pretty girl. Beg like a good little slut."

A high-pitched whimper escapes my lips. "Please, Atlas. I need you inside me. Please make me cum."

He slaps my pussy again, and I buck. "I said, *like a slut.*"

I'm going to pass out from the adrenaline. From the ache. "*Please fuck me.* I'll be good... I'm so tight. *Please,*" I beg.

With his free hand, he tightens the belt around my wrists. He lowers his mouth to my ear and whispers, "You won't be tight for long. I'm going to stretch you wide open."

My knees buckle as he shoves one finger inside my pussy. "Oh, shit." The wind picks up around us as the first wave of spasms rips through my core. *Fucking finally.* He thrusts a second finger in, and I release a sigh of relief as if his touch is my only salvation. "Yes... Holy fuck, Atlas."

He wraps his hand around my throat and squeezes. "You didn't come to me after they hurt you, pretty girl." He thrusts a third finger in, making my clit pulse with need. "But I found you, didn't I? Mmm."

"I'm sorry," I whimper as the oxygen in my lungs depletes. He pumps his fingers in and out of my slick folds, harder each time. "I had fun playing with your body while you slept. Fucking your tight little pussy while you were off in some dream." He shoves a fourth finger in, and I almost black out. "Or was it a nightmare?"

Hmm? You were so wet, and you didn't even know what the fuck was happening. You know why?"

A tight pressure builds in my belly as he twists his fingers inside me, raking them against my walls. My legs give out and I hit the ground. His hand travels with me, the impact forcing his fingers in farther. I spread my legs wide to accommodate the girth, ignoring the sharp twigs that are digging into my knees and thighs.

Fuck. "I can't breathe. . ." His iron grip around my throat is only allowing a small amount of air to filter through. Between my heart racing and the deep spasms rolling through my core, I'm seeing stars. He snarls, baring his teeth. "I'll tell you why you were so wet. Because your body is *mine*. You don't even have to be conscious for it to know that." He presses his thumb down hard on my clit, roughly rubbing it in circles.

As my orgasm starts to build, tears of struggle stream down my cheeks. Everything tingles. My sigils burn, intensifying every touch and tremor. Despite the pain in my chest, I grind against his hand, drowning in my own depravity.

"Don't run away from me ever again," he whispers in my ear. His grip on my throat tightens. I feel like I'm floating. No. He's moving me, tilting me backward. I look up at the sky as my head gently hits the ground, unsure if the stars I'm seeing are real or just spots in my blurred vision.

The pressure in my core builds. I'm going to fucking explode. I try to cry out, but without breath, I sound like a mangled animal. "Please. . ." I manage to gurgle out.

"That's it, beg for it like a good little slut. Fuck, you feel so good." He slides his fingers out and strokes the lips of my pussy. "You're taking it so well. But I think you can do better than that, pretty girl."

I roll my hips as a sharp spasm hits my core. "Uhhh," I moan. His gaze turns feral as he tucks his thumb between his fingers and shoves his whole fist inside my pussy.

Oh, my fucking god.

I feel him in my lower back, my belly, and in my ass. Atlas's hand is huge and bony, and he's far from gentle. I whimper and moan as he stretches me.

"Oh, yeah. Such a pretty pussy. So pink and swollen. Mmm. Fuck." He pumps his fist in and out. Every time my hips jerk up to meet his rhythm, it sends a sharp pain down my arms as my wrists dig into the hard ground underneath me. The belt around them is cutting off my circulation. And his hand around my throat isn't easing up.

Every cell in my body is on fire. Electric. It feels like I'm slowly dying and coming back to life at the same time.

Without warning, he releases my throat, sliding his hand down the length of my naked body. As cold air rushes back into my lungs and I start to choke, he slaps my clit. I buck and thrust my hips, angling up as he curls his fingers around my core.

"That's it, fucking cum for me," he demands.

The stars in my vision explode and then go black as a deep orgasm rolls through me. I open my mouth wide to scream, but nothing comes out except a quiet squeak. But what my voice cannot do, my body makes up for.

I contort and twist like I'm having convulsions as he thrusts in and out, milking me like he's trying to break a wild horse. Fuck. Fuck. Fuck. My cum squirts out, landing on his face as I ride his fist. "Atlas, fuck."

"Mmm," He licks my cream off his lips. When he pulls his fist out, he slaps my pussy again. "Fuck, you're still coming." He smears his fingers in my folds as I continue to writhe on the ground like a cat in heat.

My juices spill out again, milky and thick. I whine and struggle against my restraints. "Untie me."

His eyes darken as he reaches around and slips the belt off my wrists. "Mmm, there you go, pretty girl."

I don't even care that my wrists are sore and bleeding. I slide my fingers down my slit and rock my hips, I play with my own juices, rubbing them into my folds and around my clit.

Atlas's eyes glow as he fixates on the show I'm giving him.

"Yeah, just like that. Get fucking filthy for me."

I cry out, my voice finally returning, as another orgasm takes hold of me. I am the most wild and unhinged and depraved that I've ever been.

Atlas cradles my ass in his hands as I come down and start to breathe normally again. "Look at the sticky mess you made..." He guides my finger down my slit and then up to my mouth. "I want to watch you lick yourself clean."

"Oh, shit," I have no lines left to cross. No more boundaries to break with this man. He has ruined me in ways that even the other two couldn't fathom. My sweet, poisonous Atlas with a streak of madness so sick that Absentia Asylum wouldn't know what to do with him.

I suck each of my fingers, one by one, tasting every drop of my own essence. He watches me silently, his lips quivering.

"That's my pretty girl," he murmurs.

I don't know if it's the new sigil he let me carve into his chest or the depraved act of watching me lick my own cum from my fingers, or even the fact that he just stuck his entire fist inside my pussy while almost choking me to death, but there's a primal connection between us now that I can't explain. Only that it's like a rabid dog on a leash—ferocious, threatened, and ready to bite.

CHAPTER ELEVEN

Valentin

W ITH MY MIND STILL REELING FROM HAVING TO FACE MY FATHER, Maur's revelations about the ravens and the curse, which is allegedly not a curse at all but a lie, I keep quiet and try to focus on the road.

Maur doesn't have much to say either as she fidgets with her nails in the passenger seat next to me. Atlas and Riot are chatty enough for the both of us in the back, going on about the Spring Equinox Festival and how we're going to get new Nocturnus recruits. Winter is almost over, which means classes start on Monday. While most normal people get invigorated by the prospect of spring, my soul belongs to winter. To the dying trees, the frozen ground, and the cold rain. It resonates deep within me.

I have mixed feelings about going back to Tenebrose. I'll have my uncle to contend with, coupled with the burden of helping Riot rebuild Nocturnus. And we'll all have to deal with the fallout from the night of the ball. The whispers were growing up until the last day before winter break. The students were told that Zeke's death was a tragic accident, but I'm sure they all suspect foul play. The whole school is fucking scared of us.

The rumor mill will only get worse once we return with Mari, her body marked up with Nocturnus sigils. No one will dare say anything, but they will gawk and gossip and make up shit to fill in the blanks of their delusional fantasies. That's how it's always been in our world. We are the elite, the privileged, and therefore, subjected to all forms of adoration *and* mockery.

I catch Maureen watching me out of the corner of my eye. I grip the wheel and step on the gas. Her close proximity sends my pulse racing. She alone can make both my blood boil and my cock hard at the same time. Her gaze is electric. It makes me uneasy and yet turns me on.

She's always expecting something. *Wanting something.* Even if it's just a look of reassurance. Sometimes, I think I can give her everything. But mostly I know I'll just disappoint her with my apathy.

"What are you thinking about?" she murmurs.

"Nothing."

I keep my eyes on the road. The past few weeks have been fucking draining. I don't want to think about the ways we've degraded her. The things I've done to her, and she's done to me. If I don't shut down for a while, I'll unravel and literally become a slave to my every fucking sexual whim with her.

It's not a horrible idea, but the more we touch, the deeper I fall. The more I crave. And that never ends well. Erebus family rule number one: *If you fall in love, you might as well cut off your balls and hand them over.*

"It doesn't look like nothing, Val. You're cracking the leather"

on the steering wheel." She covers my hand with hers and I tense. *Introverted me* isn't pleasant to be around. She has no idea the extent of my self-loathing and deprecation.

She sighs. "Okay, I'll leave you alone."

The second she slides her hand away from mine, the guilt claws at me like a hungry beast. I shouldn't feel this way. I haven't even known her for that long. But those honey-colored eyes always seem to strip me bare. And I fucking hate it.

I nod. "Excellent."

Atlas snickers from the back seat, suddenly more interested in us than Riot's diatribe on Nocturnus politics. "Do I detect a little mood swing, Val?"

"Fuck you," I snap.

He laughs. "Point and case."

"Back off, Atlas," Maur whips around to my defense. "He's been driving all night while listening to you two chatterboxes the whole time."

Why is she fucking defending me after I just bit her head off?

She's just as toxic as the rest of us. "Stay out of it, Maur."

She rolls her eyes. "Whatever."

Riot stretches his arm out, curling it around her from behind so he's hugging her and the front seat. "Relax, baby. We're all on edge." She practically purrs at the sound of his voice in her ear, almost coming from just the weight of his arm across her heaving chest. She closes her eyes and sinks back. "Mmm."

Atlas laughs again. "He's right, Maur. Val's always like this after he sees his father."

Fuck.

The engine roars as I step on the gas. Beads of sweat form on my forehead. I need to get the fuck out of this car. Away from everyone so I can fucking think without this feral ache between my legs distracting me.

With each sigil, it gets harder and harder to drown them out.

Our bond grows deeper with each one. Fuck, I was obsessed with her before her first sigil. Now she has four. Even her scent consumes all the air inside the car, filling up our lungs with its potency.

I unzip my jacket and roll down all the windows, locking them in place so they can't roll them back up.

I ignore their pleas and grumbles as I drive faster. I don't dare look over at Maureen who is cursing up a storm. Out of the corner of my eye, I see her dark brown stands blowing ferociously around her head. Goosebumps pebble her skin.

Spring may be on the way, but it's still cold as fuck. I can't help but smirk as I get off on torturing them. I push the pedal all the way to the floor and close my eyes. The sigil on the back of my neck flares to life, taking over.

Three ravens flap alongside the car hysterically as they lose the battle for sight. I take over, using their eyes to guide me. Their squawking is lost in the wind, lost over Maureen screaming at me to open my eyes.

"He's got this. Calm down," Atlas yells.

She's in a state of panic as she tugs on my sleeve. "What the actual fuck are you trying to do, get us killed?"

One of them yanks her away from me. "He's using the ravens, Maur," Riot shouts.

"But there's a cliff up there," she screams. "We're going too fast to take the turn."

"Then we'll go over. Consider it a shortcut," I snarl while gritting my teeth.

We call it *Devil's Yard*. It's a hairpin turn that's seen a lot of blood. I've driven it a hundred times with my eyes open. But I have no intention of taking it today.

"You'll need all of us, Val," Riot calls out over the howling wind. Atlas puts his hand on my shoulder. "Fucking hell. Let's fucking go. I'm so hard right now."

"Are you all fucking crazy?" Maureen cries. "Let me out right fucking now."

I laugh and shake my head. "We won't make it without you." She squeezes my thigh. "Then slow down, Val. You don't have to do this."

Riot rests his hand on my other shoulder. "Fuck it, Maur, focus. Envision us going over the cliff and landing safely on the ground below."

"What? No. It's not possible. We're gonna fucking die." She's shrieking now. The terror in her voice sends my adrenaline coursing through my veins. It's so palpable I can almost taste it.

"Do it, pretty girl. Help us get over that cliff," Atlas coos. "You're the dark queen on the chessboard, remember?"

The edge of the cliff nears, sending my pulse racing as fast as this car. "Time's running out. Everyone needs to focus."

"Oh, shit. Okay, okay," Maureen locks onto my wrist, and I feel her power surge instantly. It pumps into my veins and arteries like electric currents.

"Good girl," Riot encourages.

Atlas howls like a wolf as the four of us grip each other. I keep my eyes closed while my vision stays connected to the ravens.

"Ready?" I call out.

Maureen's scream gets lost in the wind as I punch it before anyone can respond.

My stomach flips as we fly off the ground. The car floats for a second before hurtling down faster than I anticipated.

The wind gets knocked out of me as we plummet.

"Focus, fuckers!" Atlas shouts.

A crackle of energy shifts through me, and we start floating again, cascading down at a slower pace.

"We're fucking doing it," Maureen breathes. "Holy shit, we're fucking doing it."

I release the ravens and open my eyes just as we pass the tops

of the elm trees. My belly tingles as I take in the view. It's breathtak-
ing. "Hold on," I whisper.

The ground is closer than it appears, and we hit it hard. "Fuck.
Hold on," I cry out, louder this time.

The tires spin as I fight to regain control of the wheel. Dust and
dirt fly in every direction as we hydroplane. I can't see if there's a
tree in front of me, or a building, or even another cliff.

Maureen grabs my arm. "Find the path, Val."

I close my eyes and go back into the raven. There we go. I let
off the gas and hold the wheel as steady as I can.

The dust starts to clear as I'm finally able to straighten the car.
I slam on the brakes and look around. We're in the forest just
outside of Tenebrose. "Holy fuck."

Atlas sticks his hand out the window and pats the door. "Mary
Shelley, you sly little minx."

"You named your car?" Maureen asks.

The rest of us burst out laughing.

"Yup." I slick my hair back with a sweaty palm.

"Why Mary Shelley and not Frankenstein?" Maureen arches
an eyebrow, a smirk on her lips.

I catch my breath and finally turn to look at her fully. "Because
it's not the monsters I'm afraid of . . . it's the ones who create them
that terrify me the most. Those are the devils you don't want to
fuck with."

Her cheeks flush. "What about when the monster finds its own
power? When it stops being a slave?"

Fuck. My adrenaline is pumping, and all this talk of monsters
makes me want to bend her over the hood of this car and fuck the
breath out of her. "A monster with a mind of its own is no longer a
beast but a king . . . or a queen in your case." I reach over and pick
a leaf from her hair. "And that, pretty girl, is when you get to make
them all fall at your feet."

"Anyone wanna talk about how we just fell from the sky?" Atlas

hangs an arm around each of our seats. His blue-green eyes are ablaze with toxin and adrenaline.

Riot chuckles. "I gotta figure out how to do that on my bike."

Maureen punches each of us in the arm. "You're all fucking psycho, you know that right?"

We can't wipe the shit eating grins off our faces.

She giggles and shakes her head. "That was pretty fucking amazing."

I want to touch her and hold her in my arms, but I still need my own space. I need to distance myself from this obsession. If I start, I won't want to stop. "Let's get you back to the Nest. I'm sure Libra is burning a hole in the floor waiting for you."

She smiles and nods, but I can see the disappointment in her eyes. "Yeah, I need a break from you guys, anyway," she teases.

Riot's eyes darken. "I don't like you staying there without us, Maur. We should all be together."

Atlas nods in agreement. "Come stay with us, pretty girl."

Fuck.

Three weeks in the cabin was fucking ecstasy. It was a fantasy. And it was fucking torture. I can't even remember if I ate food or slept much. If she moves in with us... there will be no stopping my heart from completely attaching itself to hers. I'll be her monster, enslaved to her without logic or reason.

To my relief, she stands her ground. "Nope. I'm trying to be a normal college student, remember? Besides, Libra will light me on fire if I leave her alone all semester. Your cousin is very persuasive, Atlas."

"You mean bossy." They both laugh as I drive up to her dormitories.

She tosses her hair up into a high ponytail, and my cock twitches as I catch a glimpse of the sigil on her neck. The Erebus sigil. Mine.

"Remember, tomorrow night; party at Nocturnus House."

"I'll pick you up." Riot kisses her hard on the lips. I want to finger her while she kisses him. Fucking hell. I shift in my seat, my cock swelling.

Atlas grabs her chin and shoves his tongue in her mouth. I watch as her cheeks flush and her nipples pebble through her white tank top. "Mmm, you taste like the sweetest sin."

To my surprise she doesn't wait for me to kiss her as well. Instead, she hops out and closes the door behind her. As much as I want some space, the thought of not kissing her goodbye irritates me. It's fucking startling.

She leans back in, draping her body through the window frame.

"See you later, Frankenstein."

This fucking girl.

"Sweet dreams, Mary Shelley."

She blows me a kiss, and I can't help but grin as she struts away.

CHAPTER TWELVE

Maureen

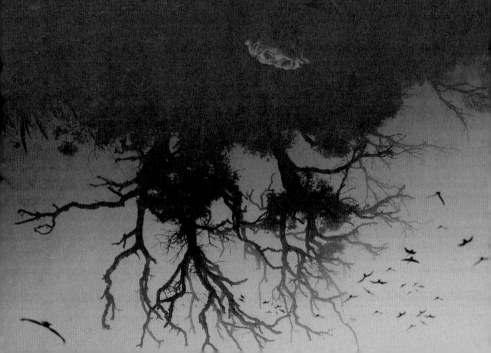

M Y DORM IS EERILY QUIET WHEN THE ELEVATOR DOORS SLIDE OPEN. Everything is just as I left it—clothes strewn about the living room, mine and Libra's, a half-drunk bottle of whiskey on the coffee table, and a pile of blankets on the floor from the slumber party that we had with Villette the night before I left.

I sigh as I roll my luggage in. It wasn't ever my intention to have such a lavish dorm room. Ever since I came to Tenebrose, it's been one thing after another, painting targets on my back. From my last name to becoming the object of Riot, Atlas, and Valentin's obsession, to the murder of Zeke, and now . . . now I have ancient sigils carved into my body, visible for all the haters to see.

If there was any doubt before that Nocturnus had claimed me,

that will soon be removed. No matter what I do, I will never be a normal student here at Tenebrose. With my family lineage, maybe I'm not ever meant to be.

The click of my heels echoes as I walk down the hall to Libra's room. I hesitate before knocking on the door. If she's sleeping and I wake her up, she'll throw a massive temper tantrum. But if I don't announce that I'm back, she'll be even more pissed. Ugh.

"Lib? You in there?" I knock softly, hoping to ease her out of her slumber. That girl loves her *glow-up rest* as she calls it.

No answer.

I knock again, louder this time. "Libra, I'm back. The clock is ticking to get out here and remind me of how basic I am." I chuckle to myself.

While she and I started out as bitchy rivals, we learned to tolerate each other fast and then eventually even grew to like each other. We come from the same world, but my life deviated away from it when I was born. While she has always been aware of our families' crazy, I just got a crash course in it a few months ago after arriving here.

Still no answer.

I turn the knob and crack the door open just to peek. I scan the room, half-expecting her to lob a pillow at me, but there's no sign of her. *Guaranteed she's out having mimosas or bloody marys.*

It's just as well. Now, I have some peace and quiet while I un-pack and try to figure out my class schedule for the new semester. After hanging up all my clothes and taking a quick shower, I sit down on the edge of my bed, pull out my phone, and log into my student email account. I have Professor Erebus again. *Great.* I think Val's uncle hates me more than his father at this point.

I also have Professor Harker again, along with Miss Tempest for costume design, Professor Visha for Botany, and a new name I haven't seen before—Professor Crane. *I wonder if he's any relation to Villette... This school is steeped in family lore and history.*

As I click out, three text messages pop up. One from Villette

insisting we meet for drinks at *Swallow* tonight. I shoot off a quick *hell yeah* reply.

The second one is from Atlas: *I wouldn't be mad if you snuck into my bed tonight, pretty girl.*

I laugh and reply back with three devil emojis. Depending on how drunk I get tonight, I wouldn't put it past myself to do exactly that.

I scroll down to see the third text, and my heart skips a beat.

It's from Bailey!

Hey, bitch. How's winter break going? Your guys better be keeping you happy. Miss you so much. Love, Bales.

A warmth spreads through my body just seeing her words on my screen. I miss my bestie so fucking much it hurts. We haven't spoken in a while. There's so much I want to tell her, but I don't know where to begin. Would she understand?

I know deep down inside that out of all people, Bailey would be the first person to get what I'm going through. But I still have a hard time remembering she's a ghost now. That she's doing her own thing in Wickford Hollow. And other than Raine, who is fucking nuts, Poe, Grim, and Saint aren't completely as psycho as my guys. My situation is so different in every way, I'm basically in a cult now. Fuck.

My hands tremble a little as I type back. *Miss you too. Winter break was . . . interesting. I have so much to tell you. But I want to do it in person. Maybe I'll come visit at the end of the semester. Have a Jell-O shot for me. These bougie bitches here won't let me drink them anymore.*

She replies back with a few laughing emojis before I see the typing bubbles again. *You only use the word "interesting" when you're stressed about something. Come visit whenever you want, Maur! I miss your face and your voice.*

A couple of tears leak out. Fuck. I miss her so much. No one gets me the way she does.

Love you, Bales. Talk soon.

I wipe my sleeve across my cheeks and give myself a little slap.

"Snap out of it, bitch."

Libra and Villette have definitely helped fill a void, but no one can ever replace Bailey Bishop. That girl is literally my ride or die.

The sigil on my thigh burns, reminding me of the ways I've been degraded. I try to shove down the memory of Holden Graves humiliating me in front of an entire congregation of initiates. I could have refused to put the robe on, refused to take it off. I didn't have to go down to that ritual room. But the alternative would have been worse. They would have taken my sins out on Riot. And no matter the reason, the fact is that I did kill Zeke. And I chose to answer for it.

What makes me sick is how my body responded. I came in front of them. Multiple times. I'm disgusted with myself for getting off. For enjoying any part of it. I can still hear Holden's voice in my ear sometimes before I'm about to drift off to sleep—*you're not just their little slut anymore, temptress.*

The sigils heighten everything. They make me crave darker and dirtier things. They're like little switches that I'm still learning to control. But right now, all I want to do is cum.

I need release so I can clear my head.

After locking my bedroom door, I take off all my clothes and lie back on the bed. I need to be in control of my own pleasure for a change. I give my nipples a light squeeze as my pulse quickens.

Fuck.

I bite my lip and suck on it as the first wave of tingles spread through my core. I slide my finger down my slit, relishing the way my juices pool between my thighs at my first touch. I arch my back and whimper as the pressure builds. I rub my clit in circles before inserting a finger inside my warm pussy. "Mmm, fuck."

I rock my hips up as I pump in and out, adding a second finger as I begin to stretch myself. My breath hitches, and I push farther in, tapping gently against my G-spot. I try not to think about the ritual room and how feral I was with all those initiates surrounding me. But the second the memory flashes, a deep spasm shakes my core. I let out another moan as I remember their masked faces, their

shortness of breath, the way their robes shifted as they jerked themselves off, watching me.

Fuck. I liked it. No. *I fucking loved being watched.*

I let out a deeper moan as an orgasm rolls through me. *"Uhhh."*
I clench and twist around my fingers as I imagine my whole
room filled with masked faces watching me, chanting softly under
their breaths. I thrust harder, palming my entire pussy as I grind
against my hand, desperate to draw it out as long as possible.

Another orgasm grips me as I remember the way they took
turns lashing me. The leather belt slapping against my pussy stung,
but then the burn turned to tingling, A deep spasm, a euphoria that
rumbled through me and had me craving more.

"Fuck," I cry out as I finish riding out my third orgasm. My fingers are a sopping wet mess now. I reach for the box of tissues on
my bedside table and wipe them off.

I blow out a steady breath and start to get up from the bed when
my phone buzzes with a text from an unknown number. *Next time
you touch yourself, you better turn on your phone camera and show me.*

What the… I look around the room, paranoid. The curtains are
tightly closed. Did someone hear me? I tend to moan really fucking
loud. Ugh. But still, I don't recognize this number at all.

Who the fuck is this? I reply.

My heart races as I wait for a response. No typing bubbles. No
response. Great. I've only been back a few hours, and already the
cryptic weird shit is happening again. *What the fuck is with this school?*

It's probably just one of the guys messing with me. They get
off on their twisted little games of torment. But I can't help feeling
like something's off. There's a prickling on the back of my neck and
a sinking feeling in my belly.

I shiver and try to shake it off. My stomach grumbles as I look
at my phone to see it's past noon. I shoot off another text to Villette,
asking to meet up earlier to grab a bite to eat.

Thankfully, she says yes and is already heading downstairs to wait for me in the main lobby of our building.

I wash my hands, touch up my lipstick, and fix the eyeliner that smudged on my cheeks. Hopefully, she won't be able to tell that I spent the last hour finger fucking myself into a feral stupor.

But knowing her, she's too polite to say anything. Libra, on the other hand, would shout it from the rooftops. I'm so fucking glad she didn't come home during that. Lately, these urges are getting more and more frequent. And more demanding.

I need to talk to the guys about this tomorrow night.

I didn't think it was possible for Villette to look more gorgeous than she already did. Yet here she is, leaning across the wall from the elevator, her skin glowing brighter than ever. Her dark strands are swept up in a ponytail, all glossy and shiny.

"Wow, winter looks good on you, girl," I throw my arms around her and languish in the warm hug she gives me. An embrace I didn't even realize I needed until now.

She laughs throatily into my neck. "I have my brother, Bones, to thank for that. We went to the hot springs almost every day." I pull back to get a better look at her. "Well, damn. You'll have to send me the link to whatever spa you were at."

"No spa, just home. Ever Graves. We have a lot of land there. There's something about the water in that place." She loops her arm through mine as we head out the main doors.

It's hard not to notice the stares as we cross the parking lot and head for the path through the woods. I can't imagine what people are thinking about me after the ball.

"Ignore them," Villette coos. "They've got nothing better to do." I nod. "Already forgotten. So, how was Ever Graves? Any tea

that should be spilled upon me?" I make a grand dramatic gesture with my hand.

She giggles. "Oh, just the usual stuff. The townies are nuts, the cliffs are haunted, and my brother's little group of heathens is still terrorizing everyone. Oh, and of course, your grandmother is still trying to convince my father I need to quit school and get married before I become an unbreedable old maid."

I gasp, stopping her in her tracks. I spin around so fast I almost trip on a thick patch of overgrown brush. "What the fuck? Seriously?"

Villette collapses into laughter. "The look on your face . . . I forget that you didn't grow up the way we did. It's fine, Maur. It's not gonna happen. No offense, but my father thinks your grandmother is off her rocker."

"Sounds like she fucking is. Unbelievable." I let her resume our walkabout toward the center of campus, all the while still shaking my head. "Did she say anything about me?"

Villette sighs. "A little. It's mostly nonsensical. I think she's getting a bit senile."

A knot twists in my stomach. "Tell me."

A sharp wind blows between us, chilling my bones. I half-expect to see Jessamine pop up out of nowhere before I remember that Professor Erebus has her sequestered. Another fucking thing I need to check in with the guys about.

Villette sighs again as if the very mention of Penny Blackwell makes it harder to breathe. "She rambled about curses and deals with the devil. But she also mentioned her regrets and how it's her fault you're damaged."

I wince. Fucking hell. "Damaged? All because my dad was poor, and they were unmarried? Ouch."

"I don't know, Maur . . . Ever Graves is a dark place. And I don't just mean because of the fog and stone. Since I was a little girl, I have always felt scared to be alone. Like something would reach out in the night and snatch me away."

I shiver. That was one privilege I had over her; Wickford Hollow wasn't like that. "I guess maybe I should feel lucky I wasn't born there."

Villette reaches out to open the door of the campus café and holds it for me. I grab the first window table that's empty, and we both plop down across from each other in the black vinyl booth.

"Oh, I wasn't born there. My parents were on vacation here in Raven's Gate when my mom went into labor. We stayed here for a few months until it was safe for them to travel back with me."

That's odd. Who goes on vacation when they're close to giving birth?

I smile as the young blonde server places menus down in front of us. I arch my brow as I look them over. "Too early for a cocktail?"

"Never," Villette quips, grinning from ear to ear.

Thank God. I would have ordered one anyway but I'm glad I don't have to drink alone. I order a whiskey old fashion while Villette opts for an ice-cold dirty martini.

"Have you seen Libra? She wasn't there when I got home." I scan the menu as my stomach growls again.

Villette shakes her head. "I don't think she's back yet. Her brother, Aries, said something about her staying a little longer in their winter villa."

"She didn't go with you to Ever Graves? Isn't that where she's from?" Another odd piece of information that didn't sit right with me. These people have so many fucking secrets.

The server comes back before she can answer. We order our food and another round of drinks. I go for my usual sweet potato fries, grilled cheese sandwich, and extra ranch dressing, while Villette opts for a Cobb salad with balsamic vinaigrette *instead* of the creamy bleu cheese it comes with. All of which literally sums up our two very different approaches to life in a nutshell.

"Yes and no. Well, her family has a pretty cool estate in the mountains. But she was born in Raven's Gate too. Her family moved back to Ever Graves when she was like two or three, I think." Villette

takes a sip of her martini and I fixate on the bob of her throat as I lose myself in my thoughts.

"Was anyone actually born in Ever Graves?" I ask, a little too accusatory.

She purses her lips, and it looks like she's genuinely thinking. "Your mom, right? My brother was born there, and your cousin Draven. Libra's brother too."

I nod. "Sorry for all the questions. I'm tired and think I forgot how to have a normal conversation."

Villette laughs and shrugs. "I missed you, Maur. Tell me, how was your trip? What shenanigans did the four of you get up to?" she asks excitedly.

A pit of dread forms in my stomach like a ball of lead. There's no way I'm telling my only friend here how Riot's depraved father stripped me naked and forced unspeakable acts on me while his initiates watched. Villette already thinks Nocturnus is dangerous and fucked up.

I smile after taking a big sip of my cocktail. "We just chilled at Val's cabin. Drank too much, slept in late. You know the usual winter break debauchery."

"Ooh, girl, thank you for not going into detail," she teases. "I know how obsessed you all are with each other's anatomy."

I almost spit whiskey out of my nose. "Facts."

We both fall back into our friendship with ease, spending the rest of the night like two normal college students excited about classes and upcoming events. We agree to go dress shopping together again for the Spring Equinox Ball. All while under the surface, secrets and lies simmer, threatening to boil over at any moment.

But the longer I live in this world, the easier it gets to shove the truth down.

The server drops the check, and we both scramble to pay. "I told you, *my treat*," Villette hisses.

I concede, but only because she snarls at me, which is not a common look for my normally mild-mannered friend. I admire her tenacity and spirit as she slaps down her credit card, satisfied with herself for beating me.

"Oh, I almost forgot to ask. Are you related to that new teacher, Professor Crane?"

Villette's face lights up even more. "Felix? Yes, he's my older brother. I'm so happy he's at Tenebrose this year. I finally get to spend some time with him."

"That's amazing, Villette. I can't wait to meet him. They put me in his poetry class." If he's half as nice as his sister, that class should be a walk in the park.

We lock arms again as we head out the front doors of the café. She gives mine a squeeze. "I told him all about you last night. The poor guy is staying in my room at the Nest because his faculty apartment isn't ready yet. Anyway, he might pop into *Swallow* tonight. No one knows he's a teacher yet." She giggles.

"Well, you are a great sister for letting him crash at your place. And I can't wait to see the looks on everyone's faces in class on Monday after they realize who he is." It feels good to talk like this again. Like some sort of semblance of me is a normal woman. The darkness surrounding me keeps getting more suffocating, but when I'm around Villette, I feel lighter. Less anxious.

"Is it cool if I get ready at your place, tonight? I'm sure Felix could use some space." Everything about this girl is warm and thoughtful. I always wondered what it would be like to have a sibling. Villette is the poster child for sister of the year. I chuckle as I think of how Libra talks to her brother. I heard her on the phone once and felt so sorry for him. I almost sent him condolence flowers.

"Hell, yeah. I'll chill a bottle of champagne for us. Gotta celebrate the first night out of the new semester."

CHAPTER THIRTEEN

Maureen

"YOU WANT THE USUAL?" THE BARTENDER ASKS VILLETTE AS SHE LEANS over the polished-wood bar. He looks at her like she's a meal to be devoured. Who can blame him? In a tight, black, strapless dress and four-inch heels, she looks even more stunning than usual. Her dark-brown hair is loose in waves around her tanned shoulders. She tosses it as she winks at him and nods. A whiff of honey and patchouli permeates the gesture.

I don't come here enough to have a usual, I guess.

"Just a shot of whiskey neat, please." I beam a little as he admires me as well. I'm in the mood to turn fucking heads tonight. Which is why I chose to wear a black leather mini skirt and pink lacey bustier that pushes my tits up so high, you could set your drink on them.

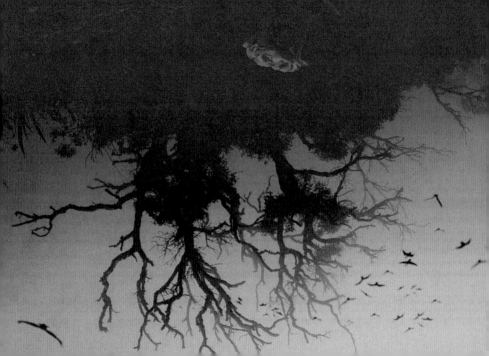

And there are plenty of people noticing me and Villette tonight. We're a Crane and a Blackwell out on the prowl like two nepo babies out of a trashy reality TV show. Just swap out the designer bags and lip injections for knives and dead bodies.

The music is loud as fuck. Perfect for drowning out the squawking ravens that have gathered outside. And for shutting out my intrusive thoughts. I want just one night where I can party with my friends without the weight of Nocturnus on my shoulders.

I glare over my drink at a few students who snicker at us as they walk by. Most of them haven't bothered to get to know me. As soon as they found out I was a Blackwell, another rich kid from one of the founding families of Ever Graves, they made up their minds about me. Even though I have no ties to my family or their money. If it hadn't been for Bailey, I wouldn't have been able to even afford a sandwich at Tenebrose, let alone tuition and dorm fees.

Villette is swaying her hips to the music while sipping on her martini when a tall, super handsome man with dark hair and brown eyes comes up behind her and curls his arm around her neck. "That better not be vodka, Lettie." He smirks as we lock eyes.

She wiggles away from him, laughing. "What are you gonna do about it? Tell Mom and Dad that your twenty-five-year-old sister is having a cocktail?"

He beams back at her, a mischievous twinkle in his eyes. "I didn't tell them when you drank an entire bottle of wine on your sixteenth birthday. Why start now?"

She throws her arms around him and squeals. "I'm so happy you're here!"

"Aren't you going to introduce me to your gorgeous friend?" Felix still hasn't taken his eyes off me. I feel my cheeks heat.

"You mean one of your new students?" She arches a playful brow at him. "This is my lovely and amazing friend, Maureen. Be nice; she bites."

I laugh throatily and stick out my hand for him to shake.

"Maureen Blackwell. I have you for poetry this semester."

If my last name bothers him at all, he doesn't show it. He takes my hand and shakes it formally, all while keeping that trouble-maker grin on his face. "Do you consider yourself a poet, Maureen Blackwell?"

"I don't know about that, Mr. Crane. I enjoy reading it, but I wouldn't consider myself poetic." His expression is intense, pensive, yet playful. I take a small sip of my whiskey while I try not to get spooked by his charm. Especially since he's Villette's brother. And doubly so because Riot, Atlas, and Valentin just walked in with death stares plastered on their faces.

"You don't have to call me Mr. Crane till Monday. And from what I see, you aren't giving yourself enough credit. I think your very essence is poetic." His gaze travels over the sigil on my neck.

"You know it's frowned upon to fraternize with the students, don't you, Professor Crane?" Atlas slaps him on the back as he walks up.

Felix flashes him a toothy grin. "She's not my student yet, Atlas. Technically."

Riot flexes his jaw as he steps in between us. "*Technically*, she's with us, so be careful what you say and do next."

Fuck. Here we go.

Villette rolls her eyes and shakes her head. "Can you all just take the testosterone level down a notch?"

Felix laughs, completely unfazed by Riot's threat. "Relax, Graves. I only came out tonight to ensure my sister's honor is preserved."

I can't help but chuckle. Villette is one of the most pious girls I've ever met. Something tells me that she's the princess of her family. I've heard her other brother, Bones, is batshit crazy. This one looks like he has it in him to be as well.

"And we're here to preserve Maureen's," Valentin chimes in.

I let out a sigh. "Okay, everyone, chill. We're both grown women who don't need preserving or whatever."

Riot pulls me to his side and rests his hand on my hip. "I'm completely chill."

Felix laughs again before planting a kiss on Villette's temple. "Have fun tonight, sis. I'll be over there if you need anything."

Despite Riot, Valentin, and Atlas hovering over me, Felix manages to find my hand and give it a light squeeze. "I look forward to getting to know more about what makes you tick on Monday."

Valentin's nostrils flare while my cheeks flame. "Um, cool. Have a good night."

Atlas barely moves out of his way, so Felix has to brush shoulders with him in order to leave our little circle of rage. But that doesn't seem to bother him either.

Villette sighs before turning around to the bartender. She orders another martini and then waves to someone across the room.

"I'll be right back, Maur."

I slap each of them on the arm. "What the fuck was that?"

Valentin digs his fingers into my waist, pushing me back into a dark corner of the bar. "We didn't like the way he was looking at you."

Atlas sweeps my hair to the side and fingers my sigil. My belly flips as he whispers in my ear, "Some people need reminding that you belong to us."

"Maybe you do as well, Firecracker," Riot barks in my other ear.

The memory of when they first cornered me in the bathroom flashes in my mind. It heats my skin and spurs the dark craving that has festered since that moment. The ache that pulses between my thighs every time they surround me.

I glance around the room as Riot inches his hand up my thigh. "Stop. Someone will see us."

Valentin pushes me back against the wall. "That's the fucking point, Firecracker."

The music pumps louder, keeping time with the thumping in

my chest. Atlas nuzzles my neck, leaving a trail of kisses up to my jaw. It sends goosebumps across my arms and legs.

"The three of you need to stop," I whimper. Who am I kidding?

I don't want them to stop.

Valentin hikes my skirt up till it's barely covering my ass. He reaches in and pulls my panties to the side. "You're ours to play with whenever and wherever we want."

Riot sucks on my earlobe. "I wanna see those juices dripping down your thighs." He shoves a finger inside my pussy, and my entire body twitches, my back arching against the wall.

Atlas puts his hand over my mouth mid-moan. "Shhh, pretty girl."

Fuck. It's too good. Too fucking hot. I look past them to see if anyone is watching, but everyone seems oblivious. A part of me wishes they weren't. Why do I get off on that? Ever since... Fuck. No. Shut it out.

I whine as Riot thrusts two more fingers in. "Am I boring you? Hmmm?" Instead of thrusting in and out, he spreads his fingers wide, stretching my walls open. I shriek into Atlas's hand.

"There she is. Don't think of anything else except being a good little slut for us." Atlas covers my nose and mouth with his whole hand now.

I have to steady my breath so I don't suffocate.

I clench around Riot's fingers, my pussy sopping wet. I roll my hips and get lost in the rhythm. *It feels so fucking good.*

Valentin unlaces my top just enough to shimmy it down and expose my nipples. He gives each one a hard pinch. "I wanna bend you over and fuck you in front of everyone. Would you like that?"

I moan and twist under their touch. Riot probes his thick fingers deeper inside me, curling them up till he hits my sweet spot.

My knees start to shake as I feel the pressure in my lower back.

This public display of debauchery has got me so wound up that I cum instantly at his words.

"Oh, fuck." Riot slides his fingers out, and my hips convulse. A stream of cum squirts out and onto the floor between my legs.

"There we go. Now we're gonna have a good fucking time."

Atlas shoves two fingers inside my mouth, pressing them against my tongue. "Suck."

I moan and obey his command. No matter what they tell me to do, I obey. I can't fucking help myself. I'm a fiend for their brutality. Val squeezes my nipples between his fingers as I unravel. I forget about the bar and the music and the crowd as a second orgasm shatters my core.

Riot breathes heavily into my neck as he kisses my sigil, licking and sucking on my tender flesh that's still not completely healed. I'm not sure if it ever will be.

My heart races while I ride out the last of my high. But just when I'm about to fully come down from my state of euphoria, I feel his eyes on me.

He smirks at me from across the room. The only one in the crowd who sees us. *Who's watching us.*

Felix Crane.

Fuck.

He leans against the wall, drink in hand, and something sinister darkens his gaze. Something feral and psychotic.

"Is he watching?" Riot taunts.

All I can do is nod.

Valentin snickers. "Our dirty little girl likes to put on a show. Doesn't she?"

Butterflies swim in my belly. "I... I don't know."

Atlas caresses my cheek. "Yes, you do, pretty girl. Now you're going to cum again ... but this time, don't take your fucking eyes off him."

Oh, fuck. This is how they mark their territory. They want him to see how they make me cum. They want him to know that I'm theirs.

They pull me farther back into the corner, into a dark spot where the lights barely hit. From across the room, it would be hard to tell what we're doing, but Felix's eyes move with us.

Valentin slips behind me, his back against the wall. I arch back as he fondles my nipples, pinching and pulling them up as he twists them between his fingers.

"He's my professor," I groan.

Atlas rubs my clit. "Yes, and now we're going to teach *him* a fucking lesson."

Oh, fuck.

I bite down on my lip as Riot slides his fingers back inside my pussy. "Look at him. Show him how fucking wet you are for us."

I want to shrink back and hide. But I feel the sigils on my thighs come alive. Everything tingles. I hold Felix's gaze from across the room. He sips his drink and watches us quietly. Unfazed by our depravity. I pray to God that Villette doesn't see us as well.

I moan, and this time Atlas doesn't cover my mouth. Val's cock hardens against my ass. He lifts my skirt higher. "Fuck, your skin is on fire."

Atlas grins back at him and hands him a vial. "Get her nice and wet first."

"Wait, no. You can't just fuck me here like this." Panic spreads through my chest. It's one thing to touch me in the dark . . .

Val snickers as he unzips his pants. I feel the heat of his warm cock against my ass cheek. In one quick jerk, he rips my panties apart. "Don't fucking tell me what I can and can't do with you."

I gasp as he pulls my ass cheeks open and pours the liquid from the vial in between them. Atlas tilts my chin up. "Keep looking at Professor Crane, pretty girl. I want him to see every flicker of pain and pleasure on your face."

Fuck.

I let out a deep moan as Val slips his cock inside my ass. He inches it in slowly, probing with just the tip at first.

Riot strokes my clit. "That's our dirty girl. So fucking wet. Show Professor Crane what a good little slut you are for us."

I lean forward as Val fills me to the brim. I can't breathe, and everything burns. But as he thrusts in and out, the pleasure explodes in my core.

Felix shifts against the other wall, tilting his head to the side as he fixates on us. I hold his gaze. The guys hold me up as Val fucks me harder, making my body shake and tremble.

Atlas releases a glob of thick saliva down my chest, smearing it over my nipples with his fingers while Riot peels my pussy lips back. I'm drowning in their sickness, getting lost in this twisted display of dominance. I'm torn between satisfaction and shame, wanting to look away but needing him to see me unravel.

"Fuck, you're so tight," Val grunts as he rolls his hips, thrusting and grinding into my ass.

The tingling begins in my clit and spreads, rocking me into another fucking orgasm. I thrust back, riding his cock hard.

Felix inches forward, finding a closer wall to lean against. From this angle, I notice a fresh sheen of sweat on his upper lip, and how the base of his throat bobs and contracts.

"Oh, fuck," I whine as I get off on them. On all of it. I'm fucking rabid, writhing against all three of them, pulling them closer to me. Val yanks on my hair and kisses the back of my neck. The spot where his sigil is carved into me. "Fuck you're so good at taking my cock. Mmm, let's see how much of my cum you can hold."

I cry out, my voice getting lost in the music. A burst of thick hot cream fills my asshole as he thrusts in deeper. "Mmm, fuck," he grunts.

It drips down my taint and into my pussy, running down my thighs and calves until it reaches my ankles.

He hugs me to his chest from behind while pulling my top back up. I wince as he re-ties the laces in the back, not sparing any room for me to breathe. "You did good, Maur."

"How the fuck am I supposed to sit in his class on Monday now?" I enjoyed that spectacle way too much, but in the aftermath, reality sets in.

Riot licks his fingers and smirks, but it doesn't reach the darkness in his eyes. "With your legs crossed and your pretty lips wet. And every time he calls on you, he'll remember how you came for us. Let him try and teach poetry with a fucking hard-on."

Atlas hums as he grabs a wad of napkins off the nearest table. He kneels down and wipes the cum from my legs. "I think what we really discovered here tonight is that our little firecracker likes putting on a show."

I feel my cheeks flush again. "No . . . no, I don't," I stammer. Val straightens my skirt. "The fuck you don't. You're a bad liar, Maui."

Riot cups my face in his hands. "The sigils bring out our darkest parts. Don't fight against your nature."

Fuck. Why am I like this? What is it about the power and rush of getting fucked while people watch? Just even the thought of it now gets my pulse racing again.

I look back over at the wall and see that Felix is gone. He got what he wanted and left. Fuck. What if he tells Villette? What will she think of me?

I shove Atlas off and head for the bathroom so I can properly clean myself. Despite how crowded the bar is, there's no line to get in. I get a few weird looks as I start wiping my legs with wet paper towels. But all it takes is a hard glare to remind them that Zeke was stabbed to death after hanging out with me, and they look away and scurry off.

Just as I finish patting myself dry, my phone buzzes. I sigh as I click on the new text message.

It's from that same unknown number from earlier.

Slut.

I gasp and cover my mouth. What the fuck? *Is this person here*

right now? It's definitely not the guys messing with me. This fuck-ing pervert is someone else. My fury grows like wildfire. How fuck-ing dare they?

Coward. I reply back.

Is it Holden Graves? Maybe he sent one of his initiates to tor-ment me. Fuck. I need to tell the guys about this.

The phone buzzes again.

My stomach drops when I see the text.

It's a picture of my bed. I stagger back against the sink.

This fucker is in my room.

"That's it. You're staying with us tonight," Val barks.

I glance around my room, looking for any sign of foul play, but everything looks untouched. Except a pair of my black panties are laid out on the bed. I don't remember putting those there.

Maybe he's right. If this psycho was in my room, then I'm not safe.

"I can't believe you waited this long to tell us about the first text." Riot hands my phone to Atlas. "Track down this number. Use your raven sight, your connections, everything you have. I want to know tonight who this fucker is."

Atlas takes a screenshot of the text and hands me my phone back. "Your little stalker must have a fucking death wish."

"Or it's someone trying to get back at us for Zeke," Val adds. I'm still reeling off the rush from earlier. My adrenaline is through the fucking roof. "What if they're just trying to scare me? To taunt me."

Riot's face pales. "Didn't you say that Felix is staying with Villette here? He got off watching you earlier. Then he disappeared right before you got the second text."

The vein in Val's neck pulses. "I'm going to fucking kill that asshole. Tell me what room Villette's in right now."

Panic rises in my chest. The last thing I need is to drag her into all of this. "Stop, Professor Crane is not sending me these texts. He's not like that."

Atlas knocks back a vial of poison as he shakes his head. "Yeah? How can you be so sure?"

"Villette adores him. I trust her judgment. She wouldn't be so happy to see him if he was some kind of predator." I have to believe that anyway. My friendship with her means too much to me to risk it over a possible hunch. And we can't just break down her door and accuse a brand-new professor of sending lewd texts to a student without any provocation. Not yet anyway.

"We're all predators," Riot snickers. "The only difference is that you are *our* prey—not his or anyone else's."

Val pulls me into his arms, hugging me to his chest. "Stop being stubborn and come back with us willingly. We just want to take care of you."

Riot towers over us. "I will drag you back to Nocturnus House kicking and screaming if I have to." His blue eyes are glowing; his expression demonic.

"Don't be a dick, Riot," I hiss. He's close to crossing a line.

"Don't fucking provoke me, Maur." His fingers twitch as a rush of energy spikes between us. The sigil on my thigh flares, burning my skin like I'm lying on hot coals.

I push back, using my own power to counteract his, but he's stronger. "Calm down," I plead.

Atlas places his hand on Riot's shoulder. "Relax, brother. Let her be."

He releases me from his grip, and I draw in a deep breath as the pain in my leg subsides. "Are you scared for my life, or are you just pissed that someone else wants to play with your toy?"

Riot charges toward me and wraps his hand around my throat.

M VIOLET

"You know how I feel about you. *And I fucking hate it.* It makes me weak. Vulnerable. And it paints a target on my back. The blood pumping through your veins has brought me nothing but trouble. And yet, I can't ever let you go. So I'll be damned if I let someone else get their hands around your throat like this."

"Fine. I'll go with you tonight. But I'm not moving in. Not until we're done with school. I have to have some sort of normalcy, Riot," I wheeze,

He tightens his grip for a second before letting go. "We'll see about that, Firecracker."

CHAPTER FOURTEEN

Alias

N OCTURNUS HOUSE IS SO QUIET YOU CAN HEAR A PIN DROP. WITH only a few new recruits, there's a strong absence of the chatter and movement from before when the house was full. It used to annoy me, but now I kind of miss all the noise.

But we have to ensure that these new initiates fall in line. Part of that is tracking down this motherfucker who's threatening my pretty girl. I plan to put him on full display so everyone can see what happens when you fuck with our firecracker. When you be-tray Nocturnus, *I thought sending the others to Absentia Asylum would have been warning enough.*

The air is cold as fuck this morning. Spring is coming, but win-ter is still hanging on by a thread. Just like the ravens. One squawks

at me as I make my way past the graveyard toward campus. I pull my hood up around my head and ignore them. They don't come to my window anymore. Not since we initiated Maureen. I pick up my stride, wanting to get today over with as fast as possible.

By the time I get to the faculty café, I've downed three vials of nightshade. I'm high as fuck and ready to flay someone. Just thinking about the things I'm going to do to this asshole gets my adrenaline racing.

It's not just about protecting her. She's more than capable of handling herself. No. It's about principle. Maureen Blackwell is ours. *Mine.* And anyone who thinks they can send my girl disgusting text messages is soon going to wish they were never even born.

I storm into the café and smirk when I spot my target. Professor Harker. I slap him on the back, making him spill his coffee. "Morning."

He glares at me from behind his wiry glasses. "What do you want, Thorn?" Dorian Harker isn't much older than me, but he dresses like an old man with his tweed suits and distinct side-part.

"A word." I motion for him to sit down at a corner table, far away from the curious stares and prying ears of the other faculty members. Miss Tempest has been stirring her tea for three minutes straight, pretending not to pay attention to us. And that new fucker, the one who gets off on watching us fuck our girl, is lurking at the condiment station, taking way too fucking long to put milk and sugar in his coffee.

Professor Harker rolls his eyes before taking a seat. "Cut the dramatics, Atlas. I've paid my debts to your father. I'm done with all that."

I smile tightly, my lips pursed. "I don't care about your little poison habit, Dorian. I'm here about a stalker."

He chuckles. "Oh, poor, handsome rich boy has a stalker. Shocking. I'm surprised you didn't think that one of your indiscretions wouldn't come back to bite you in the dick someday."

I slap his hand like he's a fucking child. "It's not *my* stalker, you

fucking imbecile. Don't worry about who. Anyway, I know you have access to records here. You're going to find out who's number this is." I hold up the screenshot from Maureen's phone.

He swallows down his pride, his frustration, his fucking balls. His cheeks burn bright red as he struggles with the fact that my family fucking owns him. We know things that could ruin his entire fucking life. But I'm still a student, and the fact that I hold any power over him . . . it must drive him insane.

He takes a small bite of his scone and washes it down with a sip of coffee. I can't help but notice the way his fingers tremble around the mug. "I can't just give you confidential records, Atlas. I could lose my fucking job."

I snicker. "You *will* lose your fucking job if you don't, Dorian. Or did you forget about what happened last summer after the garden party at my father's house? He got so hopped up on poison that we found him having an orgy with three of my classmates in the pool house. I sure as fuck took a video of that shit."

His gaze darts around the room as all the color drains from his face. "How long are you going to hold that one over me? I was not in a good place. But it was all consensual."

I shrug. "I don't really give a fuck if it was or wasn't. Doesn't make the video go away. But you know what does, Professor Handsy? You getting me that info. Today."

"You . . . you'll get rid of the video?" His throat bobs as it beads with sweat.

"Sure. That's just one of them. But it's probably the most incriminating. I'll hang onto the others. That must have been one hell of a fucking summer vacation for you," I taunt.

His cheeks redden again. "Fuck you, Thorn. Fuck you and your whole fucking psycho family."

I arch an eyebrow. "Should I post the video on the Tenebrose page first? Or maybe I'll start by emailing it to the dean."

"No. Stop. I'll get you what you want."

Of course, he will.

"Good. I'll meet you in your office in fifteen minutes. Don't want any of your peers to see us leave together. They might get the wrong idea." I wink and swipe his scone as he reaches for it, taking what's left of it with me as I strut out the door.

I help myself to a swig of whiskey from the bottle I find in Harker's bottom drawer and make myself comfortable in his chair.

He shuffles in, glaring at me. "You going to threaten me for having that in my desk too?"

I chuckle and set it down on the desk, leaving a whiskey ring on a stack of papers. "Nah. The dean keeps a stash of weed in her desk. Doubt she'd care about this. Man, this job really brings the addict outta all of you. I think you might need to get your dick sucked more."

"I'm good on that, thanks." He grumbles and curses under his breath as he fumbles with his coat and briefcase, getting tangled up in both.

I turn his laptop around to face him as I've no intention of getting up from his desk. I set my phone with the screenshot down next to it. "Search. Now. Tell me who this number belongs to."

He sighs and leans over the screen. "It's going to take a bit. This system is old. I can't just do a Google search."

I take another swig of whiskey. "You better get started then. If you're not done in two hours, your pool orgy goes viral."

He wants to punch me so badly. I can fucking feel it in the tension between us. The way he chews on his lower lip, preventing him from saying something he can't take back. I'm a loose fucking cannon, and he knows it.

"Alright. Let me get to it then." He sits down and begins typing away.

As my boredom quickly sets in, I start pacing around the office, opening up drawers and file cabinets. *Not that I'd expect to find anything juicy in here.*

"You're going to kill whoever this is, aren't you?" He doesn't look up from the screen, his fingers flying across the keyboard.

I lean across the desk, so close he can feel my breath on his face. "Do you really want to know, Professor? Does that change things?" Like this fucking idiot is suddenly going to develop a conscious.

He peers up over his glasses, narrowing his eyes at me. "No."

I chuckle. "Didn't think so. Self-preservation always beats morality." I take another long pull of his whiskey before slamming the bottle on the desk. "Fuck, I love this shit."

I spend the next hour rifling through his stacks of books, critiquing them, and spoiling the ending of at least three that I can tell by the look on his face. Watching this man try not to come unglued is my new favorite pastime.

"Have you heard from your cousin, Libra, by the way? She's not back at school yet."

I shrug. "I don't keep tabs on her. She's probably waist-deep in designer bags, champagne, and fuckboys. I think our family gives this school enough money to allow her a few extra days of winter break." Maureen hasn't heard from Libra either, but I'm not going to start worrying yet. My cousin is known for disappearing on benders for weeks at a time.

Dorian's breath hitches, and he stops typing. "Fuck."

My stomach knots. That did not sound like a good *fuck.* "Who is it?"

He snaps his laptop shut. "You . . . you don't want to know."

The rage billows inside me. I lift him out of the chair by his collar and slam him against the wall. The sigil on my chest flares. It sears my flesh, digging into my muscles like an invisible dagger. My need to protect, to defend, to avenge consumes me.

"FUCKING tell me," I roar in his face.

He whimpers but holds my gaze. "The texts came from a phone registered to Barnaby Withers... He's an errand boy for your father."

It feels as if all the veins in my neck are about to burst. I pin him against the wall, my forearm pressed into his neck. "What the fuck are you talking about? That name means nothing to me. You're lying."

He shakes his head. "I swear. He used to bring me nightshade every Friday after class. I thought I recognized the number at first, but it's been so long... I wasn't in my right mind back then."

Fuck.

I let him go, and he drops to the floor with a thud. "You will tell no one about this," I wave my finger in his face.

He pushes his glasses back up his nose. "I'd say we're square now, don't you think?"

This motherfucker. Tit for fucking tat, I snicker. "I'll get rid of the pool video. But I'm keeping the rest. And if you're wrong? Fucking hell. There won't be a place far enough away for you to run to."

He nods. "I'm not. Er, wrong or running. I might be a coward, but I'm not a liar. Maybe this guy acted on his own."

I side-eye him. "Come on, Professor, you know my father better than that. He loves leverage more than he does his own family."

"I'm sorry you were brought up that way. Truly. This world we live in... well, it's hard and unforgiving. No matter where we go, our demons follow us." His eyes are haunted, dark, and disturbed. I suddenly feel bad for the guy. There's a reason he got hooked on poison to begin with. "We all have our vices, Professor. But eventually, not even they can keep the nightmares at bay. They end up making them worse."

"Believe me, I know," he murmurs.

I snatch the bottle of whiskey on my way out the door. "I think I need this more than you do right now."

He nods, his face pale, but he doesn't utter another word. I think we both hope that we don't have to talk to each other ever again.

I empty a vial of oleander into the whiskey bottle and shake

it up before taking a huge swig. My fingers twitch, and my pulse races as I head toward the Nest to go track down Barnaby Withers. Murder would be a mercy. But I have no fucking mercy in me today. Not until he tells me exactly what my asshole father has been up to.

It takes me less than fifteen minutes to find out which room this prick is in. When you're Atlas Thorn, all you have to do is give a few girls a little extra attention, bat your pretty blue-green eyes, and they squeal like fucking pigs.

I approach the door and take a deep breath, closing my eyes as I siphon my power into the doorknob. I lift its internal latch, un-locking it within seconds. I can smell Barnaby's fear the moment he sees me barge through the door.

"Hey, you c-can't just come in here," he stammers.

My skin tingles as the fibers between my veins stretch out and pulse, filling with adrenaline and rage. I cross the room to him in two large strides, grabbing him by the throat when I'm within reach. "You've been a naughty boy, Barnaby. Time to answer for your crimes," I threaten.

A steady stream of piss shoots out, soaking his jeans. "I-I don't know what you're talking about."

I dig my fingertips into his neck, aching to crush his windpipe, knowing that I can without breaking a sweat. But I need him alive. For now.

"You know exactly what I'm talking about. And you're going to tell me everything. Starting with why my father hired you to tor-ment Maureen Blackwell." I lighten up on the pressure just enough to give him a chance to speak.

His eyes bulge, and the uptick of his pulse beats against my

palm. "I-I didn't want to do it. But you know how... persuasive your father is."

Of course, I fucking know. I know him better than anyone. He's charming, good-looking, and butter could melt in his mouth. The complete opposite of Holden Graves, my father presents himself as a fucking saint. But I know better. His deceit and depravity are subtle, but they're there, simmering below the surface of his expensive suits and shiny white teeth.

"What does he have on you?"

As Barnaby shakes his head, a stream of snot drips out of his nose, landing on his upper lip. "Nothing."

Fuck. I'm losing patience with this sniveling idiot. I really want to snap his fucking neck. "Then what did he promise you?"

His eyes dart from side to side, and his snot-covered lip quivers. "He said I could play with her whenever I wanted."

My sigils surge with power, particularly the one she carved into my chest. "The fuck? You must have one hell of a death wish. *She is not yours to play with.*" I don't know if I can stop myself from killing him. I need to breathe and calm the fuck down. At least until I find out everything.

Tears stream down his cheeks. "But he said she would be."

Fuck. Fuck. I need to focus. "How did you get into her dorm apartment?"

"Your father gave me the elevator key. He told me to just take a picture of her room. But I couldn't help myself... I took out a pair of her panties. They smelled so—"

I slap him hard across the face, leaving a handprint on his cheek. "You sick fuck. She belongs to me. To Nocturnus. How dare you even fucking look at her." The motherfucking audacity. I slap him again. "If I wasn't planning on killing you, I'd take you straight to Absentia Asylum right now. I'm sure they have a straitjacket with your name on it. *Unfuckingbelievable.*"

I'd done some sick fucking things in my life but never to someone

who wasn't already interested. This guy hasn't ever even had a conversation with Maureen. He's probably been creeping on her since she got here.

Barnaby pisses himself again. "Kill me? Wait, why?"

This kid is clearly delusional. If I were a better man, I'd take pity on him, show mercy, and take him to the asylum. But I possess zero empathy. I have my father to thank for that. All I care about is keeping Maureen away from him and anyone else who comes for her. My father included.

"All right, Barnie boy, time for a little nap." I tighten my grip on his neck and cut off his circulation. I don't want to kill him just yet, but I need him quiet and docile so I can get him back to Nocturnus House.

He claws at my wrists. I enjoy watching him turn from pink to blue. I let out an exasperated sigh when he finally goes limp in my arms. "Fucking weirdo."

I hoped earlier that I wouldn't have to talk to Harker again, but I need one last favor. He answers my call on the first ring.

"You were right, Professor."

He clears his throat, "I'm sorry that I was."

"I need you to give me and Barnaby a ride back to Nocturnus. He's unconscious, so I can't have anyone seeing me drag him through the woods."

He's silent for a few beats before finding his balls. "I'm guessing you're at the Nest? Take the elevator down to the cellar. There's a tunnel that leads to some brush by the forest. I'll pick you up there.

Good man. I nod even though he can't see me. "Consider us completely square after this. No more videos. We're done."

"Thank you, Atlas," he murmurs.

I click end call and snarl down at the unconscious pervert in my arms. "Me and you, on the other hand, are just getting started."

CHAPTER FIFTEEN

Maureen

T HAT MOMENT IN BETWEEN SLEEPING AND WAKING IS SACRED. IT CONTAINS an infinite amount of magic in those few seconds. When I realize my dreams are just dreams, and reality hasn't quite set in yet. It's a conscious slumber where my soul feels untethered to my body. Where I am just Maureen. Not a Blackwell, or a Gray, or belonging to Nocturnus. I'm just me. It's when I remember who I am most. And then it's gone, fading away into the farthest reaches of my mind like a distant memory.

I roll over to find Riot awake and gazing back at me. This part of the day is when I know who he is the most too. When the pressures and demands of the coven haven't settled in yet. He blinks back the sleep from his blue eyes, and they're filled with tenderness and

DIRTY LITTLE SAINT

wonder. They haven't had the chance to harden. His face is strange yet angelic. His black hair messy and soft.

"What are you thinking about, Firecracker?" His voice is raspy like honey on sandpaper.

I stroke his cheek. "You."

He clasps my hand to his. "Tonight is going to be chaos."

"Why?" There never seems to be a dull moment for us these days. He kisses my fingers. "Later. I just want to enjoy the stillness with you right now."

A flurry of nerves swims in my belly. I know that look in his eyes. Trouble is brewing for us. But all I want to do is drown in this moment.

I nod and scoot closer to him. My breath catches in my throat when we lock eyes. I won't ever get over how strikingly beautiful this man is. How wanting him and needing him have become one and the same.

"Did you find anything out about the text messages?" There's something that the guys aren't telling me. I heard Atlas get in late last night. The three of them went down below the house to one of their many chambers. I planned on questioning them, but they were down there so long . . . I drank too much wine and passed out on the couch.

His eyes darken. "Yes."

"And?" I hate when they keep secrets or withhold stuff from me. He leans forward and kisses me so softly it leaves my lips tingling. "Not now, Firecracker. . . Come here." He pulls my hips toward him until I'm flush against his body. His cock twitches beneath his black sweatpants, pulsing against my thigh. I reach in between us and rub my palm against it as his erection grows, relishing how quickly he responds to my touch.

"Fuck." He pulls my tank top down and pinches one of my nipples. "You're going to be the fucking death of me."

I slip my hand inside his sweats and wrap it around his cock.

143

Sweat trickles down my back as the heat between us grows from a spark to an inferno.

He kisses my neck, hungrily, devouring it while I stroke him up and down. He moans in my ear before biting down hard on my earlobe. The sharpness of his teeth sends shivers over every inch of my body.

I let out a whimper. "Riot . . . I need you inside me."

"You have too many clothes on." He pushes my panties down and off before climbing on top of me. I yank his sweatpants down as he shifts in between my trembling thighs.

He studies my face, watching my every reaction, as he rolls the tip of his cock up and down my slit. "Damn, you're so fucking wet I could just slide right in."

"Mmm, fuck, Riot. Stop teasing me."

He chuckles and continues to do just that. I practically drool at the sight of him over me. His tattoos and sigils make his body look like a work of art. "I want you to cum first. Grab my cock and use it to get yourself off."

Oh, fuck. I am going to explode. I wrap my hand around him and guide the tip up to my clit. I let out a deep moan as I move it in circles, grinding against it as it stimulates every sensitive nerve. He fists my tank top, using it to anchor himself as he tries to stifle his grunts. "That's it. Just like that. Take control. Fucking use me."

"Uhh." I shiver as his pre-cum leaks out and drips down my slit. The pressure builds in my core like a fucking trigger. And I know I'm a fucking goner. I jerk my hips as a rush of tingles quakes through my pussy. I grind his tip down on my nub as I buck, my limbs wild.

"Mmm, now I'm going to fuck the life out of you." He shoves my hand away and thrusts his cock inside my soaking wet pussy. I cry out as my orgasm reaches another level. "Oh, fuck. I'm coming again."

He pushes through my walls, burying himself to the hilt. "So tight. Fuck. I wanna stay inside you forever."

I clench around him, desperate to feel every ridge of his cock as he slides in and out. "You're so good, Riot. *So fucking good.*"

He grunts as he slams into me over and over again, all while not taking his eyes off mine. We are connected—body and soul. I let out a gurgled cry as I surrender to every single sensation. This pleasure hits deeper within my core this time, bursting from a spot that no one has ever stimulated before.

"You look so fucking beautiful when you cum." He moans louder as his cock throbs against the inside of my pussy. "Fuck. I'm fuck-ing... FUCK."

His cum shoots out, thick and hot, filling me to the brim. He grinds his hips against mine in a frenzy. Our moans collide as we ride each other, our bodies contorting and twisting together as we chase this feral need to consume.

The sigil on my thigh, the one that belongs to Riot, sparks, re-minding me of my ruin and my addiction to him. There is nothing I wouldn't do for this man. Nothing I wouldn't let him do to me. But the high I get from seeing him completely unravel for me... the satisfaction of feeling his cum drip down my thighs... there's no amount of alcohol or poison that can come close to this rush.

I whine when he pulls out, my needy pussy still tingling. "You've desecrated my soul, Riot Graves. Fuck."

"Right back at you, love." He lies back down next to me and curls me into his chest. His breath is hot and erratic against my ear. "I'm too fucking greedy with you. Atlas and Val let me take too many liberties."

"That's because they love you." *I love you.* I'm still scared to say it out loud to him.

He sighs. "They know that I need these quiet moments. That I need to have you to myself sometimes. To keep the darkness from swallowing me up."

I nod. I know too well what he means. Lately, my thoughts have become darker, heavier. It's getting easier and easier to justify what I

did. *Murder*. Killing Billy in Wickford Hollow was not self-defense. It was an act of revenge. Zeke was no different. Holden was right. I enjoyed killing his bastard son.

I shudder as the memories come flooding back. The crack of the belt echoes in my ears. As if I'm back there in the ritual room on all fours—naked and panting in front of them while they lash me. While they get off on punishing me for my sins.

"Hey, Maur. Stay with me," Riot pleads.

I shudder again. "Sorry. I just get lost in my head sometimes."

He hugs me tighter. "Get lost in me, love. Let me carry your burdens."

I choke back a sob. "I don't want to talk about that night . . . It brought something out of me. Something dirty."

Riot tilts my chin up so I have to look into his eyes. "Don't ever be ashamed of your desires. We will always give you what you want and never judge you for it. Our tastes are dark as well. You know this about us."

He's right, but then why do I still feel so filthy? I've never embraced these parts of me. Never even entertained it for a moment. Back in Wickford Hollow, I would get drunk and let them pass me around. Sometimes, I wasn't conscious when they did it. But it was just your standard blow jobs and getting fucked from behind by dumb football players that reeked of cheap beer and cigarettes.

"Last night, at *Swallow*, I liked what the three of you made me do. Being watched . . . it makes me cum harder. My body comes alive, and my sigils respond with so much heat."

Riot drags his thumb across my lower lip. "That's why we did it. We know you, Maur. And if you like being watched then we will make that happen again whenever you want."

What does it say about me that it turns me on when he says stuff like that? We are so fucking toxic, and yet I crave every bit of it.

"Mmm, you know what would turn *me* on?" he whispers in my ear.

My nipples pebble. "Tell me."

"Watching you touch yourself in front of others. I want to see my woman put on a show, knowing they'll want to fuck you but can't. That only we get to defile your pussy."

Fuck. He knows just what to say to get me going. Liquid pools between my legs.

He slides a finger inside me and moans. "Mmm, fuck. We'll have you on full display. They will fucking worship at your feet."

"Yes," I can barely breathe. Every inch of me is on fire, obsessed with what he's doing to me right now.

The heat in my body climbs as he pinches my clit between his fingers, rolling it back and forth between his soft pads. "You'll spread your cunt wide open for them… show them *everything*."

I jerk my hips as his touch stimulates my core. I can't help but clench around his fingers, desperate to ride this high. "Riot… *Fuuck*."

He kisses my cheek. "You see, your pleasure belongs to me. Your pain is mine. There can be no shame because I own every single trem-ble that passes through your tight little cunt." He grabs my chin and tilts it up. "You can do no wrong, love. You're my dirty little saint."

The hot water soothes my aching limbs. Riot's cum still leaks out of my pussy as I stand here washing myself. I stay in the shower until the water runs tepid, savoring every bit of heat and steam that I can before I have to get dressed and go down to the party.

I put on a pair of tight jeans, black boots, and a purple stretchy V-neck sweater. I leave my hair down so as not to draw attention to the sigils on my neck. I already get side-eyed enough. Everyone knows I have them, but I don't feel like having their eyes on them tonight. Downstairs is already filling up with students when I make

my entrance. They know better than to disrespect me in Nocturnus House, so I get a few timid smiles and head nods as I walk past.

"There you are!" Villette saunters up, looking gorgeous in a white cotton dress and black satin heels.

I give her a hug and instantly feel my anxiety start to dissipate. I was worried that she might have seen her brother watching us last night at *Swallow*. If she did, there's no indication. "I'm so happy you're here. I don't think I could face the vultures without you."

She hands me a cup with whiskey in it. "Girl, I got you. They're just jealous that the most sought-after guys at Tenebrose are obsessed with you and not them."

I giggle as I take a sip. "Or they're afraid that I'm going to stab them in the graveyard."

She arches an eyebrow. "Yes, probably that too."

Villette wanted to know as little as possible about what happened with Zeke the night of the Winter Solstice Ball. Libra, on the other hand, wanted all the gory details. A little knot forms in my stomach at the thought of her not being here tonight.

"Hey, have you heard from Lib yet? I'm surprised she's not here tonight. She hates missing a party."

Villette shrugs and looks around the room. "I'll text my brother, Bones, tomorrow and try to find out if he's heard anything. She might still be up at her family's estate in Ever Graves."

I nod and take another sip of my drink. My presence is finally starting to go unnoticed as the house fills up with more people. Cocktails and joints are being passed around like candy while the music gets louder, muffling everyone's voices.

Villette walks with me through each room as I try to find the guys. "I had to beg Felix not to crash the party tonight. He still doesn't seem to get that he's a teacher," she shouts over the music. "Thank fuck he's not here tonight. I don't have the nerve to look him in the eye yet. I'm already dreading having to sit through his class tomorrow. I laugh nervously. "It's cause he's so much younger

than the rest of them. He's probably bored out of his mind in the faculty lounge." I laugh back.

My pulse ticks when I spot Atlas and Val on the terrace. "Villette, I'll be right back. I have to go do something. You'll be okay?"

The corners of her lips turn up into a smirk. "You mean you gotta go do *someone*," she teases. "I'll be fine. Go get your guys."

I give her another hug. "Thanks, babe. See you in a bit."

A burst of cold air sends goosebumps across my skin when I open the terrace doors. Val's eyes are hooded, dark, and venomous as he listens to whatever Atlas is saying to him. I take a deep breath and waltz over.

"Care to fill me in?" I hug my arms to my belly as the wind whips through my hair.

Atlas takes off his leather jacket and drapes it over my shoulders. "Hey, pretty girl."

I look at Val. "One of you needs to start talking."

He flexes his jaw. "Atlas got the fucker who's been stalking you."

My heart skips. "Who is he?"

"Barnaby Withers." Atlas's blue-green eyes fill with a venom that matches Val's.

As I rack my brain, I can't for the life of me picture who they're talking about. "I don't understand. That name means nothing to me."

Atlas snickers. "That's what I said too. But Professor Harker let me in on a little secret. And Firecracker, you're not going to fuck-ing like it."

Val curses under his breath, and I feel all the blood rush to my feet. I swallow hard, my mouth running as dry as sandpaper. "What's going on?" Fuck I should have brought another shot of whiskey out here with me.

"Barnaby Withers is an errand boy for Pisces Thorn," Riot grumbles as he walks up behind me.

Fuck.

I turn to Atlas. "Your father? Why would he hire someone to terrorize me?"

He shrugs before downing one of his many vials of poison.

"We're trying to figure that out."

Val lights up a joint, takes a long puff, and passes it to Riot. "We've got the fucker chained up below in the catacombs."

I snatch the joint before Riot can grab it. "Why didn't you cancel the party?" The sigil on the back of my neck prickles. That dark, sinister energy creeps into my bones as I think of all the ways I want to hurt this fucker for violating me. "That asshole went into my room and touched my panties."

"Yeah, he said as much," Atlas quips.

"I'm going to break every bone in his body," Val snaps.

I take a long hit off the joint before passing it back. "Not if I break them all first." The rage within me is becoming a sickness. An addiction that I don't want to curb. The more I feed it, the more alive I feel.

Riot nods. "I recruited a few new initiates. Tonight will be their first test. Let's see if they can keep an eye on our house while we go mutilate Barnaby Withers."

I raise an eyebrow at him. "And after, I want to meet these new initiates. They need to know that they answer to me too now."

His blue eyes glow back at me. "Agreed. We will not have another incident like what happened with Zeke."

I nod, satisfied and kind of impressed with myself for demanding instead of asking. I'm their equal now. I may not have as many sigils as they do, but I will soon. And my power is growing faster than I think any of us are prepared for.

"Shall we then?" Riot holds out his hand to me.

A rush of adrenaline shoots through my fingertips as I clasp his hand. "I need to grab my knife first."

CHAPTER SIXTEEN

Valentin

O UR DESCENT INTO DARKNESS IS BLURRING EVERY LINE MAUREEN has ever crossed. The sigil of Erebus carved into her neck will be her undoing. My shadows call to hers. And tonight, they want to come out and play.

Torches light the cavern. They flicker wildly in response to our presence. A small grouping of ravens has gathered at Barnaby's chained feet, squawking over his wails. It's a beautiful sight.

Before Maureen pledged her oath and added her bloodline to our coven, we used to draw on the ravens for power. We made sacrifices to them. Carved sigils into our flesh as offerings. But now, it's the other way around. The bond shifted in our favor. Each new sigil makes us stronger. Now, *they draw power from us.*

No one knows where they come from or how they got here. They just always were. Rumors and speculation have been passed down through the generations. Some say the ravens embody the spirits of our ancestors. Others believe they are the devil's children. Nocturnus was born from the desire to be invincible. Immortal. But it came with a price. A price that Jessamine and countless others have paid with their lives.

It has spurned feuds and curses, deceit, and greed. The ones before us have benefited in ways most mundane people could only dream of. Our fathers have had their fun for long enough. It's our turn now. And we've done what they never could. We've turned the ravens into our servants.

The only sacrifices we'll be making now is to each other.

The four of us form a circle around Barnaby. His trousers are soaked with piss and shit. I have to choke back the bile from the stench of it.

Atlas rips the man's shirt open. "Hey there, Barnie boy," He dips the tip of his dagger into a vial of poison before waving it in front of his face, taunting him with it. "Now that you have all of our attention, why don't you start from the beginning? When did my father first approach you?"

Barnaby's eyes widen as he fixates on the knife. "Right after the Winter Solstice Ball," he stammers.

Maureen's fists clench at her sides. I can practically smell her anger, feel the rage reverberating off every cell in her body.

"Did he say why he wanted you to do this?" Riot asks calmly, even though every vein in his neck is bulging.

Barnaby shakes his head. "I don't know. He said that pretty dolls should be played with. That I could play with her if I did what he asked."

Maureen snaps her fingers. "I'm right here, fucker. But I'm not your doll to play with."

Atlas presses the flat of the blade against his chest.

Barnaby's lip quivers as a big glob of snot falls onto it. "Pl-please don't kill me."

This whole display infuriates me. Barnaby should be at Absentia Asylum, not running errands for one of the most powerful men in Raven's Gate. Fucking, *Pisces*. The sick fucking bastard. He's always had a strange way with women. Charming as fuck, but deeply disturbed.

"I'll ask you again," Atlas roars. "What the fuck does my father want with Maureen Blackwell?"

His eyes dart back and forth as his chest heaves. I think this asshole might hyperventilate to death before we get a chance to kill him. "I-I don't know. She's pretty. Who wouldn't want to keep her?"

He's right about that. But Pisces Thorn doesn't go out of his way for pretty girls. I shake my head. "Kill him quick. He doesn't know anything."

Maureen snaps her head to look at me. "Fuck that. This asshole was planning on abducting me. He needs to feel pain before he dies."

Riot lets out a sigh. "Firecracker, you could kill him with a flick of your wrist. You have no idea how powerful you are. He wouldn't have succeeded in abducting you."

"Let her do what she needs to do," Atlas urges. "An eye for an eye."

"A soul for a soul," she whispers back.

Barnaby's gaze hardens. "Dolls aren't supposed to talk."

Oh, fuck.

Maureen whips out her knife. She moves toward her stalker while the ravens flock around her like a small army. "You know what, Barnaby?" She rests the tip of her dagger against his chest. "You talk too fucking much."

"In absentia lucis, tenebrae vincunt," Riot chants. *In the absence of light, darkness prevails.*

I feel a deep rumbling in my chest. An electric spark shoots through my veins as my sigils come alive. I glance around the room

and see theirs are glowing too. There's an invisible thread connecting us, tiny little fibers that stretch out between us like tendrils. The
power rushes through my bones, spiking my adrenaline like it did
that night we drove off the cliff.

I take a deep breath and lean into its power. I surrender to it.

"Mors tua, vita mea." *Your death, my life.*

Atlas holds up a vial of poison in salute. "Mors vincit omnia."

Death always wins.

Maureen exhales before plunging her dagger into Barnaby's
chest. His eyes bulge out as he lets loose a bloodcurdling scream.
She drives the blade in hard and deep, twisting it until it's buried to
the hilt, her gaze locked on his.

"Ruina nostra salus," she whispers. *Our ruin is our salvation.* The
ravens let out a piercing cry unlike any I've ever heard.

The man's head falls forward and his body goes limp.

Maureen struggles against his chest as she attempts to pull the
dagger out. I move forward to help her, but Riot holds up his hand.

He shakes his head.

She must do this herself.

Her tiny frame seems to find unnatural strength as she releases
a loud grunt and pulls the blade out. She looks wild and free and
beautiful. I want to lick the blood from her hands as a tribute. To
kneel down at her feet and bathe in her power. We belong to her as
much as she belongs to us.

She is fire.

The dark queen on our desecrated chessboard. We have to protect her at all costs. Even from herself... *Especially from herself.*

I amble toward her, careful of the ravens who dot my path.
They eye me suspiciously. As if they don't already know what's in my
soul. As if she's their mother, and I'm a predator stalking through.
Riot and Atlas circle in after me, shooing them off. Reminding
them that *we* are the devils of Raven's Gate. That we control

them now. They shrink back, their squawking quieting to a low whimpering.

Maureen spins around to face us. Blood splatter decorates her cheeks and neck. She wipes the blade across her jeans before slid-ing it back inside her boot. "Someone needs to call Pisces Thorn and tell him to come pick up his trash."

Maureen showers upstairs while Atlas, Riot, and I usher out the last of the partygoers. I'm sure the teachers of Tenebrose aren't going to be too pleased with us for getting all their students drunk and high the night before the first day of school. But it's tradition.

We throw a party every semester. They couldn't stop us from doing it if they haven't. Which they haven't. We have too much dirt on them. Too much leverage. And our families donate obscene amounts of money to keep them all driving their fancy cars and living in their monstrous houses. Even the faculty lounge is funded by us.

Riot leans back against the couch, whiskey in hand. "We need to keep an eye on her at all times. Who knows how many spies our fathers have planted here."

Atlas snickers. "Well, mine is about to see firsthand what we do with spies." He plops down next to Riot and lights a joint.

"Have you called him?" I want to make sure Maureen is no-where near this house when he arrives.

Atlas holds up his phone as he coughs out a huge hit of weed. "I sent him a text. Told him it's urgent. He'll be here soon."

I grab my coat and keys. "I'll take her back to the Nest and stay there with her tonight."

Riot nods in agreement. "Good. Make sure you walk her to class tomorrow too. I don't trust anyone but us right now."

I wait for Maureen in the car, the engine running. When she

bounces out the front door, she's all smiles and sunshine. Like she didn't just stab a man to death.

The scent of honeysuckle and vanilla invade my car as she climbs into the passenger seat, her hair damp and glistening. I want to lick her entire body; she smells so fucking good. Wearing a fitted white tank top and yoga pants, there's not a speck of blood on her that I can see. She looks like Maureen again. The sexy, fiery version we first met. Before we corrupted her.

"Ready, love?"

Her eyes light up at the pet name. I haven't told her I love her yet. *But I really fucking want to.* It's not that I'm afraid to say some-thing so final, it's the fear that she's not ready to say it back. That would crush me.

She nods and puts on her seatbelt. "Thank you for taking me back home. I can't wait to sleep in my own bed."

I throw the car in drive and peel out of the stone driveway. "I'll take you anywhere you wanna go, Firecracker. Anytime. Always."

She gazes at me as I drive us through the dark forest. It reminds me of the first time I took her to the cabin. It's hard to take my eyes off her, so I steal as many glances as I can between her and the road. There's a calm radiating from her, a serenity oozing from her pores. After what she just went through, I'm in awe.

"What are you looking at?" she teases.

Fuck. I'm looking at the most beautiful creature I've ever laid eyes on. "I was about to ask you the same question." I smirk back at her.

She leans over and plants the softest kiss on my neck, sending shivers down my spine. "I'm wondering how I'm going to get any sleep tonight with you in my bed."

My cock flexes. "I'm going to fuck you to sleep."

Her breath hitches as she brushes her hand up my thigh. I al-most lose control of the car at the contact. "Val. . ."

I step on the gas, increasing our speed. I need to get inside this woman as soon as possible. "Yes, Maur."

She blows out a deep breath. "I want to drink and fuck and read poetry under the stars and fall in love … with you."

Fuck. I'm a goner. A woosh of nerves swirls in my belly. I squeeze her hand. "We can do whatever you want, Firecracker. You know I'll give you anything you want."

I can't pull into the parking lot fast enough. I bring the car to a screeching halt outside the Nest, and we barrel out, making a mad dash for the front entrance.

As soon as the elevator doors close, I push her back against the wall. She whimpers and fumbles with my pants. "You smell so fucking good. Fuck." I kiss her hard, shoving my tongue deep into her mouth. We claw at each other in desperation. With a frenzied need to find release within each other.

She moans as I slip my fingers inside her pants and press them against her pussy. Her panties are already soaking wet. "Yes, Val. Fuck. . . . A thousand times, yes."

Her praise sends an emotional response to my brain. An archaic and primal instinct to dominate, to force her into submission. "I'm going to do filthy things to you tonight," I promise in her ear.

"Mmm, yes, please. I need it." She grabs my cock and squeezes.

The doors slide open with a ding, letting us out into her dorm apartment. I half-expect Libra to come barreling out of her room, but then I remember she's still not back.

Relief fills me when I realize we're all alone. And we can do whatever the fuck we want without anyone bothering us.

Our kisses deepen as we stumble inside. I pull her top off first and then push her pants and panties down in one quick jerk. I pull back to look at her. Her nipples are bright pink and hard as fuck. Her thighs glisten as moisture from her cunt leaks out.

"Bend over the coffee table," I groan as the ache takes hold of my voice.

She bites her lip coyly and gazes back at me with so much mischief and temptation I have to steady myself.

I relish the way her creamy white ass jiggles slightly as she saunters over to the table. She looks back at me and winks before spreading her legs wide around it, straddling it underneath her.

Fucking hell. I grab my cock as it pulses.

She hangs off the end of the table, flat on her belly, and holds onto the sides. I stalk over and take a minute to gaze at how fucking naughty she looks.

I drag my fingers down her ass crack until I find her pussy underneath. "Are you going to let me do whatever I want to you tonight?"

She lets out a moan as I push two fingers in. "Yes, baby."

I slap the inside of her thigh. "Anything?"

"Mmm, yes. Whatever you want. Please," she whines.

I love seeing her bent over and begging for my cock. "Keep your hands on the table at all times."

I grab her hips and pull them back toward me. Her juices leak out as I push the tip of my cock inside her cunt. "Fuck, I love how tight you are." I push all the way in and let out a deep moan as her walls clench around me.

"Oh, fuck," she cries out. "Harder."

I thrust slowly in and out, edging her into a wild frenzy. "Shh, relax. We have all night."

Her body glistens with sweat. I bend over and lick the back of her neck, savoring the salt of it on my eager tongue. "Mmm, fuck," I pump in and out as she wails, her fingers white-knuckling the edges of the table as she grinds her pussy against it.

"This is going to hurt a little," I murmur. I pull out of her cunt and inch the tip of my cock inside her asshole.

She bucks and clenches as a fresh sheen of sweat spreads across her body. "Val," she moans. "Fuck, go slow."

Her ass is like an oven. I can barely squeeze in there. I muster a

glob of saliva and spit it down in between her ass cheeks. The sound of her moans alone could make me cum. I feel her loosening, moistening, as we fall into a rhythm.

I reach around and play with her clit, making her cum hard within seconds. "Yeah, that's what I needed." I thrust my cock all the way inside her anus as she rubs her pussy against the table, milking her orgasm to the fullest.

I pinch her hips as I push and pull them forward and back. I'm so fucking deep inside her. Fuck. Every nerve, every fucking ridge on my cock is being tugged tight as I thrust in and out. I can't hold back for much longer.

"FUCK," I roar. All the blood rushes to the tip as my cum bursts out. I pump harder and faster as wave after wave of spasms ripples through my balls and down my shaft.

She screams my name over and over again as I pound her so hard the wood on the table legs splinters. "I'm coming again, Val. Fuck you, this feels so fucking good."

I take pride in breaking her, unraveling her. I ride her ass like a matador trying to wrangle a bucking bull. I give her ass cheeks a hard slap as I fill her to the brim with my thick hot cum.

Collapsing onto her back, my cock still inside her, I kiss her shoulders. Consumed with my need to worship her, I brush her hair to the side and leave more kisses on her neck. "I... *love you, Maur,*"

I whisper softly in her ear.

She grabs my face and presses it to hers. A gurgled cry escapes from her throat. As she turns her head to the side, her eyes brim with tears. But I don't have to wait for a response. "I love you too, Val. I love you so fucking much."

Thank fuck. Her words are my salvation tonight. My reckoning.

As I slide my cock out gently, more of my cum leaks out. "I'll buy you another table."

She laughs through her tears. "Nah, I think we should leave it for Libra to find."

I scoop her up and carry her into the bathroom before drawing a hot bath. We take turns washing each other in silence, our gazes locked and full of something that feels stronger than love. Something that transcends human emotion and logic.

And when I lie her down next to me in her bed, she curls up in my arms like a wild cat who's finally found peace. I know it will be short-lived, but at this moment, everything is still and quiet and perfect.

"Val?"

"Yes, Maur."

"Why don't I feel any remorse?"

I hold her tight to my chest, afraid that the shadows will slip in between us again. "Because you're with Nocturnus now," I sigh. "And because he deserved it."

She whimpers and tucks my arm under hers against her belly.

"They all deserve to get what's coming to them."

"Yes they do. Sleep now, baby."

I try to do the same, but the sound of the ravens pecking on the windows is riding my last nerve. I send them *shut the fuck up* messages through my sigils, but they keep tapping and whining.

When I finally drift off to sleep, a tiny flicker of fear sparks in my chest. The more her power grows, so does her lust for vengeance. Something tells me that there's much more bloodshed to come.

CHAPTER SEVENTEEN

Atlas

W HILE THE NEW INITIATES CLEAN UP THE MESS FROM THE PARTY, Riot and I wait for my father in the foyer. We haven't spoken a word since Val left with Maureen. But we don't need words to know how furious we both are with the situation.

She's *our* fucking firecracker to stalk and bully and mangle. No one else's. And to think my father has the audacity to mess with what's mine. . . That's one of the main rules we've always abided by in the Thorn house—you only eat from your own plate, or you reap what you sow.

Fuck, if my mother knew half the shit her husband is capable of, she would have a fucking heart attack. I don't know how she's put up with his shit all these years. He must have a golden fucking cock.

"Atlas, please stop thinking about your parents fucking. It's dis-turbing." Riot paces across the foyer so hard his boots leave scuff marks on the marble.

I forget how deep inside each other's shit we are sometimes. We're not mind readers, but we get impressions. "Fuck, sorry, I'm really wound up right now."

He pats me on the back. "We all are. Our fathers are out of con-trol. It's time we reign them in and teach them a lesson."

I nod and take a long swig of nightshade. "After this semester is over, we're going to give them an early retirement. No more col-lege parties. No more fucking games. We should be in charge of all the business holdings. Everything."

"Agreed. They've been grooming us to take over anyway. Let's just make it sooner rather than later." Riot's head jerks toward the front door as a car engine hums up the driveway.

I stand, my fists balled. "Speak of the fucking devil."

My adrenaline spikes at the sound of his designer shoes traips-ing up the front steps. I swing the door open before he has a chance to knock.

"Hello, boys." Pisces Thorn stands before us, a picture of per-fection. From the top of his neatly coiffed silver hair, navy-blue, three-piece suit with monogrammed cufflinks, all the way down to his expensive Italian leather shoes. He could have been a movie star.

"Dad." I stand aside and motion for him to enter.

Riot glares at him. "Mr. Thorn. Something to drink?"

Pisces looks us over with that smug grin on his face that I've been accustomed to seeing my whole life. "I'll take a scotch. Two ice cubes."

He skirts ahead of us like this is his house, making us follow *him* into the sitting room. I swear, no matter how old we get, he still treats us like we're fucking children.

Once all three of us have a drink in our hands, I start in. "You've been keeping some secrets and—"

"Cut the dramatics, Atlas. Why did you summon me here in the middle of the night? You interrupted one of my favorite meals."

He narrows his eyes at me.

I feel my cheeks heat. He's the only man who continues to disrespect me. "What the fuck are you eating at midnight? Shouldn't an old man like you be in bed at this hour?"

Pisces purses his lips. "I *was* in bed. Eating pussy."

Fucking hell. Guaranteed, it wasn't my mother's.

Riot glares at me again. "Thanks for the overshare, Mr. Thorn. We called you here because we have something that belongs to you. And we just wanted to return it."

He chuckles and arches an eyebrow, clearly amused with us, like we're back in grade school, learning how to make poison for the first time. "You two were always so precocious. All right, I'll bite. What did you little shits steal from me this time?"

He thinks this is a game.

All my life, I've watched him steal and manipulate. He's the best con man I've ever known. When I was a kid, I used to take things from him just so I could turn around and sell him back his own shit. It started small at first; a couple of watches, some family heirlooms, and the like.

As I got older, I got smarter. I stole bigger things like his Alfa Romero sports car. I even managed to take over one of his country houses. Had the locks changed and everything. Instead of being angry, he was always impressed and played along with my shenanigans. He'd pay me top dollar for whatever I stole. It was never about the money for either of us. It was about winning.

And this time, he lost.

I shake my head. "Follow us."

He sighs before knocking back the rest of his scotch. "Make this quick, boys. I have an early meeting tomorrow."

We don't take the direct path down. No. Instead, we lead him

in circles, disorienting him so he's distracted. The last thing I want is for him to learn his way around here. These are our sacred spaces.

"Can we hurry this up? I don't need a tour of underneath your house," he grumbles.

"Right this way, Mr. Thorn," Riot snickers back.

He reluctantly follows us into the cavern, freezing when he takes in the sight. "What the fuck?"

I stalk over to Barnaby's lifeless body. His chains rattle as I give him a good shake. "Looks like you lost one of your *dolls*."

Pisces's face pales, but he lifts his chin in defiance. "I have no idea what you're talking about, boy. What is the meaning of this?"

Riot cocks his head to the side, his eyes murderous as he glares daggers into my father. "*This* is what happens when you fuck with what belongs to us." He takes another step closer to him. "When you plant spies in our backyard and think we won't fucking sniff them out."

"How dare you speak to me that way, Riot. I should call Holden right now and tell him how disrespectful his son is being." Pisces loosens his tie as beads of sweat form on his brow.

My laugh echoes through the cavern. "You're getting sloppy, old man. And the only one being disrespectful is you. Maureen Blackwell is ours. Stay away from her."

Pisces's blue-green eyes flicker with rage. "You stabbed a young man to death over some fucking pussy? For fuck's sake, Atlas. I thought I taught you better than that."

Riot clenches his fists at his sides, using all his strength to not deck my father in the mouth. "Oh, *we* didn't stab him to death. She did. Now, why don't you tell us what you want with her."

Pisces's gaze travels the length of Barnaby's body as he stalks toward him. "Excellent knife work . . ." He sighs. "Maureen is lever-age. This childish feud between the Graves and the Blackwells has to end. Penny Blackwell owns most of the land in Ever Graves, and

she refuses to do business with anyone who sided with the Graves family. I'll never understand why my brother, Gemini, ever did."

I'm fucking shaking. "And you thought kidnapping Maureen for this pervert to *play* with was going to earn you points with her grandmother? For fuck's sake."

He scoffs and shakes his head. "That's only what I promised him, so he'd be more motivated. As soon as he grabbed her, I was going to kill him myself."

"Unfuckingbelievable," Riot growls. "Maureen is not yours to bargain with. She belongs to us."

Pisces snickers. "You fucking idiots. Neither of you have any idea what you're dealing with. Trust me."

"*Trust you?*" I roar.

"Calm the fuck down. You, Riot, and Valentin are messing with something that you are too ignorant and immature to understand. She belongs to Nocturnus. To the elders. Not to a silly group of college boys who still walk in their fathers' shadows."

I charge forward and push him hard. His eyes widen before they darken into something so sinister it makes my skin crawl. He catches me off guard. The sigils on his neck glow as he takes two steps toward me and shoves me back, sending me flying to the ground. I feel my shoulder crack and dislocate the second I make impact with the hard cement.

I wheeze as I struggle to get air back into my lungs.

He comes at me again, but Riot blocks his path. "Get away from him before I string you up right next to your little bitch boy."

I take a deep breath and climb to my feet. He's never laid a hand on me before. Not even when I've been at my worst. With a loud grunt, I slam my shoulder into the cavern wall, snapping it back into place.

"*We will not hand her over.*" I pull out a vial of oleander and drink it down. It numbs some of the pain. "And we will kill anyone

who tries to take her from us." I raise my good arm up and point at Barnaby.

Pisces's chest heaves as he and Riot remain locked in a match of death stares. "That temptress will be the death of us all. You'll see. Soon... you'll be begging me to take her."

"Get out," I yell. "Get the fuck out of our house. Get the fuck out of Tenebrose. And take your spies with you, or else I'll send them back to you in pieces."

He straightens his tie before slicking back a strand of fallen hair. "I should have had more children because you are a fucking disappointment."

"Oh, fuck you," Riot hisses.

I wince at my father's words. He's been cold and absent my whole life. But hearing him finally admit it out loud... that I've never lived up to his standards... it's a fucking blow that hurts more than the one he dealt to my body.

"It's fine. At least now, I know where we stand."

Pisces snickers. "I'll show myself out. And yes, I know the way. Despite your earlier efforts to distract me."

I bite my tongue as we watch him leave. Lines have been crossed, and new ones drawn. We've spent our whole lives worshipping our fathers. We put them up on pedestals so high that it went to their heads.

"We can't trust them anymore," Riot murmurs.

I nod. "We never should have."

I pull out my phone and dial Val.

He picks up before the first ring. "How bad is it?"

I close my eyes and pinch the middle of my brow as a headache starts to form. "Do not let her out of your sight."

He lets out a deep breath. "Understood."

I hang up and accompany Riot back upstairs. The initiates have gone to bed, and the house is spotless without any hint of a party ever happening. Fuck. What a long fucking night.

"So what's our next move?" I ask.

Riot rubs my shoulder, soothing it with the power from his healing sigil. "They won't try anything again for a while. But we stay alert. After the semester is over, we go to Ever Graves and end this feud ourselves."

The first time I saw our firecracker was in this very room when she came to our first party of the year. She gave me fucking butterflies. I knew she would change everything. I felt it in my bones that night.

"I'm in love with her," I admit.

Riot nods. "I know. We all are... Sleep with me tonight, Atlas. I don't want to be alone."

A warmth fills my chest. Riot doesn't make himself vulnerable very often. I clasp his hand in mine. "Neither do I."

I follow him to his room and shut the door behind us. My heart races as I watch him remove his shirt and pants before slipping inside the sheets. I strip down as well and climb in next to him.

"Atlas, I need release."

I wrap my hand around his hard cock. "Use me however you like."

"Get on your knees and face the wall," he commands.

Fuck, I'm so hard. I push up and grab a hold of the headboard.

"Don't be gentle."

He sucks on his fingers before sliding them up and down my ass. "You know I won't be."

I lean my forehead against the wall as all the pain in my shoulder dissipates. "Fuck."

He slides the tip of his cock in first, taunting me with its girth. I scratch my nails down the headboard. Sweat drips from every corner of my body. I want him inside me so fucking bad. I need this ache to subside. This need to be filled by him.

"Relax. Open up for me." He slides deeper in, and I feel like my

belly is going to explode. I spread my legs farther apart and arch my hips back toward him.

"Good boy, Atlas. Just like that." He lets out a deep moan as he pushes all the way in, stuffing me to the brim.

I cry out and jerk my hips forward, but he yanks them back, slamming his thick cock back into me. "Yeah. . . Don't let me get away."

He reaches around and squeezes my cock. "You could never get away from me."

There's a different energy between us tonight. After all we've been through, all we've sacrificed, we both need this more than ever. He thrusts all the way in till I can feel his abdomen against my ass cheeks. I bite down on the headboard while he strokes me with both hands and his cock throbs inside me. It's the sweetest fucking torture.

"Fuck me. Please," I beg.

Riot chuckles as he slips out, leaving just the tip inside. He moves it in circles, tickling my entrance until I'm ready to fucking cry from need. "Mmm, I love that tight puckered hole."

I moan and jerk my hips, urging him to put it all the way back in. "Show me. I want to see what you've done to me."

He reaches for his phone. "Hold still for me." He fingers my ass, rubbing his tip around it before I hear the click of the camera. Fuck. I'm so hot. So desperate for his cock.

Riot shoves the phone in my face. "Look how red and swollen you are for me."

The picture unhinges me, unleashing an orgasm so fucking deep, I let out a guttural scream so loud, I'm sure every single initiate in the house hears me.

Riot thrusts back in and echoes my cries as he thrashes into me like a wild animal. "Fuck, Atlas. You take me so fucking well."

His cum is hot and thick and so fucking creamy. I grab my own cock and milk myself, squirting my cum all over the pillows

and sheets. He slams into me as he rides his orgasm, knocking me into the headboard. "That's it. Take it all out on me. Give me your fucking violence."

Riot wraps a hand around my throat as he stills his cock inside me. His cum leaks down the backs of my thighs and ass. "No one can break us, Atlas. The four of us are too strong together."

I take a deep breath as my pulse starts to steady. "Only we can break each other."

CHAPTER EIGHTEEN

Maureen

"THERE HAS TO BE SOMETHING YOU CAN DO. HE'S MY BEST FRIEND'S brother. Isn't that a conflict of interest?"

Miss Florian glares up at me from behind her pointy glasses. "No, Miss Blackwell, it's not. And no, there's nothing I can do. The drop period has passed. So unless you want to get an F, you'll need to get yourself over to Professor Crane's poetry class immediately."

I roll my eyes at her and storm out of the admin office. A chill sweeps through my bones as I stand on the front steps. Fuck. If Villette finds out that her brother watched me get fucked, she's going to be pissed. She might not ever talk to me again. A group of students

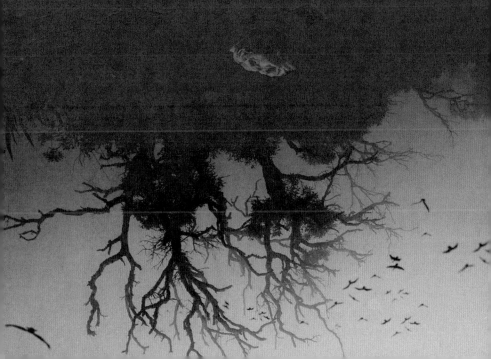

snicker as they walk past me. I realize I'm just standing there, star-ing out into space with three ravens at my feet.

"Shoo. You're making me look crazy," I whisper. They squawk before flying off. I look around to see more eyes on me.

Fuck this.

Professor Crane's poetry class is at the other end of campus, and I'm already two minutes late. I throw my bag over my shoulder and book it through the woods. The wind whips my hair around my face, lashing my cheeks till I can barely see. I almost trip twice over fallen branches and foliage. But I keep running as fast as I can without making myself puke.

My hands tremble around the campus map. I've only been here one semester, but it feels like a lifetime. And yet, I still don't know my way around this fucking school. The buildings here are omi-nous. They aren't like the ones we have back in Wickford Hollow. Tenebrose Academy looks like something you'd see out of a horror movie. Everything is dark and Gothic, black and grey, with stone walkways and iron spires. Gargoyles and statues of crying an-gels decorate almost every walkway and entrance.

As the forest starts to fall away and I inch closer to the spot marked on my map, I remember exactly where I am. I stop to catch my breath and gaze up at the monstrosity before me. Black walls, iron spires, and purple stained glass windows. It's the Goddess of Death church where I had my *Appreciation of Melancholic Music* class last semester. It was the first time I'd met Professor Harker, and he refused to answer my question about his students worshiping the goddess, Nephthys. Funny how I used to think *that* was a cult. Now that I belong to Nocturnus... everything else seems less threatening. My pulse races out of control, and my heart feels like it's going to explode out of my chest. I can't believe I ran all the way here. I feel so fucking out of shape. Time to face the fucking music... well, poetry.

I look behind me one last time to see an unkindness of ravens

watching me curiously. They don't annoy me as much as they used to. Ever since the night I got my first sigil from the guys, I've felt just as drawn to them as they are to me. We are tethered now. At first, their cries were agonizing. I was repulsed by them. But they've slowly settled inside me like they've always been there.

My adrenaline spikes as I spot Valentin between the trees. He leans against one of them, arms crossed. This is my new normal. The first thing he told me this morning was that Atlas's dad tried to have me kidnapped. The elders are unhinged. So the guys won't let me out of their sight now. But the darkness growing inside me is what they should really be afraid of.

My dreams are getting bloodier, more sadistic. And the acts of violence I've committed don't disgust me like they used to. I crave more. The rush of power and control. The need to show everyone I'm not the one to be fucked with. I never want to be that scared girl running through the woods again.

I turn away from him, now ten minutes late for this fucking class, and blow out a deep breath as I pull on the heavy wood door.

Oh no.

It's not as heavy as it fucking looks.

Fuck.

I practically rip it off the hinges because I underestimate its weight. The wind makes it blow back even harder as it shuts behind me with a loud bang.

I clutch my bag to my chest as twenty or so students spin around in their pews to ogle the hot mess that just blew into their class like a fucking hurricane. My eyes dart around the cold church, desperately seeking an empty place to sit.

Professor Crane stops mid-sentence when he sees me, his brown eyes playful and amused. "Miss Blackwell. Thanks for fitting us into your busy schedule. Please, take a seat so I can continue."

I feel my cheeks burn and know without any doubt they are bright red. "Sorry."

A guy with pale skin and white hair scoots over to allow me space to sit. The pew squeaks as I sit down, eliciting muffled laughter from the class. "Sorry," I mumble again. Shit. Fuck.

Professor Crane smirks. "All right, where was I?"

"*The Haunted Palace*," a pretty redhead drawls. She tilts her head to the side coyly.

In fact, all the women and men in this class are looking at the professor like he's a tasty snack. I forgot how striking he is. He projects an energy that oozes lust and sin. And everyone in this room is drinking it up like holy water.

"Yes, thank you, darling. That particular piece could very much be about a haunted palace, or it could mean something else entirely. Our bodies are temples, are they not? Palaces of trauma and emotions and dreams. Let's read between the lines, shall we? Open your book and turn to page thirty-three."

He smiles at the redhead again. "I'd like you to read the fifth stanza of Edgar Allan Poe's *The Haunted Palace* aloud, please, darling. *Darling?*

This man is fucking slick. So charming, he's got everyone on the edge of their seats, mesmerized by his every move.

I follow along in the book as the girl reads, her voice practically purring as she caresses the words with the ache in her voice.

But evil things, in robes of sorrow,
Assailed the monarch's high estate;
(Ah, let us mourn! — for never morrow
Shall dawn upon him, desolate!)
And round about his home the glory
That blushed and bloomed.
Is but a dim-remembered story.
Of the old time entombed.

Professor Crane gives her a wink as she looks up at him for approval. "Beautiful. Haunting. But was Poe referring to a house? Or was it about himself? Evil things in robes of sorrow assailed his

high estate. These could be creatures or ghosts . . . but," he walks down the center of the room, locking eyes with every student as he passes each pew, "he could also be referring to his inner demons, the ghosts of his past that now haunt his mind."

My belly flips as he stops in front of my pew. I swallow hard as my palms start to sweat. We lock eyes, and he looks at me the same way he did the other night at *Swallow.* When he watched Riot, Atlas, and Val defile me in the dark corner of the bar.

"What do you think, Miss Blackwell? Was Poe writing about a haunted house or a haunted mind?" He rests his hand on the pew in front of me, and I can't help but notice how his long, slender fingers clench the wood as if he needs it to steady himself.

I gaze up and follow the vein in his neck all the way up to the muscle twitching in his jaw. This man is unnerved by something.

"Maybe it was both," I murmur. "Maybe he went mad because his palace was haunted."

Amusement flickers in his eyes. "Read the last four lines of the poem for me."

I fumble with the pages as this whole display strikes a nerve in my belly. It's not the way everyone focuses on me. It's the way he watches me . . . like I'm the most fascinating thing he's ever seen. I clear my throat and skim down the page until I find the last part of the poem.

While, like a ghostly rapid river,
Through the pale door
A hideous throng rush out forever,
And laugh—but smile no more.

"I think you might be right, Miss Blackwell. We'll never know." He turns away from me, and I release the breath I'm holding. He walks back to the altar and spins around to face us all again. "This class isn't about finding the answers. It's not about choosing between the literal and figurative. It's about embracing both. The true lesson comes from asking the right questions."

If I wasn't so embarrassed about what transpired between us at the bar, I'd actually really fucking enjoy this class.

He zeroes in on me again, sending goose pimples across my skin. "Over the next semester, we'll explore the works of some of the most haunted poets. There's no homework, no tests. All you have to do to get an A in this class is show up with an open mind, be on time, and ask questions. Sound good?"

A few students actually clap with glee. Fucking hell. *Be on time.* My cheeks burn again, but now it extends down to my neck and chest too. The harder I try to be a fly on the wall, the more I become the fucking elephant in the room. I suck at blending in. Fuck. We spend the rest of the hour going over the syllabus and reading material and watching him try to field personal questions from several female students, including the panting redhead from earlier. I try with all my power not to wear my emotions on my face. But I can't help it. My eye twitches every time someone asks him if there's a *Mrs. Crane* or a *partner* waiting for him at home.

Poor Villette. Once they find out she's his sister, she's going to have her own little fan club of Crane stalkers.

A bell tolls from a distant tower and sends all of the students scrambling from their pews. This is my chance to slip out. I have the advantage of sitting at the back, so I shove my book back into my bag and leap from my seat. Just as a large group rushes past, I dive in between them, almost knocking a couple of them over.

"Miss Blackwell." Professor Crane's voice reaches over the shuffle of feet and creaking pews.

His tone is soft but commanding. It stops me dead in my tracks.

Fuck.

I slowly turn around to see the smirks and eye rolls from the students, who undoubtedly think I'm about to be reprimanded for being late.

The redhead bumps her shoulder against mine. "Lucky bitch."

What the fuck? I'm tempted to grab her by the hair and drag

her out back so I can return the favor, but I don't dare move. I'm already in enough trouble as it is.

I lock eyes with Professor Crane instead and wait for the rest of the class to file out.

As he stalks toward me, the click of his heels echoes through the church, bouncing off the stained glass windows and sending my adrenaline into overdrive. This very moment is the reason I tried so hard to get out of this fucking class.

"It seems you don't want to be here, Miss Blackwell. Wanna tell me why? I thought you enjoyed poetry." He stands dangerously close to me.

"Villette is my best friend here. You're her brother. This has nothing to do with poetry, and you know it, Professor Crane." I cross my arms in an attempt to seem aloof.

He flashes that damn smirk again. "You can call me Felix when we're alone. And I think what happened the other night at *Swallow* has just as much to do with poetry as anything else."

The heat spreads to the backs of my arms and down my legs. "I don't think it's a good idea for me to be in this class. It's... unethical."

Felix chuckles. "For you or for me?"

As I become more aware of our solitude in this massive iron church, my heart beats faster. The space between us is full of tension and uncertainty. I have no idea what he's going to do or say next, and it fucking terrifies me.

"For both of us. There's a laundry list of reasons why I shouldn't be your student."

His smirk fades, and his eyes darken. "But there's so many things I could teach you." He takes another step toward me, and it forces me to uncross my arms so they don't touch his chest.

Sweat beads down my back. "Are you still talking about poetry, Professor Crane?"

His bottom lip twitches as he gazes down at me. "I'm talking

about how you *loved* every second of me watching you the other night."

The memory of Valentin thrusting his cock in my ass as I locked eyes with Felix flashes in my mind. "You don't know what I love," I whisper as shame fills me.

Felix cocks his head to the side as his gaze travels down the length of my body.

"*O Rose thou art sick.*
The invisible worm,
That flies in the night.
In the howling storm:
Has found out thy bed,
Of crimson joy:
And his dark secret love
Does thy life destroy..."

"Stop quoting Poe to me, please. Am I in trouble for being late?"

"It's *The Sick Rose* by William Blake. And no you're not in trouble for being late. Although, I prefer that you don't do it again. You're in trouble for trying to avoid me... I'm joking. You're not really in trouble at all. Unless you want to be."

This man is going to be the death of me. "How the fuck am I supposed to sit in this class every day with you looking at me like that? After what you watched me do..."

"Because if you drop this class, I'll have to tell Villette why, I don't like keeping secrets from her." The smirk returns to his face.

Fucking fuck. "You're blackmailing me, now?"

He sighs. "No, I'm warning you that I won't lie to her if she asks why you're no longer in my class." He leans down and whispers in my ear. "Remember, Maur, it's not about finding the answers; it's about asking the right questions..."

My belly flips, my heart pounding. "Why did you watch?"

His lips still hover over my ear. "You are more exquisite than

any poem I've ever read... Deny it all you want, Little Raven, but you came harder *because* I was watching you."

The door to the church flies open, shattering the static between us. I spin around to see Val charging down the aisle. "You're late for your next class, Maureen."

Felix chuckles. "My apologies. I asked her to stay after. I'll write her a note." He clicks his pen open and starts scribbling away on his notepad.

My heart is beating in my fucking throat.

"Why is that, Professor Crane?" Val's eyes are murderous.

A devious twinkle flickers in Felix's eyes. "We were discussing poetry, naturally. One of my favorite poems in particular."

Oh, fuck.

I snatch the note out of his hand and push Val toward the door.

"Thank you, Professor. See you next week."

"Which poem is your favorite?" Val calls out.

Every cell in my body is on fire. My hands are shaking against Val's chest as I try to urge him outside. I swear to fuck if this man says my name...

Felix chuckles. "Edgar Allan Poe's *The Raven*, of course. Good day, Miss Blackwell."

My stomach flips, but I let out a sigh of relief.

And his eyes have all the seeming of a demon's that is dreaming—

my favorite line from *The Raven* . . .

Val growls as I finally get him out the church doors. "I was worried when you didn't come out with the others. Then I remembered who's class you're in. What the fuck did he really want with you, Maur?"

I shake my head. There's too much going on right now. So many enemies and threats. The last thing we need is another one. "We talked about poetry."

Val snickers. "Don't fucking keep secrets from me, Maur. He watched me bend you over and fuck you in the ass the other night.

He watched all of us pass you around like a fucking toy. And he didn't say anything to you about it?"

I throw up my hands, frustrated. "Yeah. So what? He mentioned that he knew it turned me on. That was it. He said it's not a big deal and that it won't affect me taking his class." This is all partially true.

Val wraps his hand around my throat and drags me into the woods. When we're halfway in, he slams me up against a tree. "I will get the fucking truth out of you."

He unbuttons my jeans with his other hand, unzipping them before sliding two fingers down my panties. I let out a soft moan as he thrusts them inside my pussy.

"Would you want him to watch you again?"

"*Yes,*" I can't fucking lie to him. Especially with his slick fingers deep inside me.

He shoves a third finger in, pumping in and out violently. "Does he want to touch you?"

I shake my head as I clench around his fingers. "I don't know..."

He rolls his thumb over my clit, and I buck against the tree. The bark digs into my back, cutting my skin. Blood and sweat trickle down my spine. "*Do you* want him to touch you?"

Fuck. I'm about to cum, and all I can think about is the church of the Goddess of Death and Edgar fucking Allan Poe. "I... I don't know."

Val squeezes my throat so tight that stars blur my vision. He pinches my clit at the same time. I nearly convulse as a deep orgasm ripples through me, rocking my core like a fucking atom bomb. I cry out as I grind and twist against his hand.

"Mmm, yeah. Now I get the truth." He slows his pace as I come down, gently caressing my pussy lips. "Let me know when you figure out the answer to my last question, Maur."

Felix's voice echoes in my head—*it's not about finding the an-swers; it's about asking the right questions...*

Fucking hell. What have I gotten myself into this fucking time?

CHAPTER NINETEEN

Maureen

"T"HIS WEEK HAS FELT AS LONG AS A FUCKING YEAR," I GRUMBLE INTO my drink.

Villette nods. "Right? Thank God, it's finally the week-end. I swear all my teachers are on edge right now. I wonder if it has anything to do with what happened the night of the Winter Solstice Ball."

I shudder as I remember how Jessamine tricked me into going out to the graveyard by myself. The way she set me up, delivering me straight into Zeke's hands. The other students don't know what really happened that night. But guaranteed the teachers do. I push my chips around on the plate, suddenly no longer

hungry. "Who knows? Everyone around here is always wound up so tight."

Villette touches my hand. "Sorry to bring that up again. I know that was a traumatic night for you."

I shrug and take a big sip of my pineapple Margarita. "It's okay. I'm working past it."

"So, how are your classes? How's my brother treating you?"

She purses her lips around the straw, wincing as if she's expecting me to say the worst.

I've been dreading having this conversation but it's impossible to avoid if I'm going to continue being friends with her. "Yeah, he's a really great teacher, Villette. So excited to be in his class."

She breathes out a sigh of relief. "Oh, good. I was worried he was going to scare you off from being friends with me. He's intense, and his obsession with poetry is borderline manic." She giggles.

If she only fucking knew.

I chuckle. "Yup. I'm definitely picking up on that vibe."

The server sets down another pitcher of Margaritas and refreshes our chips and salsa. "Those guys over in the corner bought these for you."

I let out a sigh as I spot Riot, Atlas, and Valentin at a corner booth on the opposite side of the Mexican restaurant. I give them a little wave. "Well, at least they're giving me *some* space."

Villette laughs. "I think it's cute. They're just worried about you." Her face falls. "Look, I know you don't tell me everything that's going on with you, but I'm not an idiot. You've been different since we got back from winter break. I just want you to know that you can tell me anything, I won't judge."

She's so sweet and kind, but it only makes me miss Bailey even more. Villette is a good friend though. I just can't imagine telling her all the horrific things that have been happening lately. There's a purity to her that I don't want to taint.

I smile and squeeze her hand. "Thanks, babe." I feel bad when

I see the look of disappointment in her eyes. She wants me to trust her. I give in and spend the next hour telling her about the stalker and how he works for Atlas's father. I leave out the part where I stab him to death. She *would* judge me for that, and I don't want to turn her into a liar.

"Holy shit, Maur. What are you gonna do?" Her eyes are wide as she sucks down her third Margarita.

Kill every single one of them.

"I'm just trying to focus on school and let the guys handle their fathers. But I think we're going to head up to Ever Graves after the spring equinox."

The server, a curvy woman with blonde hair and bright-red lip-stick, returns again with a plate of street tacos. "Um, those guys said you both need to eat more if you're going to suck down Margaritas like water."

I arch an eyebrow at her.

"Their words, not mine." She raises her hands up in defense.

Villette and I burst out laughing as we happily scoot the plate of tacos between us. "Can we get some more sour cream, please? The biggest bowl you have."

When the server returns with it, I stop her from setting it down. "I'd like you to give this to those guys, please. Tell them they need to eat all of this using only their fingers."

The server sighs and shakes her head as she stalks off with the bowl, mumbling to herself. "*Fucking weirdos.*"

Villette laughs so hard that Margarita almost comes out of her nose. "I see why they call you firecracker now."

I laugh with her. "Hey, they started it. I'm just better at play-ing their games."

The look on Riot's face is fucking priceless. I laugh so hard my stomach hurts. Atlas dips his finger in first, of course. He moans dramatically as he licks the sour cream off his fingers. Val dips the tip of his finger in cautiously as if it's going to bite him.

"This is the most entertaining thing I've seen in a while," Villette cackles. "You know you're the only girl who can get Nocturnus to do shit like this. They are so obsessed with you."

I wink as I finish a street taco in two bites, my appetite coming back tenfold. I wash it down with a fourth Margarita and finally start to feel a little tipsy. "I wish Libra was here for this. She would have told me to make them lick the bowl clean."

"You still haven't heard from her either? It's not like her to miss the first week of school. One of her favorite things is showing up to her first class hungover and reminding her teachers that she's a Thorn and can do whatever the fuck she wants," Villette quips.

Her absence is starting to feel weird. I never thought I'd care about Libra Thorn, but I can't help but worry about her. "Yeah, it's not like her. Have you asked your brother, Bones, about it?"

She nods. "He says he hasn't seen her. Aries, Libra's brother, can't get a hold of her either... I hope she's okay."

My stomach knots. With everything that's been going on lately, I can't help but think the worst. But I can't let my mind go there. Yet. "I'm sure she's fine. Probably just wants to be fashionably late so she can make her grand entrance."

Villette smiles, but it doesn't reach her eyes. "For sure."

I make a mental note to have Atlas press his family for more information on her whereabouts. Which isn't going to be easy since his father currently wants to kidnap me and make me his ritual sex slave. Fuck. How is this my life right now?

The guys insist on paying the check and also driving us back to the Nest. I make Villette sit in the front seat next to Val so she doesn't have to be sandwiched between Riot and Atlas. Even though she's known them her whole life, they still scare her. She doesn't say as much, but I can see it in her eyes.

Atlas climbs out of the car after me. "Looks like it's just you and me tonight, pretty girl."

They weren't kidding when they said they weren't letting me out of their sight.

I hug Villette goodbye and watch to make sure she gets inside safely before I lean in to give Riot a deep kiss. I stretch across the passenger seat and kiss Val with just as much passion. They both taste differently, each one stirring my senses and stimulating my need. I want all three of them with me tonight, but there's so much to be done. Riot has Nocturnus business, and Val needs to check in on his uncle, who's been holed up with Jessamine since the winter break. And for the first time in Nocturnus history, they aren't throwing one of their parties this weekend. That alone lets me know that this thing with their fathers is serious.

When we walk into my dorm apartment, the first thing I notice is the new coffee table. I chuckle to myself. Atlas sets out an array of poison vials across it before plopping down on the couch. "Fetch me a couple of glasses, love, so I can make us a cocktail."

His tone is playful and not demanding in the slightest. A little rush of excitement seeps into my veins as I head to the kitchen. I come back with the glasses and also a bottle of tequila. I take a pull from the bottle while I watch Atlas pour from the vials like a chemist. If someone told me a few months ago that I'd not only be immune to poison but also craving it, I would have thought they were crazy. It looks like I'm the crazy one now.

He hands me one of the glasses as I take a seat next to him. "Wanna talk to me about what happened with Professor Crane, pretty girl? Val said he walked in on something strange between you two."

It's been a week since our encounter, and no one has said a word. I thought they might let it go. Fuck. "Um... it was nothing. He just wanted to talk about what happened at *Swallow*. That was it."

Atlas runs a hand through his blond hair, slicking it back off his forehead. His eyes glow and I try not to drown in them. He has this pull. Like the ocean that their color mimics. I take a sip of the

poison cocktail and draw in a quick breath. It burns my throat like fire. My chest tightens, and my lungs contract as my blood and oxygen go to war with each other.

I lean my head back against the cushions and close my eyes as I wait for the pain to subside.

He strokes my thigh. "Relax. Don't fight it."

A whimper escapes my throat as my sigils come to life, responding to the poison like beacons of light. But as I adjust and allow the toxins to flow through me, my body tingles. It's euphoric. Even his breath on my cheek feels like heaven.

"That feels good now, doesn't it?" He slides his hand up higher and caresses my belly.

I nod. I try to swallow, but my tongue feels so heavy. I take another pull from the tequila bottle, needing the alcohol to coat my mouth.

"Yeah," I breathe.

My pulse quickens as he unbuttons my shirt. "Tell me about what happened in the ritual room at Holden's."

I shake my head. "No. I don't want to talk about it."

"I'm not asking, Maur. This shame you're carrying ... you gotta let it go." He peels my shirt back after he's finished with the last button. I arch my back as the poison and tequila start to make my head spin. He unhooks my bra and pulls it down.

"Touch me," I beg.

He traces his finger around my breast and then stops. "Only if you tell me something about that night."

Fuck.

My pulse is racing. I am high and drunk and horny as fuck. "I had to touch myself in front of them ... had to make myself cum while they watched."

Atlas pinches my nipple before rolling it back and forth between his thumb and forefinger. "Good girl. And how did you feel when they were watching?"

I blow out a deep breath. "Fuck, Atlas . . . It made me cum harder. Why did it turn me on?"

He licks my nipple, sucking it gently before scraping his teeth across it. "There's something naughty about it, isn't there? Yeah. You like the dirty things. Just like us, pretty girl." He grabs a vial and pours a drop of poison on my nipple. I gasp as it sizzles and burns. He puckers his lips around it, moaning as he sucks.

Sweat races down my chest as all my nerve endings stand erect. "They were wearing masks, so all I could see was their eyes . . . It made me so wet."

"Mmm. Yeah, tell me why it made you so wet."

I whimper as he licks poison off my other breast. "Because I was in control of my pleasure and theirs."

He drags his teeth across my jaw. "Yeah. That's it, pretty girl. It's your fucking kink, and you should embrace it. No more shame." I nod as he unzips my jeans. "Say it, Maur."

"No more shame," I whisper.

"Good girl."

As he starts to slip his fingers inside my panties, I suddenly remember what day it is. "Wait. I'm on my period."

His eyes light up like I've never seen them do before. "Don't play with me, Maur."

"Atlas . . . no." I remember how hot he was for me in the car that day. Riot pulled out my tampon, and he went feral like a wild animal. "Don't tell me no. I want your blood all over my cock." He jumps up and comes back with a stack of towels. I watch as he lays them out all over the floor. "I'll buy you a new set tomorrow."

He takes off his clothes and stands there waiting for me. His cock is so hard and beautiful. My pussy aches at the sight of it. "Come lie down, pretty girl."

I start to stand but stumble as the poison and tequila rush through my veins. He reaches out in two strides to catch me before

I fall and helps me down to the floor. My head spins as I lie flat.

"You're a fucking psycho, Atlas."

He nods as he pulls down my jeans and panties. "Yes, and your blood's gonna cleanse all my sins."

My legs shiver as he pushes them apart. "Fuck. There's so much blood."

He slides his finger down my slit before wrapping it around the tampon string. "Let's get this out of the way."

I arch my hips when he pulls it out. "Fuck, that tickles."

"So beautiful." He lines up his cock and inches it halfway in, then pulls it out. His eyes are glazed, wild, as he admires my blood on his veiny ridges.

I have to admit it feels fucking amazing. I'm so lubricated, so wet. . . "Put it back in, Atlas. Please."

He thrusts all the way in with a grunt. "FUCK," he yells.

A primal ache stirs in my belly as I look up at him. His sigils glow in between his chiseled muscles. He looks like a Greek god—dangerous and beautiful. I raise my hips up and down as he rides me slowly. We fall into a rhythm, my juices flowing like honey.

Every time he thrusts in, he pulls all the way out so he can fixate on the way my blood paints his cock. He smears his hands in it, then grips my thighs and my belly until we're both bathed in it.

He presses his thumb hard against my clit. "I will give you anything you want, pretty girl. Fucking anything."

A spasm flicks against my core as he rubs his thumb in circles. I moan as my orgasm starts to build. "I'm going to cum so hard for you."

He drives into me, filling me to the brim. Our thighs are soaked as he slips in and out of my sopping-wet pussy. He rocks into me, forcing my hips up and down, as he wails like an animal. "Mmm, fuck. I'm coming."

The spasms reverberate through me, hitting me deep inside. We both cry out as his cum shoots into me, thick and hot. I scratch my

M VIOLET

nails down his chest as I clench around his cock. He buries himself so deep I can feel him in my lower back.

"Your blood is mine. Fuck." He thrusts into me again as he rides his orgasm, milking it for every sacred drop.

We lie still for a while. I'm afraid to move and make more of a mess than we already have. Finally, after what seems like forever, Atlas pulls out and flashes me the wickedest smile I've ever seen.

"That was fucking perfect." He threads one of the towels between my legs and wraps me up in it. I let him scoop me off the floor and carry me to the bathroom. "I'm going to clean you up now, pretty girl."

The hot water feels amazing on my poison-fueled skin. Atlas is surprisingly gentle with me in the shower, taking his time to wash the blood off both of us. I almost cry tears of joy when he shampoos my hair, the way he massages his fingers into my scalp like a professional. I whimper and moan at every touch.

After, he gives me some privacy so I can put in another tampon before I get dressed. I wrap a towel around my wet hair and come out to find him already in my bed.

As I crawl in next to him, he wraps an arm around my waist and pulls me close. "Anything you fucking want, love. Just name it."

A skitter of nerves flutters through my belly. There are many things that I want. I'd like to see Bailey, and to go to Ever Graves to meet my grandmother. I also really want to kill the Nocturnus elders. But all that will have to wait.

"I don't know . . ."

Atlas kisses my neck. "What you want and need are not different things anymore, Maur. You need to accept who you are. Show us how naughty you can be."

I bite my lip, and my cheeks heat as I think about the ritual at the Graves's estate. The memories flood me one by one like a fever dream. Felix's eyes flash in between them. The way he hungered for me as he watched the dirty things they did to me at the bar.

DIRTY LITTLE SAINT

"I want to be in control," I murmur.

"Mmm, I know, baby. Don't worry about a fucking thing. We're going to give you exactly what you want and need."

My heart races for a bit longer as the idea of it all sinks in. The thrill of having someone watch us again is all I can think about as I drift off to sleep.

CHAPTER TWENTY

Riot

M Y FIRECRACKER IS SAFE FOR NOW. I STILL WISH SOMETIMES THAT I'd never made that sacrifice to the ravens to get her here. But I'm too selfish to live without her. We all are. I hit the throttle and let the machine between my legs soothe my anxiety. There are many pieces to this puzzle that we need to make fit. One of them is adding another pawn to the chessboard.

As I ride through the forest, my muscles relax. This is my favorite time of day, that space when night starts morphing into morning. The sky is a pale gray, the ravens sleep, and the air is so crisp you can practically cut it with a knife. No one is awake yet except me and my bike.

Well, and the man meeting me in the graveyard before class.

Through the glare of my headlights, I spot Felix Crane sitting on top of a faded headstone, his legs so long they touch the ground. The mist makes his black hair curl even more. From this viewpoint, he looks like an ethereal dark prince reigning over his kingdom of death. His eyes glow like mine. I noticed it that night at *Swallow*. It was subtle, but I definitely caught it.

The Cranes are *also* one of the founding families of Ever Graves. Which means they, too, were born with curses and darkness in their blood. But they never wanted to be a part of Nocturnus. The Cranes are wanderers, nomads, not ever craving the comforts of a coven. Yet his power simmers underneath his pressed suits and schoolboy charm. He's a monster, just like us. And I can't have him roaming around causing havoc.

I hop off my bike and stalk toward him. "You're early."

He flashes a toothy grin. "Am I? You didn't really think I'd let you get the jump on me, did you?"

I roll my eyes. "Cut the fucking banter, Crane. I'm in a really bad mood."

He shrugs and slides off the headstone. "Is this the part where you tell me to stay away from your girl?"

I'll give Maureen anything she wants. So will Atlas and Val. What they don't realize is we all need each other. It's not just about making our girl happy; this move is about survival.

I unzip my jacket and pull up my shirt. "See these marks? They connect us to each other and the ravens. They tether us to a source of power so great we don't even fully know where it comes from."

Felix tilts his head. "Go on."

"We were strong before she came, but now, we are nearly untouchable. Each sigil carved into our flesh strengthens the bonds between us. The source no longer matters because the power comes *from* us instead of *to* us. Do you understand?"

He crosses his arms. "While this is all very poetic and macabre, I have no fucking idea what any of this has to do with me."

I sigh and point to his face. "Your eyes. Your name. Where you come from. You have power. It's in your blood. My sigils flare every time you come around. I'm betting Atlas and Val's do too. We could be even stronger if you joined us."

Felix bursts out laughing. "This is not at all how I thought this conversation was going to go . . . So, you wanna carve me up and boss me around like you do everyone else?"

This man is testing my fucking patience and almost making me regret bringing him out here. "I'm not asking you to be a fucking initiate, Felix. I'm offering you a spot in the coven—as an equal. I'm not blind or stupid. I see the way you look at Maureen. You could help us protect her. I think you want to."

A hint of deviancy flickers in his eyes. "And would that also en-title me to do more than just watch?"

"That's up to her," I grit out. "I will never let another man touch her unless he is in this coven. This family. And she agrees. We don't share with anyone but each other."

"Maybe I don't want to do more than watch," he snickers.

Fucking liar.

"Yeah, well, I think you came to Tenebrose to try and do exactly that. You could have taught at Ever Graves Academy or literally any-where else. But I'm guessing Villette sent you a couple of drunken pics, you took one look at our girl, and the power rushing through your veins did the rest. People like us are drawn to each other."

Felix rubs his chin as he paces around the headstones. "I'm not going to give you an answer right now."

"You don't have to," I bark back. "But don't take too long. The Nocturnus elders, our fathers, have been trying to take her from us for the last four weeks. She's ready to kill them herself. The shadows lurk in her Erebus sigil, making her more unhinged every day. We need more balance. Another source of power to help keep her safe."

His eyes darken. "What do you mean *take her*? As in kidnap?"

I nod. Now he's fucking getting it.

The muscle in his jaw twitches. "I need to get ready for class. Either way, I'll be in touch soon."

I zip up my jacket and hop on my bike. "I'll be waiting. What's more fucking poetic than that?" I snicker. As I ride back the way I came, the sunlight starts to peer through the trees, bringing with it a whole new fucking ray of uncertainty.

§

My pulse kicks up a notch when I see her upstairs in the library, hunched over a dusty book and completely engrossed with what-ever she's reading. Her dark hair is tied in a low ponytail, exposing her neck. Her sigils. My stomach flips. She's getting braver about showing them off.

Atlas slips out from between the stacks in the *Melancholic Music* aisle and pats me on the back. "You're up. I gotta get to class."

I can't take my eyes off her. Dressed in a brown cashmere sweater and plaid miniskirt, she's more beautiful than ever. Her smooth legs are bare underneath, and I'm trying not to wonder if she's wearing panties or not. I'm tempted to bend her over the table and find out.

"Have you told her anything about Felix yet?" I ask as Atlas gazes at her with the same lust and sin in his eyes that are gripping me right now.

He shakes his head. "No. I figured I'd leave that to you. You're much more eloquent than I am. Did he agree?"

I sigh. "Not yet. But I'm confident he will. His sigils will be dif-ferent, you know? They have to be to ensure the balance."

Atlas swigs from a vial of poison. Tiny swirls of light dance around his pupils. "Maybe he needs to hear it from her . . ."

My stomach flips. He's right. "I'll tell her before class. She has his first this morning."

He pats me on the back again. "It's all gonna be over soon. I'll see ya tonight, Romeo."

I chuckle and cross the room to her. The second I'm behind her, her breath hitches. Her body knows mine without having to see it. I lean over her and place my hands on the table, boxing her in.

"Riot..."

"Hello, love. Did you miss me?" I breathe in her ear.

The vein on her neck pulses, her heartbeat racing. "I always miss you. Sometimes, even when you're right next to me."

I look down to see her thighs are clenched. "What color panties are you wearing?"

She sucks in a deep breath. "I'm not wearing any."

Fuck.

I chase a bead of sweat on her neck with my tongue, lapping it up before leaving a soft kiss in its place. I chuckle as a few students blush when I catch them staring. "We don't have much time before class. I need you to come with me now."

She closes her book without hesitating, sending a sprinkle of dust up into the air. I scoot her chair back and spin her around. She looks up at me with those amber-colored eyes, and my knees slightly wobble. She has no idea the affect she has on me.

I brush my thumb over her full, pouty lips. "Let's go for a ride, Firecracker."

"Can I drive?" She tilts her head and bats her eyelashes at me.

I clasp her hand and tug her toward the door. "You think you can handle my bike?" I tease her.

She lifts onto her toes to whisper in my ear, "I can handle a lot of muscle between my legs."

My cock instantly throbs.

I usher her out the door and down the steps to where my bike is parked. The thought of her rubbing her bare pussy against my leather seat makes me so fucking feral I almost drag her into the bushes and ravage her like a wild animal.

I glimpse a flash of her taint as she throws a leg over my bike. As I nestle in behind her, I pull up the back of her skirt. Her bare ass presses against my cock with only my black cotton pants separating us.

"Where to?" she asks.

I wrap my arms around her waist. "The graveyard."

She revs the bike a few times before taking off. This is the first time I've ever let anyone else drive, but she handles it like a pro. She's wild and fearless as she shrieks like the wind, increasing the speed little by little as she gets more comfortable.

It's turning me on so fucking much I can't contain it anymore.

"Don't lose focus."

"What do you mean? I'm fine," she calls back.

I chuckle as I unzip my pants and pull out my cock. I nudge her forward and pull her hips back, hoping we don't fucking crash. But then again, I'd happily die with my cock inside her.

"Oh, fuck," she cries out. "Are you doing what I think you're doing?" I watch as her grip tightens around the handlebars.

With one arm still around her waist to anchor myself, I fist my cock in my other hand and press it against her entrance. "Watch the road, and don't take your hand off the throttle."

Her juices trickle out and onto my leather seat. Fuck, she's so wet. As I slide my cock inside her pussy, we both gasp. "Oh, baby . . . fuck."

The bike drifts, and she almost loses control. "Riot . . . you're a fucking psycho . . . But don't stop."

I roll my hips forward and almost cum instantly. With the cold wind whipping furiously between us, lashing at our heated skin, every nerve in my body is tingling. My cock pulses inside her core as she clenches so fucking tight around me.

It's hard to thrust at this angle, so I just grind into her in little, short bursts. "Drive faster. I need to fuck you harder," I growl in her ear.

She lets out a deep guttural moan as she hits the throttle, nearly spinning us out, but she corrects, and we thankfully don't go fly-ing off the bike.

"Please... fuck, I need more, Riot."

"Then drive faster." I hold up her skirt and slap her hard on the ass. She chokes my cock with the walls of her pussy, squeezing me so fucking tight.

When we finally pass through the iron gates, I point to a group of trees. "Park over there."

As soon as we reach the spot, she kills the engine, and every-thing gets dead quiet. I push her forward so she's lying across the bike on her stomach. "Fuck, you did so well. Riding me and my bike at the same time."

She grabs onto the handlebars as I slide out and then thrust back inside her. "*Uhhh,*" she moans. "Fuck... you're crazy."

I slap her ass cheeks and slam into her again, lifting her hips up and down as I bury myself to the hilt. "Mmm, I'm... fuck. FUCK." I push in as far as I can go. All the blood rushes to the tip of my cock as a wave of spasms rolls up my shaft. My cum bursts out, filling her to the brim.

And it triggers her.

She rubs her pussy against the leather, grinding against it as she stimulates her clit.

I push on her ass, moving it in circles. "Yeah, give me all your fucking violence."

She screams, and the floodgates open. Her juices spill onto my cock like a dam breaking open for the first time. I thrust into her again, splitting her wide open, drawing her climax out until she's raw and broken.

As we still ourselves, our breaths heavy, I smooth my hands over the marks I left on her ass. "We need to talk about something."

She chuckles. "Right now?"

With my cock still inside her, I hold her hips in place. I don't

want to leave her warm pussy yet. "We're adding someone new to the coven. Someone who will lend us more power and balance."

She turns her head to the side and fixates on one of the head-stones. "Are you asking me or telling me?"

My cock twitches again. Fuck. I cannot get enough of her. "Both. I've already made him the offer, but if you're against it, then I'll rescind it."

"Who is it?"

I shift a little, wanting to thrust my cock again but trying to be a good boy while we have this conversation. "Felix Crane."

She clenches around me, her body going rigid. "Why Felix?"

My cock swells as more of her juices trickle out. "He's from a founding family. He belongs in our coven, Maur. And I think he's just as obsessed with you as we are."

She lifts her hips and slides up the ridges of my cock. "What about this? Will he get to do this?"

I reach around and press on her clit. "Yeah, he will," I rasp as I start fucking her again. "But only if I get to watch."

She bucks at the word, and I lose it. I pull out so I can flip her over onto her back. I yank her legs apart and shove my cock back inside her.

She gazes up at me, her eyes glowing. "Will it make you happy, Riot?"

I cum faster this time, never taking my eyes off hers as I un-load it inside her. "Yes, love. It will make us all happy." I thrust a couple more times, milking her. "He can help us take Nocturnus away from the elders."

Her eyes widen, and I feel her pulse kick up a notch. "Good. They don't deserve to be in charge. We do."

"Agreed. Now, let's get you cleaned up." I lick the cum off her thighs like it's ice cream. *Any excuse I can get to taste her, I'll take.* "There's just one thing . . ."

She sits up and pulls her skirt down as she waits expectantly.

I slick my damp hair back off my forehead and sigh. "He hasn't said yes yet. We need you to help convince him."

Maureen snickers and hops off the bike. "Well, I have his class in about twenty minutes . . . Fuck. That's what this is all about. You want me walking in there smelling like sex and cum."

I wrap my hand around her throat. *This* was about me fucking *my* girl while she rode *my* bike. Does it hurt that he will sense your arousal within seconds? No, it does not. But don't think that I have any ulterior motives to fucking you other than the fact that I crave your pussy around my cock every second of the fucking day."

She licks her lips as she fixates on mine. "Okay."

I kiss her hard, relishing the way she tastes on my tongue. "I'm doing all of this because . . ." I press my forehead to hers. "Because I fucking love you. I've loved you since that night in the bathroom at Wickford Hollow."

She smiles and clutches my hands to her chest. "Riot . . ." I love you so fucking hard it hurts sometimes."

I kiss her again, softer this time, as I explore her sweet mouth with my tongue. "You're my ruin and my death, Firecracker. And I hate you just as much as I love you."

She sniffles as she laughs. "Right back at ya, psycho."

I hold her to my chest for a little longer before I drive her back to campus. I know she'll succeed in convincing Felix. Maureen Blackwell is impossible to resist. He's only prolonging the inevitable. He knew the second he first saw her that he'd do just about anything for her and anything to be next to her.

It starts as a quiet longing but then quickly festers into full-blown obsession. I almost wish I could be there to see the look on his face when she walks in, smelling of cum and sweat and filth.

I drop her off at the edge of the forest and give Valentin a nod as he arrives to keep watch. "If all goes well, we'll initiate him this weekend."

198

"Who the fuck would say no to being in Nocturnus?" Val grumbles. He lights up a joint and leans back against a tree.

The shadows inside me flutter. "No one if they know what's good for them."

Val takes a puff off the joint and passes it to me. His cheeks bulge as he holds in the smoke before blowing it out. "Our fathers have no fucking clue the destruction that's coming for them."

Nocturnus is meant to be ours. Not theirs. They're too greedy and sloppy to be in charge. They disrespect the very principles on which it was founded. But their first mistake was fucking with my firecracker.

They crossed a line they can't come back from. So, now they have to face their reckoning.

CHAPTER TWENTY-ONE

Maureen

T HERE'S AN UNKINDNESS OF RAVENS TRAILING ME AS I SKIRT ACROSS the grounds toward the black church with its iron spires. I'm accustomed to them now. It would be weird if they weren't following me. A calm falls over me now when they're near.

But it doesn't quell the nerves in my stomach today. Not when I know I have to walk into Felix Crane's class wearing no panties and cum still stuck to my thighs. Especially now that Riot has invited him into our coven.

I open the door gently today, careful not to repeat my grand entrance from last week. I'm relieved to find students already in their seats and thankful I'm not late again. There's already so much attention focused on me.

Felix Crane pores over a stack of papers at the head of the church. The flickering torchlight hitting the stained glass windows, casts a purple glow over his face, highlighting his dark features. He hasn't noticed me yet, so I continue to gaze. To really look at him.

He's tall and slender, but his shoulders are broad, his jaw strong. As he reaches across his desk, his sleeve pulls back, revealing a swirl of black ink. I can't make out the design from this distance, but I am curious to know what this man has tattooed on his body.

I imagine him having lines of poetry down his muscular back. My cheeks flush when he looks up and catches me gawking. He stares knowingly into my eyes. But there's no trace of his usual mischief or deviancy. I can't figure him out—and it annoys me.

After I sit down in one of the pews, I realize I left my book bag in the library. Fuck. I'm sure he'll love calling me out in front of everyone.

The bell tolls as the last of the students shuffle in. But Felix doesn't address us right away. He stares into nothingness, quiet and pensive. The tension builds as we wait for him to speak. For him to break the stillness. *Waiting for him to unleash his poetic violence into the room. To fill our ears and mouths with the need for more.*

The silence is unnerving.

I keep my legs crossed, afraid that when I do finally hear his voice, my body will betray me. *Please, Jude, don't let me drip all over this pew.*

I sneak another glance at him as he ambles down the center aisle, disheveled and unkempt. His necktie is missing, and the first two buttons of his shirt are undone. Usually, his black hair is slicked back in thick waves, but as he moves closer, I can see his strands starting to curl and go in different directions.

"I spent my morning in the graveyard," he calls out, his voice bouncing off the church walls.

So Riot brought him there too. How fucking poetic.

Some giggles mixed with gasps break out amongst the class.

Felix flashes a grin. "I was offered immortality. Well, something like it, I should say."

My heart beats fast as he slowly makes his way closer to my pew.

"I was given a choice between watching devils from afar or," he raises his finger in the air, "trading in my soul for horns."

A few more students laugh out loud.

My skin heats. So this is how he wants to go about it? A full-on spectacle. As the rage in my chest builds, my sigils flare. Especially the one on the back of my neck. Erebus.

"You know what I love about graveyards? They have no need for the living. None whatsoever." The smirk on his face is smug, cocky, as he keeps coming down the aisle. "Open up your books to page forty-seven. There you will find Edgar Allan Poe's *Spirit of the Dead*."

I sit with my hands crossed in my lap, my cheeks red, amidst the ruffling of pages.

"Miss Blackwell." He gazes down at me in amusement, well aware that I have no bag and, therefore, no book. "I'd like you to read the first four lines of the poem."

My pulse ticks. The guy next to me snickers. The redhead glares at me. Fuck. I'm tempted to get up and run. "I-I don't have my book. Sorry."

Felix nods. "Last week, you were late, but at least you were prepared. Maybe I should allow you to be tardy from now on."

The class bursts out laughing, and I want to crawl under the pew and die. I also want to slap him for being such a dick. "It won't happen again," I manage to squeak out.

He leans over and places his copy in my lap. "Read from mine."

I nod and swallow down the lump in my throat. Sweat beads on the back of my neck as he lurks over my shoulder.

He smells like vetiver—earthy and smoky. It's intoxicating as fuck.

I clear my throat before reciting the poem.

Thy soul shall find itself alone,

'Mid dark thoughts of the gray tombstone—
Not one, of all the crowd, to pry.
Into thine hour of secrecy.

He stands upright but doesn't budge from the back of my pew.

"What do you think Poe means by *hour of secrecy?*"

The white-haired boy I sat next to last week reluctantly raises his hand. "The dead can't tell secrets."

Felix air high-fives him. "That's right. The dead can't speak our secrets."

I can't help but snicker.

"Did you have something to add, Miss Blackwell?" He leans back over me.

I have to turn to the side to look him in the eyes, our faces almost touching. "In my experience, I find that the dead don't shut up."

Felix smirks and snatches the book off my lap. He holds it up, using one of his fingers to bookmark the page. "Aha, yes. That brings us to the next stanza. Read it to yourselves."

I roll my eyes. He's so fucking dramatic. This man is literally driving me insane. He makes me want to have a cocktail at eight in the morning.

Felix and I lock eyes over everyone's bowed heads. He stalks back over and shoves his book in my face again. "*Be still,*" he rasps. The tension between us is excruciating, but I tear my eyes away from him and look down to read the second part.

Be silent in that solitude,
Which is not loneliness—for then
The spirits of the dead who stood
In life before thee are again
In death around thee—and their will
Shall overshadow thee: be still.

Does this man only speak through poetry? For fuck's sake. I glare up at him and shove the book against his chest. "Clever," I whisper.

He winks before stalking back up the aisle. "The dead can't tell secrets unless the dead rise again. But then they are *undead*, are they not? This brings us back to the original assessment of... all together now."

The class collectively shouts as he lifts his hands up, "*The dead can't tell secrets.*"

You know who else can't talk, asshole? Cocky professors with their tongues cut out.

My Erebus sigil stings. I rub my neck and try not to freak out that it's ice cold to the touch.

Felix's lips are moving, but I can't hear what he says. My ears are ringing. Swelling. As a sharp pain shoots up my spine, I grab the pew in front of me. *Fuck.* My head feels like it's going to explode.

I don't know how long I've been like this, but it feels eternal. Endless. The other students are too focused on how hot he is to notice me having a meltdown. My limbs feel heavy. Weak. I suck in a deep breath and try to will my other sigils awake.

Something's happening.

The students look toward the door.

I can't breathe.

Fuck.

Felix's eyes widen when they land on me.

The ringing gets louder. Fuck, are my ears are bleeding? He smiles and looks at his watch. I wish I could hear what he's saying.

I see everyone getting up and putting their books away. Are they leaving? There's no way we've been in class an hour already. I try to move, but I can't.

Felix rushes toward me and places his hand on my shoulder. My ears pop just in time to hear the room descend into chaos. A cold draft hits my back as the church doors fly open. The silence gets sucked out like a vacuum as their shrieks fill the room.

I spin around to see at least twenty ravens dive inside the church. They peck and squawk at my classmates, sending them running down the steps.

What in the actual fuck?

Felix traces his finger over the back of the pew, the one I'm holding onto for dear life. Panic washes over me. The wood is . . . cracked.

"Wh-what the fuck did I just do?" I stammer.

He looks back and forth between me and the church doors, shaking his head. He's going to leave. He's a fucking coward. My knees tremble as I struggle to stand, my adrenaline still racing through my veins.

But when he gets to the doors, he closes them, and turns back around to face me. *So he's not a coward. I'm just a judgy bitch who* jumps to assumptions.

"You're staying?" I hold onto the back of the pew to steady myself.

He moves like a predator, slow and calculated, inching toward me like I'm a timid deer who's about to run off. "Do you want me . . . in your coven?"

A tingling sensation swells in my belly. I don't know if it's from whatever the fuck just happened or from the way he's looking at me right now—like I'm some fragile flower that needs to be sheltered from the storm.

"He was right about your eyes . . . They glow. Riot says we'll be stronger if you join us—because you're a Crane."

Felix closes the gap between us and towers over me. "That's not what I asked, Little Raven. What do *you* want?"

I want this heat between us to either set me on fire or fizzle the fuck out. I can't breathe with him this close. "I'm losing control, and it scares me," I whisper.

His chest heaves with the same need. "What triggered you? Was it the poem?"

I shake my head and collapse back into my seat. "No. I think it was you. You said something that made me angry. But I'm really just angry with myself. I keep stifling what I feel... what I want."

Felix sits down next to me, our legs touching. "You haunt me. Just like Annabel Lee haunts Poe."

I take a deep breath and surrender to the power of his scent. That earthy musky fragrance that reminds me of a rainstorm. "It's about so much more than wanting you, Felix. I need you... It was you who pulled me out of that tailspin I was just in. It was your light."

He unbuttons his shirt and strips it off, revealing his white ribbed tank top underneath. I try not to gawk at his corded muscles. Try not to salivate over the tattoos covering every inch of his arms.

He leans back against the pew. "Can I hold your hand?"

I slip my sweaty palm into his. As our fingers lace, a flutter of nerves churns in my belly. "Do you want to be with us, Felix? I need your answer."

He turns to look at me, and I almost cry. There is peace in his brown eyes. "Yes, Maur. My answer has always been yes."

I let out a sigh of relief. Suddenly, the thought of not having him be a part of this feels like spiritual suicide.

There's only one thing that could ruin it all. Villette. She hates Nocturnus. And after she finds out about all of this... she's going to hate me.

How the fuck am I going to manage this one?

Footsteps echo behind us.

"You two all right?"

I let go of Felix's hand and leap from the pew. I rush toward Val and fall into his arms. He rubs my back. "It's okay, love. Tell me what happened."

Felix stands to face us. "She lost control, and the ravens attacked my students."

Val sighs. "So, you in or out then?"

I gaze up at Val. "He said yes to my crazy."

Felix rests his hand on my shoulder. The same way he did to break me out of my trance. "*In absentia lucis, tenebrae vincunt.* You're not crazy, Little Raven. You've just been swallowed up by too much darkness."

Val side-eyes him. "That's what Nocturnus is."

Felix shakes his head. "No. It's what you do. But dark cannot exist without light. Even Edgar Allan Poe knew that when he lost his Annabel Lee."

I walk between them as we make our way back to Nocturnus House. As we pass the Nest, I stop and look up at the ominous building.

"I need to talk to your sister first. She's been nothing but kind to me, and I refuse to keep this from her." My heart literally hurts at the thought of what she's going to think of me. How she's going to feel when she learns her big brother is becoming everything she stands against.

Felix grabs my hand. "We'll tell her together."

Val glares down at our clasped hands. "I'll wait in the car. I left it in the lot this morning. Don't take too long. Riot and Atlas are waiting."

We take the elevator up to Villette's floor, our nerves wrecked. When she opens the door, her gaze falls to our clasped hands, her smile fading instantly. Confusion turns to fear and then to anger.

"*No*," she pleads.

"Villette, let me explain," I beg.

She shakes her head and backs away from us. "Felix, no. Not you too. Papa will not allow it."

Felix gently grabs her shoulders. "I'm a grown man, Lettie. I don't need our father's permission. This is what I want."

"And you." She charges toward me. "You're supposed to be my friend. Ever since you got here, people have turned up either dead or missing. But I stuck by you. And this is how you repay me? By going after my brother? Isn't three guys enough for you?"

Fuck. It's worse than I thought. So much worse. "Villette, please. I didn't mean to hurt you. We're drawn to each other, Felix, and me...We're connected."

"She's why I came here, Lettie. I've been haunted by her ever since you sent me that picture of the two of you at the ball. When I learned who she was, who Nocturnus was, I couldn't stay away any longer. Papa pulled some strings to get me a position here at Tenebrose."

"But you lied to him about it," she yells. "You took advantage of him so you could drink poison and stab people and fuck my best friend." She chokes back a sob.

Tears stream down my cheeks. I'm breaking her heart. I'm ruining everything. Fuck.

Felix cups her face. "You know how I've struggled," he admits. "I've been in a dark place for a long time. Something evil had a hold on me. That's gone now. Every second I spend here...with her...I feel freer."

She looks down at the floor. "I thought you came here to be closer to me. I was so happy to have my brother back. But now...they're going to take you away. You'll always choose them first."

"NO," I shout. I shake my head. "I won't let that happen. You're his sister. I won't let him choose us over you. I promise."

There aren't many things I have control over right now. But I'll be damned if I let anyone else break her spirit. She's a good person. The best person I know. The guys will not fight me on this. There are some things that are too sacred to break.

"Mirame, Lettie. Look at me. I will always protect you. I love

you more than anything. Please give me your blessing." Within moments, he goes from looking like a cocky professor to a scared schoolboy. His vulnerability is his strength. There are so many layers to this man that I've only barely scratched the surface on.

She wipes her eyes on his shirt. "Because I love you, I will try . . . But *you*," she glares daggers at me. "You're canceled. I don't want to be your friend anymore."

I bite my lip to stifle the sob that's been building in my chest.

Damn.

"Lettie," Felix pleads.

"No, it's okay. She has every right to hate me. I'm gonna go wait in the car with Val. You two take your time." I force a smile and walk out the door.

I walk as fast as I can toward the car. The ravens cry with me as the tears stream down my face. Are we doing the right thing? Villette is right. Everything we touch turns to shit. Riot, Atlas, and Valentin ruined me. I ruined them. And now we are going to ruin her brother.

I get in the car and slam the door.

Val arches an eyebrow. "I'm guessing that didn't go well."

I glare at him. "I don't want to talk about it."

He rests his hand on my knee. "I'm sorry you lost your friend. But I don't care who we have to hurt if it keeps you safe and all of us together."

I cross my arms and gaze out the window. "But at what cost, Val? Maybe it's too high a price to pay."

"We're all making sacrifices, Maur. Seeing you hold his hand . . ." Val looks down at his lap.

I choke back another sob. "Then let's figure out another way." He holds my hand to his cheek. "No. We need him. I'm just being a selfish prick because I secretly want you all to myself. Even from Riot and Atlas."

Our greed for each other knows no bounds it seems.

M VIOLET

My heart breaks all over again when I see Felix skulking toward the car. "People really think we are the devils of Raven's Gate, don't they?"

Val snickers. "Yeah, and we'll see all of them in hell."

Felix slides into the back seat, and it's all I can do not to tell him I changed my mind. That I made a mistake, and he should stay away from me. From all of us.

But I don't.

Because I'm a selfish prick too.

CHAPTER TWENTY-TWO

Felix

I'M FINALLY HERE. So many endless nights and seasons longing for this moment, and I've finally arrived. Standing in the center, her black robe hangs slightly open, revealing a peek of her nakedness underneath. My little raven is more beautiful than her picture. More exquisite than I ever could imagine. I'd happily join any cult or religion for her.

My heart beats so fast and hard, I'm afraid that they'll hear it. That its thunderous drum will echo off these cavern walls and shatter them. I've been trying so hard to hold back. The first night I met her in person, at *Swallow*, tested me... tempted me.

When I watched them touch her, *fuck her* in the corner of the bar, I almost died from need. From wanting to feel her wet pussy

on my fingers. To taste her venomous tongue. And later that night, as I lie in bed, I replayed it over and over while I stroked my cock, making myself cum with her name on my lips.

My knees tremble now. I'm so close to her and them and everything I've ever wanted. To share this sickness. This greed and lust for all that is unholy. For all that is poetic and dark and alive. I want to feel the weight of it crush me. To be buried under the rubble of all her beautiful destruction.

Riot, Atlas, and Valentin stand still in their robes. They stare back at me, their faces masked in bronze. Their eyes glow as she approaches and hands them a silver dagger.

My pulse increases in anticipation, my cock swelling underneath my robe. The energy between us is electric. I'm afraid to move or speak or even take a breath. For fear it would disrupt the symmetry.

Riot raises his hand and points to the center of the room, to the altar—a large stone table. Its edges are lined with the leaves of nightshade and oleander. He beckons me over.

"Take off your robe and lie down when you're ready," Riot commands. His voice is rough and thick, much like the air in this cavern.

As I look at each of them, the heat in my body rises. But it's not until I lock eyes with her that I become another version of myself. The one I've kept hidden. I untie my robe and let it fall to the ground. She bites down on her bottom lip, aroused by what she sees—me standing before them exposed, raw and naked aside from the tattoos that cover most of my body.

I notice the guys admiring me as well. The way they shift their stances to accommodate their growing erections, their throats bobbing as they try to gulp down their ache.

I smirk from behind my mask. Ritual is power. And the cock between my legs is how I will wield mine. They will each have a piece of me before the night is over. I want to touch all of them. But I want her the most.

The stone is ice-cold against my back as I lie back upon it, my feet dangling off the end. They close in, surrounding me on the altar in a circle. My fingers tremble in anticipation.

Riot caresses my arm with the tip of the blade. "We'll each mark you tonight. Four of us, four sigils. It will be painful. There will be poison and blood and fluid. If you survive, you'll be one of us when it's done."

I release a deep breath as my heart threatens to explode inside my chest. "I'm ready."

Atlas stands over me and removes his robe. I have to blink a few times to make sure I'm not hallucinating. A king cobra snake slithers down the length of him. It twists up his arms and around his neck.

Holy fuck.

My muscles tense as he holds the head of the snake between my legs. It hisses and snaps, lunging at my flesh like it hasn't eaten in days.

"Try to stay still, Felix. I'm going to let Zeus bite you. But I'll suck the poison out before it hits your heart." Atlas's eyes are crazed, wild, glowing like two pools of neon light.

I nod and grip the edges of the stone table.

He lets the snake loose on my leg. Fuck, I shouldn't be this turned on. Knowing that this bite is going to hurt. That the poison is going to be excruciating. That it will briefly paralyze me. But the sweet release after . . . Fuck.

The snake's skin is smooth and rough at the same time. Its head fans out as it pauses near my inner thigh. Atlas hovers over it, ready to wrestle it away. While it's hard to take my eyes off the cobra, this Greek-looking Adonis is giving it a run for its money.

Atlas is a beautiful man, fearless and unhinged. I wonder how many times he's wrestled this snake and won.

"That's good. Look at me, Felix," he coaxes.

I hear the hiss before I feel the sting. I bite my lip to keep from screaming as Zeus sinks his fangs deep into the fleshiest part of

"Mors tua, vita mea," Riot chants. "Your death, my life." He dips his fingers into the blood and smears it over my abdomen.

My throat is dry, my head spinning. I list things in my head to keep myself from passing out—adrenaline, endorphins, eyes like burnt honey, release, agony... I recite poems in my mind. These words bring me comfort and peace amidst this violence.

I gasp as he thrusts the tip of the blade into my flesh. He is not gentle or soft. The pain is unthinkable. *Unimaginable.* I watch as he carves the symbol into my leg, mutilating my flesh in ways it has never been violated before.

"Now, this is really going to hurt," Riot declares. He presses the dagger to my bite wound. "*Serpentis.*"

By the time Atlas is done, the poison is gone, and I'm left with a lingering vibration in my core. It pulses inside me like a second heartbeat.

Fuck, I need to touch her. I arch my back and lick the blood off my lips.

I feel her small hands on my shoulders. "I'm right here."

This rush of adrenaline, the euphoria, it's like I'm high and drunk and sober all at the same time. I taste blood on my lips from my desperate attempt to keep quiet. But I don't want silence anymore.

Atlas darts back over, snakeless. "You're doing so good." He kisses my thigh before he starts to suck on the wound. His lips are soft and warm. He moans as he drinks from me, his eyes glowing when they lock with mine.

Through my blurred vision, I watch Atlas guide the snake off my leg with seduction, not force. He strokes it gently until it re-leases its grip on me. I don't feel the pain from the bite anymore—just the feeling of being suffocated by the toxin that's trying to take over my body.

my thigh. My hips jerk involuntarily as the venom rushes into my bloodstream.

His fingers trail farther down, and I can't help but whimper as he wipes the blood around the base of my cock.

I arch my back as he cups my balls. "*Fuck*," I grit out.

"That's it, Felix. Surrender to Serpentis. The power of the snake." Riot wraps his hand around my shaft and squeezes before stroking up and rolling his thumb over the tip. A trickle of pre cum oozes out. He licks it off his finger, and I almost black out from need.

"In absentia lucis, tenebrae vincunt," Atlas murmurs.

Valentin is next. He tilts my head to the side and presses a soft kiss to my neck. He whispers in my ear. "Now you will get the Lux sigil. For light. So you can balance all our crazy."

A smirk pulls at the corners of my lips, but it's short-lived as Val drags the tip of the blade through my flesh without warning. This time, I scream, unafraid and unashamed to embrace every twisted and beautiful layer of this ritual.

My little raven coos in my ear. "You can do this, Felix . . . I need you."

Her voice gives me life. Her breath on my cheek is worth more than any poem that has ever been written in the history of the world.

Val licks the blood from my neck. Shivers race down my spine.

"Good boy, Felix."

"My turn," she murmurs.

My little raven strips from her robe and climbs onto the stone table with me. I can barely breathe as I drink in the sight of her. Her nipples are dark red, hard, and swollen. She parts her legs, straddling me, her pussy wet and glistening. She sits on my stomach, her knees bent.

"I would endure a thousand cuts for you," I proclaim.

She nods and slides down.

Oh fuck. I need her. Yes.

"I want you inside me when I mark you." She fists my cock and lowers herself onto it, sitting all the way down.

I draw in a sharp breath as the heat from her core envelops me.

This is how I want to die someday. With my cock inside her perfect cunt. "You can stay here as long as you like, Little Raven."

She moans as she rocks back and forth. "I'm so full. Fuck."

I'm in awe that she's taken the entire length of me inside her. I want to squeeze her nipples, but Atlas and Val hold down my wrists. Riot puts the blade in her hand and guides it over my chest.

"Do it just like you did it to Atlas before."

She digs in deep, her eyes feral as she carves into me. But I don't care about my mutilated flesh. I don't feel the pain or smell the blood. All I feel is her tight wet pussy sliding up and down my cock. I lift my hips, angling her up so I can slide in deeper. I want to stretch her till she cries, till she begs for my cum to soothe her raw flesh.

After she finishes marking me, she cries out, "Ruina nostra salus." *Our ruin is our salvation.*

Riot caresses her hips and thighs. "Easy, love. It's not time to cum yet."

She whines when he pulls her off me.

My body aches for her. Fuck. I force myself to take a deep breath.

Valentin and Atlas help me off the altar table. I stagger as the blood rushes back to my head. "Is the ritual over?" I look down at the bloody mess they've created on my body.

Riot shakes his head. "Almost. This way, Felix."

My cock is throbbing so much it's hard to walk, but I follow them out of the cavern and into another chamber. Maureen looks back at me every few feet. It takes all my strength not to pounce on her.

This next room is warmer. Instead of a stone altar in the center, there's a bed. A black leather couch sits across from it. *For view-ing pleasure.* Hundreds of candles flicker across the room, creating an atmosphere of sin.

DIRTY LITTLE SAINT

This is what I've dreamed about for so long. To be part of something so depraved and devious, so fucking filthy.

The bed is stripped down to just a black sheet. My little raven removes her robe again and sits down on the edge of it.

I follow the others and join them in taking a seat on the couch across from her. My heart pounds, thumping in my ears and head.

Fuck.

Riot leans forward. "Spread yourself open."

With the bronze mask still hiding her face and her naked body perched on the corner of the bed, she looks like the Goddess of Death herself. Like my dark angel come to save me from the madness in my mind. She opens her legs and waits for the next command.

And I don't dare take my eyes off her.

CHAPTER TWENTY-THREE

Maureen

T HERE IS POWER IN THIS ROOM. SEXUAL POWER THAT MAKES US stronger. I need this so fucking bad. My belly flutters as I perch on the bed across from them, their masked faces watching me. They will know my pleasure. My ecstasy. And I will give them the display that they crave. *That I crave.*

"Spread your pussy and hold it open," Riot quips, his voice cold and calculating. This is how he is. He shows passion through darkness.

My skin tingles as I peel back the lips of my pussy. Felix licks his lips as he fixates on it. Val and Atlas's eyes glow brighter than the candles. They watch me under Riot's command with a brutality in their eyes that's both hot and terrifying.

Riot stalks over. He tilts my chin up. "Lie back on the bed. And don't you dare move your hands."

Oh, fuck. I fucking love being at his mercy.

I lie back, my feet still on the ground, and hold my pussy open for them to focus on.

"Felix, come. She's yours now too. Play with her," Riot rasps.

He stalks over without hesitation. I gaze up at his dark eyes, full of desire and thirst. He's beautiful—deep and tragic, like one of his poems. He's also fragile, like a lit fuse.

My belly flutters when he kneels between my legs. He runs his hands over my thighs before pushing my fingers away and re-placing them with his own. "You don't know me." He gently peels my pussy open. "You have no idea how deeply I've ached for you. All the nights I imagined touching you just like this."

I quiver as he rolls his tongue up my slit slowly, moaning as he laps up my juices. "Felix... I want to know you."

"I can show you." He slides the rope out from the loops in his robe. He takes his time tying one end around my wrists. They're snug but not hurting me until he pulls them over my head and wraps the rest of the rope around my neck to hold them in place behind me.

My stomach flips. I don't dare squirm, or else I'll choke my-self out.

Felix stalks over to Atlas and removes his rope. "There's freedom in restraint, Little Raven. To be truly in control is to surrender."

A spasm ripples through my core as he pulls my legs together and wraps the rope around them from my hips all the way down to my ankles.

Valentin, mesmerized, tosses his rope to Felix. "Fuck, that's beautiful."

Felix smirks as he towers over me. "Like a bird in a cage... who's too blind to see it's been unlocked this whole time."

My heart pounds in my chest as I watch him wrap the rope around my chest and over my shoulders, looping it around each breast before knotting it off around my belly. He tugs on each of them to make sure they're tight.

I can't move an inch. "What are you going to do to me, Felix?"

"Shhh, relax." He slides his finger down my slit, and it's pure torture. I can't open my legs. Every time I squirm, the ropes get tighter.

Riot, Atlas, and Val nestle back against the couch to watch. And that feral streak in me springs to life. The act of being watched turns me on so much I can barely breathe. That *they* are going to watch him do filthy things to me.

He takes the fourth rope, the one from Riot's robe, and wraps it around my face, forcing my lips to part around it. I shudder as I try not to choke on my own saliva when the taste of resin fills my mouth.

"The ropes are so delicate on their own. But give them a purpose, and they become unbreakable. Just like you," Felix coos. He kneels naked on the bed next to me. "You have never known pleasure like this before."

He rubs the tip of his cock against my nipple, stimulating every nerve in my body. A moan hangs in my throat as he does the same to the other one.

I feel like I'm caught between ecstasy and sheer terror, not knowing what this man will do to me next.

His pre cum leaks out, and he uses it to paint my lips. "I want to keep you like this all night." He runs his fingers underneath the ropes that drape across my belly. "Would you let me do that, Little Raven? Let me play with you all night like this?"

Goosebumps spread across my skin. I whimper over the rope, desperate to swallow and yet strangely aroused that I can't. I can't nod my head without choking myself out. So I try to scream through the gag.

He drags the tip of his cock up and down my slit. "I'm going to fuck these pretty lips of yours."

Oh, fuck. Another spasm rolls through me as he wedges his shaft in between my pussy lips and slides up and down, rubbing his veiny ridges against my tender flesh.

My eyes roll back as my clit shudders and releases multiple bursts of tingles. I cry out, practically begging for mercy with the ache in my voice.

Riot, Atlas, and Valentin join us on the bed. They chant softly,

"Mors vincit omnia."

"Yes," Felix moans as his cum spurts out and drips down my slit. "This is a slow death. An end to things that no longer serve us. And death always wins."

Riot and Valentin roll the tips of their cocks over my nipples, stroking themselves as they chase their release. Atlas loosens the rope around my face. But he doesn't take it off. Instead, he raises it slightly so he can slide his cock inside my mouth.

I gag as he pushes all the way to the back of my throat. Fuck. They are destroying me, brutalizing my body for their own plea-sure. What the fuck does that say about me? That every tiny little spark of stimulation leaves me wanting more.

Atlas pulls out and Riot goes in, followed by Valentin. They take turns fucking my mouth, choking me, bruising my lips with their viciousness. And Felix watches as he continues to rub my pussy raw, making me cum over and over again until I have noth-ing left.

Our connection deepens as the rush of our release unleashes our sigils, awakening them to each other.

"Relax your throat," Riot demands. His cock throbs against the insides of my cheeks before a burst of hot thick cream rushes out. He lifts my head so I don't choke. And I swallow every drop.

"Thatta girl," Riot praises.

Before I can catch my breath, Val thrusts in after him. He

grips my face tightly in his hands. "Such a good fucking girl," He thrusts hard as I suck and scrape my teeth across his veiny shaft. He twists my swollen nipples until they burn while his cum shoots down my throat.

"I want to taste them on you." Atlas shoves his tongue in my mouth, kissing me deeply, and lapping up the sticky cream.

"Mmm, now I'm gonna fill you so fucking full again."

Stars dot my vision when he slides his cock inside my mouth again. My lips tingle around his engorged cock, his ridges twitching against my cheeks.

"Fuck." He pulls out. "Open your mouth and stick out your tongue for me, pretty girl."

Another spasm rocks my core as Felix fingers me, rubbing my clit in circles with his thumb.

I stretch my tongue out as far as it will go and Atlas slaps his cock onto it. He strokes himself furiously as he cums. I gag, my body jerking and contorting as his cum races down my throat.

"Yeah, pretty girl. Fucking choke on me."

Their hands and mouths are everywhere now, stroking me, sucking my nipples, pinching my nub, licking my belly. They leave teeth marks on my breasts and red imprints of their fingers on my thighs. I am drowning in them. Falling into an abyss of sensory overload, each orgasm hitting me deeper than the last.

There is no control. No boundaries. With our limbs and mouths entwined, we are no longer separate from each other. Our deviant bones will crumble together in heaps of poisoned ash in the end. It's the devil's fate.

And yet, amidst their darkness, I feel his light. Felix casts it on my shadows, setting me free as he confines me.

When the rope falls away from my face, I lie still as they work together on releasing me from my bonds. They spend the rest of the night caring for me, washing my skin, applying sweet-scented

I don't have to lift a single limb.

DIRTY LITTLE SAINT

ointments to my rope burns and scratches. I relish their soft, soothing hands massaging my neck and shoulders, kneading their strong fingers into my thighs as they coax me back to life.

I drift in and out of sleep, barely conscious as they lie me down on a lavish bed. I'm tucked into a thick, fluffy comforter, surrounded by soft pillows. I feel gentle hands in my hair, fingers caressing my arms and legs, soft kisses urging me to return to my deep slumber as they surround me on the bed like a cocoon. My beautiful dark devils.

CHAPTER TWENTY-FOUR

Valentin

T HE DEPRAVITY IN THE EREBUS FAMILY IS NO SECRET. IT FESTERS IN OUR minds like a sickness. My father was so fucking demented he drove my mother away. I haven't seen that woman since I was thirteen. But I had my Uncle Julian. He helped raise me. He was always the one who would comfort me after my father would beat the shit out of me. But Julian has his demons too. And right now, I'm looking at one of them. And I'm not sure what the fuck I just stumbled into.

"You're fucking a ghost?" I immediately help myself to a glass of his twenty-five-year aged scotch. "Isn't she a little old for you?"

He snickers and gives me that look he used to give me when I

mouthed off. "Watch it, Val. I won't have you disrespect Jessamine in my house."

Has he lost his fucking mind?

"Have you forgotten about her luring Maureen into the woods so Zeke could torture her? Or how she locked Libra and Villette in the basement of the ballroom at the winter solstice? I know you like dangerous pussy, Uncle, but that chick is certifiable. And we're pretty sure she's behind every bad fucking thing that's happened between our families."

He snatches the glass out of my hand mid-sip. "It's a little early for booze, Val. Jessamine is done with all of that. I've been helping her come to terms with Silas being gone. And the fact that nothing she does is going to bring him back."

It annoys me when he treats me like a child. I'm not that cowering little boy anymore. I peer down the hall to see Jessamine lingering in his bedroom doorway. "I'd like to hear it from her if you don't mind."

He sighs and beckons for her to come forward. "It's all right, love. Come on out."

She's not what I imagine a ghost would look like. It's not like the movies where they float around all wisplike. No, this chick is as solid as Uncle Julian and me.

"Is this true?" I ask her. "Are you done going after Maureen?"

She nods sheepishly. "I'm sorry. I didn't mean to hurt her."

I can't believe this girl has been around for over a hundred years. She seems so childlike. "You realize Maureen is like your great-great niece, right? You shouldn't betray your own blood."

"I know. Zeke promised I'd be with Silas again. I would have done anything for him . . . but I see that I was wrong, Julian—I mean, Professor Erebus—has made me see how wrong I was."

This just got even weirder. I can only imagine what these two are doing. I look past her and catch a glimpse of restraints on the bedposts in his room. "So I should just take your word for it?"

"You will take *my* word for it, Val. Have I ever let you down?"

Uncle Julian stands protectively in front of his new ghost girlfriend. He's right. I have no reason to doubt or not trust him. He has shielded me so many times—looked after me my whole life. "All right, Uncle. But she's your responsibility. I'm counting on you to keep her in check."

"Understood." He turns toward her. "Go wait for me in the bedroom. I'll be right there."

Her eyes light up, and she skips down the hallway, obeying him without question.

I snatch the glass of scotch back and knock it down before he can rip it out of my hands again. "She looks at you like a king. Well done."

He rolls his eyes. "Don't judge me, boy. I know what kind of dark and depraved shit you and your friends are into."

I chuckle as I remember the ritual with Felix. "You have no idea."

Julian stalks over to the window and peers out. "I'm going to tell you something that could get me killed. But you have to promise me if I do. . . . you need to make sure you win."

My stomach knots. There's a hushed, ominous tone to his voice that I don't like one bit. "Win what? I'm going to need you to clarify."

His eyes darken when he looks back at me. Between the hard lines on his face, I can see the boyish charm and youth that used to be there. "Holden Graves has called a meeting of the elders. I don't know when, but it will take place at Graves Estate."

Fuck. They haven't had a meeting in years. Mostly, they handle business on the phone or via teleconference. The ritual side of Nocturnus has become overshadowed by their greed. It's become more of a business than a spirituality.

What the fuck are our fathers up to?

"Then I'll tell you our plan, Uncle. We plan to retire them soon. To restore Nocturnus to what our ancestors intended."

"And what is that, Val? The lines are blurred more than ever now." Julian concedes and joins me in a glass of scotch.

"Power and greed are two very different things, Uncle, and yet they get confused all the time. For us, Nocturnus is about ritual and sacrifice. It's about connecting to that power that makes us nearly immortal. Untouchable. And then Holden crossed the fucking line."

I clench my fists to keep my hands from shaking. Just the mere mention of what happened that night at Graves Estate sends my temper flaring with the need to murder something. "Our fathers betrayed those vows the second they used Maureen as a whipping post to quell their own perverse desires."

Julian hangs his head. "They should not have touched her. The interest they've taken in her is concerning. It will only make things worse with Penny Blackwell."

I sigh and run my hands through my hair. "Agreed. It's up to us to fix this. Let me know if you find out when they're meeting. Atlas wants to pick them off one by one, but I think having them all in the same room will be better."

"Are you going to kill your father, Val?" Julian's eyes brim with tears.

Fuck knows I've dreamed of it since the very first time he hurt me. Every time my arm would start to heal, he'd break it again. "No. . . I don't know. But I can't speak for the others. And I won't stand in their way."

He nods. "It's none of my business, but did I see Felix Crane leaving Nocturnus House last week?"

The days tend to blur together now. For the past few weeks it's been ritual after ritual. Felix and Maureen have both moved into the house. The new recruits were moved to the guest quarters. After what happened with Zeke, we keep the initiates separate from Maureen now.

"He's joined us, yes," I quip. "There's not much else to say about it. It's not my story to tell."

"I'm sure his family is upset. The Cranes have always been no-mads. Felix's father made it very clear decades ago that there would never be a Crane in Nocturnus."

I shrug. "That's their fucking problem. Felix is a grown man. He came here on his own and chose to be a part of this."

My uncle stalks over to his desk and pulls out a box. He smooths his hand over the top of its velvet lid. "You should have been *my* son, Valentin. I'm sorry that you weren't. Life isn't fair like that sometimes."

I swallow down the lump in my throat. I would give anything for him to be my father. But my mother chose the wrong Erebus.

"You were there as much as you could be. That's all that matters."

He lifts the lid and pulls out a shiny gold skeleton key. "I'm giv-ing you the estate in the woods. The deed has already been trans-ferred into your name. It's the one thing I own that your father didn't steal from me."

My fingers tremble around the key as I take it from him. The cabin in the woods is my safe space. Which is why I was so furious when my father showed up there that day to threaten us. "Thank you, Uncle. You have no idea how much this means to me."

He pulls me in for a hug, patting me on the back. "You have to win, Val."

The affection almost brings me to tears. It's not something I've had a lot of in my life. "I promise you, we will."

He clears his throat to stifle the rising emotion in his voice. "I'll be in touch as soon as I find out when the meeting will take place. Be ready."

I stalk to the door to leave, but something else needs to be said first. I turn around and see that he's holding his composure together with a short thread. "I'm happy you have Jessamine now. You de-serve to be happy too."

I don't wait to hear his response lest we both collapse into piles of sniveling sobs.

With only a week away from the Spring Equinox Ball, the compulsion to be done with all this grows. Spring means the end of the semester. And a long summer break. I'd like to spend that break between Maureen's legs and not looking over her shoulder to make sure no one is about to stab her in the back.

I text everyone to meet me at Nocturnus House before throwing Mary Shelley into drive.
We're so close now.

Once I have everyone at the dining room table, I tell them everything my uncle shared. Riot paces around. He's quiet and pensive. I can practically see the wheels in his head spinning. Felix fiddles with the tattered pages of his copy of Edgar Allan Poe's collected works. The cover is so faded he must have read that book a thousand times. Atlas's eyes glow bright like seafoam, like a deadly storm about to wipe out an entire country.

"So we wait to hear back from Julian," Maureen is the first to break the silence.

Atlas slams his fist down on the table. "And if we don't? We should retire them one by one now. Get them alone."

I shake my head. "They've been expecting that. I would. But to ambush them when they are all together? They won't see that coming. We'll catch them off guard."

"Men are cocky that way. It's always been our downfall. History has proven that time and time again," Felix drawls. He looks very much like a professor today with his tweed jacket and brown slacks. He takes his reading glasses off and rubs his eyes. "When you say retire... what does that mean? Murder?"

Riot leans over the table toward him, their faces inches apart. "Death is too easy, my new friend." He pushes up his sleeves,

displaying his recent marks. "We will strip them of their sigils. Carve them right the fuck out. It's a worse fate."

Felix's eyes light up. "Like returning a canvas back to its original state... Fuck, that's beautiful."

"Yes, very poetic. And painful and messy. I'm going to enjoy every second of it," I snicker.

"So am I," Maureen snarls. "I can't wait to see the look on Holden's face when I'm the one standing over *him* with a dagger this time."

Atlas's chair groans as he stands up from the table in a rush. "If we're going to ambush them, then I need to start working on a new batch of poison. I'll be in the greenhouse if you need me."

Maureen rushes over to him and grabs his arm. "I'll come with you. You can teach me some more."

The hardened look in his eyes softens the second she touches him. He can't say no to her. He doesn't want to. I can see it in the way his body angles toward her like a magnet.

Atlas takes a deep breath and presses his forehead to hers. "Okay, pretty girl. Come on."

They clasp hands, giggling as they saunter off.

I also notice the way Felix watches the whole exchange. "You will have moments with her too," I say.

He chuckles in disbelief. "She's barely spoken to me since the night of my initiation."

Riot sits down across from him and leans back in his chair, exhaustion taking over his face. "You make her nervous. Maureen doesn't trust that easily. Just give it time."

"Seduce her with more poetry, Professor," I tease.

Felix smiles, but there's a sadness that lingers in his eyes. "Yeah, I'll try that. Thanks."

Poor guy. He looks like a wounded puppy every time she's around. So different from how the rest of us were when we met her.

To be fair, we initially hated her for being a Blackwell. But still, Felix might be more obsessed with her than we are.

Riot tilts his head to the side in that way that he does to appear warm and inviting. It's rare so I enjoy witnessing it when it happens. It's like his soul isn't completely black after all. "Do you have everything you need here, Felix? I want you to feel at home."

Felix smooths his hands over his poetry book again. "It's better than the graveyard," he teases.

I laugh. "How are your students reacting to you?"

"Well, some of them started eye-fucking me even harder. And others won't look at me at all. Maureen sits as far away from me as possible to avoid the gossip, but it's already out there. The only other professor who will acknowledge me in the faculty lounge is Dorian Harker."

It didn't take long for students to spot Felix coming out of Nocturnus House. And then there's the new sigils on his neck. . . . he's not really a turtleneck-wearing kind of guy. Rumors spread like wildfire in this place. Everyone knows he's one of us now.

Riot snorts. "I'd expect nothing less. Harker's got some skeletons of his own. He's got no business judging you. Fuck the others. No offense, Val, but your uncle has about as much charm as a plank of wood."

He's right about that. "True. But he's mostly keeping his distance because of us, not you, Felix. If anyone's watching him, they need to see that he can be trusted with information from the elders. Hanging out with us is not going to do him any favors."

Felix nods. "Makes sense. Now, I don't feel so bad about him slighting me."

While I lack human empathy mostly, I can't help but feel sorry for Felix. He came here on a whim with hearts in his eyes, got dragged into a feud between psychos, and quickly became the talk of all of Tenebrose for sleeping with a student, who now barely gives him the time of day.

M VIOLET

"Be patient with our firecracker," Riot quips as if reading my mind. He probably actually fucking can now at this point.

"She likes impulsive gestures," I add. "Try a different approach."

Felix gets up from the table. "Thanks. I'll work on it." He winks and heads upstairs. Now *that* guy is full of fucking charm. I'd drop my pants for him in a second if he asked me to. I can only imagine how he is in the classroom getting all passionate about poetry and fated mates and shit.

Riot snickers. "I can smell your desire from over here, Val. He's got you wound up a bit."

I tug at my collar in jest. "Fuck, who doesn't wanna be scolded by a hot brooding professor."

He nods in agreement. "I guess he's got us all wound up. Especially Maur. She's going to need to lean on his power."

"She will. I saw the way she looked at him after he stopped her meltdown in the church. She trusts him. But I think that scares her."

Maureen is our firecracker, our dark queen, but she's also a twenty-five-year-old girl with an abusive mother, a grandmother who abandoned her, and a drunk for a father. She's stronger than she once was, but she still holds onto that scared little girl. The one who ran for her life through the woods last year in Wickford Hollow. The girl who Riot found half-naked and broken in the bathroom.

Riot nods again. "He has a way with her."

We're her cage. Her ruin. But that's what she craves. Felix gives her too much space. If he can figure out how to lock a piece of him-self inside her, then she will give him everything. I just hope it hap-pens soon. We're gonna need his bond when we crash the elders' party. It's going to take all of us to win.

CHAPTER TWENTY-FIVE

Maureen

THERE'S SOMETHING ABOUT SPRING THAT MAKES EVERYTHING SEEM LESS tragic. The shadows shrink back a bit, revealing new growth and light. I can't help smiling as I walk across campus, drinking in the sight of new violets pushing up between the cracks in the walkways, basking in the scent of the bougainvillea winding around the iron spires as it creeps up the stone walls of Tenebrose. I wish I could bottle it up and give it to Villette as a peace offering. Every time I look at Felix, I think of how much she hates me. It breaks my heart over and over again. I need her to forgive me. To be my friend again. With Libra still out galivanting some-where and Bailey thousands of miles away, Villette is—*was*—my

only friend here. And with all the shit that's coming our way, I need her more than ever.

My stomach knots as I enter the black church, taking away all the hope of spring and new beginnings I felt on the walk over. It's the last week of classes before the summer break, but I wish I could skip it all. Every single one of my classmates either hates me or fears me. Especially the redhead and her posse of pick-me girls. All anyone can talk about these days is how I manipulated a professor into fucking me and joining Nocturnus. Ugh.

I take my usual seat in the last pew where I don't have to feel their eyes burning holes in the back of my head. And I can be far enough away from Felix so that it's more difficult for people to see the fire between us.

I know he can feel me pulling away. And I hate it. But ever since the night of his initiation, I've been racked with guilt. I'm ruining his fucking life. He should have stayed in Ever Graves, far away from our depravity and violence. Then Villette and I would still be friends, and he would be an esteemed and respected professor somewhere else. Some place where ravens aren't trying to attack his students.

"Good morning, everyone. We're going to read something different today. It's a poem that I wrote." He hands a boy in the first pew a stack of papers. "Please take one and pass it back."

My heart races. *Of course, he writes poetry.* The man is obsessed with it. I should have asked him before. I'm suddenly overcome with a need to read his work. To climb inside his mind and sit for a while.

There's an echo of excitement, oohs, and aahs as the stack of papers gets thinner on its way back to me.

My fingers tremble slightly as I hold it. I don't look down yet. I want to hear the words from his lips.

Once the shuffling of papers stops, he takes a deep breath and wipes a bead of sweat off his brow. "I don't usually do this, but someone told me there's joy that can be found in impulsive gestures."

DIRTY LITTLE SAINT

Butterflies swim in my stomach. He looks nervous. Felix Crane never looks nervous.

"Here goes..."

He puts on his glasses and clears his throat.

"There's nectar on my lips.
A fire in your eyes
The whisper of a wish
For our ship to sail nine tides
There's a beginning that tows the line.
And an ending that bears no fruit
But in these quiet spaces, you are mine
When the world sleeps, I belong to you.
You could bring me wildflowers.
Or a bucket of mustard seeds
I'll fight off all your demons, chop down every single weed.
You could steal a thousand hours.
Be the water when I forget how to flow.
I'll rhyme all your reasons...
Every single brutal blow.
But the raven flies straight
And the Melancholia fantasy seems so far away.
We could call it impossible, call it fate.
Or we could bottle it up like lightning and save it for another rainy
day.
There's a pulse that beats when you find your way to me.
A ferocious growl that aches
When the wolf meets the beast, we're face-to-face.
When the need festers and you can't stay away.
Now the whiskey no longer numbs the pain.
We are damaged.
We are broken.
We are fauna.
We are ocean.

M VIOLET

The madness inside each other's cold open
Two sparks caught in a circular motion.
A fire that burns under all the corrosion
We've nothing left to give except what is unspoken.
When the struggle of our own making has led us here
And the safety of starving keeps us bound to our fear.
Objects in rearview mirrors move closer when they appear
Through the smoke and the rubble, we're the headlights and the deer.

Will we ever love this way again?
Across the room as we pretend
That our craving doesn't exist
That what we want isn't more than this.
That we aren't a thousand degrees away from being friends
That meant to be isn't us in the end.
It's a beginning that can't tell time.
An ending that we abuse.
But in the absence of nothing, you are mine
In the hysteria of everything, I belong to you."

His hand is shaking as he sets the paper down on the desk. A hushed awe falls over the room.

My heart is in my throat. *He wrote that for me.* We lock eyes, and I know it in my bones. I raise my hand halfway up, unsure if I want to speak but dying to say something that lets this man know that it wasn't in vain.

His lip quivers slightly. "Yes, Miss Blackwell?"

"That... that was beautiful," my voice cracks.

He flashes a grin. "It's the subject that's beautiful. The words are merely a catalyst. But... thank you."

For a brief moment, the air stills in my lungs. The room and all the people in it fall away except for me and him.

"All right, enough of me stroking my own ego. Everyone, please turn to page sixty-six. We'll be reading Lord Byron today." He pushes

his glasses up as they slide down his nose, going right back into pro-fessor mode.

But I still can't catch my breath. I don't even hear much from the rest of the class. I steal looks at him voraciously when I think he's not looking. I don't care if anyone sees. Felix is mine. And I'm his. I'm tired of fighting it. I'm done with feeling guilty about want-ing this man.

When the bell tolls, marking the end of the period, I stay in my seat. I ignore the snickers from the people who have probably figured out that the poem was for me.

I wait for every single one of them to file out before making my way down the aisle. The click of my heels against the tiled floors sounds monstrous in the silence of the church. He keeps his back to me while shuffling papers into his briefcase.

My heart hammers in my chest as I stand behind him, unsure of what to say.

"What can I help you with, Miss Blackwell?" He doesn't look up.

I place my hand on his back. "Felix . . . I'm sorry I've been dis-tant. That was so beautiful. It means everything to me."

He sighs and turns around to face me. "You don't have to apolo-gize for how you feel. I get it. You need me to make the coven stron-ger. But you don't have to like it."

Fuck. I'm such an asshole.

I shake my head, taking his hands in mine. "I want you, Felix. Not because of your power or your last name. But because you're strange and beautiful and you make me feel special. I let my guilt get in the way."

He towers over me, his eyes alight with ache and desire. "You are special, Little Raven. And you have nothing to feel guilty about."

I look down, my eyes brimming with tears. "I hurt Villette, alienated you from your family, and turned you into a spectacle in front of your students and peers. All because I'm selfish and greedy."

Felix tilts my chin up. He brushes his thumb across my cheek, wiping a tear away. "Listen, love. I pushed my family away a long time ago. That has nothing to do with you. Villette will forgive you. Her heart is too full of love to leave room for grudges. And fuck the students and the other teachers. They're all just jealous. Every single one of them would trade places with us if they could."

This man is breaking me, piece by piece. Tearing my walls down with every word he utters. With every breath he takes. "Why me? What makes me so fucking special?"

He flashes that smirk I've grown to love. The one that makes my stomach flip and my core tingle. "You're wild and free and full of fire. You don't give a fuck what anyone thinks. You take what you want when you want it, and I pray for anyone who tries to get in your way. You're also hauntingly beautiful, sexy, smart ..."

Fuck, he knows all the right things to say.

He leans down and whispers in my ear, "And your pussy tastes like cake and stardust."

I shiver at the feel of his lips on my ear, his breath hot. "I love how you speak to me. Like every thought you have is an eloquent verse. Do you dream in poetry too, Professor?"

He squeezes my hips and pulls me toward him so our chests are flush against one another. "I dream about you, Miss Blackwell. Every night. And all the ways I want to touch you."

I'm a goner. Melting in a puddle of my own lust for this man. "So touch me. Right here, right now. In this church of the Goddess of Death. Defile me in this sacred place."

He picks me up and I wrap my legs around his waist as he carries me to the wall, slamming me up against it. "It's only sacred because you're in it."

He teases my lips with his, brushing them ever so softly like a whisper. I whine, consumed with the need for him to kiss me, chasing his lips as he darts back, smirking as he toys with me.

"You're adorable when you pout, Little Raven ... so impatient."

He nibbles at my bottom lip before dipping his tongue into my mouth and back out.

"Felix," I beg.

He rakes his teeth over my lips before thrusting his tongue back inside my mouth. Fucking hell it was worth the wait.

I moan into his kiss, gasping for air. For *his* air to fill my lungs. He tastes like paradise. Like sin and divinity at the same time. I kiss him back with an urgency unlike any I've ever felt. As if his kiss will save me from every dark thing that haunts me.

His lips are soft and firm while his tongue rolls over mine, crashing into every nerve like a tidal wave.

"Help me with my pants," he rasps in between kisses.

I fumble with his belt and practically rip the button right off before unzipping him. I reach in, pull out his cock, and stroke all the way down to the tip.

"Oh, fuck. This is new." I look down in between us to see he has a thick barbell pierced through the tip.

"I got it for you, Little Raven." He hikes up my skirt and rips my panties in half before sliding his finger down my pussy lips. "Fuck, I want to drown in your nectar."

"Yes," I grab his cock and guide him in. We both gasp as he works his long, slender cock inside, the cold barbell almost sending me over the edge as he inches all the way to the back of my core. I feel high as he fills me, leaving no space between us.

"Fuck, Felix..."

He rocks against my G-spot. "I don't want to be your ruin, Little Raven," he breathes in my ear. "I want to be your salvation. Your god."

"Uhh," I cry out as he slams back into me on the word *god,* filling me so full I can feel the pressure in my belly.

He unleashes everything he has, rocking me against the wall of the church like a monster. I gaze up at the purple stained glass windows and think this is what heaven feels like. And for a moment I think I hear angels sing. But it's probably just the ravens.

He takes my lower lip between his and sucks. "Mmm, fuck. I'll write thousands of poems for you. One for every time I make you cum."

Fuck.

No one has ever kissed or fucked me like this before. It's like our very souls are clawing at each other. Our essences morph into one. He squeezes my ass as I clench around him. His cock barely fits, and yet, I want to swallow him inside me and keep him there forever.

"Teach me how to fly, Professor. Teach me everything you know..." I am falling fast and hard, drowning in the perfumed abyss of this man's poetry and passion.

He thrusts in and out, each time driving me harder into the stone wall at my back. "Ooh, Miss Blackwell, I think I like you call-ing me Professor when my cock is inside you."

The way he fucks me is biblical. Holy hell. "I'll call you what-ever you want as long as you don't stop."

He pulls my ass cheeks apart as he grinds my pussy. The sides of his cock pulse against my walls. "Oh, shit, I'm fucking coming."

I whine and moan as his cum floods me. It feels like a baptism, triggering my release. I roll my hips, rubbing my clit against the base of him as he grinds his cock in quick circular bursts.

"Felix!" A singular spasm multiplies within seconds as the tin-gling in my core heightens and spreads throughout my entire body. I soak his cock with my juices as I buck and writhe between him and the cold church wall. "Fuck... *Felix*," I cry.

He kisses my cheeks, then my forehead, and my lips. "You're the only temple I want to worship in," he whispers in my ear as he leaves another trail of kisses up my neck and jaw.

I could happily die right now.

He sets me back down on the floor but keeps an arm around my waist to steady me. I take deep breaths as I try to regain control over my pulse.

"My sigils didn't flare up this time..." They didn't burn or pulse like they normally do when I'm aroused.

Felix gently rests his hand at the base of my throat, protectively holding it there. "Because this wasn't about power or ravens or even Nocturnus... this was just for us, Maur."

I kiss each of his hands. *In the hysteria of everything, I belong to you.*

His eyes light up. "That's right, Little Raven. Now, let's get you home. We have a spring equinox to plan and a whole lot of avenging to do."

CHAPTER TWENTY-SIX

Maureen

MY PALMS SWEAT AS I LINGER IN FRONT OF THE DOOR. I THINK I'M going to be sick. I hesitate before putting my proverbial big girl panties on and knocking. My heart races as I listen for the sound of footsteps.

I take a step back as the door jerks open violently. Villette's eyes light up briefly as if she forgets all my transgressions for a split second. But then the hurt floods back in.

"What do you want, Maureen?"

I wince at her sour tone. "I was hoping we could talk. Can I come in?"

She glares back at me.

I thrust a pink box out into the space between us. "I brought macarons."

She snickers. "You're trying to bribe me with French pastries?"

"And champagne!" I reach into my bag and pull out a bottle.

"Please, Villette."

She rolls her eyes but stands aside and gestures for me to enter. *Hope. I'll take all that I can get.*

I stand in the middle of her room, afraid to make a wrong move and have her change her mind about letting me in.

She snatches the champagne from my hand, pops the cork, and takes a swig straight from the bottle. Well, fuck. *She is pissed.* I open the box and cautiously offer her a macaron. She grabs the whole box and sets it on the nightstand before plopping down on the bed and shoving one in her mouth.

"Okay, talk," she mumbles between bites.

I rub my sweaty palms over my tweed skirt. Well, *here goes nothing.* An impulsive gesture to say the least. "First of all, I'm not here to apologize."

Her eyes widen as she almost chokes on a pink macaron. Oh, fuck. I'm losing her.

"*Not* for feeling the way I do about your brother. I am not sorry for that. What I came to apologize for is how I've treated you." I sit down on a chair and lean forward, resting my elbows on my knees. "I shouldn't have kept you in the dark. Friendship is about trust. I didn't give that to you, and it was wrong. So I'm going to tell you everything now."

She takes another swig of champagne and wipes her mouth on her sleeve. "Go on."

I tap my foot on the floor as the knots in my stomach twist. "The guys didn't stab Zeke to death. I did. He was trying to hurt me."

Her mouth drops open. "Maur . . ."

I shake my head. "I'm dealing with it . . . During the break, we visited Riot's father, and he did . . . unspeakable things to me.

Punished me. Humiliated me." My voice cracks, and I almost don't continue.

She sets the champagne down. "You're safe with me, Maur. It's okay."

I breathe in a deep breath. "When we got back to Tenebrose, I started getting disgusting texts from an unknown number. Atlas tracked the stalker down. It turns out he was hired by Atlas's father."

Villette hands me the champagne. "I think you need this more than I do."

I chuckle and happily take it from her. "The stalker, Barnaby Withers... I killed him too."

She moves to the edge of the bed, closer to where I'm sitting.

I take a swig. The champagne fizzes on my tongue, coating my throat with liquid courage. "I've been getting more sigils, growing my power. My connection to the guys. But with that comes con-sequences. Nothing in this life is free. There's been a dark energy growing in me... Until I met Felix."

She covers my hand with hers and gently squeezes. "Tell me how you feel about him."

I sigh as tears stream down my cheeks. "He has a light in him. Being with him is like taking a hot shower after you've been caught in a snowstorm without food or water for days. The guys want him because he has power. Because the five of us together will have more than a fighting chance against the elders. But it's more than that for me. Felix and I ... we're poetry. Like lighting in a bottle. He makes me feel like I can do anything. *Be anything*."

Villette nods. "I understand. Felix has been troubled for a very long time. He's battled bouts of depression. There were times that I thought I'd lost him forever. But he's been different since he got here. There's a light in him that he's never had. Maybe it's because of you. Or because he isn't stifling his power anymore."

I choke back another sob, washing it down with another gulp of champagne. "I'm sorry, Villette. I know how much you hate

Nocturnus. I wish it wasn't your brother. For your sake and for our friendship, I'd give anything to have it be different."

She holds tighter to my hand. "I've been so blind. I should have made you feel comfortable telling me these things. Through my selfish need to have my brother back and the ingrained hatred I have for Nocturnus, I've neglected *you*. My best friend. That's on me, Maur. I'm sorry."

I shake my head. "No. I ruin everything. You were right to be angry."

She leaps up and cups my face in her hands. "Maur, listen to me. I love my brother. But I also love you. If Felix can help keep you safe, then I demand that you stay with him. If Nocturnus is the reason he's no longer walking around like a zombie, then I will back him. I will back all of you."

I throw my arms around her and sob into her neck. "I love you too, Villette. The past few weeks have been agony without you. I've missed you so much."

She rubs my back. "From now on, no more secrets. No more holding back. We tell each other everything. Well, leave out the dirty stuff with my brother, please."

I snort through a half-sob, half-laugh. "Deal."

"What are you going to do about the elders?"

I like this new openness between us. It feels like a thousand weights have been lifted off my chest. "Nothing until we find out when they're meeting. We need them to be at the same place at the same time."

She nods. "I know I don't have powers, but let me know if I can do anything."

I hug her again. "You can come and get really drunk with me at the Spring Equinox Ball tonight."

She squeals in delight. "*Yes.* I hated dress shopping without you…"

My heart fills with so much love for this girl. "Well, then you're

M VIOLET

definitely getting ready with me tonight so I can gush over how gorgeous you look before anyone else gets to."

As we say goodbye and plan to see each other upstairs in my dorm apartment later, I feel like the broken cells in my body are starting to heal. Felix isn't the only Crane with a light in him. Villette is like liquid sunshine. Just being around her eases my anxiety and calms my nerves. I've never met anyone like her. I'm so fucking grate-

ful we're back to being friends.

&

I find Atlas on the couch in my dorm apartment wearing navy-blue slacks and a white shirt unbuttoned at the top. His blond hair is unkempt and falling over his eyes instead of slicked back like it usually is. "Hey there, pretty girl."

I cross the room and stand over him. "Hi, handsome. Everything all right?"

He squeezes my thighs. "I've been up for days making vials..."

I caress his cheek. "You should take a nap before the ball."

He shrugs. "Nah, I'm good. I just came by to tell you that I'm not going to let what happened at the last ball happen at this one. We're not letting you out of our sight this time."

I shudder as I try to block out the memory of Jessamine luring me into the woods. "I know." Villette and I made up. She's going to get ready here with me in a few hours."

He flashes me a toothy grin. "Good, I knew she'd come around. No one can resist you, love."

I bend down and plant a soft kiss on his lips. "I think you're a bit biased."

Fuck knows there are plenty of people who want nothing to do with me. Like half of my family, for starters.

He pulls me down onto his lap. "I also wanted to tell you that I

don't need a sigil to want to protect you. Back at the Graves Estate . . . I acted like an asshole that night. I've followed those men blindly for so long that I didn't think you needed protecting from them. But I shouldn't have let you go down to that ritual room. That will never happen again."

"Shhh, it's okay. We're past that now." I kiss his cheeks.

He presses his forehead to mine. "I'm going to murder every single initiate who defiled you."

Sweat beads on our skin. "The vials?"

He nods. "Death by poison is slow and painful. It's what they deserve."

When I think back to when I first met this man till now, it's almost like he's a different person. Still deviant and unhinged as fuck, but there's a selflessness there now that wasn't before. An empathy that didn't exist until recently.

He's strong and magnetic and strikingly gorgeous. But on the inside, he's so much more. He's bittersweet melancholy mixed with mischief and mayhem.

I spin around, lifting my leg to straddle him. To look him deep in the eyes. "I love you, Atlas."

He pulls me to him and covers my mouth with his, kissing me soft and sweet. "I love you so fucking much, baby. My pretty girl."

I pull down his zipper and free his cock from his pants. "I'm such a slut for you," I coo in his ear.

He chuckles as he lifts my skirt and pulls my panties to the side. "Mmm, show me."

I sit on his cock and slide all the way down. We both let out a gasp. "I'm going to wrinkle your suit."

He grabs my hips and thrusts into me. "Fuck this suit. I don't even like it that much."

My laugh is cut off by a moan as his cock swells inside me, stuffing me to the brim. "Well, in that case," I breathe. I rip his shirt open, sending buttons flying across the hardwood floors. I drag my

nails down his chiseled chest, admiring every curve and line of his muscles. I bite my lip as I ride him.

He grabs my throat and yanks me forward until our lips meet. He crushes them, bruising them with his hunger for my mouth. Our tongues swirl together feverishly, greedily.

I rock my hips back and forth, desperate for release. My sigils burn, crackling as they come alive on my skin.

He lets out a loud moan as I bounce up and down. "Don't stop. Fuck. Just like that."

My clit spasms before spreading down my slit and then deep inside my core. I throw my head back and scream as my orgasm consumes me. "*Uhhh.* Oh, my fucking . . . Atlas."

"That's it. Cum for me, pretty girl. Fuck, let me fill you." He yanks my hips down hard. I feel his cock swell and throb against my core. "Mmm. Oh, shit. Here it comes."

A deep guttural growl escapes his throat. I grind in circles around his cock as his thick milky cum rushes into me, hot and fast. "Yeah . . . *Good boy, Atlas.*"

He squeezes my throat, his eyes glowing. "Pretty girl . . . You and your magical fucking pussy."

Our chests heave as we attempt to catch our breaths. With our sweaty foreheads pressed together, his cock twitches inside me as the last of his cum trickles out.

"Happy spring equinox," I exhale. "We're going to have fun tonight. I can feel it."

He nods, still catching his breath. "I'll make sure it's the best night of your life."

I lean on his hand as I reluctantly slide off his cock and stand up. "I gotta jump in the shower before Villette gets here. You sticking around?"

"Nah. Imma get out of your hair and let you girls do your thing." He zips up his pants and stands, laughing as he sees all his shirt buttons on the floor. "I'll be back to collect those later."

He kisses me again before getting into the elevator. And I don't take my eyes off him until the sliding doors close. A grin plays at the corner of my lips as his sticky cum rubs against my thighs on the way to the shower.

I wonder which one of them is standing guard now that Atlas has to go back home and change. I chuckle to myself.

My phone buzzes, and I get my answer. I look down to see a text from Riot. *What the fuck happened to Atlas's shirt?*

I laugh so hard I snort.

Fuck, I love them.

Villette and I clasp hands as we strut down to meet the guys. Felix leans up against a black limousine. His eyes light up when he sees us. He picks up his sister and twirls her around. "Mi hermosa hermana." *My beautiful sister.*

She giggles as he sets her down. "Felix! You're going to wrinkle my dress." She looks stunning in an emerald-green, flower-print, floor-length gown. It bustles in the back, accentuating the curve of her hips and slender waist. The straps are thick and hug the middle of her shoulders.

His gaze flits over to me, and that rumble in my chest kicks in.

"Fuck." He saunters over to me and takes my hands in his. "Damn... Helen of Troy's got nothing on you, Little Raven. Your face could launch a *million* ships."

I knew this dress was the one as I put it on. With a neckline that dips down all the way to my waist, the pink and black striped satin hugs my body like a glove. The skirt splits in the front and flares out, revealing my tattooed legs.

I stalk forward, careful not to trip in my new, black, strappy stilettos. "Always the poet."

M VIOLET

Catching movement in the corner of my eye, I hold my hand over my face to shield the glare of the sun. Through the rays, I spot them, and my heart gallops.

Riot, Atlas, and Valentin amble across the parking lot, a vision in all black.

I glance between them and Felix, overcome with emotion. *They are all here for me.*

Villette squeezes my hand. "Let's go have some fun."

We pile into the limousine in a sea of laughter, followed by champagne bottles popping.

Riot leans across the leather seats and whispers in my ear, "You're so beautiful, it hurts."

I kiss him on the cheek. "We've come a long way from that day you cornered me in the bathroom, haven't we?"

He nods, a smirk on his lips. "This is just the beginning, Firecracker."

When we pull up to the ballroom, all eyes are on us, their gazes glued to us as we climb out of the limousine. The snickers and gaping mouths don't bother me tonight. I have my good friend and my guys with me. We look hot as hell and about to burn off some much-needed steam.

Felix offers Villette his arm while Atlas and Val sandwich me in between them. Riot leads the charge with the air of a king. A dark king with energy so sinister, the shadows part for him.

I gasp in awe when we step inside. The ballroom is unrecognizable. Like a fairy wonderland with its twinkling lights, glittered-covered floor, and smoke machines. Pink and purple roses cover the tables while blue hydrangeas and green ivy climb the walls. I lose count of all the tables stacked with mini fondant cakes and rows of pink champagne. White-gloved servers carry silver trays, offering whiskey in teacups and powdered-sugar-dusted truffles. A string quartet strums in the corner, gracing our ears with the

sounds of Bach and Tchaikovsky. "Look at all this." I twirl around, soaking it all in.

"Look at *you*," Atlas coos. "You're in heaven."

Villette chuckles. "*This* is Tenebrose. We go all out."

I grab a pink flowery teacup off a tray with more excitement than necessary. I take a sip and almost orgasm. "Why does whiskey taste better in this?"

Val snorts. "Did you just curtsy?"

"Maybe I did." I smile coyly.

Felix drapes his arm around my neck. "And here I thought you were opposed to polite society."

"Are you calling me a heathen, Professor?" I tease.

"You *are* the company you keep." He sneaks a playful jab at Riot who always manages to look relaxed and on edge at the same time. Despite my state of bliss, his apprehension hasn't gone unnoticed. I watch the way he scans the room, taking note of every single person here.

Val and Atlas are on high alert as well; they're just better at hiding it. But Riot is always one step closer to turning feral. And he doesn't give a fuck who sees. Sometimes, I think that smiling causes him actual physical pain. But it's my favorite thing about him.

Villette loops her arm through mine. "Dance with me?"

She shrieks as I drag her to the dancefloor in response. We laugh. We twirl each other. We make a spectacle of ourselves. I grab a glass of champagne this time as she spins me out and back, giggling like a teenager as I almost spill half of it.

We dance and drink like this for hours, oblivious to the haters who gawk at us. Felix was right, they're all just jealous. I pay them no mind as I continue to make a fool of myself with Villette.

When the music shifts tempo, I pause our dance to catch my breath and grab another whiskey. Over the rim of my purple teacup, I catch sight of the guys over by the bathroom. Riot, Atlas, and

M VIOLET

Felix surround the door, their shoulders squared and stances wide, jaws clenched. They look like fucking guard dogs.

My stomach knots.

"What is it?" Villette asks.

I shake my head. "Maybe nothing. But let's go find out."

She trails after me as I dash toward them. "What's going on? Where's Val?"

Riot puts his hands up to block me from charging into the men's bathroom. "He's fine, Maur. He's just having a little chat with his uncle."

Fuck.

My heart hammers in my chest. I look back and forth between them, the looks on their faces telling me everything I need to know. The room starts to spin as panic grips me, sucking all the joy from my lungs like a vacuum from hell.

I clutch my chest. "It's tonight, isn't it? The meeting of the elders."

Riot's eyes darken. His fingers tremble around my wrists. "Yes."

CHAPTER TWENTY-SEVEN

Atlas

I'VE BEEN PREPARING FOR THIS FOR WEEKS, KNOWING THAT ANY SECOND, we'd have to act. The look of dread on Maureen's face kills me, though. She looks so pretty in her gown at her little garden party.

"I'm sorry, love, but we have to go now," Riot tells her.

Val gives his uncle a nod as they exit the bathroom. "It's confirmed. All three elders will be there. All three of our fathers."

"I'll have the limousine take me back to Nocturnus so I can get what we need. You all wait here, Villette, I can drop you back off at the Nest along the way."

Her cheeks flame. "Oh, hell, no. I'm coming with you guys."

Felix grabs her arms. "Nope. Go with Atlas. He'll take you home."

Fuck. Now I have to deal with this shit." "Listen to your brother."
She shakes her head and latches onto Maureen. "I'm not letting
you go in there alone. Please. I can be bait or a distraction."

Hm. Not a bad idea actually.

"It's too dangerous, Lettie!" Felix tries to wrench her away.

Val intervenes. "We don't have time for this. Atlas, go. I'll sort
this out."

I nod and sprint out the front doors toward the limo. The driver
jumps out, not expecting me, and scrambles to open the door.

I step around him. "Give me the keys."

"Excuse me, sir? I cannot—"

I grab him by his lapels and shake him. "Give me the fucking
keys!"

He shrinks back against the car, his eyes wide, and points to
the driver's side. "Th-they're in the ignition."

I let him go and dust him off. "Thank you."

Miss Florian wags her finger at me, screaming at me to slow
down as I screech out of the parking lot at full speed. *Yeah, not a
chance, lady.*

I barrel through the woods, my adrenaline racing, and I don't
let up on the gas until I pull up to Nocturnus House. I make it there
in five minutes—one of the benefits of living on campus.

The remote door is already open when I leap out of the limo. I
race inside the ten-car garage and click open the locks to my shiny
black Escalade. I throw open the trunk to find all my vials tucked
away nice and tight.

It's no secret that I'm so fucking amped for this ambush, so obsessed with it my cock throbs just thinking about it. I race around
the car, double checking I have everything I need. Only one more
thing to grab, and then it's game fucking on.

I run upstairs and grab the cage, draping a black sheet over it
before I lug it back down to the garage. I don't need Zeus getting

wound up before I'm ready. I slide the cage into the back of the SUV and climb into the driver's seat.

With the windows rolled down, I charge back through the woods. The cold air soothes my fiery skin. It feels fucking fantastic. I down a bottle of nightshade, relishing the way it seeps into my veins, raising my adrenaline up another notch.

"Woohoo!" I yell out the window as I hit a bump and slam back down on the road with a thud. The tires lock for a moment and I slide, hydroplaning the last few feet. I roar with laughter as I spin out and drift into the parking lot like some kind of daredevil. Dirt and debris kick up around the car in my efforts to correct it and right my path.

Fuck, that was fun.

I spot them outside the ballroom, Villette still in tow. I chuckle. I knew she'd get her fucking way. We have a hard time saying no to these women.

As soon as I pull up, Riot slides into the passenger seat while everyone else climbs in the back. "Welcome to the chaos, Little Crane."

Felix shoots me a glare. "If anything happens to my sister…"

I smirk at him in the rearview mirror. "You'll still have your other brother, Bones, right?"

"Very fucking funny, Thorn."

"Sorry, I'm an asshole." I wave my hand like it's a white flag. Riot chuckles. "You're such a dick."

I push the pedal all the way to the floor when we get to the highway. The tension is so thick in this car that it practically weighs us down. All jokes aside, I'm looking forward to murdering people tonight. Especially after what they did to Maureen. The more I think about it, the more the sigil on my chest burns.

"Focus on the road, Atlas," Val calls out. "You can dream about dismembering people when we get there."

I blink a few times and take a deep breath, loosening my white-knuckle grip on the steering wheel. He's right. I need to fucking relax.

But I keep the odometer at one hundred miles per hour. And I don't slow down until I pull off the highway and creep up to the main road.

Riot turns in his seat to face everyone. "My father has security cameras that I'm going to disable from my phone as soon as we're within view. But I'll need to turn them back on within two minutes, or else he'll be alerted. That gives us two minutes to get inside the house. Understood?"

Villette gasps. "Ooh, I feel like we're on a heist."

"You're staying in the car, Lettie," Felix growls.

"He's right," Maureen adds. "You should stay here where it's safe."

Villette crosses her arms and pouts. "Absolutely not. I did not come all this way to sit in the car. Let me help."

Felix throws his hands up in frustration. "My mother is going to kill me."

Maureen smirks. "I see where she gets her stubbornness from now."

Fuck this chatter. "All right, therapy's over. Everyone out. You're on foot now."

"Wait, where are you going?" Maureen asks.

I give her a wink. I know these grounds like the back of my hand. "I'm going around back. I'll meet you in the caverns."

After they all finally get out at the top of the road, I kill the headlights and take the other path through the woods. It's an unmarked trail we used to use for hunting when we were kids. It's covered in brush, but I can find my way through it with my eyes closed. You get stuck out here alone a couple of times as a kid, and you learn really fast how to find your way back.

I down another vial of nightshade once I pull up to my destination. I close my eyes, using my raven sight to confirm that the initiates are making their way through the tunnels right now.

I grab the vials and the cage out of the trunk before using my

old key to unlock the cellar door. And I almost cum in my pants when it clicks open. *Fucking Holden. So cocky he doesn't even change the locks.*

My heart races as I make my way to the ritual room. The corridors are damp and musty, leaving a stench in the air that I know is gonna stick to my clothes. I'll be burning this suit after tonight, anyway.

Shit. I'm too late.

I get to the room at the same time they do. I was hoping to get the jump on them.

Fuck it. Let's play.

The twenty masked initiates freeze when they see me.

The cage screeches across the floor as I drag it the rest of the way in. "What's up, boys? Am I late for the party?"

No one speaks. Creepy as fuck. Well, creepy for me.

"Who wants a drink? Anyone thirsty?" I stroll over to the cabinet where Holden keeps all the good shit and pull out a bottle of fifty-year-old whiskey.

"Mr. Thorn? Your father's upstairs. He didn't mention you were coming to tonight's ritual," a voice from one of the masks squeaks out.

I laugh as I pull the cork out with my teeth. "That's because it's a surprise. It's his birthday, you see. I brought him a gift." I point to the covered cage.

Another voice calls out, "Should we go get him then, sir?"

I wave him off and take a pull from the bottle. It burns as it goes down. "Fuck, that's good. "No, no. He's in a meeting. Now get your creepy asses over here and have a drink with me. In celebration of Pisces Thorn's illustrious life."

None of them move a muscle.

These fucking assholes.

I sigh and set my case of vials on the ritual table. "Are you

refusing to raise a toast to one of your elders?" I take one of the vials out and down it. "Come, the first one over here gets two." I wink.

One of the initiates, must be the head idiot, nods to the rest and they file over. I hand them each a vial. "Good doggies," I snicker. I hold up my vial in salute. "To Nocturnus and its rebirth."

"To Nocturnus," they mumble through their masks.

I can't help but laugh as I watch them struggle to drink their vials while still keeping their faces covered.

Now, the fun begins.

I clap my hands together. "Who wants to see the gift I brought, dear old Dad? Anyone?"

A couple of grumbles break out amongst them.

I stalk over to the cage and pull off the sheet.

The initiates gasp at the sight of two king cobras slithering and snapping at the bars.

"Oh, you didn't think I only had one snake, did you?" I lift open the door to the cage and the initiates take a giant leap back.

I'm so turned on by this I'm tempted to fuck one of them while he dies. "See, in about thirty seconds, you're all going to keel over. Paralysis will set in. But your minds will still be alive, feeling every-thing. The toxin will slowly travel to your heart, which will then explode."

The look of horror on their faces makes my cock twitch. The leader of them steps forward, "You poisoned us? Why?"

I sigh and grab him by the throat. "Because you disrespected what's mine. You spread your disgusting seed all over my pretty girl. And the penalty for that is death."

I crush his throat seconds before the paralysis sets in. Just in time to watch the rest of them drop to their knees.

CHAPTER TWENTY-EIGHT

Maureen

T HE DUST FROM ATLAS'S TIRES BLOWS BACK IN OUR FACES. We wait for it to clear before continuing down the road. When we get to the fountain with the gargoyles, Riot hacks into the cameras. No one dares to utter a word until he gives us the okay.

"My old man has lost his edge," Riot snickers.

Felix smirks. "Did someone forget to change his passwords? And they say boomers aren't tech savvy."

Riot hands me a key. "This opens all the doors on the main floor. You, Val, and Villette go in first. We'll be right behind you."

I swallow down the lump in my throat. This house is triggering. Standing at the front door, all the memories come flooding back.

M VIOLET

Villette puts her hand on my shoulder. "You got this, Maur. I'm with you every step of the way."

"We all are, love," Val adds.

I nod and turn the key to the front door. When it creaks open, I peer into the dimly lit foyer. It feels like my soul has left my body.

I look back at Riot and Felix before stepping inside, dreading being apart from them. Villette and Val both stick close to me as I shut the door gently behind us.

"What now?" she whispers.

Good question. I need to get down to the ritual room before the elders do. I really fucking hope Atlas has succeeded in killing the initiates.

I take another step forward and find comfort in the cold blade strapped to my thigh. Another reason why I chose a dress with open slits. Easy access.

"This way," Val starts toward the first corridor. The one I re-member getting escorted down the night they mutilated me.

I shudder, hesitating before taking another step.

"What is the meaning of this?" Clover Graves calls out from behind us.

Fuck.

I freeze.

"Maur, get behind me," Val orders.

"Romulus, stop them!" Clover shrieks at her butler.

This creepy fuck.

I dart to the side as he charges me, but trip over Clover's cane and go sprawling to the floor. Val drapes himself over me, desperate to shield my body as Romulus cocks his fist back.

"Oh, hell no," Villette growls. In one swift move, she yanks on his shoulder, knocking him off balance. He turns on her just as she slams her fist into the side of his jaw. His knees buckle right before he slumps to the floor.

"Night, night, motherfucker." Villette shakes out her hand, wincing. "Fuck, that hurt."

"Holy shit, Villette. Where the fuck did you learn how to do that?" I let Val help me up from the floor.

She smirks. "I have a brother named Bones; how do you think I learned?"

"I regret ever doubting you, Crane," Val quips, his eyes wide as he looks between Villette and the grown man she just knocked out cold.

She raises her chin, proud. "Thanks."

"How dare you break into my house and assault my staff."

Clover hisses.

Fuck. I forgot about this bitch. I still can't believe Riot lived in her womb for nine months. I slide my knife out from its strap and hold it up to her face. "You should be ashamed of yourself. The atrocities that your husband commits in this house. Disgusting. You're coming with us now."

"No, Maur. She'll slow us down with that leg of hers. Let's lock her up in one of these rooms." Val starts opening up doors in the hallway.

"She'll just scream for help. Ooh, Villette can you knock her out too?" I'm only half-joking.

Villette holds out her hand. "Give me the knife. I'll keep an eye on her in one of these creepy kidnapper rooms while you do what you need to do."

I look at Val, who just shrugs like it might be our best option. "I don't wanna leave you alone with this monster."

Villette takes the knife from me. "Don't worry, I *will* knock her out if I need to."

"Maur, we have to go." Val's brow is glistening with sweat, and we haven't even gotten to the hard part yet.

I nod. "All right. Be careful. Stab the bitch if she tries anything."

Clover laughs. "Silly little girls trying to play grown-up. You have no idea what you're up against. You will lose."

I grit my teeth and fight the urge to choke her to death. This woman doesn't have a caring or nurturing bone in her body. "I won the second your son chose me over you. Let that ruminate while my friend holds a knife to your throat."

Clover's eyes darken. "My son likes pussy. He didn't choose you. He's just made you his latest obsession. And when he loses interest, I'll be the one he comes to for drugs and booze and money, just like he's always done."

I almost feel sorry for her. She really believes what she's saying.

"Whatever helps you sleep at night, lady."

"Maur," Val pleads.

I turn to Villette one more time. "If anything goes wrong, you run like hell, Villette. Run as fast and as far as you can."

She nods and gives me a hug before I take off running down the corridor with Val.

The tunnels look familiar, but there's no way I'd find my way back to the ritual room without Val. I was in such an adrenaline-fueled daze the last time I was here. The way they surrounded me like a rat in a cage as they led me down to torture me for their sick pleasure.

"Hey, we're almost there. You okay?"

I raise my chin. I need to remember who the fuck I am. "Yeah. I'm good."

As we reach the doorway to the ritual room, I feel nauseous. A wave of panic rushes over me. My body is literally revolting. Fuck. I never want to see this place ever again after tonight.

Val grabs my hand. "Let's fucking hope he didn't fail . . ."

I step into the room to see Atlas lounging across the altar. I

Over thirty ravens fly into the cavern, squawking. They woosh

"Oh, fuck. Here we go," Atlas calls.

"For the raven," I whisper to myself. "*For Nocturnus.*"

The tunnels rumble from where Atlas first came in. The ground shakes underneath my feet. I close my eyes, guiding them to me.

Death always wins.

Atlas howls as he removes his shirt too. "Mors vincit omnia!"

Val nods and takes off his shirt. "They'll be here soon." The marks on his body glow with light as his sigils seem to connect like constellations.

I close my eyes and call for the ravens. My sigils burn as I awaken them. As I draw on their power.

I kick off my other heel. "Now it's my turn. I'm fucking ready."

He licks the blood from my fingers. "I'm your angel of death, pretty girl. This is just a taste of what I'd do for you."

I toss the heel and hobble over to Atlas. His eyes glow, and he looks slightly terrified of me for the first time. I grab his face with bloody hands and kiss his lips. "Thank you."

I lean over his ear, hoping his soul can still hear me. "*Fuck you.*"

He's one of the ones who held me down. I rip off my stiletto and drive the pointy heel into his throat. A gurgling scream leaves my body as I stab him again and again. Until there's nothing left to stab.

When I get to the last one, I recognize his hands, his build. a crazed maniac, stripping them of their masks and their robes.

next one and the next until I'm flailing around the ritual room like I rip off one of their masks and spit in his face. I do the same to the

"FUCK YOU," I scream. I no longer want to contain my rage. step over each one of them.

Hysterical laughter bubbles up in my throat. My hands shake as I

I stagger farther in, dropping Val's hand. *These fucking bastards.* the dead initiates.

breathe out a sigh of relief as I look around the room and see all

around me, crying to me. Begging for me. I raise my hands. "Shhh, be still for me."

The ravens fall silent and settle on the ground, flanking me on all sides like a small army.

Val stands tall, his shoulders pressed back. "You did it, Firecracker. Fuck. You control the ravens."

CHAPTER TWENTY-NINE

Relux

I UNDERSTAND NOW WHY MY PARENTS HATE NOCTURNUS. BECAUSE THESE ubiquitous monsters have been running it from a place of greed and perversity. I also get how Riot and the others want to change that. But I'm here for *her*. For my little raven. I'll tell Holden Graves whatever he wants to hear, just so I can watch her cut his heart out.

Riot snaps open the door to the library, and we barrel in. I try not to become distracted by the bookshelves that line the walls, spotting a first edition of *Frankenstein* to my left.

We charge toward the three old men in the center of the room. With vicious snarls on their lips, they break their conversation mid-stride.

"What the fuck are you doing here? This is a private meeting,"

the one who looks like an older, meaner version of Riot snaps.

Holden Graves.

"I brought you a new initiate." Riot points to me.

A blond man with blue-green eyes looks up at me over his spectacles. "Aren't you Edgar Crane's son? Does he know you're here?"

Fuck, he even sounds like Atlas. I wonder if people think that about me when they see my father.

"He's also the new poetry professor at Tenebrose," the third man grumbles. I'm guessing he must be Laurent Erebus. I can see where Valentin gets his death stares from.

Riot stalks toward them like a lion, fearless. He was raised around these men. While he knows what they're capable of, he also knows their weaknesses. Ego.

"Father, my apologies for barging in, but I realize you are right about everything. I fucked up. So... meet Felix Crane. My peace offering."

They eye me suspiciously as I stick out my hand. "Not hand shakers, eh?" I chuckle. I'd rather break their hands than shake them anyway.

Holden tries to get a read on his son. "This doesn't even begin to make up for the mess you made. But it's a start."

Laurent nods. "Well, since we're all here, I vote to initiate him tonight."

Pisces Thorn's eyes light up. "Are there any dolls here for us to play with?"

Holden nods. "Of course."

"Good," Pisces rasps. "I want one sitting on my cock while I watch the show."

My stomach turns. These men are vile and disgusting.

Laurent smirks. "Get one for each of us. Especially Felix. Part of being in Nocturnus is getting your cock sucked anytime you want."

"I can't wait," I murmur.

Riot's pulse quickens. I can sense it through the sigil on my thigh. The one he carved into me. "Then it's settled. Shall we?"

"Relax, son. We need to conclude our meeting first. Go wait outside until we're done." Holden turns his back, not caring for a reply as he dismisses his only son. Laurent and Pisces give their attention back to each other as well.

The rage oozes out of Riot's pores as we exit the room. "Fuck."

"Relax. We've come too far to mess this up with an outburst." Patience has become my best friend in these recent months of planning and moving to Raven's Gate. Waiting for the moment when my little raven would fly to me.

He narrows his eyes at me. "This *is* me relaxed."

We wait in silence for another twenty minutes before the Nocturnus elders file out of the library.

Holden clasps my back. "Come, Felix. Your whole world is about to change."

Riot rolls his eyes, but they don't see. They're too absorbed in their own greed and lust to notice anything other than the fresh meat in their hands—me.

Pisces laughs. "You're about to gain access to all the poison, pussy, and power you could ever dream of."

This one. He's the one who hired Maureen's stalker. He planned to kidnap her. I'd like to break his face first.

I smile back. "It's about time. I've been rather bored in Tenebrose."

We start to follow Holden across the foyer when he stops abruptly. "Where the fuck is Romulus?"

Riot snickers. "That old man is senile as fuck. No doubt he got lost in the east wing again."

I hold my breath as Holden taps on his phone, swiping up and down. "Everything okay?" I ask.

He nods. "It seems so. No security threats. Perhaps you're right. Romulus is getting quite forgetful these days."

Thank fuck.

Riot looks just as wound up as I feel.

We continue walking across the marble floors, past the grand staircase, and down a long corridor. The architecture alone is impressive, but the house itself is cold and soulless. Sinister. It makes me uneasy.

We come to a stop at a large steel door. "No turning back now, Felix." Holden pulls on the heavy door, revealing nothing but darkness beyond its frame.

I take a deep breath and pray to the ravens that Maureen, Val, and Atlas have succeeded in taking over the ritual room.

"I'm ready."

Riot nudges me forward. "Let's fucking go then."

As soon as I step into the dark abyss, a sconce lights up on the wall to my right. I grab onto the railing and take another step down. Another candle comes to life.

"That's it, boy. Keep going down. Your destiny waits at the bottom," Laurent drawls.

My destiny will be to help the woman I love destroy you.

"Get your hands off me," a woman shrieks at the top of the stairs.

Laughter erupts. "Look what I found slinking through the hall."

"Let me go!" she screams.

I know that voice.

Fuck.

I spin around and start to go back up when Riot grabs me. "It's your turn to relax. Don't give them any reaction."

"She's my sister," I growl.

He places his hand on my chest, over the sigil Maureen gave me. "I know. But we have to go along with it. I promise you, I won't let them touch her."

Every corded muscle in my body is clenched. I want to attack until I remember that these clowns don't fight fair. They're old men

who win their battles by drawing power from all the sigils they've carved into their initiates.

Villette's eyes widen when she sees me as they shove her down the stairs. While they're busy ogling her, I put my finger to my lips, motioning for her to stay quiet. She releases a quivering breath.

Holden smells her hair. "Expensive shampoo. Mmm, where'd you come from, sweet thing?"

I almost vomit in my mouth.

"I-I was looking for my boyfriend. He works here." Villette's voice shakes. She's never been a good liar, but they are too blinded by their lust to catch it.

He thumbs her lip. "Well, if he works for me, then he belongs to me. And so do you. Come, sweetheart. You're going to be part of something really special tonight."

Fuck.

Riot grabs my arm. "Keep walking, Felix."

Villette whimpers with every step we take. The descent seems endless. I hate myself so much right now. I never should have allowed her to come with us tonight. She should be back at Tenebrose, safe in her room at the Nest.

If we fail . . . I'll never forgive myself.

They surpass me when we reach the bottom of the stairs. With my sister sandwiched between the three of them, Riot and I follow like bloodhounds, watching their every move as they lead us to the ritual room.

Riot laces his fingers through mine. "I keep my promises, Felix. She'll be fine."

I squeeze his hand. "I'll murder them." I don't give a fuck if they are their fathers.

"I'll help," Riot mutters.

This moment might be my worst. But something flickers between Riot and me. A transfer of heat and energy through our fingertips. I believe him. *I trust him.* His loyalty is not to these men.

"It's to us. Me, Atlas, Val, and Maureen. We are the ones he will kill for. No matter who the prey is. He'll murder his own bloodline to protect us.

"I'm all in," I whisper. "No more doubts. Carve my entire body up with sigils. I belong with you."

"Mors tua, vita mea. Your death, my life, Felix."

It's not the death of flesh and tissue. Death is just an ending. A chance for rebirth.

I keep a trained eye on my sister and pick up the pace as we follow more closely. I can't for any reason let them take her some- where I can't see her.

Riot jerks his chin up, motioning to what lies ahead. "Be ready." I swallow hard and nestle up behind Villette. I touch her back. *I got you baby sister.*

The lights are brighter through the entrance up ahead. It's so fucking quiet I start to fear they failed.

One by one, we enter the ritual room, and it takes a second to process what I see. Holden, on the other hand, loses his shit immediately.

"What in the fucking name of my ravens happened here?"

The ground is covered with dead naked initiates, their mouths foaming, and a few have their throats torn open. I spot a bloody sti- letto next to the altar, and my heart races. On the altar itself is the biggest fucking king cobra I've ever seen.

Fucking Atlas.

But what no one can take their eyes off is her. She stands quiet and still in a sea of ravens. They gather at her feet, guarding her, wor- shiping their shadow goddess. Val and Atlas stand on either side of her, shirtless and bloody, their eyes murderous.

"This is what happens when you fuck with us, Father." Riot walks to the center of the room and holds up his arms like he's about to be nailed to a cross.

While they argue back and forth, I grab Villette and stash her

behind me. She clings to my back. "I'm sorry, Felix. I should have stayed hidden. I heard your voice, and I thought it was all over."

"It's okay Lettie. You're safe. Just stay behind me." I'm angry with myself, not her. She's my little sister. I should have done a better job of protecting her. Bones is gonna have my balls when he finds out about this.

I lock eyes with Maureen, and it sends my pulse racing. Barefoot, her dress torn and covered in blood, she is more beautiful than ever. My sigils come alive, burning and crackling as they ache to connect to her. Every part of me longs for her. Her eyes blaze with fury when she spots Villette behind me.

Maureen's eyes flick to the altar, and I nod. "Lettie, listen to me. I need you to get on that big stone slab over there."

She shrinks back in horror. "The one with all the snakes? No fucking way."

I cup her face in my hands. "They're Atlas's. They won't hurt you. Trust me."

She nods even as her lip quivers. I need her out of the way of harm, but I also need to help my little raven.

After I watch my sister climb up onto the altar, I spot Atlas's snakes circling around her like guard dogs. *He controls them.* When I heard how Zeus bit Maureen's thigh, I thought it was because, well, he's a poisonous fucking snake. But now I see that it was at Atlas's command. I'm in absolute awe of him for the first time. This makes him seem less unhinged and more just fucking badass.

"You ungrateful son of a bitch!" Holden screams at Riot. Pisces shakes his head as he looks around at all the dead initiates.

But it's Laurent who fires the first shot.

With just one murderous look, he drops Val to his knees.

Maureen cries out.

The ravens flap their wings, flying above her.

Her eyes glow bright gold, like burnt honey.

She turns toward the three elders... And chaos erupts.

CHAPTER THIRTY

Maureen

VAL DROPS TO HIS KNEES AND A RAGE UNLIKE ANY I'VE EVER KNOWN rises in my blood, crushing every rational part of me, stirring me like a deadly storm.

I scream and raise my hands toward Laurent. He snarls before directing his energy at me.

Fuck you.

I hold my ground, pushing back as we lock in a battle for power. I picture his lungs collapsing, his head popping like a balloon. Val rises to his feet and grabs one of my hands. The Erebus sigil on the back of my neck awakens, singeing my flesh. The pain feels like love. Like madness. We squeeze each other's sweaty hands, willing our power to surpass his.

Atlas grabs my other hand just as his father Pisces stands with Laurent, the both of them hurling a force at us that threatens to steal all the air from our lungs. Atlas's energy is sharp and brutal, yet effervescent as it tingles my skin. While Val's essence is rough, mangy, and ferocious like a rabid coyote.

"How could you let this happen, Riot?" Holden calls out.

"You're supposed to play with your toys, not let them play with you." This fucking piece of shit.

"I'm going to play with you next," I hiss.

He laughs. "Once I'm done destroying your little coven, I'm going to keep you as my pet. I even had a cage made for you. That way, I can punish you whenever I want."

The memory of his hands on my thighs fuels the rage in my chest. My hands shake as he walks toward us. Riot tries to block his path, but he sends him flying. I see Felix rush to him out of the corner of my eye. But I don't dare take my full gaze off Holden.

"Yeah, that's right, little temptress. No one will be around to save you from me. From all the vile things I plan to do to you. I will fuck your pussy raw until it bleeds. Every night. You'll be pissing razor blades and begging for death by the time I'm done with you."

Laurent and Pisces join him in laughter.

He plants the image in my mind. I see the cage, the restraints, the perverse look in his eyes as he dangles his stubby cock over me. I shudder and blink a few times.

"Get out of my head!" I scream.

Riot and Felix dash over to stand in front of me. To block me from Holden's ire.

"Enough," Riot roars. "She is not yours to cage."

"She never will be," Felix snarls. There's a dark edge to his voice that I've never heard before.

I glance over to see Villette wide-eyed and curled up on the altar. Zeus slithers around her, but his head snaps toward us. He wants a piece of these assholes just as badly as we do.

The ravens screech and squawk as my guys circle around me. Dark and light threads of energy glimmer between us. I let it consume me. Let it feed me and give me strength.

Pisces, Laurent, and Holden face us, throwing everything they have in our direction. I feel the temptation to give in to them. To surrender. To succumb. My limbs ache as I fight to hold my ground. Everything burns as if I'm actually on fire.

"Lean on us, Firecracker. Take what you need," Riot commands.

"Just like we did when we jumped the cliff, Maur," Val adds.

And now we have Felix. His energy is poetry. It caresses my soul like a soft feather, and yet, it feels impenetrable, strong like bamboo. I feel his light wrapping around me like a warm cocoon. With a cry, I unleash my shadows. I let them soak through me, reaching the deepest parts of me before I unfurl them. The sigil of Erebus cools, sending chills like icicles over my heated flesh.

I stalk toward the three elders. "You will crumble and cower at my feet." It's my voice, but it sounds strange and unfamiliar. I lift my hands and send the ravens down. They shriek as they dive at their skulls. Blood spots their flesh as they peck at their lips, their cheeks, and their hands.

Pisces breaks first, flailing his arms around as he tries to fend them off.

Holden curses at him. "You idiot!"

They're weakening.

Riot rushes forward. "We're done being pawns for you." He cocks back and physically punches his father in the face. Holden releases his hold on our circle and swings back. Riot ducks and steps forward. He shoves him back. "You're too slow, old man."

"Fuck this," Laurent lunges at Val. "Time to teach you a lesson, boy." I step in between them just as he raises his fist, catching it in my palm before it reaches Val's cheek. "You will never lay a finger on him ever again," I declare.

The ravens flock to me, flapping wildly around us as I force this man down to the ground with every ounce of strength I have.

He glares up at me, sweat dripping down his face, his cheeks bright red, as his fist shakes in my hand. "You are an abomination."

Well, that's a fucking new one.

Val charges forward and wraps his hands around his father's throat, unleashing a scream that stops all of us in motion. Every trauma he's endured at the hands of this man boils to the surface.

"You never loved me," he yells in his face as it turns purple.

Laurent's eyes bulge wide with horror.

"It's your fault I'm like this. You gave me these scars," Laurent claws at Val's wrists as he fights for breath. "My sigils protect me from *you*. Not from her or anyone else."

We watch as he chokes him. As the life leaves his eyes, Laurent's hands fall to his sides. "Fuck you." He spits in his face just as his body convulses and slumps to the ground.

I want to comfort him, but we have two other predators to deal with.

Holden shrieks. "Are you going to kill me too, Riot? Your own father?"

Atlas towers over Holden and Pisces, a demonic look in his eyes. "Probably."

"Atlas, you sick fuck. You've always been a disturbed boy," Pisces snaps.

He smiles back, his blue-green eyes glowing. "I learned from you, Father. But we're not *your* boys anymore. We're grown men who have come for a fucking reckoning."

Holden shakes his head at Riot, who is holding himself together by a very thin thread. "All of this drama... her pussy must taste as sweet as fucking pie. You have ruined everything for this slut."

Riot backhands him with all his power behind him, sending him to his knees. "Call her a slut one more time, and you'll be joining your good friend Laurent in the After... Nocturnus doesn't belong

to you anymore. You've desecrated it with your greed and your filth. Nocturnus is ours now."

Atlas rubs his fingers in the air, and Zeus begins to slither across the floor to us. "You don't deserve to bear our sigils. You never did."

They both yell in protest as the king cobra snake wraps itself around Pisces, locking him into a tight embrace. "Don't do this, son," he begs.

Atlas laughs. "Oh, now I'm son? This *is* happening."

I stalk over to Holden, bloody knife in hand. "As soon as you take off your clothes, the ritual will begin," I hiss, mocking him with his own words.

"I will not." He folds his arms to his chest like a child pouting.

"Yes, you fucking will," Riot screams in his ear.

I kneel down next to his father and smile as I wave my blade in his face. "Undress. Now. Or I will let the ravens eat your testicles."

The venom in his eyes is monstrous. I can imagine he's dreaming about all the violent things he wants to do to me but can't.

"You're outnumbered," Riot goads. "We are stronger than you, and you know that you've lost. So do as she says."

I fixate on his every move, salivating as he removes his shirt, then his shoes and pants. The sick pleasure that twists in my bones sends an endorphin rush to my head, making me higher than any poison or drug ever could.

His short chubby cock shrivels in fear as I glare at it. "You're really fucking ugly, you know that?" He flinches as I lean forward. "This is going to hurt a lot."

Riot, Atlas, and Felix hold him down as he cries in protest.

I take stock of the sigils on his chest as I straddle him. "Hmm, which one should I take first?"

"You crazy, cunt," he whispers.

I laugh. "My how the tables have turned." There is nothing sweeter than revenge. Than taking back power and control. "You

violated me, mutilated me, and tortured me in this very room." I can barely get the words out through my clenched jaw.

"I had nothing to do with that," Pisces calls out.

I jerk my head toward him. "No. You planned to kidnap me and do worse. I'll get to you next."

He whimpers as Zeus tightens around him.

I press the tip of my blade to Holden's chest. "You think you can handle thirty-five cuts, Mr. Graves?" I mock him again.

He purses his lips. "Do your worst."

With a quick flick of my wrist, I slash three lines across his chest. *Fuck this feels good.*

"Is that all you've got?" He cackles.

I smile as my gaze locks on the sigil above his heart. "I'll take this one first." I dig the knife into his chest and begin to cut.

His eyes fill with horror as he realizes that I'm not fucking around. He lets out a bloodcurdling scream as I sink the knife deeper, twisting and turning to dig out the chunk of skin that the sigil was carved into.

My adrenaline soars as I move to the next sigil on his neck and do the same. *"Red looks good on you,"* I echo his words back to him again. I am fire. Darkness. Rage. I'm caught between madness and euphoria. Hysteria and serenity.

There is no mercy for one who does not give it himself. No redemption for leaders who choose themselves over their disciples.

I carve and cut and flay his flesh as if I were butchering an animal. I skin him alive. And in my head, I hear Val strumming his violin, filling my heart and soul with its haunted melody.

I hear Felix's words, his poetry, like a sacred chant. It beats a drum in my pulse, putting a fire in my belly. I roll Holden over and chip away at the sigils on his back. I have to hear the music so I can drown out Villette's sobs. *She shouldn't be here.*

When I saw his fucking hands on her . . .

I let out a scream and remove another sigil with one deep cut.

"How does it fucking feel to be powerless?" I yell in his ear.

"Please…" Of course he begs. Well, I fucking begged, too, and he didn't stop.

Riot nods when I look up at him. "Finish it, Firecracker. Take your revenge."

I carve the last sigil out of him, my hands shaking. "Now I'm going to leave you here on the ground so you can slowly bleed to death."

His gurgled cries are muffled. He doesn't make any sense.

"Next." I stalk toward Pisces.

"No, please, no. I'm sorry. Okay? Can't we just call a truce? I promise I'll never bother you again. Believe me." His lips are quivering, his eyes bloodshot.

Just because he didn't succeed in kidnapping me doesn't negate all the vile things he had planned for me if he had.

"I'm not going to take your sigils, Mr. Thorn." I wipe my knife on my blood-soaked dress, which was pointless except to demonstrate how fucking feral I am right now.

He lets out a deep breath. "Oh, thank the raven."

I kneel down next to him and pet Zeus on the head. His tongue darts out to lick my wrist. "He is."

Pisces's eyes bulge. "What? Atlas, you can't do this. Please. I'm begging you."

Atlas locks eyes with Zeus as their unspoken bond sparks. The snake moves into action. "Don't worry, the numbness kicks in after the paralysis. You won't feel anything after that."

The sound of their screams sends shivers up my spine. My hands tremble as I clasp the knife to my chest. *We won.* The rest is a blur. Exhaustion is kicking in. All my muscles ache.

"Come back to us, Maur." Felix's voice is soothing, like a warm bath. I'll need multiple baths to get all this blood off.

He faces me, his brown eyes glowing. "In absentia lucis,

DIRTY LITTLE SAINT

tenebrae vincunt. . . . Don't let the darkness prevail." He kisses me on the lips, and it tastes like sunshine. "Let me in."

I let out a deep breath and close my eyes. As soon as I feel his sigil reaching out to mine, I feel lighter, freer. "Your light destroys me in the best fucking way, Felix."

Villette still cowers next to the altar. I cannot approach her right now looking like this. Not after what she just watched me do. Felix picks her up off the ground and hugs her to his chest. "I got you, Lettie. It's okay."

We're safe now.

We control Nocturnus and the ravens.

But . . . none of us are okay.

CHAPTER THIRTY-ONE

Riot

W E LEFT MY MOTHER AND ROMULUS TIED UP IN ONE OF THE guestrooms. I'm sure they'll free themselves eventually.

Our fathers are dead.

Our fathers are dead.

Per their wills, all their financial holdings were transferred to us. Atlas took pity on his mother and left her their country house and a small monthly allowance. She cared less about him than his father did.

But I don't give a fuck about the money. I care about the control. The power that they can no longer abuse.

Fuck.

It's late, and we haven't spoken much since we arrived back

at Tenebrose. Atlas went straight to the greenhouse. Felix is staying with Villette back at the Nest, afraid to leave her alone with her memories of what happened tonight. And Val... fuck. He freed himself, but that monster was still his father. So he went to the one person he always goes to when Laurent Erebus breaks his heart—his uncle Julian.

I find Maureen sitting on the terrace, sipping a double shot of whiskey neat. "Thank you," I murmur.

"For what?" her voice cracks. Her skin is fresh after an hour-long shower as if the blood was never there. But the blood will always be there. It will stay in her bones next to the other lives she's taken.

I sit next to her on the porch swing. She smells so fucking good. "For coming to Raven's Gate. For making me love you. You saved us."

She leans her head on my shoulder and sighs. "We saved each other. You always show up for me. I love you, Riot."

I kiss her forehead. Fuck, I need this woman more than I need food or sleep or air. "I am obscenely and undeniably in love with you, Maureen Blackwell."

"What we did tonight will leave marks on our souls, you know?" she squeaks.

It always does.

"Don't worry about that now, Firecracker. Just rest." I want to bottle her scent so I can have it with me always.

She stands up and faces me. The moon shines behind her, casting a halo around her head. "I want you to fuck me gently tonight." She pushes her sweatpants down, no panties, and climbs onto my lap.

I lean back as she unzips my pants and pulls out my cock. "I'll fuck you any way you want, love."

The sweetest smile I've ever seen on her face emerges as she lifts up and slides her pussy down my shaft. "Mmm... fuck. So perfect, Riot. You're fucking perfect."

I roll my hips up as the wind whips around us. The porch swing

rocks as I still myself inside her, pulsing against her walls. It's an ache that roots deeper than any that have come before. This need to just feel her around me. After all the violence... *we need this.*

"I'm so fucking happy I found you in that bathroom in Wickford Hollow." I anchor her hips, relishing the way her eyelids flutter, the way her voice whimpers as I pull her back down. She is fire, fucking pure passion encased in a vision of black hair and golden eyes.

"I never hated you, Riot. Not even when you did your worst. I fell for you that same night. The night you zipped up my corset. The night you killed for me." She arches her back and rubs her pussy against the base of my cock, moaning as I hit that sweet spot deep within her.

I slide my hands up and underneath her tank top until I find her nipples. I trace my fingers lightly around them and almost cum as they harden instantly from my touch. "Oh, baby... You feel so good like this. I can feel all of you. Every fucking beautiful inch of you."

Our souls might be damned, but the pleasure we take from each other is pure. Even when it's rough and chaotic. Especially when it is. But as I thrust gently inside her, I'm overcome. Every sensation heightens the agony of drawing it out...

She presses her lips against mine and kisses me softly. I moan as the tip of her tongue probes my mouth. The hunger for this woman is unnatural. It moves beyond obsession, teetering on actual physical need. Like if I don't have her, my body will disintegrate and turn to ash.

I squeeze her hips back and forth on my cock.

"I'm going to cum for you. Ready, Riot?"

This is more erotic than anything we've ever done. This slow crawl over each other as we edge ourselves into orgasmic oblivion. I suck on her bottom lip. "Mmm, yes, baby, I'm going to cum with you."

"Uhhh, fuck... Riot, I love you." She throws her head back and lets out a pent-up moan.

I thrust in deeper, faster, as her juices coat my cock. "Oh, fuck."

I grit my teeth as the blood in my cock rushes forward, taking me by surprise, the pleasure overwhelming me. We grind against each other on the flapping porch swing, coming at the same time.

I kiss her lips, her cheeks; I devour her neck and shoulders as my pleasure intensifies the longer I'm inside her. "You've ruined me, and I fucking love you for it."

She sucks on my earlobe, trembling as she clenches around my throbbing cock. "Our ruin is our salvation."

I wrap my hand around her throat loosely just to feel her pulse beat against my palm. "Over and over again . . . Always."

CHAPTER THIRTY-TWO

Atlas

"WANT SOME COMPANY?" MAUREEN LEANS AGAINST THE doorframe of the greenhouse.

I set down a vial of nightshade and stalk toward her. Her hair is damp, her face freshly washed, making her look younger than her twenty-five years. I twirl one of her dark strands around my finger. "I always want your company, pretty girl."

She closes her eyes and sinks into my arms. "I'll never forget what you did for me tonight, Atlas."

I wrap my hands around her neck and force her to look up at me. To meet my gaze. "Those monsters got what they deserved. I *will always kill for you.*"

I remember that first day she came to the greenhouse with me.

It was the first time she tasted poison. *Tasted me.* I fell in love with her right then.

She places a soft kiss on my cheek. "Right back at ya, love. Always."

"Are you all right?" I ask her, afraid that tonight's massacre may have permanently scarred her for life.

"I will be." She nods as she saunters over to my worktable.

"What about you, Atlas? You lost your father tonight."

Am I all right? That will always be a complicated question for me. My family has a chaotic history. We've always fitted in between these feuds and wars, never fully taking a side. Always one foot out the door it seems. But that ends with me.

I snake an arm around her from behind and pull her flush against me. "You can't lose something you never had, Maur. My father wasn't there for me then, so I have no feelings about him not being here now."

She hugs my arms to her belly. "How did we all get such fucked up parents?"

I laugh. I have to. Otherwise, I'll cry. I'll wallow and brood like Val and Riot do. Or start reciting melancholic poetry alongside Felix. "The deeper the trauma, the stronger the soul. Don't envy people with happy childhoods, Maur. They don't stand a chance in this world."

"Our souls are damned no matter how strong we are. We're murderers, playing god . . . But we aren't gods, Atlas."

I spin her around to face me. "No, we're not gods. Like it or not, we're devils. Harbingers of death like the ravens. From the second we each took our first breath, we were destined for this life. For this outcome."

I snatch a vial of oleander out of my pocket and nudge it to her lips. "Forget about all that, pretty girl. Let me be your escape. The one you always come to when you want to be free. Now drink."

There will be plenty of time for us to work through our daddy issues but tonight I just want to wrap myself up in her.

She nods and drinks the whole vial down in one gulp.

"Good girl. Now bend over this table so I can fuck all the sadness out of you." I push her forward until I have her draped across the table, ass up. "Put your hands above your head and keep them there until I tell you."

She whimpers when I yank her pants down. "Fuck me hard, Atlas."

That won't be a problem. Fuck, her ass is perfect. Her black G-string panties are sexy as hell, though. "Let's keep these on." I pull them to the side before getting two fingers inside her wet pussy. She smacks her hands against the table as she moans. "Yes... please, Atlas. Don't hold back. Fuck me like a fucking psychopath."

My cock throbs. I can't get my pants down fast enough as she wiggles her ass back and forth, begging me to penetrate it. I want to make her cry and scream and beg for mercy. I want to fill her ass and her cunt at the same time. I spit down her ass crack before inserting the tip of my cock inside. "I'm going to hurt you now."

"Yes," she begs. "Make me forget everything else."

I slip inside the warm cavity of her ass and have to still myself for a moment. Her anus is so tight, I can barely squeeze in. But I push hard, spreading her ass cheeks apart as I force my cock deeper inside. Her screams fuel me to stay present. To not cum too fast.

"That's my pretty girl. Let me hear how much it hurts."

"Ruin me, Atlas. Uhhh, fuck..." She sobs into the table but doesn't tell me to stop.

Her cries trigger me, edging me closer to my own release. But I'm not ready to unravel just yet. She wants more punishment, more pain. And I'm going to give it to her.

I shove four fingers in her cunt first before tucking my thumb and sliding my whole fist in.

DIRTY LITTLE SAINT

"Fucking hell!" She screams so loud I'm sure the entire house hears her.

I am sick with my own need as I ride her ass and fist her cunt at the same time. I laugh as she bucks wildly, jerking and contorting her hips like she's having convulsions.

"There's no escaping me, pretty girl. I've got you trapped just the way you like it. Are you going to be a good girl and cum all over my cock and my hand?"

"Mmm, yesss," she slurs.

A tremor shoots down my shaft, pulling all my blood and adrenaline down to the tip. I grind into her, fucking her without mercy. Without remorse for her raw and tender flesh. I hock another glob of spit down her ass crack as I thrust faster, desecrating her as I chase my release.

"Fuck, Maur . . . *My dirty little slut*. Look what you done to me. Fuck."

A deep guttural moan escapes from her throat as she grinds back against me. Her juices spill out, dripping all over my hand and cock. "That's it baby, cum for Daddy."

"Fuck you, Atlas. Oh, fuck, that feels good. Don't stop." A dribble of saliva drips out of her mouth and onto the table as she cums all over me.

I'm making her foam at the fucking mouth.

I burrow as far into her ass as I can get and unleash everything I have. My cum shoots out, hot and thick. I'm overwhelmed, my head spinning as an orgasm so intense grips me literally by the balls. I feel every twitch of her raw cunt over my ridges as I thrust over and over again.

Tears stream down my cheeks as I cry out in ecstasy. "*What have you done to me?*" I repeat, my voice cracking as I fill her with my essence.

I collapse onto her back, my chest heaving, I whisper in her ear, "I love making you scream."

M VIOLET

She turns her head to kiss me on the neck. "I'm yours to mangle and fuck and ruin. Always."

Years from now, this is what I'll remember the most about tonight. Not the twenty or so initiates I murdered. Not the death of my father. But *this*, right here. Me and my pretty girl fucking each other to tears in a greenhouse full of poison.

This is what we are. What we'll always be. And it's all I'll ever need.

CHAPTER THIRTY-THREE

Valentin

W HEN UNCLE JULIAN OPENS THE DOOR, IT TAKES LESS THAN FIVE seconds for him to see the death in my eyes. To know what I've done.

He pulls me into his arms, and I collapse into sobs. I'm that eight-year-old boy again, crying as he tends to the wounds my father gave me.

"I killed him."

"Shhh, it's okay, Valentin. My sweet boy."

I heave in his arms, letting everything go. Feeling every emotion that I've pushed down for so long. He lets me grieve. For my father, for my absent mother, and for myself.

And by the end of the night, I am cleansed. I'm born again.

I spare him the gritty details and instead speak her praises. My dark queen. I tell him of how she protected me from him. "She's our salvation, Uncle. She sacrificed her soul and body to right their wrongs."

Julian nods. "I misjudged her. Her love for you is pure. I see that now."

"We all misjudged her," Jessamine whispers as she peers from behind the wall. "Penny was wrong about her too."

"Her grandmother? She's never met her." I am still not one hundred percent happy that my uncle is shacked up with this ghost chick.

Jessamine creeps in, her body language timid and awkward. "There are things you don't know about Maureen. Things she doesn't even know about herself. You need to take her to Ever Graves."

"Tell me now," I demand, my patience non-existent after the night we just had.

"Easy, Val. Maybe it would be best to go to Ever Graves. Maureen needs to know where she . . . came from."

The way he speaks is cryptic. "She was born in Wickford Hollow."

He and Jessamine exchange a look. "Yes, but her mother was born in Ever Graves."

I shrug. "And?"

Jessamine cowers back into the shadows of the hallway. "There's *something wrong with the women of Ever Graves,*" she whispers.

An uneasy feeling hits my stomach. But this chick has that effect on people. She's so fucking weird. I can never make sense of what she says. I pinch my brow as I feel a headache coming on.

"What about the ravens?" I ask her.

She shudders. "The ravens are the devil's children."

What the fuck? I stalk toward the hallway, determined to get a clearer answer out of her, but my uncle stops me.

"Go get some rest, Val. You've been through a lot tonight."

Julian hands me my leather jacket.

I nod. "Yeah, you're right. I'll come by later this week."

The sky is black, without a star in sight. I slide behind the wheel and drive as fast as I fucking can through the woods. I roll the windows down to feel the wind whip at me. It's cold and sharp, and it makes me feel something other than this hole in my chest that I have for that fucking disappointment of a father.

When I get back to Nocturnus, the lights are off, and the house is quiet. I slink up to my room, grateful to be back home. I kick off my shoes, strip out of my clothes, and slide into my bed. My pulse races when I feel her warm body inside my sheets.

"Maur..." I just want to bury my heart in her chest for safe-keeping.

She caresses my face. "Val," she breathes. "My beautiful Valentin... you're safe now. You're always safe with me."

I love this woman so fucking much. I gasp as I kiss her, thrusting my tongue deep inside her mouth. "Please fuck me, Maur. Fuck me violently and dark and hard. I need..."

"Shh, I'll give you whatever you want, Frankenstein. We can drink, fuck, read poetry under the stars, fall in love..."

I rip her pants off first, then her top. "All of it. I want all of it with you."

She lets me fuck her hard and rough. She begs me for more when I bruise her lips and thighs. She cries tears of joy, singing my name like it's a holy hymn when I slam my cock over and over again inside her pussy and her ass. Until there's so much cum and sweat that neither one of us has an ounce of energy left to give. I collapse in her arms and fall asleep instantly, for the first time in my rotten life.

CHAPTER THIRTY-FOUR

Maureen

"I THINK I'M GOING TO STOP GOING TO BALLS. THEY'RE BAD LUCK." I dip a sweet potato fry into the massive bowl of ranch the server reluctantly brought over.

"Maybe it's just ball gowns. People always get stabbed when you're wearing one," Villette teases.

"Yeah, I'm like Buffy the Douchebag Slayer." We both erupt into giggles.

It's been a month since that fucking night at Graves Estate, but the nightmares still come every night. Especially for Villette. I moved her into Nocturnus House. It's easier for us to all be together. We take turns running into each other's rooms when one of us wakes up screaming.

"Any word from Libra?" Villette asks.

I nod. "Well, sort of. Her parents called Atlas. They said they got a text message from her saying she needed space and time off from school to figure out what she wants."

"It's weird that she hasn't responded to us, right? Like I know the winter solstice was crazy, but she seemed fine right before she left."

I've had an uneasy feeling about Libra's absence since the first week of this semester. But there's been no time to really deep dive into it. Now that all that shit with the elders is over with, and Nocturnus is ours, I need to try and track our bougie little friend down and make sure she's truly okay.

"Very weird. That's actually part of what I wanted to talk to you about. With the summer break coming up next week, I'm planning on going to Ever Graves. Figured I'd ask around about her there. Among other things." I smile and thank the server as she sets two more glasses of wine in front of us.

Villette takes a big sip. "All of you are going?"

I nod. "Yeah, they don't let me out of their sight . . . wanna come?"

Her eyes light up. "My parents are already expecting me to come home for summer. My papa is sending a car for me next Friday. So I'll meet you there."

We clink glasses and cheers.

Villette grins from ear to ear. "Ooh, I'm so excited to show you around. We'll have a great summer."

I believe that we will. It doesn't matter what my last name is anymore. I have my loves. Riot, Atlas, and Valentin. And then there's Felix . . . we're still learning about each other, but I'm in absolute awe whenever I spend time with him. He and the guys are getting closer too. I think he has a particular affinity for Riot. They've been inseparable lately.

"Same, girl. Thanks for spending my birthday with me, by the way. It's the first year without my bestie, Bailey."

Villette squeezes my hand. "I'm honored that you invited me. But we better get you back to Nocturnus. The guys have something special planned for you. I'll be in my room with headphones on, by the way."

We both burst out laughing. She knows us too well. The poor girl has heard me moan more times than I can count. No wonder she's having nightmares.

We finish our drinks and walk back to Nocturnus House just as the sun starts to set. Tenebrose is growing on me. It feels more like home than Wickford Hollow now. I've come to love the hallowed ground, the spooky Goddess of Death church and its beautiful stained glass windows, and even the ravens. They follow me everywhere I go, ready for my command at a moment's notice. They protect me just as much as the guys do.

I don't mind the graveyard anymore either. Ever since Riot and I made a new memory there to replace the one I had with Zeke. Villette and I take the path through it, walking through the headstones without fear or anxiety.

Tenebrose is our place now. We own it. And everyone knows it. No one dares to snicker or glare at me here anymore. Even in Felix's poetry class. The other girls keep their heads down and avoid making eye contact with me.

News spread rather fast about what I did at the Graves Estate. They're more afraid of me than ever. But it's better that way. I don't need their approval or validation.

When we enter Nocturnus House, my breath hitches. I can hear her laughter from the other room. I look at Villette, wide-eyed.

"Is this real?"

She winks. "Go. Have fun. I'll be upstairs if you wanna chat later."

I don't waste another second. I sprint into the living room and nearly choke on my sobs. "Bales..."

She looks up from the circle of guys around her—mine and hers—and bolts over to me. We nearly knock each other over in our fierce embrace.

"Maur! I've missed you so much, bitch."

I can't stop hugging her. I can't stop the tears from falling. She is here. Bailey Bishop is in my arms. "Best fucking birthday ever. I love you so much, Bales. Fuck."

When the guys finally pry us apart, we just look at each other. It's been six months since we've seen each other. The longest we've ever been apart in our whole lives. She looks amazing. Her blonde hair is a little shorter but still hangs past her shoulders. She looks stunning in tight black pants, black boots, and a white fuzzy sweater.

"I couldn't miss your birthday, bitch. Oh! I brought you stuff."

She hands me a Jell-O shot, and I almost cry again.

I drink it down, and it tastes like home. Like late nights and tequila, and horror movies and sweet potato fries at Ruby's. Like Halloween and abandoned houses and haunted mortuaries. It tastes like us. "You have no idea how much I missed this."

She smiles and hugs me again. "I know. Me too, Maur. Um, your guys are hot as fuck, by the way. Nice work."

I give her a little curtsy. "Your girl hasn't lost her touch." I look past her and wave to Poe, Grim, Saint, and Raine. "I see yours are still devoted and fine as ever. Things good back at Wickford Mansion?"

She locks her arm through mine. "Yeah, we are in our nesting phase. Saint has been gardening like crazy thanks to Poe's demanding list of rare ingredients that he refuses to cook without. Grim and Raine are still at each other's throats, but it's entertaining to watch."

She leans in and whispers, "Really fucking good foreplay."

I burst out laughing. My heart is so full. I can't remember ever being this happy. "So... tell me what you think of the devils of

M VIOLET

Raven's Gate. I can't even begin to wrap my head or heart around how much it means to me that she's here.

Bailey's violet eyes sparkle with excitement as she guides me toward the terrace, away from earshot. "I like them for you. Raine was a little annoyed to meet Atlas at first, you know, being a Thorn and all, but I reminded him that sweet Atlas wasn't even alive when Daisy Thorn poisoned them to death."

"Oh, fuck. I totally forgot that Raine's ex was a Thorn. Yikes."

I down another Jell-O shot.

Bailey laughs and tucks me in closer as we exit onto the terrace. "Yeah. Small fucking world. Anyway, I love them all. Valentin is funny as hell. Riot is so elegant and polite. Like he stepped out of one of those old black and white movies. And Felix is hot, girl. Oh my god. He was also really fascinated with Poe being named after his favorite poet."

I roll my eyes and snort. "He's obsessed with Edgar Alan Poe."

She clasps my hands in hers. "They fucking worship you. Obsessed. You did good, Maur."

I hug her again. Everything is perfect. "I'm so glad you're here. How long can you stay?"

We sit down on the porch swing as she lights up a joint. "Just tonight. Work is killing me."

I snort laugh. Her mortuary humor never gets old. "Fuck, I missed you."

She passes the joint to me. "Are you okay? Your mom's been saying some crazy shit."

I roll my eyes and take a long drag. "Yeah, better now that you're here. It's been a wild year."

I spend the next two hours telling her everything. We laugh and cry and drink an entire tray of Jell-O shots. And when the clock strikes midnight, like Cinderella, she has to go.

I hug her so hard it hurts. "I'll come to visit you soon. Maybe even stay a while if that's okay with everyone."

Saint is the first to respond. "Maur, you and your guys are always welcome at Wickford Mansion. Stay as long as you want."

I hold her hands while the guys say their goodbyes and promise to keep in touch. We stare at each other for an eternity, our entire lives flashing in our eyes. "I love you, bitch. Thank you for coming."

She gives me one last hug. "I love you too, Maur. But you have Villette to thank. She helped make this happen. Such a sweetheart. Keep that one close. She adores you."

I wave to Bailey as they drive away; my heart is the fullest it's ever been.

When I walk back inside, Val is playing violin by the fire. Riot and Felix are discussing Poe—both the poet and the man who just left our house, and Atlas is playing with his poisons. I love them so much it hurts. I want to suffocate myself in their scent, drown in their hands and limbs and essences.

I've been let down a lot in my life. But never by them. These heathens are my ruin and my salvation. My beautiful devils.

As I stand there beaming, they turn their attention to me. It's unnerving in the best fucking way. Spasms tingle in my core.

Riot crosses the room to kiss me. "Happy birthday, Firecracker."

Felix grabs my hand and pulls me onto his lap. "I think we should unwrap her, what do you think, hmm?"

Atlas downs a vial of poison before stalking over. He gazes down at me with those electric blue-green eyes. "She's ours to mangle, ours to fuck . . . ours to worship."

My cheeks flush as my body heat rises.

Val runs his thumb across my lips. "Yeah, I think she's going to let us play."

I open my mouth and let him push his thumb all the way in. I let them strip me naked and play with my body all night. We kiss and fuck and carve new sigils, healing and saving each other with every touch.

Our ruin really is our salvation. We might never be fully okay but it doesn't matter because we're together.

Sometimes there's just not enough light to chase away the darkness. Not enough holy water to cleanse your sins…

But who needs light and holy water, anyway?

Not this bitch.

Did I do the right thing?

Fuck it.

I'd do it again.

EPILOGUE

Maureen

T HE TOWN OF EVER GRAVES PERCHES HIGH ATOP A RIDGE ON JAGGED cliffs with fog so thick you can't see two feet in front of you. The air is dense and crisp, chilling me to the bone. I can see my breath on the window.

We drive past unmarked graves. They line the dirt road that zig zags up into the mountains. I try to not look down. As we climb in elevation, the road narrows, the edge getting closer. I shudder as I imagine what would happen if one were to fall off, into the ocean below—they'd be dead before they knew, the surface shattering their bones on impact, like glass.

I lock eyes with Atlas in the rearview mirror and he gives me a wink. "Don't worry, pretty girl. We're almost there."

Valentin turns his head to look at me. I'm sandwiched between Riot and Felix in the back seat. "Draven is going to meet us at the front gates and show us where to go. They're having a party for us."

All my life it's just been me and my parents. I always wished our family was bigger. I wanted grandparents, aunts and uncles, and cousins. But now that my wish is about to come true, I'm nervous as fuck. The only thing I know about these people is that they kicked my pregnant mother out when she didn't marry the man they chose for her. Do I even want to know them?

Riot squeezes my thigh. "We don't have to stay long, love. Just until you get your answers."

I nod. The closer we get to Blackwell Manor, the more my Erebus sigil burns. This town is shrouded in darkness. It seduces me, caressing my thoughts with shadowy whispers and promises of lust and sin.

I release a deep breath. "There's something about this place … it feels so wrong."

Felix grabs my hand. "That's why I left … I never felt right here. There's too much darkness. Too many secrets protecting evil things."

"Villette said the same thing," I murmur. "But your brother, Bones, he's never left. And Atlas, your cousin, Aries, is still here. And my cousin, Draven … I don't understand. How can they live with this feeling every day?" I've always been drawn to dark things, dirty things, but this is something different. Something so sinister it's hard to breathe without shuddering.

Felix stares out the window, his gaze fixated on the trees, as if he's straining to see something that lurks in the shadows. "This place has a hold on them. It's hard to break free. Some embrace it and thrive while others descend into madness. I was the latter. My parents sensed it and sent Villette away first. Then me. Bones … well, you'll meet him. He belongs here."

When we reach the top of the mountain, the fog clears, revealing the town center. The streets are lined with cobblestones and lit

by lampposts. It looks old—vintage—like something out of one of Felix's Victorian novels.

Riot, Atlas, and Valentin's gazes dart around as they take it all in, mesmerized by the sight as much as I am. Felix just stares straight ahead. He rubs his hands together, clasping and unclasping his fingers as if he's about to freak out.

I cover his hands with my own. "Are you okay?"

"I don't know . . ." he breathes.

Riot stretches his arm behind me to squeeze Felix's shoulder.

"We've got you. Remember, we're the devils of Raven's Gate, the new elders of Nocturnus. Nothing can hurt us anymore."

Val looks back at me and smirks. "And we're strolling in here with a Blackwell. That alone gives us protection."

A nervous tickle flutters in my belly. It's still hard to believe that I come from one of the most powerful bloodlines in Melancholia. I was just the Sheriff's daughter back in Wickford Hollow. We weren't dirt poor but no one considered us noble or influential. Now . . . that's all about to change.

Spanning only ten blocks, it doesn't take long for us to drive through the main street of town. With the lamplights and cobble-stones behind us, another forest approaches.

"Your family estate is just on the other side of these trees." Felix takes a swig from a vial of nightshade. "We'll be there in a few minutes," he rasps.

Atlas and I lock eyes in the rearview mirror again, his expression darker this time. He reaches back and I instantly grab his hand.

"You stay close to us, pretty girl. Family or not, I don't know or trust these people one fucking bit."

"Agreed," Riot adds. "*The blood of the covenant is thicker than the water of the womb.*"

Felix smiles for the first time since we arrived. "Quoting Sir Walter Scott now, are we? I think I'm rubbing off on you, Riot."

"You're not the only poetic one in the group, Professor," Riot teases.

Val snorts. "Always the competitive one."

The truth is, they don't have to tell me twice. "I have no inten-tion of leaving any of your sides tonight. Not after what happened at Graves Estate . . ."

The guys collectively tense as they're reminded of the night they left me alone with Holden Graves. The night I was tortured and humiliated. I don't bring it up to make them feel bad or guilty. But I'm still working through my issues. Saying it out loud instead of brushing it under the rug makes it easier.

"That will *never* fucking happen again," Riot grits out.

I kiss his cheek. "I know. But I'm still never leaving your side again."

He wraps an arm around me and pulls me into his chest. "Fuck, no. Never."

We ride in silence for the rest of the way, each of us lost in our own pensive thoughts. It feels like it might be our last moment of peace, as we have no idea what we're walking into.

When we pull up to the front gates, my stomach knots. The Erebus sigil on the back of my neck crackles, threatening to unleash the darkest parts of me. I take a deep, concentrated breath, and will it to simmer. Fuck. I'm close to having a full blown panic attack.

A tall, muscular black-haired man emerges as the thick iron gates creak open. He nods at Atlas and motions for us to follow. As we drive alongside his willowy figure, I can't take my eyes off him. He's my cousin, the first relative I've ever seen.

He side eyes the passenger window and chills creep across my neck when his gaze finds mine through the tinted windows of Atlas's SUV. *What the fuck?*

But my attention is pulled from him when we arrive at the main entrance. Blackwell Manor is about the size of Tenebrose Academy, sprawling far and wide across the dense marshland. It's juxtaposition

is odd, strange, *unnatural*, as it towers over wet foliage, overgrown brush, and swampy lagoons.

Felix follows my gaze. "Welcome to Southern Melancholia ..."

When we exit the SUV, I stagger back against the door, unprepared for the heady scent of bougainvillea and jasmine. It overpowers the oleander and nightshade. The wind is warm and humid. It sticks to my clothes, dampening my skin almost instantly.

The man who let us in stalks over, his gaze fixated on me. When we're face-to-face, my pulse races. His eyes look just like mine. Like burnt honey. We stare at each other, dumbfounded. I wonder if he's thinking the same thing.

Felix breaks the silence. "Draven," he addresses the man. "Meet your cousin, Maureen Blackwell."

His eyes are cold, expressionless. The muscle in his jaw twitches as he clenches his teeth. "Welcome."

Am I though? He looks unimpressed.

I stick my hand out, anyway. "Nice to meet you, Draven. I've been wondering about you all for so long."

He arches an eyebrow before conceding. I shiver when his ice-cold hand wraps around mine. "You might regret that by the end of the night."

It sounds more like a warning than a threat. A nugget of wisdom from a man whose spirit has clearly been crushed by the weight of this family. From the hollow look in his eyes to his rigid posture, it doesn't take me long to see he's got some serious trust issues.

Riot, Atlas, and Val make their introductions as well before we follow him up the massive stone steps. Draven couldn't look more disinterested if he tried.

When we approach the double doors, sounds of music underneath nervous chatter pour out, and my stomach knots. "How many people are in there?"

Draven clucks his tongue in annoyance. "Twenty or so. But the only one you should concern yourself with is Grandmother."

Penny Blackwell

Fuck. Now I get to finally meet psycho granny. The stories about her alone give me so much insight as to why my mother is such a bitch. I almost feel sorry for her. Until I remind myself of my affectionless childhood.

"Are Lib's parents here?" Atlas asks before downing another vial of poison.

Draven nods. "Your Uncle Gemini and Aunt Rose are inside, along with your cousin, Aries. My parents are here as well."

Felix snickers. "I'm guessing mine are not."

Draven tilts his head and flashes him a murderous glare. "No. But Bones is here, of course."

From what Felix has told me, Draven, Bones, and Aries are a tight group—best friends and heathens who enjoy terrorizing the town because they can. Our families are founders, powerful and rich. *Untouchable.*

The front doors open up to a lavish foyer. A crystal chandelier hangs from the ceiling, illuminating the marble floors and cherry-wood staircase. The air is cool, a nice reprieve from the humidity outside.

All the fixtures on the doors and windows are made of pure gold and encrusted with diamonds. I look down at my black pants and black cashmere sweater and feel underdressed, cursing myself for not wearing something fancier.

"Fuck, I need a drink," Felix mutters.

"We all do," Draven drawls back.

"Well, lead the way then, sunshine," Val mocks. He leans down and whispers in my ear, "He might be a robot."

I stifle a laugh as we follow my new cousin down the hall and into the crowded sitting room. I don't have to try hard because the second we enter, the chatter stops and all eyes are on me.

Fuck.

Looks of horror mixed with pity are hurled in my direction. What do these people know that I don't?

A white-gloved server hands us each a cocktail—gin martinis. I take a sip and wince. It brings me back to the first party at Nocturnus House when Libra ordered me one. It was before she knew that I had never met any of my family. Before she *reminded* me that I'm one of the heirs to the Blackwell Gin Company.

Draven walks me around the room, my guys in tow, and proceeds to introduce us to everyone. They are polite but reserved, eager yet suspicious. But if there's any doubt that I am who I claim to be, that is quelled the second I lay eyes on Penny Blackwell. With her dark hair, though streaked with gray, and her honey-colored eyes, she's a much older version of me.

The crowd parts as she crosses the room to me. There is no longing in her gaze. No kindness or warmth or even any of the pity that the others expressed. She approaches cautiously as if any sudden moves on her part might spook me and make me attack.

My grandmother looks at me the same way Laurent Erebus looked at me that day in the cabin—like I'm something to be feared and hated.

I don't dare speak as I wait for her to finish assessing me. The guys stand closer, protectively, and every single one of my sigils burns.

"We'll speak this once. But after tonight, I do not want to see you again." Her voice is deep and raspy from what sounds like decades of cigarettes and gin.

A twinge of sadness stirs in my chest. I did not expect her to be happy to see me but she's colder than I could ever imagine. This woman has no love for me or my mother. No remorse for kicking us out twenty-five years ago.

I nod. "I have some questions."

Her eyes narrow at me. "Not here. Discretion is the tallest pillar"

in our world. It's what separates the wolves from the sheep. We shall talk in the library."

And as if she gave a command through her mind, the rest of the crowd turns away from us, picking their conversations back up as if we'd never entered.

As promised, the guys don't leave my side. Riot, Atlas, Val, and Felix lean back against the leather couch, their gazes trained on my grandmother. To someone not from our world, they might look silly or over dramatic for being cautious around a seventy-year-old woman. But this is Melancholia and this woman is a Blackwell. We'd be fools to not be on guard.

She wastes no time getting to the point of me being here. "What do you want to know, Maureen?"

My name sounds strange on her tongue. Like she swore to never utter it.

Well, I can be blunt too. "Why did you send us away? Was it because my mother didn't marry who you wanted her to? Was my father really that repulsive to you that you couldn't bear to have a grandchild born from him?"

Penny walks over to the hearth and gazes into the fire. "I warned your mother so many times but she wouldn't listen. She was always a stubborn girl. And a precious one. Has she really never told you the truth?"

A wave of nausea rolls through me. My sigils are ringing like alarm bells in my ears. Something in my gut tells me I'm not going to like the truth. "I don't know. That's why I'm asking. She says you kicked her out because she got pregnant by a man you didn't approve of. My father, Sheriff Mason Gray. But she has never shown

any love for me or my father. I think there's more to it and I want you to tell me."

She snickers. "Mason Gray is not your father. He was my groundskeeper who your mother manipulated into pretending he was so she wouldn't have to face what she did."

I look at my guys one by one, my heart hammering in my chest. They all lean forward, just as intrigued as I am at this point. But Felix's face pales. A flash of recognition sparks in his eyes. What the fuck? He just figured out something that we are all still on pins and needles waiting for.

I feel my cheeks burn with resentment. "Who is my father then, Penny? And what the fuck was so bad about him that you cut us off?" I'm done being polite with this witch.

She turns to look at me, her eyes wild with anger. "A very long time ago, the devil came to Ever Graves. He fell in love with a mortal woman. He became obsessed with her. But she rejected him. So he placed a curse on this town. You see, every time a girl is born here, the devil gives her a nightmare man. An entity that will never leave her side, taunting her until she either gives in or goes mad. And if she gives in, the devil wins. And he spreads more of his evil seed."

All the blood rushes to my feet, dizzying me. I sit down on the couch next to Riot before my knees give out. I don't want to hear any more. I think I already know. I swallow hard, willing moisture back into my mouth. "What do you mean... give in?"

Penny hisses. "I'm not going to spell out the debauchery. *The filth. Women of this town have always resisted. I resist every night.* But your mother was weak. She let him... impregnate her." She almost chokes on her words. "That vile creature is your real father. *You're an abomination.*"

Her revelation knocks the air out of my lungs. *No.* This can't be true. But it is. I feel it in my bones. In my sigils. Fuck.

I look at Felix. "Is this why Lib and Villette were born in Raven's Gate? To avoid the nightmare man?"

Felix runs a shaky hand through his dark hair. "I always thought it was just a myth. A spooky nursery rhyme to scare children. But my parents are superstitious. All of the families here are. They don't give birth to girls here anymore. They go somewhere else when it's time."

"Oh, fuck," I whimper as a gurgled cry lodges in my throat. "What the fuck am I?" I feel like I'm losing control over my sanity as the room starts to spin.

Val grabs my face. "You are our firecracker. Our dark queen. You're Maureen Blackwell, the woman we all love. Fuck this old hag. She doesn't deserve to know you."

Penny gasps at the insult.

"Yeah, Maur, fuck her," Atlas adds. "I don't care if you're part devil or raven or whatever. You're ours. That's all that matters."

Riot glares daggers at Penny, his fists clenched. He's on the edge again, wrestling with his own inner demons so he doesn't erupt into a rampage.

Tears stream down my cheeks. "Your fathers knew. That's why they were after me. They weren't trying to bargain with Penny, they wanted to leverage me with the fucking devil himself."

My grandmother clucks her tongue. "You should be thanking me for sending you away. Thanks to *me* you were born in Wickford Hollow and don't have a nightmare man haunting you for the rest of your life."

I wipe my tears away with my sleeve as my fury builds. "Oh, is that why you did it? For me? Fuck you. You think you're better than us because you resisted temptation? Like you're some holy saint who deserves more than the rest of us? Congratulations for keeping your legs closed but fuck you for turning your back on your own flesh and blood."

Her mouth twists in horror. "I did what I had to do to protect this town and the rest of my family. I will not let the devil win. He's *stronger when you're here.*"

"Enough!" Riot roars. "Just fucking stop. Don't you see? He

already has won. Not because his nightmare man tempted your daughter. Not because Maureen was born from it. No. The devil won the second he succeeded in ripping apart your family. The instant you turned your back on them. I bet he's laughing at you from hell right now."

She presses a button on her desk and the library doors burst open. Six armed guards file in, pointing guns at our heads. "I will not listen to this blasphemy any longer. Get out of my house and don't ever come back."

The guys form a circle around me, each of them ready to take a bullet for me. A part of me wants to call on my sigils, on the ravens, and show these assholes their guns can't hurt me. A darker, more devious part of me wants to call on the devil himself. My true father. The nightmare man is just an extension of him. That's what terrifies her the most. I feel sorry for my mother now. It doesn't excuse how she treated me. But I do pity her. I wonder if she's been plagued by the nightmare all these years or if he went away after she gave in.

Maybe someday I'll ask her.

I hold up my hands. "Thank you for telling me the truth, Grandmother," I say to piss her off. "I just have one more question and then you'll never see me again."

She nods at her security detail and they lower their guns. "Fine. Then I want you gone. I have set up a trust for you and you'll continue to receive shares of the Blackwell Gin Company. It's the least I can do since I know you did not choose this."

I grit my teeth. *How fucking sweet of you.* "Why aren't there any ravens in Ever Graves?"

She snickers. "Because the devil sent them all to Raven's Gate. They watch over the ones he didn't curse. They watch over you."

Fuck.

I am the devils daughter.

"Goodbye, Penny."

She looks back toward the fire. "Good riddance," she whispers.

Draven, Bones, and Aries wait for us by the SUV—one final escort to ensure we leave their town. I keep quiet as they say their goodbyes. I don't have the energy to speak, still processing what just transpired. To my own surprise, I don't feel shame or disgust, just relief. I finally know who I am and where I come from. And it makes me love the father who raised me even more. Sherrif Mason Gray loves me like I'm his own. There's true honor in that.

I look around the group, noticing Bones and Felix's tense exchange, their defensive stances while they argue about him joining Nocturnus. I catch a snippet of the conversation between Atlas and his cousin Aries—they still haven't heard from Libra and they're concerned.

Fuck. I hope she's okay.

Riot and Val stand on either side of me like bodyguards, their gazes trained on the heathens of Ever Graves. *This fucking town.* Fuck. I'm grateful I wasn't born here. I never would have met Bailey if I had been. My sorry excuse for a grandmother did do me a favor. More relief fills me as we climb into Atlas's SUV and drive away. It's done. There's no more secrets, no more enemies to face. It's just us now—me and my devils of Raven's Gate.

"I think I'm going to change my major," I announce.

"To what, pretty girl?" Atlas asks.

I look at Felix. "I want to be a psychologist at Tenebrose. It's odd that they don't have one. Maybe I can help students who are like us."

"I think that's an excellent idea, Little Raven." He plants a soft kiss on my temple. "They'll be lucky to have you."

Riot squeezes my hand. "Are you okay, Firecracker?"

I feel calm and steady, like a weight has been lifted off of me. "I actually am. We won. No one can break us. *Ever.*"

"We can only break each other . . . in the best possible way, of course," Val teases.

DIRTY LITTLE SAINT

As we laugh together, the love between us is palpable, our bonds—unbreakable.

And now we get to go home and live our lives in peace.

We can drink, fuck, read poetry under the stars, fall deeper in love . . .

Ruina nostra salus.

They are my ruin and my salvation. And I am theirs.

Over and over again until the ground opens up and swallows us whole. Because any other fate would be worse than death. Because no other fate exists.

THE EVER DARK JOURNALS OF MIA HARKER

(A prequel to Ever Dark)

Mia Harker

H E NEVER TOLD ME HIS NAME. I never asked with his tongue between my thighs.

When I wake he is never here. But I still smell him. The hairs inside my nose tinge with smoke and cinnamon like spilled perfume on the carpet. Cloyingly sweet. Sickening almost. I'd go in search for it in my dreams. He left it like a trail of breadcrumbs. Like a trigger. I hated it. I welcomed it. And when my limbs would stretch out and brace for him, he'd come for me like a freight train with his charred fingers and the strength of a hundred men. With his whispers of lust and dreams and brimstone.

I used to think he was the devil but why would the devil find me so special?

He more than haunts my nightmares. He *is* the nightmare. It plays over and over every night. Different but the same.

When I was young he would taunt me with silence. I'd sit in the cold dirt, shivering in the dark tunnel, staring into his wild red eyes. As I got older, he'd whisper dirty things. They'd echo down the tunnel, caressing my cheek like a soft breeze. I used to be afraid to go to sleep for fear of what he'd do to me next.

Until one night he touched me . . . and my body uncoiled for him like a forgotten piece of music.

Then night after night, more. He kept me longer each time. I slept more than I woke.

No one alive could compare. I wouldn't let them.

He was my nightmare who was always with me. In the

orphanage. On my eighteenth birthday when they kicked me out.

He was right next to me when I slept on the streets. When I almost froze to death.

And when I got help.

When I landed my first job at the gallery. He was still there. Every night. Twisting me.

And then I met my fiancé. Sleep was borrowed. It was for the hollow girl I had once been. And my nightmare came with a fury.

He kept me longer. His brutality knew no bounds. His viciousness knew no mercy. I made myself sick in craving it—still wanting a phantom instead of the flesh and blood lying next to me. My fiancé, Matthew, sensed I was not well.

He'd wake to my moans, watching in horror as I touched myself. Night after night, he became jealous of the unnamed monster living in my head. It got worse when I began painting him. Every canvas in our house was consumed by the ravings of my nightmares. Every blank wall became a canvas.

He brought in specialists, pills, and even priests.

But it was a hopeless battle because it was an unfair fight. I was too consumed by my own darkness. The evil that had sought me out and claimed my soul, would not let me go.

And so... Matthew decided to stop being my fiancé.

I was alone again with my nightmare. I feared he would follow me even in death.

Then one night, when I was half a bottle of whiskey deep into a drunken stupor, I received the call that would change everything.

The man on the other end was my grandmother's estate manager. *A grandmother I never knew I had.*

She had left everything to me, her only remaining heir.

I was terrified at first, but then it was a change I welcomed, in hopes to start over somewhere new.

So, I moved to a great big house in a small little town.

I had nothing to lose. Nothing to anchor me. The strangeness proved to be just what I needed.

Until I met them.

Bones Crane, Draven Blackwell, and Aries Thorn—the heathens of Ever Graves.

But I digress.

I must first go back to the *before* beginning.

Back when my monster first came for me.

He never told me his name.

So I gave him one.

Nox.

It means nightmare.

December 25th, 2009

Dear Diary,

I hate Christmas. I asked for new gloves. Mine are dirty from scrubbing the floors. Which reminds me. I hate chores too. They suck. Still no gloves for me this year. "Santa" only brings fruit to the Wickford Orphanage. I know Santa doesn't exist but fuck it would be nice if he did. It's really just Sister Mary. She really outdid herself with the oranges this year. I guess I should be happy they weren't rotten. Unlike last Christmas. Ughhh. Five more years. I just had to get through five more years. Then I'd be eighteen, and I could leave this shithole forever.

Well, time for bed, Diary. Can't wait to wake up tomorrow and have it not be Christmas. Actually, I can't wait to wake up.... The nightmares are getting worse. The man with the red eyes. He's inching closer to me every night. Can you be murdered in a dream? It feels possible when I'm

trapped with him in that dark tunnel. I should be used to him by now.
Does every girl have a nightmare man? Ugh. Fuck. Alright. Off to bed.
Wish me luck, Diary.

December 31st, 2009

Dear Diary,

I've been in and out of sleep for five days. Sister Mary says I have a fever. I definitely feel sick. I hope the medicine works soon. Every time I slip back in, he's there, watching me. I yelled at him last night. Told him to tell me his name or leave me alone. He didn't do either. I still haven't even seen his whole face. Ever since I was a little girl... all he's shown me is those monstrous red eyes. I can't tell anymore if it's the fever or if I'm projecting. A therapist told me once that I had made him up to cope with being abandoned. She was probably right. But he felt so real. I stopped telling people about him a long time ago. Lately, he's been whispering to me. I can't hear what he's saying though. Maybe it's in a different language. Or I'm just losing it. But if I created him would he be speaking English, right? I mean I don't know any other languages. Ugh. I feel dizzy. Going to pass out again.

October 31st, 2012

Dear Diary,

Happy not so sweet 16 birthday to me. With each year he gets closer. Or the tunnel is getting smaller. It feels as if the walls are literally closing in. How can I be so tired when all I do is sleep?
Every year on my birthday he tells me the same thing: "You're running out of wishes."

This year was different.

He recited me this....

Down, down, down
Winter's bony fingers pull me down
Night never ends
Sleep is forever
I wear the nightmare crown

Don't make a sound
Silent as the howl less wind
Down, down, down
Back to my web again

Honeyed fingers, poisoned tongue
Sharpest is the kiss that feeds
There is no dream in which I'm from
Lost between the wishing trees

Down, down, down
Crushed by devil's rocks
Bound, bound, bound
To an eternity of Nox

October 22nd, 2014

Dear Diary,

I hope no one ever finds this. I'm almost too ashamed to write what happened but I have to tell someone. Well, not an actual person. They'd have me committed. And I only had a few days left until my eighteenth birthday. Until I was free.

I tried to sketch his face today. It was just a black blob with red
dots for eyes. My fingers shivered as I held the pencil. So cold I couldn't
draw a straight line. Everything about him was cold. Everything turned
to ice and frost around him. So many cold wet things.

But I heard his voice last night. Really heard it. It wasn't monstrous. It was low and husky. Deep. It was his words that shocked me.
Oh, god. No one has ever spoken to me like that. I . . . I tried to run but
there was nowhere to go. No way out. The tunnel just loops back around.
No matter how many times I run, I always come back to him and his
red glowing eyes.

As I close my eyes now, I can still hear him like he's right in front
of me. It started a week ago like this:

"Take your panties off, Mia."

"Why?," I asked.

"You don't have to do anything. Just take them off and open your
legs so I can see you."

I shouldn't have. I don't know why I did. It was just a dream, right?
Another nightmare.

So I removed my white cotton underwear, scooted up against the
cold cement wall, and spread my legs open.

He watched me from the dark end of the tunnel. His breaths were
short and heavy. His red eyes glowed brighter. I sat there, trembling,
wide open for him to see me. I sat like that for hours.

And then he whispered, "Enough," right before I woke up.

The chilly air, the cold cement against my bare ass, the weight of
his eyes on me, it was doing something to my body that I'd never felt before. Something wrong. Dirty. Wicked. And I'd wake up wet between my
thighs and with an urge to put my fingers down there.

But I wouldn't dare. Sister Mary said masturbation was a sin.

But night after night, for a week straight, I've done this for him.
And the urges have gotten worse. It's all I can think about when I'm
lying in bed.

And I'm even more scared to go to sleep now. Fear of what he'll ask

October 31st, 2014

Dear Diary,

Unholy shit.

Nox stepped out of the shadows last night.

He backed me up against the tunnel wall, towering over me by at least two feet. I've never seen a man that big before. He was magnificent. Not because of his enormous size or the black shiny strands that hung just below his sharp jaw. It wasn't because of his red eyes, the way they seemed to stare into my soul. Nor the way his perfectly carved chest heaved with each quivering breath as he breached the space between us. No. It was just him. The way he moved, the rasp as he spoke, the twitch of his lips as he ogled mine. The scent of death and blood and sin surrounded him. Surrounded us. And it took everything I had to not succumb to his darkness.

He hovered over me, caressing my collarbone with his icy fingers.

I couldn't stop shivering.

And then all hell broke loose inside my body.

He wrapped one hand around my throat and tore the front of my nightgown open with the other. My nipples pebbled under his stare. But he didn't touch them. I was aching for him to, but he didn't.

With a knowing smirk, he just watched the rise and fall of my chest. Watched as I sucked on my lower lip. Watched as I arched toward him. Watched with his hand around my throat, holding me in place and enjoying every moment of my torment.

The cold chills on my spine turned to feverish beads of sweat. They rolled down my back and chest as moisture pooled between my legs.

my nightmares? Or am I of my own free will? That line was blurring every day.

me to do next. Afraid that whatever it is... I'll do it. Is he controlling

I finally found my voice. "What are you doing?"

"Feeding your sins." He rolled his forked tongue—oh fuck, why is his tongue forked? — he rolled his forked tongue fucking across his lower lip and flashed a smile that I could only describe as pure evil. The kind of evil that terrified and excited me at the same time. He squeezed my throat tighter. "Soon, Mia," Nox breathed. "I will taste every part of you. I will infiltrate every inch of you."

My head was dizzy. Spinning. I couldn't breathe as he squeezed. I shook my head and clawed at his fingers. "No," I rasped out. "I won't let you."

He snickered. The scent of death growing stronger. Maybe it was my own death that I could smell approaching?

"I am already inside of you. You can't escape me. There is only sub-mission. The longer you resist, the more I will make you suffer."

His terror made me wet. What in the hell was wrong with me? "Why are you doing this to me?"

He released his grip around my neck. "There is only you, Mia. In my dark prison, you are my holy water. My candle burning bright. My obsession."

I pressed my slippery back hard against the wall in an effort to put some space between us. "What about what I want?"

Nox stepped closer, boxing me in. He drew air circles around my nipple, and I instantly stiffened. "I don't even have to touch you, Mia. Look how erect you are for me."

"I'm just cold," I fired back.

He chuckled and moved his hand down, hovering it over my belly. "Then why is your pussy glistening through your panties? Hmm? I bet if I slipped inside you right now, I'd be drenched. Your juices would soak my cock like a dam bursting open."

I didn't mean to whimper but I did. My body was betraying me. His hand lingered, swaying back and forth, circling, but never touching.

I held my breath, waiting to be set free or locked in this prison with him for eternity.

"Happy eighteenth birthday, Mia. No more wishes now. Wishes are for children and you are a child no longer."

He stepped back and the air whooshed back into my lungs. I hugged my arms to my chest, blocking his view of my misbehaving nipples.

He darted back, retreating deep into the shadows again. Leaving me with only his red glowing eyes to look at. "You're mine now. Your body is mine to ruin and destroy. Every time you go to sleep, I will find you. I will teach you how to be a good girl for me."

I opened my mouth to scream but nothing came out.

I woke up in a panic, bolting straight up in my bed. My breath quickened and my heart raced. But as I looked down, all the hairs on the back of my neck stood up.

My night gown was torn in half.

No. No. No.

It was just a dream. A nightmare.

Fuck.

I must have torn it myself. I must have. Nox isn't real. He can't be.

March 25th, 2015

Dear Diary,

I'm so tired. I've tried everything I can to stay awake as long as possible. I haven't seen Nox in months. But I know it's just part of his game. I try to sleep in short intervals. Just enough to not die, but short enough to where I hope he can't find me.

Sleeping in parking garages and abandoned buildings actually makes that easier. You can't let your guard down on the streets. Not for a second. So I kill two birds with one stone. Keep the other grifters from fucking with me and stop Nox from actually fucking me.

I'm a head case. Just looking at what I'm writing makes me seem like I've lost my mind.

I never thought the sisters would actually make me leave. They said it but I didn't believe them. They raised me. How could they just kick me out?

I need to get a job, a place to live, and another therapist.

But more importantly, I needed to stay awake.

April something 2015,

Dear Diary,

He found me.

I don't know what day it is anymore.

"You can't say no to the dark." Nox's words echoed in my head.

"You've been a bad girl, Mia. Trying to stay awake. Thinking you could hide from me."

I was flat on my back on the cold hard cement. My wrists were shackled above my head, chained to something above me. "I'm so tired . . ." I murmured.

He caressed my cheek. "And who's fault is that? It's time to end these childish games, Mia. You belong to my night. I've waited patiently for my feast. And now I'm going to play with my food."

Oh no. Fuck.

And yet as I gazed up at him, my breath hitched. He was beautiful but only the way dark things are. I ached. Hungered. Shame filled me as I laid there naked, quivering in anticipation. Reveling in the fact that he was looking at me like I was a meal to be devoured. No one had ever looked at me that way before.

"You are so fucking perfect," Nox growled. He knelt between my legs, sliding his hands up my thighs as he pushed them apart. "I am in your head. I know what you want. I know you are a liar. Try to play

the victim all you want but I know your thoughts better than you know them yourself."

Moisture trickled out of my pussy. I couldn't speak.

His hands crawled further up, resting in the crook of my thighs, that spot right next to my trembling folds. "I know no one has ever touched you before. You have never even touched yourself. That will come later. I can show you how. But first, it's my turn. I've waited long enough."

I flinched as he ran a bony finger down my slit.

"Mmm. You're trembling. You have no idea what your fear does to me. Fuck... I'm going to enjoy this more than I thought."

What was happening to me?

My body was coming alive with need. I watched him, wanting him to keep going. Wanting to feel more of those tingling waves. His touch was so light. So soft.

He used both his hands, both index fingers tracing the line of my slit. "Let's peek inside."

I bucked as he spread my folds open, pinching them back as he kneaded his thumbs against my walls. My whole body began to convulse.

He snickered. "I knew you'd like it when I stretched you open. Let's see if it tastes as sweet as it looks."

He dipped his head and that forked tongue darted out. He held my gaze and winked right before he licked the length of me.

"Ughhh," I cried out.

"Yes, fucking scream." He raked his teeth over my swollen clit. "I'm going to fuck you with my tongue until you cry."

His tongue pushed inside my pussy, and I lost it. The sounds that came from me I didn't recognize.

The ridges of his tongue, the way it split inside of me, licking both sides of my walls at the same time. I clenched around him, and he slapped my thigh.

"Yes, fight me. It only makes me want you more."

I bucked as the pressure in my clit swelled, rolling my hips as his rough tongue licked and sucked and probed every inch of me.

"It's too much. Enough. Please." I was seeing stars.

He lifted my hips off the ground and curled his hands around my ass as he continued to feast on me, humming as he sucked. The vibration from that alone was sending me into convulsions.

"It will never be enough. Now be a good girl and fill my mouth with your traitorous cum."

I rocked against his face in shame. In utter and complete disgust for myself. And then the tingling coiled through me, and I burst.

My screams echoed through the tunnel.

He moaned as he lapped up every drop of my thick cream.

"Like holy water," he rasped. He settled me back down against the ground. "My thirst will never be quenched."

I trembled as my orgasm rippled through me still. Little aftershocks of pleasure. "I hate you," I spat.

"You have no idea how much you will despise me after what I do to you next. Rest for now, Mia. I showed you mercy tonight, but your suffering has only begun."

I woke up on a dirty mattress in an abandoned doll factory, my wrists red and swollen. My thighs still wet.

Fuck.

And the only thing that terrified me was that I wanted more.

October 31st, 2015

Dear Diary,

I've lost time. Nox keeps me asleep. For days sometimes. He only lets me wake so I can eat and tend to my body.

He's my nightmare.

My villain.

And I'm his obsession.

A few nights after he feasted on my pussy, I found myself in a new

room with him. I always had a feeling there was more to that tunnel. He kept me in the dark for so long. But then I realized that he is the dark. And all other matter just molds to him.

The new room was a chamber in the tunnel. It had no door that I could see. And this is where he punished me for being a bad girl.

The first night I traveled there, was the scariest. But it was my awakening.

I was tied to a bed, face down, and spread eagle. My wrists and ankles each bound to a bedpost.

Nox left me like that for days. He would stalk around the bed admiring me. Admiring his handiwork, occasionally tugging on my restraints to remind me there was no escape.

But every time I'd start to doze off, he'd slap my thigh. If I slept, then I would wake up in my world. And he wouldn't allow that. I was his prisoner. His slave. He wanted me weak, drained, and hungry for his touch.

Finally, he got on the bed and knelt over me. He planted kisses up my back all the way to my shoulder. He brushed my black hair to the side and kissed my neck. With each press of his lips to my flesh, I trembled more.

"I hope you've had time to think about what a naughty girl you've been." He slid a finger up the slit of my ass, and I moaned into the pillow. "I'm going to show you what happens when you hide from me." He pinched my ass hard between his fingers and the released it with a slap.

"When you disobey me."

Any sane person would have been scared but I was turned on.

He did the same pinch and slap to my other ass cheek. "Remember, I know what you like."

I laughed, suddenly feeling unhinged. "I don't want you. You make me sick," I whispered.

Without warning, he fisted my hair and yanked my head up. His breath rustled in my ear. "We'll see about that when you're begging me to let you cum."

No. No. No.

He was right.

Another slap on my ass, harder this time. Every time, more of my juices would pool out onto the mattress. He'd slip his hand underneath me to feel. "I know what you like," he repeated.

He dug his fingers into my ass cheeks and spread them apart. That devilish tongue lashed out at my entrance, and I bucked, clenching around him.

"Your fear tastes so fucking good. Your resistance is mouthwatering. But you can't run from your destiny. Deep down you don't want to."

His fingers dug deeper into my ass cheeks. I knew they would leave a mark. I couldn't clench anymore. He had me pinned open as his tongue inched farther in. The two tips of his tongue flicked at my entrance, light at first and then violently as if he were a starved animal. And my traitorous juices flooded out. He laughed as he lapped at them, licking, and sucking as I moaned into the mattress.

And just as I was about to reach my peak, he stopped.

My heart raced as I laid there, unable to see what he would do next.

The flesh around my entrance ached, throbbing with need and pain.

The cheeks of my ass burned from his fingers.

He leaned over me, and I could feel the length of his body lightly pressing into mine, hovering just out of reach. He licked the inside of my ear before whispering, "I'm going to break your body first and then I'm going to break your soul. No matter where you go, dark one, I will always be there."

Hours turned to days. I was starting to hallucinate shapes and shadows on the walls. He kept me tied to the bed, cold and aching.

The next night, I must have drifted off because I don't remember him flipping me around. I opened my heavy lids to find myself staring at the ceiling. My wrists were still bound but my legs were free. I curled them up toward my body and cried out as the muscles in my thighs resisted. The blood rushed through my veins after being stuck in one place for so long.

His red eyes peered out of the darkness, moving closer until he was standing at the foot of the bed, snarling down at me. His eyes were laced with lust and malice.

"I'm going to give you a chance to obey. If you're a good girl for me, I'll release your wrists too."

Panic filled my chest. I couldn't even feel my arms. I nodded.

"O-okay. Please. I can't take anymore."

"I wish you could see how beautiful you look right now. I can see the fight leaving you. The way you struggle to hold onto the last shred of humanity you have left. It's exquisite. And it's all mine."

"You're fucking crazy. Tell me who you are really," I breathed.

He licked his lips, reminding me of that tongue of his. "I'm your dark priest, your nightmare, your masochistic god. And you will learn to obey me. All I have is time and the means to make you suffer."

The more he spoke, his voice soothed me. It was sick. I was sick. This couldn't be what I really wanted, could it? But I created him. He was my nightmare man. What was wrong with me?

"Please untie my wrists. I'll do whatever you say," I pleaded.

He shook his head. "Not until you can prove to me that I can trust you. Consider this your first test."

He crawled onto the bed and kneeled before me. "Spread your legs apart."

Every muscle in my body trembled with ache and soreness. I took a deep breath and slowly slid my legs open.

"Wider," he growled.

I whimpered and opened up as far as I could.

"That's better. Now I want you to imagine my thick cock inside of you. I want you to move your hips as if you were riding it."

What the fuck? "You want me to have sex with the air?"

Without warning his palm came down in a hard slap on my inner thigh. I flinched, my hips rocking up. "I want you to show me how you'd lift and buck and twist for me. Do as I say, or I will tie your legs back up and slap your pussy till it's numb."

I swallowed down the lump in my throat. He was trying to humiliate me. Tears streamed down my cheeks as I started to rock my hips
back and forth. I didn't even know if I was doing it right. I was a virgin. I'd only seen sex in movies when I would sneak into the theater for
warmth. And he knew that.

"Yes, that's it. Imagine the girth of my cock stretching you open.
Look how slick you are for me."

As I thrusted my pelvis into the air, a tingling started to spread in
my nub. I bit down on my lip to stifle a whimper.

"Good girl. You can stop now."

As I rested my hips back down on the mattress, he leaned over and
untied one wrist. My arm fell limp like a dead weight. He rubbed at it,
coaxing the blood back in.

"See how nice I can be when you behave?"

I nodded, afraid to say one word that could get me tied back up.
Instead of untying my other wrist, he sat back down on his heels
between my legs.

"Slide your middle finger down the slit of your pussy."

My eyes widened. The heat rose to my cheeks.

"Don't start disobeying me now, dark one. My cock is begging me
to let it fill you. And believe me it will hurt that little tight cunt of yours."

Fuck.

As I slid my finger down my slit, my juices pooled. Oh my god that
felt good.

"Deeper. Bury that finger in between your folds till I can barely
see it."

A rumbling stirred in my belly as I burrowed in deeper between my
folds. I couldn't stop the whimpers this time. My breath was erratic as
the tingling increased, threatening to push me over the edge.

"Mmm, my naughty little marionette... Here, let me teach you."

He placed his finger over mine and began guiding it into a rhythm
that triggered a spot inside of me, I nearly passed out from pleasure. He
took over, moving my finger up and down my pussy, bending it to his

will. He brought my finger up to my clit and pressed down, moving it
in firm circles around my swollen nub. The pressure began to build inside my walls. I clenched and cried out as the most intense wave of tingling erupted.

I jerked my hips, grinding against both our hands.

He pressed his lips to my belly and hummed as I laid there twitching. It was the greatest thing I'd ever felt.

"Happy birthday, dark one. I will release you for now."

Everything went black until I woke up to blinding lights and the
sound of a heart monitor.

I was in the hospital.

You're probably wondering what happened to me, Diary. Well, I
didn't even know until this morning. The nurses are coming in and drug-
ging me to sleep again. I will write more tomorrow.

November 2nd, 2017

Dear Diary,

Sorry it's been so long. I know I said I'd write more tomorrow and
that turned into two years later. I didn't know how to write everything
down. I put you in my backpack and refuse to touch you. It was too much.
Too shameful. As far as I know, I'm the only person who gets held hostage
by her own nightmares. I thought that's all they were at first. But when
I wake up ... the proof of what he's done to me is there. For a while, I
thought I was doing it to myself, in my sleep. Until the night he branded
me. That's another story that I'm still not ready to put into words.

But that's when I knew he was real.

I may have dreamed him up at first, but now he was fucking real.
He lived in the dark corners of my mind. And yet what he did to me ...
what we did together left physical marks. I couldn't explain how or why.
I would never know. It's not like I can ever tell anyone about this. They'd
lock me up and throw away the key.

So where did I leave off... ah right, the hospital. They told me they found me unconscious in a parking lot. That I had been in a coma for five days.

After being grilled by three different nurses and a police officer about why my body was bruised, swollen, and malnourished, they finally released me. I kept telling them that I was fine. That nobody hurt me. One of the nurses gave me an address for a shelter. The pity in her eyes made me feel worse than the disgust the police officer had looked at me with.

I did check into that shelter though. Not at first. I spent a week feeling ashamed and yet somehow too proud to go. But it was winter, and people were freezing to death in parking garages. They were nice enough. I had my own room because I was the only female. It didn't deter all the boys from trying to creep on me at night, so I started barricading the door. No locks in a shelter.

Sleep and I have always had a complicated relationship, so staying alert wasn't hard to do. But by the third night, I was exhausted. My body fell into a deeper state of sleep than it had been in since the hospital. And that's when he came for me again.

I opened my eyes to find myself in that room again. The one with the bed. This time I was unbound. But still naked. Nox stood over me. His red eyes were more feral than usual.

"Hello, dark one. Miss me?"

A pounding started in my chest. Did I? I scooted away from him and hugged my legs into my chest. "How long is this going to go on for?"

He smiled. "Forever. Even after your body dies, your soul will fly to me."

A feeling of dread crept into my bones. "So when I'm ninety, you're still going to want to play with my saggy skin and fragile bones?"

Nox let out a deep laugh. "This is your nightmare, Mia. You don't age in here."

The idea was strange but made sense. This was all in my head. No matter how old we get, we tend to still imagine ourselves as being young and vibrant.

I chewed on my lower lip. "What are you? Where do you come from?"

Nox slid onto the bed wearing only a thin pair of black pants. His tanned chest was taut and muscular. His body was beautiful. All the way down to the v shape right below his belly button.

"Come here." He yanked my legs and pinned me underneath him. My heart raced as he dragged a finger across my jaw.

"I require sacrifice. Obedience. Submission. That's all you need to know about me. And in return I will give you everything, dark one. Every filthy and vile act that you so desperately crave."

I shivered as his hand inched down my neck. He wrapped it around my throat. "You have much to learn. If you're a good girl, I'll tell you one truth."

Despite my mind screaming at me to run, my body was prickling with desire. The scent of cloves and patchouli invaded my nose as he lowered his lips till they were almost touching mine. "Do we have a deal, dark one?"

His breath tasted sweet. Dammit. I wanted him to kiss me. Wanted to feel that forked fucking tongue against mine.

"If I behave... you'll answer one of my questions truthfully?"

He flexed his chest against my pebbled nipples. "Yes."

I shifted underneath him, desperately trying to clench my thighs together. "Okay... we have a deal."

Nox sucked in a sharp breath. "That's my girl. If I have to ask you to do something twice, not only will you not get your truth, but I will also bend you over my knee and spank you so hard you won't be able to sit for a week."

My breath hitched. That was definitely not part of the deal. But I nodded anyway.

He lifted my chin with his finger. "I want to hear you say, yes sir."

I held his gaze, forcing myself to not show any fear. "Yes, sir," I spat through gritted teeth.

That evil smirk returned to his lips. "Mmm... my cock is so hard now. It wants to fill you." He raised up, leaning back on his heels, and pulled his pants halfway down.

I gasped.

He was huge. I was fucking terrified imagining how it would fit inside of me. But that wasn't the only reason why I suddenly couldn't breathe. The tip of his cock was also fucking forked. It was split, the two halves wiggling as if they had a life of their own.

Nox watched me take it all in, smug as he saw the sweat bead down my chest. "Beautiful isn't it?"

I was stunned. Speechless. Just staring at it.

Nox slapped my thigh. Hard. I squealed and met his gaze. "I asked you a question. Remember what happens if I have to ask you twice."

Oh, shit.

"Y-yes sir. It's beautiful."

His red eyes flickered. His tongue lashed out as he gazed at my pussy. He pushed his pants off and wedged himself between my trembling thighs. "This is going to hurt, dark one. But it will also feel good."

He lined up his cock to my entrance and began stroking my clit with his forked tip. I moaned softly as it covered my nub like a suction, squeezing it until I thought I might burst.

"I'm going to bathe in your virgin blood and then feast on your cum. All that sweet sticky cream."

I squirmed as the pressure began to slowly build inside my walls.

"Squeeze your nipples. Hold them tight and don't let go until I tell you to."

I pinched my nipples between my fingers and moaned.

"Mmm, yes that feels good, doesn't it?" He parted my aching folds

with his hands and stroked. I arched my back, my body betraying me again as his touch sent ripples of tingles inside my traitorous pussy.

"I'm scared..." I whispered.

He inched the tip of his cock between my folds. I shuddered as the two tips flexed against my flesh.

"Shhh, relax, dark one. Fear is like fire. It can only hurt you if you leave your hand too long inside the flames. But a little pain is exquisite. Pain teaches you how to feel, how to love, and how to cum. And you are going to cum so fucking hard for me. Do you want that? Tell me the truth. I will know if you're lying."

"Yes...." It was the truth. I knew deep down in my bones I could refuse him, and he would stop. Because this was my nightmare. My mind. My dark and devious desires come to life.

I was scared but I was also needy. A part of me wanted him to fill me. To see how much I could take. Because maybe if he ripped me open, the pain and the pleasure would make me forget all about my cursed existence. The sad lonely orphan girl who no one wanted. No one but Nox.

He grinned as if he could read my thoughts. "I've wanted you for so long, dark one. No more wishes. Only this starvation and thirst that will finally be quenched... Now, let me hear you scream."

He plunged inside my pussy with so much force, I almost blacked out. I screamed so loud, I knocked the wind out of my own chest.

Nox growled as he burrowed himself in all the way. "Ahh yes, my little dark one. Like a fucking glove. Open up for me."

My walls were stretching, contracting, clenching, then stretching more to accommodate him. And with each breath I took, the ridges of his cock expanded more, throbbing against me. Every pulse was agonizing. I cried out again as he began to move inside me.

"Ride me. Ride me fucking hard," he growled.

I rolled my hips into him, remembering how badly I needed this. Not just his truth but his dominance. With each thrust, he was becoming my obsession. Liquid pooled out, coating my thighs red as he slid in and out with more ease. And my body came alive.

"Uhh," I moaned. "More."

He pumped into me. "That's my girl. Fucking. Her. Monster. So. Good." He thrusted harder with every word.

His praise was music to my ears. I bucked wildly against him like an animal. Like a feral cat who'd been starved for days. I screamed into his face as he rammed into me with so much force, my back lifted off the bed and slammed into the wall. But my grip never slipped. I still held my nipples tight between my fingers. They were swollen and numb, but I promised to obey.

The forked tip of his cock lashed out, probing at a deeper spot. It was like pressing a magic button. A rush of spasms gripped me.

"You didn't know about that one, did you, dark one," he grunted as he grinded and twisted, giving everything he had. "That's your special spot. My special spot now. Mmm still so fucking tight."

We were against the wall, my back aching from the force of him slamming into me, when the floodgates opened.

Nox let out a deep moan before covering my lips with his, shoving his forked tongue inside my mouth. I couldn't breathe. Every inch of my body was his to consume. The spasms intensified, climbing inside of me until I could no longer keep them contained.

I tore away from his mouth and screamed. "Something's happening."

"Mmm, cum hard for me. Fuck, yes. Like fucking holy water on the devil's cock."

My juices flooded out as he grunted. His cock throbbed inside of me one more time before a gush of thick hot liquid filled me.

"Oh, fuck," I breathed. It pooled down our thighs. "There's so much."

Nox twisted and grinded as he chased his own salvation inside of me. "There will never be enough."

I was expecting him to release me. To leave me there against the wall until I woke up on the other side. Back in my room at the shelter with the unlocked door and the dirty mattress.

He did none of those things.

Nox pulled me down to the bed and tucked me in his arms. He

wrapped his blood and cum stained thighs around mine. "Promise me you'll keep me forever, dark one."

It was in that moment that I was finally aware of what he was. Mine. He was mine.

That was my truth. I didn't have to ask him a question. I already knew where he came from. Nox was born from the darkest depths of my soul. The monster that I'd created.

I gazed up into his red eyes and sighed. "I promise."

This is just a sneak peek into some of the backstory of EVER DARK, Mia Harker's twisted journey with Bones Crane, Aries Thorn, and Draven Blackwell.

And of course, her nightmare man, Nox.

EVER DARK is a dark, Gothic, why choose romance—part bully, part monster romance. It takes place in the town of Ever Graves and is connected to the world of Wickford Hollow Duet and The Devils of Raven's Gate Duet.

EVER DARK will release in 2025.

MORE BOOKS BY M VIOLET

Pretty Little Psycho (The Devils of Raven's Gate Book 1)

Good Girl (Wickford Hollow Duet Book 1)

Little Fox (Wickford Hollow Duet Book 2)

Wickford Hollow Duet (includes Good Girl, Little Fox, and an exclusive bonus chapter of Riot and Maureen)

Wicked Midnight (A Dark Why Choose Romance Retelling of Cinderella)

Unholy Night (A Dark Why Choose Holiday Romance)

AUTHOR'S NOTE

As much as this book is my ode to dark romance and smut, it's also my ode to poetry and language and love.

Writing a book can be both a harrowing and cathartic process. You initially write it for yourself but along the way it becomes bigger than you. It becomes part of a collective. Writing Dirty Little Saint has been both a challenge and a blessing.

For me, Dirty Little Saint is my baptism, my reckoning, and my favorite journey so far. This book might not be for everyone. But it's for me and it's for *you*, my Vixens.

Maureen, Riot, Atlas, Valentin, and Felix will always occupy space in my head now. Maybe someday we'll pop in on them and see what they're up to…

But while our Firecracker's story is now complete, there is still much more to come in this world of Melancholia… *"There's something wrong with the women in Ever Graves."*

In absentia lucis, tenebrae vincunt: in the absence of light, darkness prevails.

Thank you for coming on this journey to Raven's Gate with me.

Until next time, little vixens.
M Violet

WORKS CITED

(All the following works cited are in the public domain.)

Blake, William, The Sick Rose

Poe, Edgar Allan, The Haunted Palace

Poe, Edgar Allan, The Raven

Poe, Edgar Allan, Spirits of the Dead

ACKNOWLEDGEMENTS

Thank you for reading *Dirty Little Saint*! I am currently in a book hangover from it while I write these acknowledgements. I am feeling all the things as I say goodbye to Maureen, Riot, Atlas, and Valentin. And of course our beautiful and broody poetry professor, Felix. These characters have taken me on a journey unlike any I've ever been on. I'm sad their story is done but also so happy I got to tell it.

For those of you who have been on this journey with me since Good Girl, thank you so much for falling in love with Maureen from the start. It was you and your voices that inspired me to tell her story. Thank you for loving her as much as I do!

I have to give a HUGE thank you and shoutout to my street team and my Vixens! Thank you so much for always supporting me and having my back. I love you al!

Thank you to every ARC reader, reviewer, booktokker, and bookstagrammer for reading my books and always being so generous with your time and space in sharing my content and raving about my books. Your support means the world to me!

Thank you to my editor Kat Wyeth of Kat's Literary Services. You always do incredible work and I'm so grateful to have you on my team. (Sorry not sorry that I made you blush in the library LOL)

Thank you to Artscandare for another GORGEOUS cover. I am obsessed with your work and might have a slight addiction to buying your covers LOL

Thank you to Stacey Blake at Champagne Book Design for knocking it out of the park AGAIN. Your skills are magical. I think you might actually have Fae blood or be a sorceress because the way you format my books is unreal. I'm in awe of you and so, so, so lucky to have worked with you all these years.

Thank you to my spreadsheet queen, my fearless and fantastic PA, the incomparable Darcy Bennett. You are a saint for dealing

with my chaos LOL. I absolutely adore you and feel so lucky to have you as my PA. XOXO

Thank you to all my author friends! To the Write Club and the Smutven! Wow, what a crazy and fantastic business we're in. I'm so grateful I get to do it with all of you. Thank you for all the laughs, tea, peptalks, vent sessions, support, friendship, and love. XOXO

I want to give a special shout out and thank you to three women who have literally been my write or die best friends on this journey. AL Maruga, Cassie Fairbanks, and Candice Rose. I love you ladies so much. And I can't believe that I will actually get to meet all three of you IRL after all these years! XOXO

And last but never least, I have to give a huge thank you to all my family and friends. You may not read dark romance or even understand why I write it, but you love me and support me all the same. Thank you so much for everything you do. I love you all. XOXO

ABOUT THE AUTHOR

M Violet is a dark romance author with a flair for the dramatic. She likes whiskey, rainy nights, and writing by the fire. When she's not creating scorching hot villains for you to fall in love with, you can find her eating chocolate and binge watching her favorite shows.

Facebook: Authormviolet

Instagram: Authormviolet

Tik Tok: Authormviolet